The Judas Cup

Shaun Ivory

For Edith
whose support never wavered

Author's Note

Any novel with specialist skills involved means a great deal of reliance on the experts. This one is no different. Without the expertise of forensics, advances in brain research and the occult this one – such as it is – would be less than gripping.

I therefore dip my head in gratitude to the following. Ian Pepper, Principal Lecturer in Policing at Teesside University, who was ever-patient to my somewhat at times naïve questioning. Also articles concerning the human brain, usually in *The Sunday Times* and made lucid by people such as Bryan Appleyard; internet info published by the universities of Wisconsin-Madison and Tottori in Japan. I hope I have interpreted them – if not accurately – then at least coherently.

As to the occult… well, where can one start, or end? From Aleister Crowley downwards, it was a dizzying spiral to depths mercifully denied me hitherto. I confess I plundered liberally. If there are adepts out there who feel I have misrepresented them, I apologise. I am still waiting to be convinced, if not converted.

And of course Helen Hart of SilverWood Books, whose gentle but insistent wisdom and business sense made me believe there was dog in the old life yet. Without ignition, the rocket remains on the launch pad. She lit the blue touch paper. She also left me feeling that perhaps it is not yet time to retire!

Shaun Ivory
Redcar, 2009

1: DISTURBANCE

The two figures off to the west of the Whitby moor road could have been erecting their tent for the night. Although still only late afternoon, the September sky was darkening dramatically – clouds piling up, the distant rumble of thunder hastening their efforts. But the more observant of the passing motorists might have judged it less than sensible to pitch a tent atop Hobb's Barrow in the teeth of an approaching storm. And those spindly struts – a frame perhaps? No, an instrument of some kind. Ah! Those surveying teams for the new reservoir. No problem. Wonder what's for tea?

All of which did little to console the two men up there, struggling to keep the flimsy structure upright.

"For God's sake, Alec, keep it steady while I get the beam lined up, will you?" The exasperation in the older man's voice was tinged with anxiety. He was unsure of his ground here, literally. The new laser beam geodolite had been part of his equipment for weeks but this was its first time out of the box. He knew he was being stubborn, almost Luddite, in his attitude to what was obviously going to be another tool of the future. His resistance had been eroded throughout the day by his young assistant's reasoned argument that this was actually their last full day on the project and their boss, Stuart Becker, had requested a report on its handling by the end of the week.

George Bennett's mood had consequently suited the weather: dark and brooding. They had worked in tight-lipped silence most of the afternoon, except for George's initial declaration that the new instrument was 'way over spec for the job'. He was hurrying this final phase before daylight faded, re-checking the alignment data across the valley that would soon become an artificial lake, a direct result of the ongoing controversy over global warming.

A gust of wind clawed at them on their exposed vantage point, an historical landmark, whose top had been flattened to a tiny plateau by the feet of countless pilgrims. George zipped his ancient anorak all the way up before kneeling to re-position the instrument's four legs. This, too, was a departure from the traditional design and he grumbled at the awkward arrangement, his normally practised movements hampered by the battering wind.

"Right, George. I think I've got it now," Alec yelled, blowing on his hands as the last warmth seemed to follow the sun over the horizon. He stepped back to allow his colleague sufficient room to manoeuvre around the splayed carbon-fibre legs. The older man trod on an egg-shaped stone, brought there and left with the bearer's initials scratched on the smooth grey surface in time-honoured manner. His right foot slid away and he began to topple. No longer nimble, he instinctively strove to deny the crumbling edge an easy victim; his flailing hand struck the geodolite and he clutched momentarily at the instrument but it was too smooth. He was only briefly aware of Alec's startled expression and crucial hesitation as the cold slowed his reflexes. Then the youth lunged, just in time to get a fistful of anorak as George began to roll down the steep, gravelly slope. He lay there for a few seconds, winded, trying not to wince at the small flints digging into his bared forearm.

"You okay, George?" Alec gasped. The senior surveyor looked almost comical, with his mouth wide open and stiff grey hair standing up in the wind like Hergé's Tintin. The look on his face seemed to say, 'This can't be happening to me'. But then his gaze shifted, past his rescuer. His futile grab for the instrument's support had dislodged the locking clamp: the top-heavy, yellow body had swung down, the red beam seeming to focus with burning intensity on a crack in the ground. It looked somehow incongruous and for all his discomfiture and lack of breath he was about to upbraid his assistant for not securing it correctly when he felt something – what? – stir beneath him.

It happened again, longer this time, and Alec's face told him it wasn't just imagination. A slow vibration started to shake the tumulus, unnerving in its rhythm, unlike anything he'd ever experienced before. Then it altered, grew stronger, shifting almost imperceptibly.

Alec pulled George to his feet but the older man immediately wished he hadn't. He swayed and an abhorrent, noxious smell surrounded them, too strong even for such a wind to dispel easily.

"What the hell is that, George?" Alec's eyes were wide open, staring, gusts flattening the dark, wavy hair about his head. "An earthquake or what?"

For answer George looked about him, across the fields, still just visible from this elevation. Cars were moving along the road as usual, some with lights now on. It all appeared so - so normal. And yet this truncated top of a man-made burial mound was apparently trying to tear itself to pieces. He was frightened.

"Let's get out of here, laddie, sod Becker's report!" They held onto each other, gathering up the equipment, the use and feel of familiar objects restoring some of their self-control. Then the whole tumulus seemed too lean over and the last of the old surveyor's equilibrium deserted him; he reached for the instrument stand just as there was a terrible cracking sound from beneath them, as though the very earth itself was splitting asunder. George fell against the geodolite, knocking it sideways. He grabbed it with both hands, quickly folding the telescopic legs and clamping its body in position.

He was still involved in this when Alec tugged at his sleeve.

3

"Wha –?" He glanced up, uncomprehending, his speech shredding in the wind.

"It's easing off, George. Whatever it is, it's going. Look!"

It was true, the tremors were subsiding and the awful ripples that had been coursing through their insides like a bad meal fading fast. Alec's face mirrored his own relief.

"Yes, well, I'm going too before it returns!" Suiting action to the words he swung his legs over the edge and slithered down the slope with undignified haste.

Alec overtook him halfway down.

2: EMERGENCE

Down in the valley, where the officially doomed village of Helmington lay, the process of evacuation was reaching its sad conclusion before the entire valley of Helmsdale was flooded. The resistant but unsupported inhabitants, most of whom were in sheep and dairy farming, hadn't stood a chance against the combined forces of council greed and a neighbouring valley's tourist draw: a ruined abbey by a gently winding river with adjacent free parking facilities. Nobody famous had been born, lived or murdered in Helmsdale, and whatever heated debates the regional television company had generated over the previous months had mainly centred on the justification for the reservoir, rather than the ultimate destinations of the evicted.

The only genuine human tragedy had been the discovery of Father Hugh Scanlon's body on the altar steps of St Michael's church a week previously. His heart attack had sparked the inevitable dire predictions of ill-omen from those few people still left in the village. But as he had been aged seventy-two and already quite exhausted by his crusade against 'those modernists of Mammon' it hadn't been entirely unexpected. There were even some who said the old priest had died of a broken heart.

But the required de-consecration of the medieval church had not been performed when Father Scanlon had died. The diocesan trouble-shooter already delegated to assist him in winding up the parish's affairs for the previous three weeks, Father Renton Cappel, had carried on alone since then. Young and 'too good-looking by half' he was everything the elderly incumbent had not been. Insensitive to the needs of the remaining parishioners at such a traumatic time, he had incurred their collective displeasure by denying them the use of what had become almost a sanctuary in the final days. His reason: too busy removing and transporting the contents of the building for safekeeping. The 'building'! More mutterings. The final service had been sombre, with the bishop and local dignitaries dominating what should have been a more intimate farewell.

"…a sad day… Oh, well, progress, you know…must move with the times… Benefit in the long term… Goodness, is that the time?"

Old Sam Branthwaite had been scathing in his comments to his wife, Sarah, as they'd trudged back to the cottage. "Bluidy faces there I've never seen afore!" he'd growled. "Lucky t'get a pew, 'n' you wi' more right'n any on 'em."

His wife pressed his arm, knowing his anger was really hurt, a deep-down wounding sort of hurt. These strangers were putting a seal on something they didn't know or understand. Their home, for instance, had been in her family for over five generations. Births, marriages, deaths, disasters and desires…its thick stone walls had seen them all.

Sarah Branthwaite sighed, accepting the finality although still bewildered at the speed of it all once the initial notice had dropped through their letterbox. For folks whose lives were determined by the seasons, the sight of the mounting activity – the thundering lorries and the smart young men with their satnavs in their 4x4s – was a forewarning of what to expect when they moved to Leeds to live with their eldest son.

Sarah had been a Christian all her life, the last eighteen years an unpaid but willing helper at St Michael's. General dogsbody, she good-naturedly called herself when asked, just something to fill her days after their last child had upped and married. For that reason perhaps she'd felt more and more drawn to the old church's comforting interior as the deadline grew closer. The shock of Father Scanlon's death had sharpened that need, which made it all the more intolerable to be denied access at such a time. The doors were shut and locked between services, something unheard of before he had taken over. She knew it was wrong to forswear the use of the new priest's name but it was her natural reserve, her country ways. Besides, there was something not quite right there, she sensed it.

Barred to all comers now, to 'make an inventory', he'd said. And 'clear up any remaining church business', whatever that might mean. She sniffed, choosing to disregard Sam's rejoinder as she'd left him to visit the church one last time. She knew the priest was inside; there was light and she could detect movement. The high, stained-glass windows were beyond her reach, even on tiptoe. The only spy-point was on top of the ancient standing stone that was actually set in the east wall of the church, on the graveyard side. Over ten feet high, they used to scale it as children for a dare. Well, that was well beyond her creaky old joints now. But those self-same bones were telling her that *something* was not quite right about it all. Each afternoon and evening she had attempted to gain entrance, to say farewell to her forebears, those generations long gone, and her reason for being. She felt a strong, almost overpowering, urge to speak to them from what – to her – was still hallowed ground. To try to explain somehow why she and Sam had to leave in this way.

The locked doors made her angry; they were something tangible to rail against and she was stubborn. Oh, yes, that streak was in her as it was in most country folk, inured as they were to the vagaries of nature, its savage winters and very often disappointing summers. If you let go just once in this part of the world, you could be lost for good.

So she would try once more, although it was getting late and she had to prepare Sam's tea, their last proper meal here before departing tomorrow forever. And the weather was worsening too, great black clouds piling up over Craw Fell, portending a wet, blustery night.

She hurried through the churchyard, past the leaning head-stones of her great-great grandparents, the lettering no longer decipherable but the names handed down through the years. The leaves of early autumn were on the move, seeming to sense that for them too the end was nigh. They whispered around the lichen-covered stones, there to gossip conspiratorially before being shepherded on by a fussy gust of wind. Sarah didn't like it when the church spoke to her in this way, undisciplined and somehow destructive, like mischievous imps bent on terror and disorder. She preferred the gentler, soothing murmur of the giant yews as they swayed towards each other like courtly latter-day gentlemen, yielding to the air but only so far, firmly resisting pressure to move with every passing fancy. But this scurrying presence beneath her feet unnerved her.

Reaching the shelter of the porch she absentmindedly searched the pocket of her shabby duffel coat for the key she habitually kept there, then stopped, mindful of his edict. As the unfairness of it all struck her, her face hardened. Why not? He's forgotten I possess this spare key to the front doors.

But what if he was in there? The taboos of a lifetime assailed her for a moment. But he's a stranger to me. And so what? By this time tomorrow we'll be gone, Sam and me. What's he going to do, ban me from ever coming back? She smiled at the thought, then inserted the heavy iron key in the lock and turned it very slowly.

Sarah pushed one half of the great double doors, with its corroded metal studs and bands, and eased her comfortable bulk through the small opening, leaving the door ajar in case she needed to retreat in a hurry. Some of her confidence drained away in the familiar surroundings but she felt committed now. There was a light from the candle-lit altar…but they weren't the usual candles. Instead of the tall, golden wax she was used to setting out, these were shorter, fat almost, and there were more on the floor, placed in some sort of order, creating a glowing circle of light. He was standing in front of the altar with his back to her.

Nervous now that she was close to his authority, she had her doubts. Should she back away and close the door, then knock as usual? A mood of defiance took hold; she touched her grey hair where it had been plucked by the wind, shoved some wisps back under the head square. No! Who better? As Sam had said, who better had the right to kneel one last time before forever became a realistic prospect? Besides, he was performing some kind of service, his murmuring barely audible at this distance. She crept quietly to the end pew, genuflected and sank to her knees.

She prayed for perhaps a minute, then something – what? – made her look up. The words…? No, the sounds! She could not distinguish anything of what he was intoning but those sounds, those syllables, were alien to her ears. Over the years she'd been present at just about every different church service performed – baptisms, high nuptials, funerals, benediction, novenas. Even once an exorcism, up at old Bernie Winston's place. And now that the Latin was barred she was still trying to get used to the somehow unfamiliar English version. But this sounded like mumbo-jumbo to her old but still keen ears. She looked at the dark, sleek head of the young priest, suddenly apprehensive, forgetting the more tangible fear of having trespassed. She flinched as lightning flickered through the stained glass, throwing elongated shadows across the interior. The statue of the Guardian Angel appeared to beckon and the outstretched wings of the carved lectern to flap as the following thunder startled it into imaginary flight.

It appeared to affect Father Cappel too, for he glanced up at the nearest window and shifted a little to his right, exposing what should have been the gold and gilt crucifix in front of the tabernacle. But the crucifix was gone. In its place was a strange device outlined in flat shiny metal. A five-pointed star!

Sarah felt her sanity slipping, her breath coming in short gulps, a tight band pressing round her chest.

The priest stepped back, raising his arms and his voice. "Master…Master…hear me and grant this desire. I will obey your commands even unto death."

There was a brilliant flash to the left of the altar, followed by a fearful cracking sound. Sarah screamed. Cappel whirled, his arms still raised, face white, eyes black as jet. A column of grey smoke snaked up from the source of the flash, slowly drifting in the draught from the open door. She whimpered as a form appeared through the smoke; black, blacker than night itself, a gigantic dog stood there, trembling. Its head was equally huge, lean-jawed and slavering as it turned from side to side. It seemed confused. Then it either saw or sensed Sarah's presence, quivered along its shaggy back. Its short powerful tail lashed as it stared down the length of the darkened church.

Sarah recoiled in horror at the great burning-red eyes. Like live coals, they appeared to swell and pulse as its gaze locked on her. With a bound it leapt into the aisle, its nails rattling on the worn flagstones. The priest – until now transfixed – broke from his spell. He shouted, something like despair in his voice, but the creature paid no heed, it raced towards Sarah.

She screamed again, pure terror ripping through her. She turned, a kind of numbness hampering her movements, in an effort to gain the doorway and escape from the nightmare. She managed a few tottering steps, heard the beast's panting, turned to see the enormous head, wide-open drooling mouth and those saucer-like eyes about to reach her.

"Holy Mary, Mother of God," she whimpered. But then her heart failed and she fell in the creature's path, oblivious to the impact as it swept her aside like a broken doll.

The priest called out again, his strength returning. "Stop! In the name of the Master I command you…"

But the creature was gone, out through the open doorway and into the darkness beyond, in its wake a peculiar burning odour that was quickly dispelled in the cool night air.

Father Cappel fell to his knees, face buried in his hands. After a long silence he raised his head. Terror of a very different kind to Sarah's began to creep across his saturnine features.

3: DEFIANCE

The ambulance, lights flashing and siren wailing, had departed, as had the police. Jake Ransome, aspiring news reporter for the *Clarion*, shivered in the gusting rain. He was a long way from being the hard-bitten cynic of his favourite American fiction, but one of the personal safeguards he'd learnt early on was an impassive outlook on the seamier side of human frailty in all its aspects.

Luckily, this one fell into the plus category. He'd picked up on the police frequency almost subconsciously, while what he liked to call his 'main brain' grappled with the habitual problem of making the borough council's debate on vandalism read as interesting as it was serious, without incurring the wrath of his sub-editor.

He cocked an ear as the soft, susurration from the receiver impinged more deeply on his awareness. "…at St Michael's church, Helmington…" Hell, he thought, that's where the new reservoir is. Didn't know there was anybody left out there. He fine-tuned, slid the volume up. "…investigate an accident to elderly female inside…circumstances from local curate unclear. Contact a Father Cappel C-A-P-P-E-L for details. Ambulance on way. Copy? Over."

By the time he'd arrived in his exhaust-rich '93 Ford Escort whatever human drama there may have been was gone. Only a distraught old man with that all-too-familiar expression of loss and confusion remained. The paramedic had skilfully fielded his stammering questions and pleas for reassurance, whilst helping him up the steps of the ambulance. Even the construction company's own security people weren't interested.

Jake looked around. The place was like a ghost town, which – in a way, he supposed – it was. Not yet six and the village street was deserted. No lights in front windows, no slamming of car doors, no barking dogs. Brown leaves blew along the road surface. It was creepy somehow. Common sense told him it would look like this anyhow, however populated, but it didn't help. Perhaps it was the unlit pedestrian crossing.

He shook himself, zipped up his leather parka and ran, head down, across the road, angling towards the lych-gate. The church door was ajar, a dim light inside. He paused before pushing it further. He wasn't a Catholic, wasn't much of anything these days but even so… He shrugged and entered, then almost recoiled – a priest was standing just inside the entrance, eyes staring out from a long, pale face. The moment of mutual surprise passed, the young reporter's reflexes marginally faster.

"Good evening, Father. I hope I didn't startle you."

"Who are you? What do you want?" The other's tone was defensive, almost rude.

Jake surreptitiously felt for the BlackBerry in his pocket, fingered it to 'record' mode in a well-practised movement. He slid his hand out with the phone in it, confident it would pick up well enough to transcribe later.

"Jake Ransome, Father," he said, "with the *Clarion*. We've never actually met but I did speak with you on the phone a little while ago, when I did a piece on Father Scanlon. You remember…?"

"What? Oh, yes, of course. I'm sorry, please come in." The priest retreated a few steps. "This whole business has…" He passed a hand across his brow. "Terrible, especially after – after…"

"Father Scanlon's death…the de-consecration service, was it?" Jake prompted, his eyes roving, reporter's nose a-twitch.

There were no bloodstains, no damaged furniture. But what did he expect? It was simply an 'old folks accident' item, only good for a slow news day, unless it had a criminal slant, like a mugging or a break-in. This didn't look like either of those and yet…this young cleric was definitely edgy, more agitated than the situation seemed to warrant. Or did they not include crisis management on the theological syllabus?

"What are you doing here, Mr Ransome?" the priest demanded suddenly. "What possible interest could your paper have in Sarah Branthwaite's attack -"

"Attack?"

"Attack, seizure, collapse, call it what you will." He waved a hand impatiently. "She was obviously under a certain amount of stress to begin with, being uprooted so late in life. And of course she was devoted to Father Scanlon and this church. It all proved too much, poor soul."

"Where did it happen, Father?"

"By this pew." The priest placed a hand on the carved end. "She was saying a last prayer before leaving tomorrow. She and Mr Branthwaite were due to leave the village in the morning."

"Were you conducting a service then, Father? I thought, once the de-consecration ceremony was completed…you know?" Jake broke off awkwardly, disconcerted by the priest's uncompromising stare.

"There was no service," the priest said firmly. "Sarah Branthwaite was in here without permission. I was up at the altar, checking for any leftover items. I had locked the doors, forgetting she still had a key from her caretaking role -"

"Why locked, Father? I mean, if there is virtually nobody left in the village and everything of value removed…" Jake thought there was something strange about the priest's behaviour, but perhaps that was reasonable under the circumstances.

"The building has to be locked because it isn't safe!" Father

Cappel was quite agitated. "That was a contributing factor in Mrs Branthwaite's collapse. But I've told all this to the police, Mr Ransome. Now, if you will be so good -"

"Please, Father, bear with me. I'm just doing my job. The situation does have a certain news value. Your predecessor found lying here a week ago, now this old lady... You do see that some readers – especially friends of hers and locals generally – would find the details of some interest? Best they get the true facts from the principals involved, rather than a distorted version that only gets wilder from pub to pub." Jake moved a little closer, aiding his recording a touch. "Now, you say something triggered Mrs Branthwaite's collapse?"

Father Cappel looked at the floor and Jake assumed he was praying. The silence lasted for perhaps half a minute. Then: "Shock," he said firmly. "It was shock that caused her condition. It's the roof, you see. That's why I locked the church – to stop anyone coming in. There was a particularly strong flash of lightning and then a great thunderclap. It must have struck the roof – I know the copper conductor up there is not as it should be. Some material came down, accompanied by clouds of dust. I heard a scream behind me and turned, only then seeing Mrs Branthwaite. She clutched at her chest before collapsing and striking her head on the flags here." He pointed to a dark stain on the centuries-old flagstone, still wet. "I – I was somewhat disoriented myself, I can tell you! Being almost buried beneath the debris was bad enough and then the shock of discovering I was not after all alone, closely followed by..." He drew a hand across his brow. "She made an awful sound as she crashed down. I was dreadfully upset. In fact, I thought she was dead and instead of running back to the presbytery to ring for an ambulance I could only think of poor Sam across the road in their cottage, wondering where his lady wife was. So it was a double shock for him when I barged in..."

"It's all right, Father, don't upset yourself. I think I've got the picture. Any further details I can get from the police. Just one final point, if I may." The priest gazed at him. "Was there much damage? I mean, I can't see any debris -"

"I've cleared it away. Sorry. Force of habit. I used to work in a youth club and it became second nature to sweep up after every session. If I didn't…" He shrugged.

Jake nodded. "I'll not take up any more of your time, Father. I can tell there was a lightning flash hereabouts – a definite smell of scorching. Yes?"

But the priest's eyes were no longer on him; he seemed to have already dismissed this minor irritation. Probably thinking what else he might have done for the poor old dear…like going along with Sam in the ambulance. Jake made his excuses and left.

Outside, the rain was blustering even more strongly. Wet leaves flapped about Jake's face like tiny drowning bats as he ran to the car.

4: MALEVOLENCE

Cappel waited several minutes, only venturing outside when he heard the car moving off. Carefully locking the double doors with Sarah Branthwaite's key, he then made his way quickly through the east side of the churchyard. He skirted the bole of the fallen yew where it lay by the boundary wall and slipped through the old kissing gate that led to the presbytery. He paused for a moment to look around, particularly into the areas of deepest shadow. But there was nothing there to alarm him, only the familiar black bulk of the medieval Norman building, the tall, shapely sentinels of the ancient yews and the uneven silhouettes of the gravestones which marked the mortal remains of a dozen generations. No sign of that creature…yet.

He turned and hurried into the presbytery porch, fumbled with the keys to the heavy, glass-panelled door. Inside, he leaned back for a moment, relieved to feel a material barrier behind him before his reason screamed, 'Beware! The demon is out there and you – YOU! – have summoned it up from the depths of hell.'

"Oh, God," he whispered, his confusion complete. "What have I done?"

But then the realization of a much closer and higher form of punishment jerked him into action. He raced up the stairs, not bothering with lights until he reached the upper storey. The room at the end of the gloomy passage, facing north, was locked as usual, since Father Scanlon's death had left him the sole occupant. Once inside he flicked on the lights and shot the bolt. The rectangular room was virtually bare; heavy dark blue curtains hung across the recess of the only window, facing north. The windows on the two long sides were similarly draped.

Striding towards the far end, Cappel quickly undressed, flinging the clerical garb into the recess. Naked now he drew on a simple black cotton robe, tied the white cord round his waist. He dragged two tea chests to the centre of the room; painted white outside, black within, the colours representing the ethereal and materialistic worlds. Pushing them together to form his altar, he then reached inside for the artifacts necessary to the purification ceremony. This was essential if he was to succeed in what was to follow. He would have to perform a stronger version of the interrupted ritual quickly, before the conditions became even less propitious.

He'd cleansed himself thoroughly earlier, fasting all day in preparation, to deny malevolent elements access in the course of the invocation. He could not afford any more errors tonight, the powers of darkness would show scant regard for excuses once invoked. Already one breach in the requirements – having to converse – had been created by Sarah Branthwaite's unwitting intervention. He was almost certain the appearance of the creature had not been due to her presence, so something had gone drastically wrong with the conjuration. The exact place, chosen with great care, the church being literally built around the standing stone indicating a strong vortex effect of converging forces. Nevertheless, he daren't risk resuming the ritual there in case someone else came snooping around. Having being used before by him, this place would have to do.

He stood up straight and inhaled deeply several times to gain self-control before commencing the ceremony. As the haunting music from Sibelius' Finlandia began to fill the room he sprinkled the prepared incense of cinnamon, myrrh and cloves on the heated charcoal in the earthenware bowl. He laid white string in a large circle on the scrubbed floorboards, enclosing the altar but leaving the ends untied. The usual homage of the four basic elements to the four archangels – Uriel, Michael, Gabriel and

Raphael – would need to be demonstrated, but in this special 'Calling up of Demons' he left the north unsecured by its guardian. Placing a lighted candle at this station, he then drew out a small knife and carefully made one small incision to the inner side of his wrist, allowing several drops of blood into the flame whilst reciting the name of the demon he wished to invoke - Asmodeus.

The power words of God – TETRAGRAMMATON, ARA-RITA, SHADDAI EL CHAI – were already printed on white cards he positioned just inside the string's boundary. On the eastern side, beyond the circle, he drew the Triangle of Art. It was here that the spirit form would hopefully materialize. It could prove to be the most dangerous aspect of the ceremony; in the battle of wills it would try to confuse, overcome and ultimately gain access to the physical body and personality of the adept. Once that happened Cappel knew that he, like so many before, would be destroyed.

A second triangle inside the first, this time with salt, reinforced the barrier. When he judged all was ready, he extinguished the room lights and stepped inside the circle, tying the string's ends together. Working now in candlelight he performed the purification rite, using the sword he'd fashioned from the church crucifix to trace a pentagram in the air whilst uttering the most holy of God's names, YOD-HE-VAU-HE. Knowing it was essential, he infused and reinforced the astral barriers against assault by repeating the pentagrammatic tracery over each compass point.

Moving through the Lesser Pentagram he conjured up the imagery of the archangels, declaring his confidence in their protection. Facing east he focused now on the Tree of Life card. This depicted the various paths he would travel along, once his mission was sanctioned. Satisfied, he now progressed from Malkuth, the sphere of Earth, to Yasod, the silver gateway to the astral world. Invoking the demon's name eleven times he stood on the threshold and recited the names of the Six Authors of Wickedness.

Anointing himself for the journey, he sprinkled more incense in the bowl until it built up in the airless chamber to an almost intoxicating level, making the room almost disappear. The temperature began to rise. He stepped out onto the astral path, his earthly body still firmly anchored within the circle. Along with the music and the emergent power in the correctly sounded words, it all combined to exert and release forces normally latent. His other self, intuitive and subconscious, had progressed through a succession of states, each one a challenge, a test to be overcome before being passed on by – sometimes strange, sometimes recognizable – spirit forms. If his nerve or his knowledge were to falter at any requested password then his failure would be total.

Already physically drained by the day's events, Cappel realized the task of compelling an entity to appear in recognizable shape could prove too daunting. He silently called upon the guardian angel Shinanim to aid him. This seemed to work; he sensed the demon's presence in the room. It paced the outside of the circle, seeking a weakness, stalking, probing. The smoke from the incense began to swirl, twisting and roiling as though in torment. The temperature that had been steadily rising within the sealed room now noticeably dropped.

"Spirit of the Ethereal Realm, I command you by the powers invested in me and through me. Raphael, Host of the Upper Regions and protector of all against evil, he who is ever-watchful of all who disobey the astral laws will hold all dissent as rebellion. Be advised that in such matters I have his blessing. Again I command you to appear."

Cappel had no illusions about what he had to achieve. He knew the next few seconds would be crucial. If the spirit summoned had been responsible for the black dog's uncalled-for manifestation then it was likely that its malevolence was still present. There were so many out there, and unless called by name would remain elusive, evading all commands unless a higher authority was ultimately invoked. To do that unnecessarily would incur monumental displeasure from those far more powerful than he.

Something was forming within the triangle, a shimmering that quickly solidified into a figure…

"Oh, my God," Cappel moaned.

It was his mother, long dead but exactly as he always remembered her; the heavy black brocade dress she invariably affected in perpetual mourning for his father. Her white hair was the same, as were the thin, severe features that stared out at him disapprovingly, as if she were only now aware of her son's defection, subverting his vocation for – for this.

She held out her hands in a silent but unmistakable plea. Come to me, my son, I forgive you; I will make it all right again. Come.

The realization that he was being drawn forward jarred Cappel back to his senses. In ringing tones he commanded the entity to assume its own form. His mother's likeness disappeared instantly. He ran a hand over his perspiring face and waited. A shape began to form once more. This time it was a beautiful child, golden-haired, blue-eyed, with chubby apple cheeks. She smiled at him, the most radiant of smiles, and he felt himself slipping.

You fool! It is merely demonstrating its own powers. The child's face crumpled into tears as it found itself confined within the triangular prison. It cried piteously, wringing his heart.

"No, no!" Cappel cried out. "Asmodeus, I command you to assume that shape ordained by the Almighty Himself at the time of the Great Betrayal. I have the power, the conjuration, to constrain you for a thousand kalpas within the triangle if you resist me. I command you!"

With a sizzling flash the apparition vanished. Cappel waited for what seemed an interminable length of time, imagining himself cast freely in space, the incense thickening and swirling about the circle. He knew this to be more machinations of the spirit form he was summoning up, but it was difficult not to loosen his grip on reality. He was caught up in his own ritualistic guidelines, formalized and known to others on the astral plane. Should he disregard certain aspects, then he would have to accept the consequences.

Then the triangle seemed to quaver, flickering in the uncertain light. Something was externalizing itself within its borders. Cappel braced himself, willing his positive thoughts forward, all negativity suppressed to more easily gain mastery over whatever should materialize.

He gasped; the form was hideous, some nightmare mutation. It crouched, almost a metre high, snarling and drooling at its invisible but tangible restraint. Its scaly surface was dark green, shiny-wet and covered in lumpy, running sores. From its back protruded stunted leathery wings; front feet that ended in claws; a spiky, curved back and a sharp, thin tail flicking like that of some angry cat. But it was the head and face that was the abomination. The appearance was dog-like though strangely human – a pointed snout, with wet quivering nostrils and carmine lips peeled back to reveal several rows of sharp yellow teeth. The ears were in keeping with the face – pointed and laid back flat against the scalp.

But those eyes…slanted and glowing faintly with a red, flickering stare across the intervening space. It was a look of such concentrated evil that Cappel felt his nerve dissolving before it. He rallied just in time, remembering this was a battle of wills, and commanded the thing to speak. It twisted and turned like some recalcitrant child, showing him hind legs ending in hooves. Suddenly the air about him filled with a horrible stench. Without actually seeing them he was aware of shapes and a sense of malevolence all around the circle as the demon called upon the forces of evil to aid it in its dominance over whatever was inside the protective ring. Cappel seized the pentacle he'd brought with him for just such an eventuality. It was one of the higher forms of defence against elementals of the astral planes, and he called upon the holy names within the circle.

This appeared to hit the beast from the lower reaches of the pit, Asmodeus, physically; it writhed about, showing Cappel its soil-encrusted rear before turning back to claw at the defensive triangle in a frenzied attack.

Finally it spoke in a deep, arrogant voice: "I FEED UPON THE NAMES OF THE MOST HIGH. I CHURN THEM IN MY JAWS AND VOID THEM FROM MY FUNDAMENT…"

Asmodeus bellowed with laughter, a sound that chilled Cappel's blood. He knew he was losing the battle – that he had taken on more than he should. An errant demon was the last thing he wanted right now. He raised the pentacle again, that most potent of Solomonic symbols, and called upon all guardians of the watchtowers to assist him in controlling the disobedient spirit form. He chanted the required words over and over, and gradually the atmosphere ceased its turbulence. Finally, he dared to look at the triangle.

Asmodeus was no longer snarling and drooling, simply levelling that terrible stare at him. He took this to indicate some form of compliance.

"Asmodeus, will you obey?"

"I…will…obey…"

Cappel breathed easier. He'd come this far, now was the moment that would prove if it all had been worth it – for there would be some price to pay, he knew that. "Where is the chalice of Julius Marr?"

He waited.

Time appeared to stand still and yet somehow expand. The room contracted, swelled, the only reality the palpable malevolence that lay beyond that – as yet – unbridgeable space. The creature moved and once more Cappel sensed it was seeking some means of escape, for to yield was to lose. Always the battle against rival forces, the eternal struggle of one over another. But no matter how it twisted the gaze somehow held his own throughout.

He was about to repeat the question when it spoke. "It…is…beneath…me…"

"Do not disobey, Asmodeus."

The demon laughed that terrible laugh once more. "I…obey…and…you…still…disbelieve…
It…is…beneath…me…and…you!"

The creature let out a raucous bellow that echoed and re-echoed around the room.

Dizzily, Cappel clapped his hands over his ears. "What do you mean?" he screamed at his tormentor, realizing he was losing the upper hand. Then, with a flash and spiralling of green smoke, Asmodeus vanished.

Cappel sank to his knees, mentally and physically exhausted, wanting to cry as he cast about for some meaning to what had just happened. The walls flickered in the guttering candlelight and he shivered as the sweat began to cool on his body, distractedly rubbing at the new wound on his wrist. He was barely aware that the music had stopped, then the click of the tape's ending startled him.

"It is beneath me…and you…" He whispered the words over and over.

Then it struck him and his head came up. "Beneath *us*… Oh, my God, yes!"

24

5: VIOLENCE

Sister Dymphna was at peace with her world. The turbulent, early years of doubt concerning her vocation had eventually faded into, if not quite acceptance, then a re-affirmation of her original beliefs. She had always been a woman with normal, healthy appetites and, coming into the order rather late in life, had sometimes found it all an uphill task. But now she was sure. She was finally winning, especially after being allowed to strike the correct balance between the sectarian and the secular. Since transferring to Lowbeck Convent her whole horizon had expanded, filling her waking hours with work of such a beneficial nature that she could at last say she was truly happy.

The life of prayer to which she had devoted herself was still the major part of each day, but the increasing influx of technology necessary to administer even a modest establishment such as theirs had uncovered skills in her that had surprised her. The laptop was exciting, so colourful and non-threatening to her theological doctrine; it only gave out what you put in – oops!..inputted! What was it the young computer expert had said...? 'Just think GIGO, Sister. Garbage In equals Garbage Out!'

She smiled at her shadowy reflection in the rear view mirror of the old Bedford van. That had been a further opening to other worlds, finding it in one of the outbuildings of the convent. A local garage owner had tried all ways to buy it from the order, finally offering a sum of money that had initiated and extraordinary meeting among the sisters.

The consensus had been to resist the temptation of immediate profit (much as it would have aided the new roof fund) and instead regard it as a bonus, a tool to ease the pressure from the outside world. Rather than have supplies delivered, with its attendant distractions on young novitiates, someone could venture out and fetch them. And that someone had turned out to be Sister Dymphna, the only nun with a current driving license. It was also felt that, at age 59, she was firmly beyond the temptations that might be presented by cheeky young 'white van' suppliers. She might have argued with that last one on principle but let it go in case it swung the vote against her.

Use of the van had also opened another door. The parish priest of St Michael of All Angels had approached Mother Superior with a request for someone to assist at the youth centre, mainly helping out with girls from broken homes. Today had been particularly fulfilling, placing Cherie Gilbert with the family of a newly-arrived American executive to the nearby chemical plant.

Sister Dymphna was heading back now for the Novena and Benediction, followed by warm milk, prayer and bed. A big day tomorrow, organizing the convent's annual audit with their accountants. She damped down the urge to coax more speed from the van's geriatric engine. The night was becoming wilder, the worn wipers failing miserably against the lashing rain. Noticing the country road's surface was slicked with leaves she eased the van round the trickier bends.

Ah, she was nearly home – and still dry! There was the old stone cross straight ahead, with the lights of the convent just visible a half mile further on. She had encountered no other traffic for a good ten minutes and would feel happier once past this particular stretch; for some unaccountable reason it always made her slightly uneasy, and she invariably felt better when it was in her rear mirror. Silly Dymps!

The wind was becoming much stronger now, the rain sheeting down. She flicked the lights to high beam, wishing the convent's resources ran to a car radio, especially at times like this.

Suddenly – as if from nowhere - a gigantic black hound appeared ahead of her, standing in the centre of the road, full in the headlights, looming large, eyes enormous, red and glowing.

"Oh, sweet Jesus -" The nun stamped on the brake pedal, but she had no chance on the slippery surface. The van started to swerve but uncannily the dog was still there, resolutely in her path and seemingly doubled in size. Desperately she tried to correct the skid, had a moment's self-recrimination for not clipping in her seat belt...and then the animal was over the bonnet and on top of her.

She screamed once before the van slammed sideways into the high stone wall. Her head smashed through the glass of the side window, a shard slicing her carotid artery as she hit the wall's jagged edge.

Oblivion was swift, and kinder than the secondary injuries that would only have prolonged her agony.

6: IGNORANCE

"Now let's get this straight, son," Gus growled. "Some old dear out at Helmsdale took a heart attack in the church and fell down, currently lying comatose in the hospital, mm?" He held one hand up before continuing. "You don't much like the look of the clerical incumbent but you can't say why, exactly. Oh, and there was a smell of burning…which isn't surprising, given said maligned minister's statement that lightning had struck the roof just prior to the incident. That's it?"

The editor of the *Clarion* then proceeded slowly – theatrically – to go through his pipe routine. Sniffing and reaming before knocking the filthy dottle out onto the large glass ashtray, separating the components parts and clearing the stem. He looked to Jake like some gnarled, over-large pygmy preparing a blowgun for battle.

Jake moved out of the line of fire and waited impatiently, mustering his debating points, aware that this performance was not even necessary, given that Gus could only smoke the damned thing outside the building and all this was only his one-man little rebellion against the ' the system'.

But as usual, when the old newspaper man raised one bushy eyebrow as his cue to answer, Jake's confidence deserted him. "But if you had been there, Gus – sir!" He corrected himself, realizing he hadn't quite attained those lofty heights whereby he could lean, elbow to elbow, on the bar of the Wig & Pen, swapping news scoops. "The atmosphere, his eyes…" His voice tailed off as the other's eyes hardened. He knew he'd lost whatever little initiative he might have had.

"We don't deal in fiction here, laddie, as even you must be

aware by now." Gus Beaney was a failed novelist and though it was a long time back he knew that every intern was appraised of this fact and been seriously advised to avoid embellishment and speculation as though it were a norovirus. "We have a deadline to meet. You have some copy that's relevant to what we do here, I trust."

Jake felt himself flush under the scorn but held his ground. "Yessir! But–but could I pursue this between other assignments…sir?"

Gus nodded curtly. "Go!"

All the way back to his desk he muttered, "He didn't say no…he didn't say no."

But that was the extent of his good fortune. The micro-fiche turned up nothing and Shirley in Archives had merely shrugged. "Saint who?" She waved wearily at the dusty shelves – or was she just drying her nail varnish? – indicating the enormity of the task. Apart from their alphabetical coding the anonymous brown envelopes always seemed to be laughing at him, inviting him to place his money and take a chance. Is it here, or here…? Or perhaps this one? When do we go digital?

He was gloomily snapping elastic bands when Gerry Malone, on the crime desk, flopped onto the seat across from him.

"Cheer up, Jake! Has the bountiful Belinda finally twigged just how high up the career ladder you really are?" Gerry ran his fingers through already unruly grey curls and loosened his tie. "You're better off than that poor nun, any road," he added, reaching for the keyboard.

"Nun? What nun?"

"That unfortunate they've just scraped off the Lawnwood Estate wall, out by Hayman's Cross. A victim of last night's storm, looks like. Hell of a way to get to heaven huh? A sixty-year old nun in a thirty-year old banger can be a pretty deadly combination. Ah, well, everyone wants to go to heaven but nobody wants to die. Wonder if that's true for nuns, eh?" He quickly sketched in the details for Jake as he played the keys.

Something about Jake's lack of response seemed to stop him and he glanced up. "What the hell's the matter with you?"

"Gerry… What time did this happen? I mean, was it late?" Jake waited, not really sure why he was asking. There was certainly no legitimate reason to connect a tragic car accident with a cardiac arrest in an old church, especially when the culprit – the weather – appeared to be the same in each case.

"Oh…" Gerry flipped through his notes. "Quite early, as it happens, she wasn't coming from the pub or anything." His usual irreverence faltered at the intense expression on his young colleague's face. "Between six and six-fifteen, near as dammit. A shop assistant driving home from Stockton was first on the scene. Wheels still spinning, so…" He shrugged. "No other person or vehicle involved, one set of skid marks on the road. Forensic reckons it's your proverbial 'open and shut, accident waiting to happen' thing. Slick road surface due to extreme weather conditions plus the aforementioned recipe for disaster…if our sexist friend over there will allow." He leered across the busy news room at Alison Grune of the fashion page.

She – out of earshot but watching and painfully conscious of Gerry's views on 'glass ceilings and gender pressure' – gave him the stiff finger on principle.

Gerry smiled beatifically back. "Of course, the dodgy brakes and steering will feature large at the inquest." He turned back to Jake. "Surprised, really, there wasn't more" – he clawed quotation marks in the air with his fingers – "statistical news."

Jake had to laugh. This was a reference to Gus's latest buzz word. 'Statistical' news was his term for news items that could be predicted, even pre-empted; snowy pile-ups and hypothermia cases in winter; forest fires and skin cancer scares in summer. Some copy on these general themes could therefore be filed in readiness, thus minimizing costs in money, manpower and time. Or, as one office wag put it, "His story repeating itself."

Gerry went on: "It was pretty wild there, but only for a very short period. Our pet weather man says such a storm at this time of year fits no known pattern and wasn't predicted by anyone."

"Just as if -" Jake stopped, shook his head.

"What?" Gerry looked up.

"Gerry, who would have an encyclopaedic knowledge of this area's folklore and customs?"

"Well, there's always Joan Winspear."

"Who? Oh, that old trout who used to write an occasional piece on the ghosts and ghoulies of North Yorkshire. Thought she died."

"She's not dead and if she hears you talking about her like that there could be a new ghost with no goolies out there!" Gerry returned to his screen. "Now sod off, I've got work to do even if you haven't."

7: RESURGENCE

Cromleac, guardian hound of Ruagh, the chieftain of all the northern tribes, stirred uneasily. It was time to resume his search. He could feel the strength building within him as darkness fell. The stones' power brought not only renewed life but form and substance also. He could not understand this but accepted his altered state. Without their aid he sensed the quest could not continue, and whined softly at the thought of never again seeing his master. Each sun's passing left him further from Ruagh's side. He could not rest until he had fulfilled his task. A gathering would occur and he must not fail his master again.

The centres of power were all around him, he could feel them. But which one held his master? How many suns had passed since his awakening…two…three? Why had he been brought back before The Time? And why him alone? The red rage that had made him feared from moorland to coastline rumbled in the mighty chest. It had been the one garbed in black who had separated him from his master, wrenching him from his vigil to an unfamiliar place of high stone walls and flickering light. Instinct told him to find space before turning to face his enemies; the old female human barring his path had proved no obstacle.

But once outside he became confused. Nothing was as he remembered; so many strange and unnameable forces on all sides – in the air, in the ground beneath him, vibrating. Once again his instinct was for flight, only realizing too late that his strength was waning the further he got from the source of his materialization.

In the world he now inhabited, there was no night and day,

only periods of weakness and energy, doubt and confidence, as he traversed the terrain. He was torn between the need to rejoin his master and the concentrations of power that sustained him in his quest. The sudden materializations frightened him, making him react instinctively – with savagery. The great metal beast with the glaring white eyes and roaring noise, rushing at him out of the darkness had contained a black-cowled human. He had hoped it was the one but it had smelt different…female. He would know when it was the right one, Cromleac had been renowned for his keen nose. Ruagh, the red-haired one, leader of men, fearsome in battle, respected in council, the human that was his life – and death – had selected him from the litter personally.

"This one!" He had reached down and gripped the small black bundle by the scruff, raising him high. The rough-haired puppy yelped and tried to bite the hand that swung him aloft. Ruagh laughed, his strong teeth showing through the bushy beard. "I will take him and teach him how to hunt and kill for Ruagh the Red. He will sit at my feet in council and stand by my side in war. He will hunt down the elk and gnaw on the bones of my foes."

And so it had been; Ruagh could envision, just as well as he could dominate events, so that people lost sight of what was practical and what was possible, his eloquence in the council chamber and ruthless warrior code quelling all but the most foolhardy dissenters. A natural leader, he revoked laws that had stood for generations, striking fear in his enemies by denying them a formal burial or funeral urn. No trace was ever left of those who defied Ruagh, a prospect more terrible for them than death itself.

He changed the tribal laws regarding life and death, food and shelter, even easing the old ones' departure when a harsh winter made their bones too painful to endure. He introduced the Cup of Everlasting Sleep, decreeing there was no dishonour in seeking to join one's ancestors when fighting and child-minding days were done.

Then the Ceremony of the Stones was revived. The stones were old, went far back to when the tribe was a miserable collection of reed shelters, foraging for food. The power of the stone circles had been discovered by one of Ruagh's forefathers. At first people had died screaming or been afflicted with the loss of speech before the stones' mysteries had been fully understood. For hundreds of moons then the tribe had prospered, gaining mastery over those who sought to subdue and steal their women. To a chosen few, the stones would speak, revealing the thoughts of others, infusing warriors with strengthened spear arms and healing wounds held within the invisible circle of power.

Those who did fall in battle were placed within a different arrangement of stones, erected under the guidance of The Chosen One. The dead warrior's body would not rot or fall away as others did, but slowly lose its juices, till on a given day, when the sun was low in the sky, the stones' alignment proved propitious and the burial mound commenced. During the course of the interment the warrior's exploits would be recounted, songs of praise composed and his weapons distributed by the elders of the tribe. His woman and offspring would be cared for until the first-born son had proven himself worthy.

In times of crisis The Chosen One could communicate with those who were now with the gods, although this could prove a perilous course; the mighty forces within the stones sometimes exacting the ultimate tribute if called incorrectly.

This had been an accepted way for Ruagh and his people, no other being known to them. Then one day the tribe who lived by the sea had been driven inland, looking for food, a season of endless storms having wrecked their homes and taken their nets.

Their soothsayers had said it was an evil placed upon them by the northern tribes' secret powers.

Ruagh sent word to the coastal tribe that he wanted to help them in their need. This wisdom was construed as weakness by the coastal tribe and, swayed by the young men's taunts, they decided to sweep their enemies away once and for all. A mighty gathering ensued and great was the killing. Cromleac had never smelt so much blood.

Urged on by Ruagh's, "Drink blood, Cromleac, drink deep!" the shaggy black hound, half a spear high and protected by overlapping bullhide strips and a fearsome metal spiked collar, joyfully plunged into the fray. Opening his mighty jaws he crunched arms and legs, tore throats out as the victims fell before his master's thrusts. Hour after hour the battle raged; knowing the northern tribes' cruel reputation in victory left them little choice other than leave their bones to bleach on the wild moorland.

Ruagh fought better than he had ever done; being at the height of his powers, tall as a rowan and just as hard he hacked and speared till the bodies lay in heaps about him. But as the sun dipped across the purple hills the many wounds he had sustained began to take their toll. Cromleac had never smelt his master's blood before and it made him whine; he retreated to Ruagh's side, wanting to protect him from further injury. His master roared at him to maintain his station, which he did, but then the over-riding love that was such a bond between them soon had him edging back again. Ruagh – in his pain and weariness – mistook his faithful hound's action. Bellowing his anger, he cursed Cromleac as craven, fit only for crow bait.

Before Cromleac could communicate in the way he knew how, Ruagh struck him a telling blow with the spear shaft, cracking his skull. The great dog shuddered under the impact, whimpered once and fell to the ground. Stricken with remorse at what he had done the warrior chief momentarily lowered his shield. Swift as striking snakes, three of the enemy ran him through, their cruel fishing barbs ripping into Ruagh's flesh. He fell across the prostrate body of Cromleac.

When the great hound regained his senses it was dark and cold, and his master was nowhere around. Only the smell of death was left on the torn and bloodied gorse. Dazed, sorely wounded but somehow still breathing Cromleac managed to drag himself across the heath to the tribe's encampment. It took all of that night and most of the following day.

Instead of being greeted as of old, with a rough hug and slap on the flanks, he heard the chant for the dead, Ruagh's name among them. The shock of his grief brought back the memory of those last moments together.

Instinctively he knew he was the cause of his master's death. Inconsolable, howling, determined never again to desert his post he bestrode the cold body, baring those ferocious fangs at any who approached. When the ritual interment ceremony was signalled to begin no man could get near to drag the snarling brute away.

To commit violence over a leader's newly-dead corpse was against their laws, so it was agreed that Cromleac be allowed the honour of dying as he had lived, by his master's side. The construction of the mound commenced.

So the concentration of forces that reduced Ruagh to an essence also acted upon the dog, not yet dead. The result was a creature held somewhere between life and death, aware of both but fully assigned to neither.

Down the long centuries Cromleac's spirit guarded Ruagh, the bond between them so strong it transcended death itself, the manner of their journey into the great unknown instilling in Cromleac an eternal stewardship over his master's presence. For this reason he must return to Ruagh's side before something similar occurred. If Ruagh was awakened and he too followed these strange and conflicting energies then they might never be re-united, a prospect that set the great beast howling once more, the blood-curdling sound rolling across the moorland, a cry not so much of despair as a rallying call, as of yore, when the world was new and they were its masters.

8: INCIDENCE

Finding out where Joan Winspear lived wasn't too difficult, locating her was the problem. Jake finally tracked her down that evening to a local school, where she was lecturing on her favourite subject. He sidled in at the back of the room and sat on a chair that creaked. Several heads turned disapprovingly and he managed a weak smile. The dragon lady on the dais ignored him completely.

"...so going back over the centuries one can see, just as in the geological layers that came to produce our land, the chroniclers of the past have built up for us a picture of what we now call our heritage. It's a legacy that holds something for everybody – romance, betrayal, corruption and family feuds. In fact, not too different from today!" A few sycophantic simpers came from the audience, which also left her unmoved. "Those of you who are local born and bred will perhaps identify more easily with some of the names and places I have mentioned. But whoever you are and whatever your origins I think you will find the premise holds good that a knowledge of what has gone before will help you cope with the present...and in some cases even determine your future. I will be giving you examples of this next week, when I refer to specific family names and properties." She placed one hand on the table as though to steady herself, before letting her gaze fall in turn on each of her listeners. She adjusted a pair of battered spectacles with the other hand. "Well, that's it for this evening, ladies and gentlemen, I hope to see you all next Thursday. Thank you."

There was a general scraping of chairs and some throat-clearing as the small group, mostly middle-aged and female, broke up. Jake shrank his athletic frame as far as possible into the chair as the members of the evening class filed past him. They all glanced down at him curiously, some inexplicably resentful-looking, one or two smiling to redress the balance. His return smile was automatic, until he perked up at sight of a slim, very dark-haired girl with large blue eyes and a friendly smile, walking down the aisle. She regarded him just as boldly as he did her – so much so it was he who dropped his gaze first.

Annoyed at himself he raised his head to re-engage but she was gone. Before he could twist around to get a glimpse of her legs beneath the dark green coat Joan Winspear spoke.

"Can I help you, young man, or have you wandered into the wrong class?" Were her eyes twinkling or just watery?

"No! I mean yes…that is, can you help me…? If you wouldn't mind, that is." Jake stood up, cursing his lack of poise in such situations. "Look, I'm sorry, I'd better introduce myself. Jake Ransome of the *Clarion*."

She turned her back on him and proceeded to wipe the white-board. "Can you be brief, Mr Ransome? I have a bus to catch."

He noticed the hem of her tweed skirt was unstitched part-way along and one of her sturdy legs was bandaged beneath the thick woollen stockings. The elbows of her fawn Aran cardigan were almost worn through.

"Perhaps I can give you a lift?" he ventured. "Where d'you live?"

She finished what she was doing and put the duster down before turning, favouring her good right leg. The glasses caught the light as she stared at him. "Young man, I am not in the habit of divulging my address to strangers, much less go home with them - no matter how harmless they may appear."

Jake winced. This wasn't going the way he had intended.

"Mr Ransome, why don't you simply tell me why you are here and let me decide how I get home."

"Alright then, I wondered if there is anything you could tell me about St Michael's…out at Helmsdale."

"St Michael's…" She looked down at him keenly, then away for a moment. "You mean apart from it becoming submerged within the next few days?"

He must have presented such a picture of misery that in the end she relented. "Mr Ransome, why don't you tell me what you know and then perhaps I can fill in any missing pieces."

At first she merely heard him out, evincing no emotion, collecting her things together as he went through the sequence of events, sometimes referring to her notes. It was only when he came to the part about the nun that she gave him all her attention. "Where, you say?"

"Hayman's Cross, out near -"

"Yes, yes, I know precisely where it is," she rejoined testily. "Go on…please."

"There's not much more really," Jake ended lamely. "Until the inquest we won't know anything definite about Sister Dymphna's death. Look, I realize this must all sound weird, outlandish, but if you'd been there – at the church – and felt what I…well, what I believe I felt -"

"Is this official, young man? Are you writing up some piece for your paper?"

"No, Miss Winspear," he replied wearily. "I simply had this wild, crazy idea that something wasn't quite right about the whole of last evening. Maybe it was just the storm, the charged atmosphere -"

"If that offer of a ride home still obtains then I'll take you up on it. Come along."

Shaking his head and thinking that she might be slightly crazy, Jake followed her out to the deserted car park. With a sigh of relief he managed to start the car first time and, taking her directions, headed out towards Skelton. She didn't speak at all on the short journey and he didn't broach the subject again, stopping by the ironstone miners' cottages on Swilly Lane, high above the surrounding countryside.

She clambered laboriously from the Escort, banging the car door on the nearby wall. Jake took a deep breath. Forget it, he told himself, it's not really a 'classic'. He got out and traipsed into the tiny terraced house, wrinkling his nose at the smells that assailed him. Just as she switched on the light something furry leapt at him before streaking out through the still-open doorway. He flattened himself against the mildewed wallpaper, heart pounding.

"Dammit, Cicero, where's your manners?" Miss Winspear cried. "We have company. When's the last time that happened?" She disappeared further into the house, calling to Jake. "Come through to the kitchen. I'll put some coffee on."

Reluctantly Jake complied, feeling somehow captive to this strange female person. The equally small front room was reduced further by the amount of clutter squeezed into it. A sagging settee took up almost the length of one wall; a mismatched armchair across from it jostled a sideboard of Victorian proportions, which in turn elbowed a teetering standard lamp in the far corner. The chimney breast and adjacent alcove were almost obliterated by books, creating the kind of fire hazard that Fire Services safety officers love to photograph – but are usually too late to do so. In the corner nearest the front window a parrot regarded him rheumily from its cage on a shelf. No TV. The carpet stuck to his leather soles.

"Where are you, young man?"

"Coming!"

The kitchen was better, larger, with less furniture. An Aga range filled the chimney recess with – on the far wall – a varnished dresser crammed with crockery, none of which appeared to match. The centre of the room was taken up with a table and four chairs; a cathedral-shaped radio cabinet stood at one end.

He stood there awkwardly, watching her back as she busied herself at the draining board. He resisted the urge to recoup some brownie points by employing a few tricks of the trade to tip the balance back his way. But he sensed vulnerability here. The clues said it all: the pets, no framed memories, no visitors to tidy up for, and besides, he knew he didn't have the heart to do it.

"You were lecturing on local history back there," he ventured. "I thought you specialized in the – er, more esoteric aspects of the North York moors?"

"You're not from around here, are you, young man?" She turned her head and gave him another of those keen looks. Before he could respond she went back to her coffee making. "I've always felt it a mistake to specialize, become a pundit…a pedant, more like, who invariably gets trundled out whenever an expert opinion is required. After a while you begin to believe in your own importance. It shows. You become…what's the term, a turn-off?" She squinted sideways at him. "But if pressed I'd have to confess a preference for the paranormal." She pushed a space clear on the table and splashed the mugs of steaming coffee down, motioning him to sit.

He complied gingerly, resigned by now to the inevitability of departing with some evidence of his visit clinging to his clothes. The coffee was scalding and bitter; he daren't risk asking for sugar in case it lay in one of those unsavoury-looking tin containers that seemed to be stuck in place on the table.

He sipped, grimaced, and then said, "But surely there has been a lessening of interest in such things. There's always something or other in the news – clairvoyance, telepathy, psychokinesis. And as you say, panels of pundits all airing their conflicting views and pet theories. The literature too is having something of a renaissance -"

"Oh, I can't deny any of that, Mr Ransome. It even extends to children's television. Even before they set off for school they can watch some mythical or cartoon hero – or more likely these day, heroine – over their breakfast of munchies, up against the forces of evil. And they always win!" The old lady angrily thumped the table, making everything jump – including Jake.

Her face coloured up, eyes alight and grey hair escaping the pins at the back. "That's the problem, it's all being trivialized for commercial profit, and in so doing we're falling into the trap that's being laid."

"I'm sorry, Miss Winspear, I don't understand. Surely if such things do exist then ridicule is the perfect antidote."

"You see! You too commit the same error!" She leaned across the sticky surface, coffee forgotten. "For evil to flourish it is simply enough that good men do nothing. All these films being pumped out from Hollywood are de-sensitising the masses. One might almost say they are *preparing* us. Young people – usually – being murdered and hacked about, all the gory special effects…and that's all they know it is – special effects. They don't relate it to reality. They finish their popcorn, scrunch up the bag and chuck it on the floor on the way out of the cinema and say things like 'Awesome' or 'Mega' and then forget about it. It's merely a noisier, bigger version of their computer games back in their bedroom. Or those forensic dramas, where the criminal always gets tripped up by the brilliant use of modern science and DNA. Then there are those best-selling books rubbishing God and hardly a word from the established church to refute or denounce their arguments, for fear of upsetting some minority ethnic group. Or perhaps they no longer have a faith strong enough to counter such attacks. Pah!" She struggled upright, scraping the chair backwards. "Come!"

Jake stood up slowly, unsure what was required of him. She

hobbled to the back door, fiddled with the key and two bolts, then opened it and went outside. She gestured at him to follow. The cool night air after the ambience within was dramatic; the sky clear, without the cold sharpness that would bring extra clarity later on. He hadn't realized how high up here they were; in daylight the panorama must be impressive. He could see the running lights of the bulk carriers riding at anchor outside Teesmouth, awaiting berths. The serried ranks of the off-shore wind farm. On the darkened land there seemed to be a street light for every one of the half million people living there. Almost beneath their feet her garden dropped in a steep terrace towards the road.

She gripped his arm and he winced, surprised at the strength in it. "Look! It's all down there – muggings, rape, racial intolerance, child abuse, animal mutilation…murder. At this very moment things are being done to people that animals are not capable of. Why? Stress, mental illness, envy, greed? Yes, all of those and many more, but from time to time an act occurs whose very mindlessness defies belief. It is usually done without remorse or real motive other than the pleasure derived from inflicting pain or depriving someone of that most precious gift – life! And we shake our heads and feel somehow guilty for being a member of the same species. Bring back the lash, hard labour, capital punishment, all expressions of our horror, our inability to understand such bestiality. But what do we actually do? What *can* we do? We're slowly being conditioned to accept anything, because experience has shown us how elusive the apportioning of guilt is; the bureaucracy that messes up your tax code; the anonymous bank clerk who's mistakenly transferred your account; the faulty goods you invariably end up with. You can never really get to grips with the ones who are responsible, can you? It's the computer; we're having staffing problems, sir; no, the manager's off today, can you come back later…next week?

So you end up shrugging resignedly, whilst inwardly damning systems to hell." She sighed. "Even Victor Meldrew ran out of steam eventually."

She stopped, her ample chest heaving, then pulled the cardigan more tightly about her and went back inside. Jake felt confused, unsure whether he had triggered something in her which she would later regret, or feel a little privileged, for he sensed that she didn't do this very often. He hoped not. She looked tired as she gulped her coffee, made a face and went over to the old dresser. Retrieving a bottle of brandy she poured a hefty measure into her mug, before peering quizzically over at him, waggling the bottle.

"N-no, thanks, I'm driving." Jake held both hands up.

She grunted and stoppered the bottle. "Nobody's really interested in the ghosts of the past any more, Mr Ransome. That's why my lectures have changed direction. They're not colourful or exciting...or resolved between the spaces of two or three commercial breaks. And that's the way whatever's out there likes it."

"I'm sorry, Miss Winspear, what was that?" He'd eased himself against the dresser, not trusting the proximity of her across the table. For all her shabby exterior this woman exerted a force of will, a personality, that he was unable to quantify. He'd made a mistake in categorizing her as just an old dear who was a bit flaky but easy for him to handle. Now...he'd almost forgotten the reason for his visit. *Had* there been a reason, other than the offer of a free ride and another dent in his car door?

"I wonder if some whiz kid with a computer can calculate the exact point at which the rising tide of evil will interface with the falling level of morality?"

He blinked; if that was meant to shock it almost succeeded. He pushed himself upright, took his hands out of his pockets and glanced at his watch. She saw his action and smiled tiredly before pulling out the table drawer. He watched, amazed, as she unwrapped a Mars bar and took a bite.

"I should mention that I have diabetes and sometimes forget. Now, you really wanted something out of the ordinary on that church, hmm?"

He nodded, watching her chewing, wondering if it was all part of a cultivated persona. He'd never been in a situation where a simple consumption of a confection took on the mantle of medication.

She went into a front room and he could hear her rummaging among the books; there was a series of dull thuds and the jangle of a telephone receiver being dislodged. Some muttered curses followed and then she returned, wheezing, clutching a musty-looking old diary that was held together with some string. She flopped down, wiped her face with one hand and began to untie the knot.

Fetching her spectacles from her cardigan pocket she put them on and riffled through the pages. She stopped, peered over her spectacles at him for a moment before starting to read: "May twenty-third, eighteen twenty-four. Reverend Marr's scandalous behaviour has this day reached a point where no decent member of the parish can allow it to go unpunished. Beulah Branthwaite" – he started, but she held a hand up and continued – "spinster and daughter of Jacob and Anne, staggered home this evening in a pitiable condition. Of the clothes she had gone to church in to rehearse her wedding vows there was no sign. Her under shift barely covered her modesty and her shoes and stockings were nowhere in evidence. The distraught parents could not calm her and immediately sent for me, as her family doctor, to minister to her needs. At first incoherent and wild-eyed it took a good hour of much soothing talk and the constant application of various medicaments before the poor girl could be understood. She then cried a lot and confessed to a terrifying experience. For some reason her intended husband, Henry Pennick, had failed to arrive at the appointed hour. Reverend Marr urged her to linger awhile, against her wishes. He pressed some lemonade upon her as the evening was unseasonably warm. She says she then felt herself being helped to a long seat. What followed next must have constituted a nightmare for the poor child, reared as she was in the protective love of elderly parents. She awoke to pain and terror, lying on the seat with the priest on top of her, his face on hers, snarling and eyes popping, a ripping pain inside her almost naked body. She screamed and threw him from her, the move evidently taking the devil's spawn by surprise. Before he could recover the shocked creature fled, leaving her clothes on the vestry floor."

She slowly closed the diary and removed her spectacles. "Several entries on, May twenty-sixth, Dr Carfax reports the presbytery of St Michael's was burnt to the ground, with Julius Marr still inside. Word of his despicable crime had leaked out, probably through the poor girl's fiancée. Any road, the villagers evidently had had enough. Apparently Marr had abused his office for years, practising his lechery on young and old alike, male and female. He set up his own version of the Hellfire Club, holding wild orgies out on the moors, till in time there were children who neither knew nor cared who their true fathers were. How did he continue undetected for so long? He had a strange power over people; some said he possessed the evil eye. And there was talk of a religious receptacle, a silver chalice of some sort which seemed to figure significantly in the rituals. This was jealously guarded by Marr at all times; only he was allowed to handle it. He was wont to consult this object during high points in his occult practices. Whatever it was, it seemed to control his actions, selecting this girl or that to be initiated…or sacrificed."

"Sacrificed?" Jake was enthralled by it all, a child once more, sitting at his Aunt Julia's knee on a winter's night before being shushed to bed by his flustered mother.

She shrugged. "Talk again, of such excesses that some victims failed to recover and were – are – buried…out there, somewhere on the moors."

Jake tried not to shudder. "So was that the end of this man Marr? He didn't re-appear or anything? Or were his remains scattered far and wide to prevent a recurrence?"

"Ha! That's the big one. When the villagers sifted through the ashes there was no sign of Julius Marr, although he had definitely been in there – they'd seen and heard him laughing crazily amid the flames. But not a fragment of human bones. The remains of a pig, yes. But that's all."

"And the chalice?"

"Same story – disappeared. The next morning the principals involved went to the church, searched everywhere, even to the extent of moving the altar base in case there was a secret compartment." She smiled wryly and continued. "I suspect, however, their actions were becoming less motivated by moral outrage by then, as such an artifact must have been quite valuable for those times. But that too was never seen again."

"But none of this is on the record," Jake protested. "Surely someone…is that the only source?" He nodded at the diary.

"The local bishop took swift action, threatening excommunication should word of this leave the valley. The suppression of the press presumably much easier in those, ah – unenlightened times." She gave him that smile again. "This and a few other brief details are in my sole possession."

"And the name Branthwaite?"

"Pure coincidence, I would suggest. It's a family name in these parts."

"So where does that leave us?"

"I don't know, young man, unless there is an element to this

– other than a heart attack in a freak storm." She shrugged. "Unless…?"

"Yes? Unless what?" Jake leaned forward, watching her.

"The only link that I can see between the two events is their geographical locations." She noted his blank expression. "Let me explain: there is a standing stone set in the wall of the church. This means it was – is – reckoned to be a source of great natural power."

She went on to explain about ley lines and the way the ancients used such points of converging forces to channel earth energies for their own rituals. When so-called paganism had been swamped in the tide of New Age Christianity the highest concentrations of these ley lines vortices had been utilized as centres of prayer and learning – Salisbury Cathedral, Glastonbury Abbey, for instance.

"But how does this power manifest itself?"

"You could read a dozen books and get a dozen theories. What is certain is that it is measurable and varies from mere ultrasonics through electromagnetism and even beta-radiation. It can twist in a spiral, pulse, indicate hot and cold spots. It gives cones of silence and varying magnetic intensity. And that's just so far. Just imagine a person or people who understand such forces intimately and could control them. These ley lines form a network, like our national grid, and if they could be turned on and off at will… Are you starting to get the picture?"

"And Hayman's Cross?"

"You mean Hangman's Cross. It's altered over the years. A place of execution in the old days for criminals, who were often buried there." She paused. "That too is a ley lines convergence point. I should add that isn't the first accident along that stretch of road."

"So…" Jake placed his hands together and brought them to his face slowly, the gesture an unconscious and prayer-like one as he pondered. "Two tragedies, one link…no logical explanation, no proof. So where does that leave us – me?"

"Well, I don't know about you, young man, but if *I* was a journalist - which God forbid! – I would be finding out exactly how that poor nun met her end. In my experience the paranormal is not all that bothered about the clues it leaves behind."

9: SUBSERVIENCE

The Reverend Renton Cappel felt like weeping as he gazed about him. His anguish was not for the ripped-out ruin that had been the ground floor of the presbytery, with its rolled-back carpets, tumbled furniture and piles of rubble. His despair lay in his failure to sustain some belief in what he was doing. He had to meet Sir Nicholas tomorrow and he knew only too well the response he would receive from that frightening, forceful man. He was not sure whether the greater danger lay in going back to Asmodeus, with all that that entailed in terms of will-power, stamina and, yes – faith.

He had so convinced himself two nights ago that he had immediately set to work with a pickaxe, shattering the floor of the study in a welter of concrete shards until he had reached the centuries-old stones below. His interest quickened by the sight of what must be the original footings he had levered and tugged, splitting finger ends and blistering palms in his efforts to dig deeper. The irregularly-shaped flagstones, settled by countless feet, lifted as if in protest at his manic energy, only to reveal more stones set in mortar.

It took most of that first night to satisfy himself no secret passage led from what had been the study. Weary to his bones, hands and arms aching to a degree he wouldn't have believed, he had fallen into a fitful sleep, clutching the smooth handle of the pickaxe to his chest. He awoke with a start, for a few seconds totally disorientated. It was light outside. Memory returned; he rose stiffly from the pillow of stones, switched off the lights and raised the window shades. He surveyed the damage he had wreaked on the room and his hands, the latter now throbbing painfully. It must have been that that had awakened him. Then he heard the insistent buzz of the helicopter, a sound now familiar as the planners did another survey or Hi-Sec monitored the progress of evacuation.

He sighed dejectedly. His reasoning powers seemed to have dissipated with the retreating darkness. He limped into the kitchen and switched on the kettle, soaking his hands in the sink as he waited for it to boil. The pain of the warm water was at first excruciating and then almost sensual in its spreading sensation. Tea made, he sat at the well-scrubbed table and, gingerly cupping the steaming brew, set himself to seriously consider his situation. If only he hadn't wasted so much time on those other St Michaels... But how was he to know? One reference in an old diocesan record, a bit of gossip really, had provided the slim but crucial clue that had sent him scampering through sneeze-making tomes and applying for locum posts whilst fending off the curiosity of clerical colleagues, canons and bishops as he delved into the history of each parish. Considering his length of stay, they had intimated, was such diligence necessary? Unable to risk investigating each St Michael's in consecutive order had necessitated the tiresome business of contriving and visiting other churches in between.

The irony of the right church being last on his list had merely further compounded the fact of its imminent inaccessibility. One way or another his quest was almost over. He shivered and pressed his throbbing palms to the residual warmth of the mug.

Digging Julius Marr's name from the local diocesan files had clinched his findings, dropping the final piece into place. But it had all taken so long. And then Father Scanlon had proved a far greater obstacle than anticipated. The upset and trauma of the irrevocable abandonment of the valley – *his* valley, he'd querulously proclaimed – had unfortunately jerked him out of his decades-old routine and lethargy. He'd become suspicious and sly, characteristics only newly apparent, one villager had confided. This altered behaviour had turned on Cappel, commenting on his trips away at such a time. A couple of snoopy phone calls had disclosed the younger cleric's duplicity; a series of rows, accusations and a wholly unpleasant atmosphere had developed, with Scanlon threatening to expose him unless he revealed his secret. Desperate, Cappel almost had, only to be interrupted by Sir Nicholas Brookes's unheralded arrival at the presbytery. The old priest had then stormed out, apparently liking the billionaire even less than his new assistant.

Sir Nicholas, a large, florid man with swept-back overlong black hair and curiously hooded eyes, had introduced himself. Cappel had stammered his apologies for his superior's rude departure but the other had waved it aside, saying he'd really come to see him! Cappel, bewildered but intrigued, invited Sir Nicholas inside, the priest proffering some refreshment, which the other politely declined, before seating himself at the far side of the room, the ancient leather chair creaking slightly beneath the weight of his ample form. He unbuttoned the jacket of the double-breasted grey Armani suit.

"How-how can I help you, Sir Nicholas. We haven't met before…have we? I'm sure I would have remembered…"

"A mutual acquaintance, my boy, simple enough." The voice – though low – had a power, a resonance that compelled one to listen. The sunlight coming in from behind him created a hazy silhouette, leaving only the whites of his eyes as a centre of focus. "Fennella Franklyn phoned me." He paused, allowing the name to produce the desired effect. He was not disappointed; Cappel's face lost what little colour there was, and yet he felt hot all over as the memory of Fennella flooded through him. The subject of a thousand liquid dreams since he had fled her soft, seductive embrace, he always thought of her charm as a sort of debilitation, a draining of everything that went to make a person

53

– vitality, resistance, memory of all except her, her, her! That generous body – so pliable and willing and somehow always smelling of a forest glade in summer – had drawn him down, down into a morass of such shuddering excess that even he had finally revolted at its seemingly limitless depths. Each session of her coven seemed to demand ever-greater participation, more input, as if testing the boundaries of his desire. At last the uncertainty of where he was heading, coupled with the dread of exposure, had forced him to flee. A parish in Lancashire had required a locum urgently. His superior, a wise old canon, had guessed some but not all of the young man's frailties, suggesting the change of scene might do him good, and promising not to divulge his whereabouts to anyone other than those in an official capacity.

But he should have known there was no escape, no complete disappearing act, when the forces these people controlled were unleashed.

"How did…? I haven't seen Mrs Franklyn for quite some time now, Sir Nicholas. I – I'm surprised she remembered me, she was always involved in so many aspects of the community in and around Bristol." He tried to keep his voice neutral but those eyes seemed to mock. "You've spoken with her recently?" Stupid question, he realised, as soon as he spoke.

"Fennella and I are old friends, Father Cappel." Sir Nicholas said, still in that soft sonorous tone. "I spent a lot of years in the West Country newspaper business before my father died, and I had to come north to claim the family inheritance." He laughed gently. "But we keep in touch, Fennella and I. When I heard the name Renton Cappel mentioned by one of my features editors it rang a bell somewhere. An uncommon name…then it came to me. Fennella and I had talked on the phone about our mutual interests…oh, it would be three years ago now. Yes?" His voice grew quieter, harsher, the eyes seeming to glow, collecting all the available light, like some cat. "You and she had been enthusiastic participants in what some might describe as somewhat unorthodox practices for one of your calling. She was a little put out, to say the least, by your abrupt and mysterious departure."

"I'm sorry. I suppose I should have contacted her before I left, but Bishop Downham felt I needed a complete change. He insisted on a clean break from whatever I was doing -"

"Whatever you were doing...? Oh, you mean in the ecclesiastical sense?" Sir Nicholas leaned forward, his eyes narrowing as he stared across the room.

Cappel sat as one transfixed, wanting to run but realizing the futility of such an action. He'd had a reprieve, a few short years to attempt to repair the damage he had done to himself before the wrong people found him once more. But he'd lost and now there would be a price to pay; the eternal law. "What is it – exactly – that you require of me, Sir Nicholas?" His fingers dug deep into the chair arms.

"I want you to complete your task, Brother Cappel, that is all. You had a crucial part to play in our plan to recover the Unholy Grail of Akeldama. Only someone like you, in your unique position within the clergy, your reputation for research, could help us."

"But -"

"But nothing!" Sir Nicholas thundered, suddenly standing. He seemed to swell, grow taller in the cramped, dimly-lit room. "You took a blood oath on the altar, swore before the Master you would devote your time, your energies - your life - to accomplishing his work. Your disappearance left the Order in considerable confusion. The ritualistic ascension was almost complete, one more sacrifice and the knowledge of the cup's whereabouts could have been ours. Instead..." The man's hands clenched and he took a step forward. Cappel shrank away, his back pressing into the chair's restraint. Brookes recovered himself; he took a large white silk handkerchief from his breast pocket and wiped his hands, all the while staring down at his victim. He calmed down, smiled, revealing small teeth for such a big man. He proceeded to pace the room, composing himself. He feigned interest in the sheet music on the old upright piano, inspected the marks on a vase base. He straightened the old foxhunting print on the wall. Cappel followed his every move, noting almost subconsciously that never once did the man allow Cappel direct access to the door. When he finally spoke the younger man almost jumped.

"We've been monitoring your progress, of course."

"What?"

"These last three years, we've tagged your every move…a lot better than the police could have done!" He turned to gaze benignly at the seated figure. "You didn't really believe we would give up that easily, did you? Tut-tut!" He shook his head. "Oh, dear no. A chance like you comes along only – what – once in a lifetime. But then" – he chuckled – "what's a lifetime to people such as we, hmm?" Cappel shuddered. "No, foolish boy, we have eyes everywhere; our troops, foot soldiers if you will, carry out orders in the expectation of recognition and better standing within the Order. But it's a cell-like structure, they get no further than the generally accepted notion of what goes on in such covens – sexual cavortings and the proof of minor spell work, with career advancement and romantic enticement dominating their thoughts. It gives them a *frisson*, they usually want little more than a low level of sin to enliven their hum-drum lives. You and I are different - we direct, control. They follow orders, as they did in this case. Your first flight – to Formby, was it? – took a little while to pinpoint. But after that it wasn't too difficult. It was frustrating, however. We could watch but we couldn't touch, as it were. Our bad luck was in finding a subject suitable enough but with such a – shall we say? – delicate stomach. We trailed you a year, looking for signs that you were becoming calmer, more receptive to renewed contact. You may have noticed a few subtle overtures… No?"

Cappel shook his head, numb, trying to recall his behaviour over that period. But he had been like some frightened rabbit trapped in a car's headlights, too petrified to glance anywhere but over the next horizon.

"Then someone noticed a pattern in your…wanderings. The name St Michael's began to recur up and down the country. Could it be, we pondered, you were going freelance? Very audacious and if I may say so, ver-r-ry dangerous! Tell me, Father, what was your plan? I use the past tense because the game – serious though it is – is over. You must see that."

He came over to Cappel and placed both hands on the wrists of the priest, clamping them firmly to the chair's arms. His eyes seemed to grow larger and larger. With startling clarity every feature of the media magnate's face sprang into focus; the almost olive, Mediterranean complexion; the prominent nose and brown eyes. There was a tiny crescent-shaped scar on his left cheek. "We were prepared to indulge you at first but naturally couldn't leave it all up to you. Your first clue in naming the church allowed us to exert some of our own power in narrowing the list. Using the aforementioned network we did some backtracking of our own. I didn't even know we had a St Michael's around here until the computer spewed it out."

Brookes stood up and abruptly returned to his seat but still somehow holding Cappel's gaze. The latter relaxed a shade, realizing the tightness around his chest was his own suspended breathing. He exhaled slowly, lest some overt movement of his body triggered off another outburst. This man terrified him, even more than the habitual terror which had been the norm these last few years. His sleep tortured and shallow, the fear of discovery, the conviction of pursuit, had never left him. Now he knew why. His only chance for the salvation of his soul lay in convincing Brookes that his future obedience was unequivocal, absolute. Something, somehow, somewhere, might occur to grant him freedom from damnation through all eternity. But not now, not here! This devil was reading his thoughts, probing his brain, altering his very perception of right and wrong, just like the group in Bristol. Then it had been less subtle perhaps, appealing to his released sexual desires, but the objective was identical – subjugation, manipulation…destruction. He must play along, gain time – what little there was.

"So…you know?"

"Know? About Julius Marr? Oh, yes, we eventually came up with a name. The business I'm in made that somewhat easier. But only the name and the man's reputation, nothing concrete. Even with my vast resources it was…ah, sensitive. Nobody I could trust. I mean, if I gain access so can others, that's the two-edged sword of the information highway. Frustrating in the extreme… Anyway, he seemed a most likely candidate. We waited. After all, he might not be the right one and you could conceivably stumble across the real custodian before we did. But we helped…"

"Helped?"

"Even the church is not immune to infiltration at a certain level, my boy. We decided to – ah, accelerate the process." Sir Nicholas's fingers tapped his knee impatiently; a man not used to immobility. "We assumed time was on our side – it usually is. Then this damned appropriation order descended on the area. It was a shock, I confess it freely." He laughed harshly. "I don't think I've ever editorialized more vociferously on an issue. You may even have seen me on television. I brought every journalistic gun to bear on the government – environmental vandalism, endangered species, national heritage, demographical imbalance, tourism, human hardship…you name it, I flayed the authorities with it. I couldn't personally be too strident, you understand, allowing my ancestral home's proximity as the tacitly accepted reason for the crusade. 'The Guv'nor's got a bee in his bonnet, et cetera.'" He snorted. "All to no avail. Even lobbied the PM himself. All he said was, 'Now, now, Sir Nicholas, think of the long-term benefits.' Ha! Little does the fool know! We – I need the Unholy Grail. Without it…"

"But is it so important, Sir Nicholas?" Cappel ventured, trying to ignore the other's glare before plunging on. "I know it represents a powerful talismanic force but there have been others -"

"You fool! As I expected you have been dabbling in matters that are way beyond your capacity to comprehend or control." Brookes paused, sank back against the chair, pondering. He seemed to reach a decision and leaned forward, the hooded eyes glowing. "The thirty pieces of silver that Judas Iscariot was paid for the supreme act of betrayal…what happened to them?"

"What?" Cappel was confused by the question, its seeming irrelevance. But the man opposite was such a potent force in the room he felt like a callow, theological student again, in thrall to his Jesuit teacher. Almost automatically he responded. "Matthew records in scripture that Judas, stricken with remorse at what he had done, tried to atone by taking the money to the temple elders and casting it down, before going away to hang himself. They subsequently rejected his blood money but sought counsel before deciding what should be done with it." He paused, then continued more slowly, "The purse of silver coins was used to purchase a potter's field on the slopes of the Valley of Hinnom, there to be used for the burial of unclaimed wretches such as Judas. This piece of ground was referred to as the Field of Blood…" His face drained and his head jerked up. "In Aramaic – Akeldama! You mean…? Oh, my God!"

59

"Well, I would have used a somewhat different expletive, but yes, Akeldama it is. Now, do you begin to appreciate what we are dealing with here? The potter, one Salem el-Hakim, was a crypto-Christian and appalled when he realized where the money had come from. He refused to use it and apparently kept it separately in a labelled purse until he, too, could determine how best to dispose of such a symbol of evil. You can imagine his dilemma as a less-than-courageous follower of this ill-starred and disappointing Messiah. But the force imbued in the metal was already at work; he was murdered and robbed, the culprit quickly caught by the Roman police and crucified. The contents of the purse was noted by the treasury and the Governor, Festus, thought it mildly amusing to have an ornamental dagger fashioned from the silver as a gift to Nero in Rome. It was said the Emperor liked to inform selected doomed Christians of the dagger's origin before watching it being plunged into them. Caligula is supposed to have murdered his pregnant sister, Drusilla, with it. Some fifty years after Nero, the Emperor Trajan – in an attempt to appease the still burgeoning Christian movement – had the dagger melted down and made into a goblet or chalice. His plan backfired, the gift was reviled and cast from them. In this way it fell into the hands of a breakaway religious sect, who re-fashioned it for distinctly un-Christian practices."

Brookes went on to recount how the chalice's course had been traced since then, chiefly through those written sources who have followed the Left Hand Path. It had had a somewhat chequered history, being successively held by Christians, the Knights Templars and various Satanists down the ages. How Julius Marr acquired it wasn't certain, except to say that the Vatican possessed it just prior to him. When it went missing they were alarmed enough to issue a Europe-wide quest for its urgent recovery.

"But why – if it's *so* influential – hasn't the Church, for instance, destroyed it or somehow neutralized its effects by burying it somewhere securely?" Cappel was as much perplexed as intrigued by this revelation of such enduring evil.

"Because, Brother Cappel, it requires blood – a blood sacrifice, seemingly, to activate its full powers. If that isn't known..." He shrugged. "As to its destruction...what man who covets power – in any form – would easily set aside such an opportunity? And in any event, how would one set about destroying such an object without some guarantee of its neutralization...or protection from retribution should they fail? Remember, the earlier churches were just as corrupt as anybody else. Nobody gets to a position of power without a good deal of ruthlessness." He looked directly at Cappel. "Believe me, I know whereof I speak."

Sir Nicholas was visibly affected by his own oratory; the tension seemed to spring from him as he spoke, the electricity filling the small study like some giant Leyden jar.

"And what happens then, Sir Nicholas? I mean, when blood...human blood?" – the other nodded – "is introduced into the chalice?"

"It confers power, power in the form of knowledge, perhaps even alters events, a prospect incalculable in the media business, not to mention other influential members of our group – police chiefs, judges...even a cabinet minister or two who could benefit. Nobody who hasn't proven their commitment to the Order is permitted to the Inner Circle. You must appreciate the dangers, Brother Cappel, and the honour bestowed upon you by our faith in your abilities. With our support and guidance there is nothing you cannot achieve, no heights to which you cannot aspire. Do this and your future is assured...forever!"

10: RELEVANCE

Jake replaced the receiver with a sigh that went unnoticed in the busy, open-plan newsroom and returned to his screen. But somehow his piece for stronger dog control laws failed to grip. Sarah Branthwaite, the hospital said, was 'as well as could be expected', that most irritating and uninformative of medical dismissals. And his fabled charm fell somewhere between awful and abysmal over the phone, somehow disastrously amplifying his shyness and northern accent.

Then there was the 'jungle telegraph'; even in the age of the super-highway, gossip was still the fastest method of communication and word had spread about his 'personal assignment'. There were sly digs at the morning meeting, conspiratorial whispers by the water cooler.

Trouble was, who could really blame them? From their viewpoint he was acting just a little unprofessionally. He sighed again, a vertical furrow creasing the normally smooth brow as he tried to concentrate on the monitor. He pecked at a key.

Gerry Malone picked up his own keyboard and made a two-handed swipe across the desk at him, exasperation plain on his wide, pleasant features. "For Jasus' sake, will ye get a grip on yerself, Jake. Ye're sendin' out so many negative vibes me solar-powered caculator's goin' haywire!"

Jake ducked instinctively before realizing he was in no real danger, and then grinned sheepishly.

"That's better." Gerry replaced the keyboard. He grabbed his little calculator and shook it vigorously before squinting at it and then holding it to his ear. "I think I've just caught it in time." He winked at his friend. "How is the old dear, then?"

"Still the same, Ger, you know what those nurses are like when it comes to divulging quote confidential information unquote."

"I know, I know, and your ineffable good looks are totally ineffective over more than one point five metres."

While he was talking, Gerry was doing his party piece to distract and cheer Jake up. His remarkable dexterity with paper clips was all the more effective for its manipulation whilst out of sight, all the while looking at the intended recipient. Then suddenly – as now – the artistic result would come sailing across; the almost exact replication in profile of the much-teased Alison Grune, with just enough caricature for effect.

Jake laughed outright and the unwitting original glanced sharply over at them, somehow certain but unable to prove she was once more their target.

"So what about old Shakes – sorry, Winspear, then? Or have you too fallen foul of the wicked witch of the north?"

"What?" Jake gave up trying to improve on Gerry's latest masterpiece. "Why'd you call her that?"

"Don't you know?" Gerry demanded, some of the banter gone, the heavy lines settling in his leathery face. "A strange one, that, and no mistake. I'd take some salt and water if I was visiting her."

Jake had to chuckle. "You're just an old religious bigot at heart, Gerry Malone. I knew you had an Achilles heel somewhere. It's that convent upbringing, all that kneeling with your head on the pew, does something to the brain. And then there was that time you got kicked in the head watching that rugby match from the sideline. Extremely heroic injury, that – Hey!"

Gerry flicked across another of his creations, a fair representation of a witch on a broomstick.

"Y'know, Gerry, when I've got a drawer full of these I'm going to set up a stall on Stockton market." Despite himself Jake felt his mood lightening, as it always did when his exuberant colleague decided to pull him out of what Gerry referred to as his 'northern blights'.

"Ah, c'mon, Jake, the Wig and Pen's been open for minutes by now. As me ould Da useta say…"

"Frequently!" the other interjected, grinning.

"…the brain is a very complex organism, designed to work at incredible speed and generating extremely high temperatures. This demands a constant cooling process, best assisted by imbibing copious amounts of fluid. If you'll only read Professor Beerman's paper on the liquid technology of the human brain you'll find the recommended specific gravity of the ideal cranial coolant corresponds almost exactly to a certain alcoholic beverage – dark, smooth, creamy in texture…"

In this manner they traversed the few side streets that separated the newspaper building from their favourite pub, an establishment frequented by the town's younger and aggressively confident business set. The original legal and literary fraternity were now little in evidence, supplanted by estate agents' staff and financial analysts just out of their teens and learning how to cope without daddy's allowance. The place was filling up rapidly and Jake nodded to a few regulars as he ordered two doses of Gerry's brain brew. He, ever the optimist though twice divorced, was sizing up the talent, preferring to ignore the fact that the generation gap was more like a gulf in his case. They sipped, looking around.

"What? Are you expectin' that pouter pigeon Belinda to float in here? The Blue Lagoon's more her style, wouldn'tcha say?" Guileless brown eyes above the froth. Jake mouthed a silent obscenity as he moved away from the bar. He spied an upraised hand, turned and pulled at Gerry's sleeve before weaving his way to the window seat.

"Hello, Alec, long time no see, et cetera. How's things?" Gerry pulled up a stool, winked at the young, intense face as his colleague slid onto the corner seat. "Oh, Gerry, this is an old school and rugby chum, Alec Daker. Alec, Gerry Malone, news hound *ordinaire* -" He pulled away from the playful punch. They all sipped their beer for a few seconds, Alec and Jake updating while Gerry continued his romantic roving. Rebuffed visually three times in as many minutes, he sniffed and returned his attention to his companions. When he could detect no mention of crime he pulled out a paper clip and began idly to twist and turn it.

"Gerry…" The warning from Jake stopped him short, Alec staring at the obvious rendition of a set of male genitalia – exaggerated as usual. A girl nearby giggled as the crime reporter rapidly reduced his Freudian slip to a metallic squiggle and dropped it on the table top .

"So…" Gerry said brightly. "When can we expect to do a piece on the first drowned water skier with this new reservoir… Alec?"

"What? Oh, yes." The young surveyor tore his gaze away from the bent wire, as though expecting it to do a latter-day version of Moses's staff. "The reservoir…" He took a gulp from his beer, finished the last of his cheese and onion pasty and dabbed at his lips with a tissue. "Well, that could be in some doubt -"

"What?" Both reporters' antennae went up; Jake got in first. "You mean there's something wrong with the foundations…the funding…what?"

"Oh, I suppose not really." Alec looked embarrassed, obviously regretting his *faux pas*. "It's just my immediate superior, old George Bennett… Know him? Oh, well, he's a good sort, actually, knows his job and all that, but he won't change, y'know, won't go with the flow of progress."

"Yes, yes, Alec, but you said…"

"Well, that was a bit strong. The only doubt is in George's mind, after what happened the other day. He reckons we should do some more soundings, run another scan -"

"Alec…" Jake muttered through gritted teeth.

Alec told them about their experience on the tumulus top. His audience subsided as the scaled-down potential of the account unfolded. The surveyor concluded on a lame note, trying to convey the humour of their undignified rout down the barrow's side. "Any road, it seemed funny at the time…"

"Yes, well, earth tremors are hardly all that rare now, even in these parts, are they, Gerry? What is it…a thousand…a million a day worldwide? I suppose it's a bit like those dozens of tiny heart attacks some experts say we all go through in the course of our lives." Jake looked at his foam-flecked glass. "Your round, I believe, Mr Malone -"

"No, no, Jake, you don't understand. The surrounding countryside wasn't trembling, just that sodding mound…as though some – some *thing* was trying to get out. I tell you, it was weird. And then that awful crack – as though something really solid was being literally ripped apart by a tremendous force…and– and a godawful terrible stench. Anyway, George called in sick yesterday, that's why I'm here now, chasing up old drawings at the office for something to do." He reached for his glass, finding to his surprise it was already empty.

Gerry saw his friend's face change. "Okay, okay, I'll get 'em in -"

Jake turned to Alec and said slowly and evenly. "Alec, think carefully… When, exactly, on Monday did this happen? I mean, was it in the late afternoon, by any chance?"

Alec's expression pre-empted his reply. "How did you know, Jake? I know the time exactly – my bloody watch stopped then and hasn't gone since. Look!" He fished out the chunky, military-style watch from his jacket pocket. "The shop says the warranty doesn't begin to cover such damage. See how the once-luminous hands have somehow been fused into the face at the very moment – Hey!"

But Jake was already gone, his hand groping for the car keys he hoped were there and not back on his desk. Gerry's lugubrious features went even slacker; he waggled his empty pint glass a few times before turning to his bewildered new friend.

"Lager, is it?"

11: SURVEILLANCE

It all looked so different in the clear, early autumn sunshine; gone the creepiness, with its dark, dank, whispering atmosphere – a ready-made recipe for susceptibility. Just a sad, abandoned village now, the victim of geo-politics and demographic change. *What am I doing here?* The engine was still running – and smoking – an indication of his reluctance to pursue whatever had impelled him from the pub.

The trip to the tumulus had been a waste of time; nothing there except a fine view of the surrounding countryside. No cracks, no smell, but then, given its prominence and the weather at the time it was hardly the place for odours to linger. The noise? Thunder, possibly. And yet…*there* was the church tower, barely visible above the trees. The start of it all. Start of what, for God's sake? No, it had to be more than coincidence, two events within throwing distance and at the same time. And the poor nun…although he would never know exactly when that crash occurred. There *was* a story there. The big question was whether he was the one to cover – or more to the point, uncover – it.

He switched the engine off, stepped out of the car and into the deserted street. He breathed deeply, the air was sweet here, away from the atmospheric cocktail that was industrial Teesside…or Tees Valley, as it was now more grandly touted. Hard to accept that all this part of his world would soon be submerged for ever – barring drought or some cataclysmic change. The birds – always first to notice Man's retreat from nature – seemed to be out in force. He wished he'd listened more to old McMasters in 4B when they'd gone out on nature trails. But what did it matter? Birds didn't know how or why we categorized them – or cared. They sang between their brief periods of sleeping, breeding, feeding and fighting. This seemed to be one of the good times.

"Oh, shut up, you noisy buggers!" he yelled cheerily.

"Shut up the'sen!"

Jake whirled, his face colouring. Where the hell did he spring – no, hobble – from? The elderly gentleman leaning on a twisted hawthorn walking stick regarded him suspiciously. Sweat-stained tweed trilby, almost identical jacket and green, baggy cords above scuffed brown leather boots. The face, saggy and weather-beaten, still possessed vitality, with bristling white eyebrows and a proud, hooked nose. The eyes were watery but alert, looking him up and down.

"You one on 'em?" He waved his stick up the valley. "Lot up thair?"

"N-no…Look, I'm sorry, I was just -"

"Talkin' t'birds, seems like. You city folk do a lot o' that, then? They bin 'ere longer'n you, all on 'em."

"I–I'm from the paper…the *Clarion*." He fumbled for his card. Some ace reporter, being wound up by a rural octogenarian. Good job Gerry's not here to see this. "I came to look at the church and – and generally wander around before…before… Shouldn't you be away by now, sir…?"

"What'n hell you mean, eh?" He waved his stick at Jake this time. "This 'ere's my home. Gran'fayther's, aye, 'n' 'is too afore 'im. All gone…all gone." His voice faded and the old head slumped forward. He wiped a hand across his cheeks for a few moments and then glanced up defiantly at the young journalist. "Look around 'ere. See all these roofs? I put 'em on – me an' my lad Jacob. Harold Chambers, dry stone walls 'n' slater, gentry or otherwise. You pays, I'll put roof o'er yer head come nightfall. That was my motto 'n' on'y ever failed once, that terrible storm o' seventy-eight."

Jake didn't dare ask *which* seventy-eight. "Oh, so did you do the church over there too?"

"You stupid or summat? 'Ow old you reckon I am?" He snorted, obviously now bored with this young whippersnapper. "But if askin' if I maintained it then answer's yes…kept a roof o'er God's head for nigh on sixty year now, on'y ever charged materials."

"It's just that the padre – Father Cappel, said part of the roof came down in that storm the other night. It wasn't safe -"

"Rubbish!" Another indignant snort. "I replaced all cracked slates three – no, four month ago. Right as rain, that roof, an' t'lightnin' rod too. You go 'ave a look."

"But -"

"Go on, round back there's small door, key's above lintel. Don't matter 'oo knows now, do it?" Without waiting for a reply he shuffled off and disappeared round a corner. In a matter of seconds Jake heard an engine cough into life and then an equally ancient Land Rover came in sight, driven by his son; the resemblance was clear. It went past and they both stared out at him but made no sign, vanishing in a blue haze down the street.

The lintel was there all right, and the key, the abode of spiders who knew not the end was nigh. The door opened slowly but quietly, recently used. The steep wooden stairs creaked at every step and he soon emerged from the gloom into bright sunshine. There was a narrow walkway between the church roof and the waist-high parapet. As the old man had said, it all appeared well maintained; lead flashing in place, the new slates showing up easily on the pitched roof, gargoyle spouts clog-free. He checked the whole area, running his hand along the parapet, brushing the almost sensual lichened surface, till he came to the lightning conductor. There, too, the man's skill was in evidence; new cleats holding the squared copper rod fast as it ran down the time-worn stone wall.

Curiouser and curiouser...and then, perhaps not, if one could fit the pieces together. Why would the priest lie? Why did Sarah Branthwaite's last act of worship end so dramatically? What was it that Joan Winspear had been *really* trying to tell him?

Jake gazed out over the valley, up to where the new pumping station – environmentally green and low profile – just broke the skyline, and then traced the four parallel pipes snaked down, following the River Helm, past him via a dip in the ground, to re-appear by the bright grey concrete of the containment dam.

He turned slowly, his gaze sweeping the tiny valley, taking in the huddled farms that had escaped the expulsion order, clinging almost desperately to the slopes of Craw Fell, lest they too join those below, drowned for the common good, a kind of Herriot-on-the-water for the modern tourist. He could see why it had succumbed; too small to command any significant support from outside – no industry, a few honeysuckle-covered cottages in a straggling row, a general dealer's, a pub and a church. The largest house the least lived-in; he put a hand up to his brow and peered down and across to where the presbytery lay, just visible through the ancient yews. All curtained tightly...

Hello, that front window curtain on the ground floor twitched. He straightened. No, must have been mistaken, the priest will surely have vacated the premises by now. He stared for several seconds before giving up. Probably a draught...and that's it for up here.

He carefully closed and bolted the trapdoor behind him, whilst feeling slightly foolish as he did so. The main front doors were firmly secured; he pushed ineffectually at them and was about to turn away when he sniffed, glancing down. The memory of that evening, standing just inside the doorway, came back with a rush. He could still smell that burning, whatever it was.

He bent lower, ran his hand along the rough surface near the bottom of the left-hand side. The wood had been scorched recently, patches of black – almost charred – sections showing quite clearly. No definite pattern, just two streaks about three centimetres wide by fifteen long, and an oval the size of his hand. He hunkered down, sniffed again. Yes, definitely it – whatever *it* was. He straightened up and sighed, brushed at his trousers and walked slowly back to his car. Still pondering this new twist to the puzzle he headed on up the valley for the want of anything better to do, loath to return to Gerry's grinning mug across the desk.

Up near the pumping station he stopped the car and got out to look back down the valley, probably the last time he would do so before the flooding on Sunday. He could foresee no possibility of justifying a return on professional grounds. He was stumped, plain and simple, unwilling to go back to the old dragon lady with…what? An indication – not even proof – that the priest had lied? Scorch marks on the church door that simply had to be the result of lightning that night? And that was it. Zip, as they said in the movies.

The *No Trespass* signs were just ahead and he fancied he could see and hear a helicopter beating its way into the sky just on the horizon. Time to fly right enough. He turned to get in the car when suddenly a different sound stopped him. With disbelief he flinched as the dapple grey hunter with a slim figure astride it burst out of the thicket above and behind him and clattered onto the road. The rider yanked on the reins in an attempt to control the fractious animal as it snorted and rolled its eyeballs at this added menace confronting it.

"Whoa, girl, dammit, whoa!" The girl's voice was shrill with annoyance. Her face was strangely reminiscent and quite beautiful, pale but for two spots of colour on her cheeks. She displayed white even teeth as she hauled back on the reins. Her black riding jacket and cream jodhpurs showed her figure off to advantage as rider and beast fought for supremacy, kicking up the gravel in front of the car. She finally brought the animal to some measure of obedience; it stood, trembling, as she made friends with it once more, talking softly and stroking its sweat-slicked neck.

She finally had time to glance down at him. "I – I'm terribly sorry. Did we startle you?"

Jake had to assume it was a rhetorical question, backed up as he was against the car door, one hand scrabbling for the handle. "Not startle exactly, try petrify!"

"What? Oh, I see, a joke. Good." She removed the riding hat and shook free her thick dark hair, finger-combing it unselfconsciously.

"You're the girl who was at Miss Winspear's evening. I remember because you stuck out – I mean…"

"Like a sore thumb?" Her smile was impish and he had to laugh with her. "I was there because I needed a crash course in this region's history and Uncle Nicky assured me Joan Winspear was the northern equivalent of Simon Schama where local matters were concerned."

He reached forward to shake her hand before realizing the obvious difficulties involved. "I'm Jake Ransome, sometime features reporter and general gofer at the local paper…the *Clarion*."

The high colour had faded and she now appeared almost anaemic; complexion chalk-white, with startling blue eyes. The lustrous black hair falling to her shoulders completed a picture that took his breath away as she gazed imperiously down at him. "Oh, yes, I do believe Uncle Nicky has shares in that or something. We have a place over there." A toss of her head in the same lofty manner. "But he doesn't come up here much except for business."

"And that's why he's...you are...? I mean..." Dammit, why couldn't he handle these situations with more élan, more flair, instead of acting like some love-struck juvenile? Which he had to admit to himself he felt like.

"I trust you write more commandingly than you speak, Mr...Ransome?" She was mocking him. "I have to believe you perform well in other areas. Whoa there, girl, easy." She gentled the mare as the sound of the helicopter became more insistent.

Jake looked to where it was coming fast up the valley, making straight for them. In thirty seconds, max, Jake calculated, they would be bull-horned away from each other, perhaps never to meet again. The prospect filled him with an unaccustomed urgency that drove all else from his mind.

"Why don't you try to find out?" He was yelling now. "Meet me at Eleanor Rigby's this evening."

"What?" She was having great problems with her mount now, as the chopper banked and its engine note increased. Jake felt desperate; it would soon hover, prior to investigation.

"It's a club in town, anybody will tell you where."

Too late; she jerked the reins, dug her heels in and they were off, the great hooves pounding the road. Then a mighty leap as they were over the perimeter fence and galloping over the rise, that tantalizing bottom bouncing out of sight in a matter of seconds.

"*You down there! Identify yourself!*"

With a weary wave Jake took out his Press card and made a throat-cutting gesture with it.

12: ALLIANCE

Sir Nicholas Brookes handed the phone back to his valet and returned drumming fingers to one well-clad knee. The valet – sixty-ish, grey-ish and with a discretion born of thirty years' survival in the service of his master – replaced the instrument back in the documents case and waited patiently for further orders. He chose to ignore the heat, noise and smell that threatened to stifle him and instead pondered the reasons for using the taxi as a means of transport in Rome. The motorists were insane and suicidal with it, something that appeared to have escaped Sir Nicholas, angry as usual, mega-making something or other from the far side of the world. He sighed, shifted queasily on the sticky rear seat and waited for the lights to change. Who knows, on green they might actually make it all the way across the Victor Emmanuel Bridge.

The media peer's thoughts would have surprised his servant; he had reckoned on the usual roadworks and the Roman propensity for making a meal out of a mouthful. Crossing the Tiber here was always a bastard at this time of day. But it did give him the excuse he needed to change the route. At least *that* part of the plan was working! The real reason for his ire was the news from England. It was not good, not business-like, and that offended his professionalism, that *frisson* before reaching a decision that could affect thousands of people. Meat and drink to him, the reason also for three wrecked marriages and count-less failed affairs. Women were attracted to him not only because of the obvious power factor that went with great wealth, but also through his sheer physical presence. Fleshy without being fat, breadth balancing height, he tended to dominate without intimidating. But none of them stayed the course, even if he'd wanted them to. His mercurial – sometimes frightening – moods and travel schedules left them exhausted en route, with an expensive trinket or piece of property to ease their departure.

But his most enduring and rewarding relationship was separate from all those others – and for a vastly different reason. For her to take off now was most inappropriate. Inappropriate, ha! There's typical British understatement, Nicholas thought. How appropriate! Damn her, why did she have to resist so much? His most difficult subject to date, she was also the most satisfying. Where *could* she be? If he didn't find out soon then this trip to the City of the Seven Hills could prove very expensive indeed.

They moved off as the flow south along the Tiber Embankment lessened for a few brief moments. He tapped the garlicky shoulder and in fluent Italian told the driver he had precisely two minutes to earn his promised tip by getting him to the Piazza San Pietro on time. Antonio Fabrizi threw up both hands and cursed this mad Inglesi who seemed to know the city, *his* city, better than he did, and lurched the battered Fiat left into the Via Della Conciliazione. The broad avenue led them quickly onto the open expanse of St Peter's Square, with the great domed basilica rising up magnificently in the background.

They drew up at the taxi rank to the left of the square's opening. Sir Nicholas – after giving his valet instructions to meet him by the official entrance in an hour with the company's Daimler – got out. He negotiated the traffic flow as decorously as his bulk would allow without hurrying and made it safely to the north side of the Bernini colonnade, striding purposefully along its pillared length until he came to the shallow steps leading to the Bronze Door, one of the entrances to the Apostolic Palace proper. The door was unlocked but a young Swiss guard stood to one side, halberd at the ready. The medieval weapon was lowered enough to bar the peer's path and the cry, "Alt!" rang out. He showed the sentry his pass and the man seemed disposed to question its validity. He already knew he should have been at St Anne's Gate but his traffic explanation seemed to satisfy his interrogator. He was telephoned through to the next stage and took the lift to the Third Loggia. More sentries, further scrutiny before progress was sanctioned.

The large entrance hall of the Secretariat of State was guarded by *uscieri*, two doormen in dark suits and unctuous tones who were the final obstacles to his objective. He was smoothly ushered into a small reception room, where he lowered his ample frame onto a flimsy antique chair in pink and gold. A bare two minutes later a young plump monsignor in scarlet-edged cassock and purple sash swept in, greeted him respectfully, begged to be excused for a "Momento". He swished back into the inner chamber, leaving Sir Nicholas feeling vaguely ridiculous at being left halfway out of the chair.

"Sir Nicholas, His Excellency will see you now. This way, please."

The prelate did not rise to greet him, an ominous sign, and one that did not go unnoticed by the younger cleric.

"Cardinal, so good of you to see me before His Holiness grants an audience. I bring a special greeting from Arundel." This last could be construed as something official from the Archbishopric of Arundel and Brighton or even Arundel Castle, home of the Norfolks, Britain's premier Catholic family.

"Will ten minutes be sufficient, Sir Nicholas? I have rather a full schedule this morning." He nodded a dismissal at his assistant, who dipped his head deferentially, smiled thinly at their visitor and retreated, closing the door with a soft but definite click.

The sigh from across the large, leather-topped desk was – what? Resigned? Testy? Sir Nicholas settled in another of the delicately ornate chairs and took a deep breath. The man seated before him was impressive with the weight of years in office; slender in form and face, the skin clear, features bony, with deep-set blue eyes that had lost little of their youthful quality. The hair and eyebrows were silver, the former brushed back from the high forehead and topped with the *zucchetto*, the colourful skull cap of his station. The scarlet-edged cape and purple sash with the brass pectoral cross tucked into it completed a picture of power far different to his visitor's but no less potent in its own right. As *sostituto* or substitute to the Secretary of State he was almost at the very centre of an organization that could influence the behaviour and moral direction of a fifth of the world's population.

"I sincerely hope, Nicholas, this visit is necessary and not a resumption of our previous – ah, dialogue. I told you then I could see no further use in going over old ground. The world you inhabit seems to preclude the acceptance of an unambiguous refusal in business matters. I am bound by more – ah, spiritual constraints, not only through canon law, tradition and simple morality, but by conscience. So…" He spread his hands, fingers downward, palms upward, in a gesture that could have signified his own particular brand of ambiguity.

"Still the same little Franzl" – the prelate flushed and put his hands down, out of sight – "appealing to the gallery. Remember how Momma used to pull you to her when you did that? Declaring your innocence to all and sundry when I – and your sisters – knew full well you'd been dipping into our chocolate treats jar. Those baby blue eyes always melted her heart far faster than the sweets did, hidden by your hand."

"How dare you bring the name of our revered mother into this – this sordid meeting?" The cardinal raised his hand as though to strike the media magnate, caught himself in time and sank back in the tall chair. He fished out a linen handkerchief from his sleeve and held it to his lips, as though to impede some noxious odour. He quickly recovered and composed himself but the eyes were no longer mildly blue; a coldness had crept in which few around him ever saw. "You always had the knack of doing that, Nicholas. I suppose all brothers possess that to some degree but I have been out of practice for so long."

"I'm sorry, Franz, perhaps it was a little strong, but it doesn't do to forget one's roots. A lot may separate us but blood is blood -"

"I thought we agreed – *you* agreed! – when we parted that our new identities must become as one with our new lives. Ferenc and Miklos Moricz must no longer exist, only that way could we hope to escape the same fate as our parents and Marya and Lenni. I know that was wrong but when you're only eight and your whole world has disappeared, with only a big brother to cling to and then he, too, vanishes from your life…"

The anguish on the distinguished churchman's face almost affected Brookes. The memories came flooding back in a way they hadn't for many years now; the Displaced Persons camp outside Vienna in that winter of '45 as they'd staggered through the gate, starving and in rags. His younger brother had been struck dumb by the horrors they had endured, with no Hungarian interpreters being available. For weeks they had languished in hospital, slowly recovering, the ulcers healing and their emaciated little frames filling out. Food was still a wonder, the bowls and cutlery having to be prised from their fingers after every meal, being told gently not to hide crusts underneath the mattress; it attracted mice. Mice! They'd eaten mice.

"It was right at the time, Franz, we were alone, we could never go back…to what? You couldn't speak. I told you how I overheard them talking about our kind…how they were going to send us to 'special centres'. Where had we heard *that* before? And nobody was even taking siblings together for adoption. We would have been left, overlooked, until our true identities were discovered and then shipped out. I had to make a decision, Franz, and I was only ten, remember. That British officer had just received word about his only son – my age – dying from rheumatic fever back in England. I looked like him, he said, so I followed him around every day. Don't look at me like that, Franz, you can't have forgotten what the conditions were like. I meant to come back somehow when we were fully recovered but it wasn't so easy. My new mother hated me, hated her husband even more for daring to try and supplant her dead son's memory with a scruffy little Hungarian refugee…" He sighed. His brother was almost weeping now, his hand across his face, head shaking from side to side. "The old Austrian couple who took you in saved your life. I found that out much later."

"It was many years before I could speak again, Nicholas." The cardinal raised his head, eyes red. He stood up and went to the window, allowing the white net curtains to waft across his face, the sensation triggering his own memories of warm, pillowed fabric, the ample bosom of his adoptive mother, rocking him gently to sleep night after night as the terrible dreams howled and gibbered through his tortured mind. He was losing the faces of his parents and older sisters, and there was no way he could prevent it; they were becoming all mixed up with the grinning skulls by the roadsides; the corpses swinging grotesquely in the winds that swept the Hungarian plains as they scrabbled for roots in the hedgerows, or a precious potato his brother had filched from God knows where.

And the nights… Oh, those nights when hunger kept the sleep at bay and his child's imagination conjured up what might have befallen the rest of their family, after their father had forced them through the splintered planking of the rail car on the way to the death camps.

"I'm sure she knew – my new mother – there were so many things that I later came to realize as recognition signals in the

80

way she gazed at me in the bath…or brushed my hair back as I lay in bed, and she got me to at least mouth a new word each night before I went to sleep. There was a kind of sadness in her eyes – a knowing – then, that I was never to see again as I grew older. That's why I went into the church, Miklos, it was no vocation, no fervent flash of awareness to be at one with the Godhead." He turned and the eyes were mild blue once more, in control. "I simply had to repay her for drawing on her well of emotion and love all those years. She died a happy woman when I was ordained and the impetus she gave me then sustained me until I really did discover the love of Christ. You who have researched my life so well must know and believe that at least."

"I do, my brother, I sincerely do," the media mogul hastened to reassure the cardinal, this man who had never resembled himself in any way. He, Miklos, was always dark to the point of swarthiness and brawny, quick to fight and slow to forget any slight to him. Ferenc, on the other hand, had pale skin and bright red hair, a genetic descent from the true European Jew. Very delicate but clever and articulate, he would have succeeded in whatever endeavour he embarked upon. Why not the church? It was a business, just like any other, when you came right down to it. His brother might delude himself but there was no denying his gene pool, and in the right hands any instrument could be made to play. "I've told you before, you misconstrue my motives." The cardinal made an impatient gesture as he returned to his seat. "No, no, Franz, my reasoning is sound, believe me. If there's one thing I know, it's finance, and whether you admit to it or not, the Holy Church is in crisis." Again that brushing motion from the other. "Hear me out, Franz, please. The Catholic Church is assailed on all sides by forces outside its control -"

"Yes, and your media networks are a great contributory factor there! We're drowning in a sea of filth and people like you are making millions – billions! – out of it, pandering to those unfortunates' basest urges -"

"I'm not pandering, Franz, I'm controlling, d'you hear me? Controlling. Think about it…the networks I own are by no means the worst. I have to balance decency against deficit, shining examples against shareholders. But the point is, I'm in profit, the Vatican is not! The Vatican Bank almost collapsed after the Calvi scandal and now there is even worse coming out of America – billion dollar law suits for child abuse, gay priests, nuns on the run, monasteries and convents going it alone. Now the sleeping giant – China – is giving grave cause for concern, with the Catholics there breaking away. Your one remaining annual stipend, Peter's Pence, has dropped by well over a third -"

"How do you know –?"

"Franz, Franz, it's my business to know. Account number…ah, five zeros-five-three-two-double nine-six-five, Unicredit Banca D'Impreza, isn't it? You think you people here in this hub of the universe are impervious to my sort of technology? I have controlling interests in a lot of the Italian media too." His brother shuddered and shakily touched his left cheekbone, as though to convince himself he was still there. "And most significant of all, your Radio Vatican is haemorrhaging to death. At this most important time, with the European Union opening the floodgates to Eastern Europe, the Baltic States…Muslim Turkey. And now the Italian government stab you in the back."

The cardinal started and then turned pale. Sir Nicholas smiled inwardly; he well knew the Vatican Radio was a project close to his heart. He still clung to an almost touching faith in the power of radio reaching every corner of the church's global empire. He believed that with the right voice he could touch the very heart and soul of each listener, no matter where they were –

out jogging, stuck in a car jam, lying on a beach. With the right voice – he was a secret fan of Billy Graham's taped sermons – people listened without seeming to, whilst doing other things; their own, individualistic secret. Different times called for different strategy and tactics.

And now the very nucleus – the source – of this 'reaching out' was being attacked in almost 'Trojan Horse' fashion. The Italian Environment Minister had just gone public with a vitriolic broadside against the Vatican's transmitting complex at Santa Maria di Galeria. A special enclave, some thirty kilometres north of Rome, it had been built in 1951, exempt from Italian law, like the rest of the City State. Then a sparsely populated area, the population had mushroomed to some 100,000 locals. The 21st century had caught up with it; reports of magnetic pollution and electrical interference on humans and property; leukaemia; electric lights switching themselves on; Vatican broadcasts blasting out of opened refrigerators and pressed doorbells.

For all these reasons the government had acted with environmental zeal; they decreed that transmission power be reduced. This at a time when the Holy City was desperately concerned at losing souls from their long-held, if once physically inaccessible, demographic areas in Eastern Europe. It was more, not less, range they now required. In fact, given the nature of this new diaspora, their transmissions needed to reach the farthest corners of the globe.

"Whatever the outcome of this legal battle I'm sure you will want to remove any taint of harming people from possible magnetic radiation. Even if the Vatican wins this battle we both know we are in the world of compensation culture. How much more money can the church pay out?"

Brookes paused and leaned back in the flimsy chair, allowing the uncertainty to hang there as the prelate's imagination took up the baton. It was true, he had spent many sleepless nights seeking a solution. And Peter's Pence – that hitherto monetary rock on which the Vatican traditionally relied – was drying up.

"You have a suggestion?" His voice was dreadfully tired.

"Well, I know you will not accept a loan."

"Impossible! Have you any conception of what that would mean? You…of all people…wanting to buy into the Holy Roman Church! The mere fact that you visited me at home last time – at the Palazzo San Carlo – was picked up by the religious correspondent for Le Figaro and relayed to Cardinal Solti. I am against all this – this subterfuge… It's – it's…"

"But nobody need know, Franz, there are ways of doing such things." Sir Nicholas tried to soothe his brother.

"Then why not a simple donation?" countered the cardinal triumphantly.

"Ah! I'm afraid at my level of finance there's no such thing as a simple donation. I'm a businessman first, a philanthropist second. And like I said, I have shareholders to answer to."

"And I to a somewhat higher arbiter of human behaviour, mm?" returned the other dryly.

"You speak of higher things, Franz, so let's take it literally, shall we?"

The other's puzzled look gave Brookes that little thrill it always did when he felt about to reveal his ace.

"As I said, this Radio Vatican thing won't go away…but it could – with my help." He had him now; that look he remembered so well – part curiosity but also part calculating, preparing his sharp mind for a challenge to his intellect. "What if you could physically move your radio station to a place where it would not only be safe from further claims on it but also in a geographical position to maximize the transmissions? Would that interest you?" What a question! Franz's face was a study in bafflement and greed.

"I have a fairly large section of land – real estate – that I acquired many years ago as a sort-of ambitious high class leisure community. I didn't come to anything, in fact I almost forgot about it back there, with so many other deals in the pot."

"In Italy? I really cannot see how that will -"

"Andorra."

The other sat up straight for perhaps the first time in minutes, eyes large and mouth slightly open. Brookes savoured the moment; he knew they didn't often come like this. "Andorra. It has everything – isolation, an easy shared administration system by two Catholic countries, low taxes, commanding altitude, guarantee of no population influx...ever! And it's yours, figuratively speaking; you only have to nod your head. How grateful the church – the Italians – would be at such a solution. You could be speaking for...Him, Franz." Sir Nicholas put as much sincerity into his voice that he could. He leaned forward in his chair as the other recoiled. "As the Vicar of Christ on Earth your word would be law – without reproach. What then?"

"Nicholas, you are in peril of your very soul when you voice such thoughts," his brother said harshly. "I will not endanger mine by even contemplating them. I have taken the papal vow of obedience, as do all who enter the service of the Vatican. It is unremitting: I do as I am told."

"Good answer, brother, your diplomatic training was not wasted. But only the pontiff is infallible. Even cardinals must harbour some...shall we say, aspirations? The present Secretary of State, Cardinal Denton, is said to be thinking of retiring. The smart money's on you as front runner for that slot-" He held up his hand as his brother started to speak. "I've told you, Franz, I know these things. His Holiness is frail and close studies of his recent TV appearances by commissioned gerontologists and one top American psychologist have reported to me that he is exhibiting neurological lapses consistent with a possible brain tumour, but more likely early Alzheimer's. Given the awesome responsibility he bears, that doesn't leave too many options -"

"What – what are you saying, Nicholas?" The prelate could barely speak the words, not wanting to believe but neither doubting his brother's resources. He *had* heard rumours.

"I'm saying, Franz, that this time next year could see white smoke and a new face on the balcony… It could be you."

"But I'm…"

"What? A Jew by birth?" Sir Nicholas laughed without humour, the heavy dark face showing no emotion. "There's only one other person in the world who knows that…and why should I tell? Besides, it could work for you, a sign from God. What greater symbolism could He show to unite the world against fundamentalism and terrorism? Jews and Gentiles facing the same way for once, proving that with God's providence anything is possible. Think of it, Franz, such an announcement at the right time could literally change the world."

"I can see where you've got your reputation from, Nicholas," Franz said a little shakily. "You seem to talk in headlines. No, no, that's not a criticism, I assure you." He got up and came round the desk, stood near his brother, closer both physically and emotionally than he had for fifty years. "Even allowing for such hyperbole to be melted down in the crucible of reason the fact remains… I simply don't have what you call in the temporal world 'political clout'. I am thought of as somewhat liberal in my views for the future of our church and too close ethnically to the present pontiff. Those two facts alone lengthen the odds against me somewhat, yes?"

"So you need an edge, is that what you're saying, Franz?" Sir Nicholas looked up keenly at his brother.

"Um, yes…" Franz smiled, ruefully, for the first time. "Given the expected *papabili* resistance at the voting conclave, an edge would be putting it mildly."

"Is the authenticated Holy Grail still in the strongroom in Valencia?"

"Of course." His brother's brow creased slightly. "Why?"

"How about its counterpart...the Judas Cup?"

The cardinal flinched; he seemed to shrink away from the question, his fingers clutching at the pectoral cross. "What – what do you know of the Judas Cup?"

"Everything." Starting with the potter's field he quickly ran through the little-known facts, right up to the crucial Napoleonic period of 1810, when the Emperor had ordered all the secret archives of the Holy See be removed to Paris. After Napoleon's downfall in 1815 the Vatican reclaimed their missing artifacts. But not all found their way back; the Judas Cup was just one of many priceless items that were never to return. "So you see, Franz, the person who restores such a dangerously potent symbol to the Vatican strongroom would be most highly regarded in the Roman Curia, throughout all twenty-four dicasteries...if presented at the right moment. Like I said, timing is all."

"Do you have it?" Ferenc Morisz, late of Budapest, Archbishop of Vienna and now successor to the most powerful man in the Vatican, would not have thanked anyone for taking his photograph at that precise moment; leaning forward, blue eyes fixed on his despised sibling, a look of naked greed in every line of his ascetic features.

"I can get it. Is it a deal?"

13: CONVERGENCE

Eleanor Rigby's was not the ideal place to meet someone you wanted to impress. The laser lights, floor smoke and stroboscopic effects seemed more like a *son et lumiere* of hell than the town's latest 'in' spot as Jake slid nervously past the four burly doormen.

He suppressed the inner voice that inevitably mocked him on such occasions, an unwelcome reminder of a lonely childhood spent in fantasies about knights and distressed damsels. Most of the so-called damsels he'd had experience with during adolescence seemed to be the ones doing the distressing. Now that at last he had met someone who might make him lower his visor and raise his lance he wasn't sure if he could hack it. That was of course if he could locate her in this flashing darkness –

"So you were serious."

She was standing by a mirrored pillar that reflected her profile to best advantage. Contrived? Who cares, he thought. Sod off, inner voice!

"Of course I was serious." He smiled his relief. "I hope you haven't been waiting long. I had some last minute work to do for tomorrow's edition. Can I get you a drink?"

"I haven't been waiting, as you so ungallantly put it. I was bored and remembered the name of this – this…" she waved her hand dismissively – "whatever it's supposed to be. Is this the best you can do around here?"

The arrogance was still there, not her most attractive trait, he had to concede. Apart from that she was still as stunning as he remembered; the shining, thick black hair swirled like liquid about her face; the eyes seemed to absorb all the available light, lending them a glow that was outside his experience. A simple white satin top that showed she was bra-less; he fancied he could hear the soft whisper of flesh on fabric as she moved. Tight black cords that reminded him of his first pubescent crush – Catwoman from the Batman TV series. His throat suddenly went dry.

"We can go somewhere else," he suggested, racking his brain for an alternative. There was really only the Cambridge, not a good move, given that it was the bouncy Belinda's posing pub.

"Just get me a spritzer first, will you, we'll consider a change of venue later." As he moved away she added. "And make sure they don't put ice in it, for God's sake. This looks like the kind of place where they'd stir a Tequila Sunrise!"

It can only get better, Jake, he muttered as he squeezed his way to the bar. His inner voice tried to suggest otherwise but even it had to succumb to the sonic saturation as he shouted his order.

When he got back to the pillar she had vanished. His multi-faceted reflection mocked him as he frantically cast about for the satin marker. Eventually he spotted her, sitting beneath a wall speaker that resembled an upended cattle grid. He pulled a stool across, placed their drinks on the mirrored table top.

"I thought" – An Arctic Monkeys number started up and he tried again, louder. "I thought you'd left."

"Left? I'm not sure if you have to pay to get *out* of here!" She sampled her drink, made a face, sighed and sat back, gazing at him. The look said, "Okay, what now?' Jake felt the first flutter-fingers of panic. Despite some active bedroom service the Book of Life still had too many blank pages for his liking. How to cope with the *frisson* and fascination of a female like this one was not yet in his lexicon for lovers. Besides, let's face it…why me?

"I had nothing better to do." Her head came up as she spoke and he received the full brilliance of those amazing eyes.

He gulped. "I – I'm sorry?"

"You asked why you…didn't you?" Her exasperation was

getting the better of whatever quirk of curiosity had impelled her here.

"Look." He took a deep breath. "Let's start again, shall we?" Taking her silence for acquiescence he ploughed on. "I asked you out because I very much wanted to. This" – he waved a hand – "was the only place I could think of on the spur of the moment. You must admit it wasn't exactly a controlled situation this afternoon. If you only knew how terrified I am of large quadrupeds -"

She burst out laughing, the memory breaking down her reserve. "You did look rather terrified, Jake."

The use of his name and the laughter transformed her; she became girlish, sipping her drink and pushing the thick black hair from one side of her face. The tip of her tongue flicked along already glistening lips as she regarded him with something approaching interest. Knowing at least the rudiments of body language he retained the initiative.

"What were you doing in the zoned area, anyway? Don't you know how many rules and local by-laws you broke back there?"

She shook her head, grinning, so he told her about the reservoir and evacuation. She appeared only mildly concerned.

"Is this your first time in these parts, Carolyn? You did mention something about an uncle but your accent indicates a life spent a lot further south than the River Tees."

"Yes, he's my mother's cousin…well, adopted cousin, really. Both my parents died in a car crash when I was very young. He wasn't all that keen on having a snivelling, pigtailed orphan foisted on him, with his extensive business interests world-wide. So I never really got close to him until fairly recently. But he's based in London, so when I got this job in market analysis I began to see a lot more of him." She paused and those perfectly formed teeth bit her lower lip for a moment. "But then I became ill…some strange debilitating condition that attacks without warning, draining me of energy. My uncle attributes it all to too many late nights and insufficient nutrition." She waggled her glass and took a sip.

So that explains her pallor, he thought, a rush of sympathy making him want to reach out and touch her. She suddenly looked very vulnerable, the previous haughty demeanour a probable defence mechanism. Poor little rich girl, got it all except where it really matters.

"I'm sorry, what d'you think it could be…M.E.? Myalgic-something or other?"

"What? Yuppie flu, you mean? No, nothing as fashionable as that." She laughed a little self-consciously. "Whatever it is, it appears to be filling the minds and wallets of several Harley Street specialists at the moment. Blood, brain, bone, organ function, you name it, they've tested it."

"So why are you up here, Carolyn? I mean, is it some treatment…what?" His obvious concern reached her in a way she did not quite understand. What *had* led her to respond to such a – a boy? No, that was unwarranted, and probably untrue. Boyish he certainly looked, but that was genetic, not choice and something he would cherish more as the years went by, she felt. There was a determined tilt to the chin she hadn't noticed earlier.

"No, no treatment, more like a retreat." She gathered her thoughts, weighing various factors. Her steady gaze began to unnerve him, but before he could react she continued, "I quite suddenly had a sense of revulsion at all the prodding and poking, the hemming and hawing. I guess I just took off…anywhere as long as it meant no more clinics and antiseptic. This childhood hideaway almost automatically suggested itself. I knew it would be unoccupied, and Mrs Sykes – the housekeeper – has always been more than happy to see me. We've always got on well together."

"So how long are you staying?" He tried to make it sound

casual. She was the sort of fabulous creature whose absence would not go long unnoticed. She must have a lover – more likely plural. The thought made him wince.

"I really should be getting back tomorrow," she said, with a reluctance that appeared genuine to the young journalist. "There will be hell to pay if Uncle Nicky finds out I've gone over the wall."

"Tomorrow!" The shock was real; he looked about him wildly, only noticing for the fist time the pulsating music and zombie-like figures dipping and weaving around them. *What are we doing here when time is so precious?* "Look, let's get out of here, Carolyn. There's someone I have to see…it won't take long and then perhaps we can have a meal and maybe – well, maybe…"

"Get to know each other a little better?" she prompted, the half-serious, half-mocking gaze difficult for him to fathom. "I'm afraid I may not last out the evening. I really do get tired very easily, Jake."

"I'll take that chance," Jake replied firmly, reaching across and gripping her hand. "Let's go."

His confidence faltered when they reached the pavement and he remembered he'd left his car at home, an instinctive move motivated by shame. But then she said she had hers parked around the rear of the club. When he took in the predatory profile of the crimson 911 Porsche Turbo cabriolet he had to restrain himself from salivating.

"This is yours?"

"A twenty-first birthday present from my uncle," she replied defensively. *From the registration plate that made her at most twenty-two,* his investigative instinct working automatically as he climbed in beside her. The interior had that wonderful woman smell of its owner, and something else less definable. *Ah, yes, he had it…money!* He luxuriated despite its somewhat cramped dimensions as it surged out of town, the muffled thunder of its exhaust bouncing back from deserted side streets as she played Amber Gambler at every intersection with consummate ease. The former twenty minutes drive was almost halved, climbing up through the old ironstone mining villages with throttled-back impatience. Joan Winspear's light was on as promised in the cryptic note left on his desk.

He eased stiffly out of the passenger seat as the elderly spinster opened the front door of the cottage, her beret still in place. She registered surprise at sight of the girl, ignoring the sight of such a car in such a setting.

"I'm sorry, Miss Winspear, I hope you don't mind my bringing a friend along. I had a prior engagement when I got your message..." He moved quickly to help Carolyn alight and led her into the musty hallway, conveying a sense of urgency that succeeded in overcoming the girl's obvious reluctance to enter such an alien place. He tried to ignore her distaste at the proximity of the mildewed walls as she brushed past.

The kitchen was still as he remembered it, nothing seemed to have been moved from table, sink or floor. As Joan Winspear turned to confront them he quickly made the introductions, already sensing an error of judgement in bringing Carolyn along. His idea of impressing this enigmatic and beautiful creature with an example of the sort of bizarre characters he habitually dealt with had all the elements of a backfire. He'd mentioned the purpose of his visit briefly on the way over but she had not responded positively. Her mind had seemed to be elsewhere as she'd powered her wicked machine through the unfamiliar streets. Now she appeared as some exotic orchid on a rubbish tip, destined to blossom quickly and fade. Was that what was filling him with this unaccustomed urgency, the fear that she would shortly disappear before he could get to know her better? He grimaced at the memory of her words; her statement about returning to London could actually be motivated by a lack of anything to keep her here...maybe even accelerated by his uncouth company.

He drew Carolyn towards the cluttered kitchen table, brushed at a wooden chair seat with one sleeve before gently but firmly pressing her down on to it. The girl was too surprised at his determination to resist. He quickly sat next to her, gave her what he hoped was a winning smile and turned back to Joan.

"I've told Carolyn something of our mutual interest in the old church at Helmington, Miss Winspear -"

"Did you say your name was Draycott? Are you local, lass?" The historian's truculence was almost palpable

"No, she's not," Jake said. "She's just up from London for a few days. Probably going back tomorrow...unless I can persuade her otherwise." He turned to Carolyn, searching her beautiful features for some sign of reassurance.

"I apologise for Jake, Miss Winspear. His male chauvinism sits uneasily on his shoulders, like a real head on Wurzel Gummidge. I wonder if he always behaves so oddly in company?" She gazed back directly at Jake, ready and capable of duelling with him on any level he cared to choose.

The victim coloured, appealed to the old historian for succour but there was none there. She gave a barking laugh and plonked her shapeless body down opposite them, began unwrapping one of her chcolate bars.

"You'll do, lass, aye, you'll do. When I was younger..." Her good humour faded at some recollection less sweet than she had at first thought. "So!" She slapped the table with a red-raw hand. "Do you have anything to report, young man?"

Jake proceeded to tell her of his meeting with friend Alec and the results of his return to the church. The old lady's eyes began to gleam halfway through his narrative. He paused for a few moments to see if any of this was having an effect on Carolyn.

She seemed more interested in the kitchen's general ambience.

"Anything else?"

"What?" The half-closed left eye was beginning to distract him. "Oh…well, my colleague Gerry Malone reports a higher than normal incidence of dog attacks – large dog attacks. The police have initially put it down to released or escaped pets of uncertain breed, y'know? A lot of recent pit bull tragedies with kids haven't helped." Her other eyelid began to droop. "What else…? Yes, it seems the convent that Sister Dymphna came from was in an uproar last night when a large dog was found on the premises. It somehow appears to have gained access to the sleeping quarters -" He stopped, grinned. "Not sure if the dog was male or…anyway, the Mother Superior was adamant that all windows and doors were secured against intruders. It tried to attack several nuns but didn't actually bite anyone before 'vanishing' -" he made quotation marks in the air -"as mysteriously as it appeared. Three nuns taken to hospital suffering from shock. Expert opinion – both medical and police – regards it as a type of hysteria brought about by the tragic Sister's death." Seeing Carolyn's puzzled expression he quickly told her about the car smash. "Oh, and Gerry said forensics reported a peculiar thing…they found strange markings on the car bonnet… Said the only way they could describe it was like paw marks burnt into the paintwork."

"Barguest!" The old lady breathed the word, both eyes now wide open. She stopped chewing, her gaze fixed at some point above and beyond the young couple.

"Pardon?" Jake glanced at Carolyn and shrugged apologetically.

But Joan had already lumbered to her feet and was making her way painfully to the front room, where he heard remembered sounds - books, phone, muttered curses. She reappeared, panting but triumphant, brandishing a book. She shuffled back to her seat, spectacles now in place and began flipping the pages. "Ah!" she grunted and looked across at them. "Here, you read it."

Jake took the book carefully; although not old its dilapidated state seemed to have been accelerated by the same process as everything else in the house. He was very conscious of Carolyn watching him.

He nevertheless took the time to scan the page quickly before clearing his throat and starting, his lips moving silently before realizing his error and speaking the words. "…the unusual events which took place at Blythburgh church and also Bungay church on 4th August 1577. During that morning, when people were attending the usual Sunday service a terrible storm rose up and – taking Bungay first – a gigantic black dog suddenly appeared in their midst. This manifestation proved fatal to two members of the congregation for 'as they were kneeling upon their knees and occupied in prayer as it seemed, wrung the necks of them at one instant clean backward, insomuch, that even at a moment where they kneeled, they strangely died'. A further man was injured when the black dog 'gave him such a grip on the back, that therewith all he was presently drawn together and shrunk up, as it were a piece of leather scorched in a hot fire; or as the mouth of a purse or bag drawn together with a string. The man, albeit he was in so strange a taking died not, but as it is thought is yet alive'. Abraham Fleming who reported this event in 'A Strange and Terrible Wonder', has also this to say of Blythburgh."

Jake looked up, first at Carolyn and then Joan, but before he could do or say anything the latter impatiently waved him on. He sighed. "On the self-same day, in like manner, into the parish church of another town called Blibery, not above seven miles distant from Bongay above said, 'The like thing entered, in the same shape and similitude, where placing himself upon a main balk or beam, whereon some ye Rood did stand, suddenly he gave a swing down through the church, and there also as before, slew two men and a lad, and burned the hand of another person that was among the rest of the company, of whom divers were blasted. This mischief thus wrought, he flew with wonderful force to no little fear of the assembly, out of the church in a hideous and hellish likeness. The only physical evidence of this event are the scorch marks on the door as it quitted the church."

Jake turned the page and started, glancing up quickly, then back to the book. Carolyn said, "What is it, Jake?" but he didn't answer right away, staring at some monochrome photographs, one of the sixteenth century notice relating to the Bungay incident, the other a close-up of the church door at Blythburgh.

A strange tingle coursed down his spine. "This photo…"

"Yes?" Joan Winspear squinted sharply at him

"One thing I forgot to mention just now – I didn't think it relevant to what I was after…There are some scorch marks on the door of St Michael's, very similar to these." He noticed the old spinster's fists clench for a moment. "I assumed somehow that the lightning…" He stopped as Joan slowly shook her head.

"It's the Barguest, resurrected, recalled from whatever dark pit of hell has been its home." Her eyes glittered as though with some kind of fever.

"I'm sorry, am I missing something here?" Carolyn's caustic tone broke the spell, cutting the febrile link the last few seconds had established. "Who or what – when it's at home – is a –a barguest?"

In response Jake handed the book across, waited for her reaction. Joan took another pull at her Mars bar. Carolyn flicked the illustration page over to check there were no more, closed the book and gave them both the benefit of those beautiful eyes. "Am I supposed to believe any of this?"

"Why not? It's happened before – and since – in various

forms. Here, let me." She reached across for the book, turned a few pages, then read out: "Bertin, a twelfth century French historian who compiled the *Annales Francorum Regum*, wrote that in the year 856 a storm arose at Trier during a service". She glanced up at them briefly. "And the church was, quote, 'filled with such a dense darkness that one and another could hardly see him or her neighbour. On a sudden there was seen a dog of immense size in a' – she held up a finger – 'sudden opening of the floor or earth, and it ran to and fro around the altar'." She closed the book. "Again at Trier in 867 according to the *Chronicon Saxonicus*, then 1171 at Andover. The testimonies come down the centuries, usually black dogs as big as a calf, with great red saucer-like eyes, evil-smelling, harbingers of death or disaster. There are a few rare cases of the creature helping humans who have, say, lost their way in fog or darkness, but in the main it bodes ill for those it sees or touches."

"Like Sarah Branthwaite?"

Joan squinted at Jake before answering, assessing how much to tell him. Then: "You're the journalist, assemble the facts," she growled defiantly.

"Just a minute…please!" Carolyn's exasperation was surfacing rapidly. "Are you suggesting this – these medieval accounts of religious hysteria are to be taken seriously, even to the extent of rolling them up with some elderly church cleaner's heart attack during an electrical storm?"

"Why not, Carolyn?" Jake replied quietly. He tilted his chin. "There is a reason for everything; the obvious explanation does not necessarily have to be the correct one."

"But-but you're deliberately going out of your way to misconstrue the facts."

"Perhaps, young lady, you are deliberately going out of your way to ignore them."

"Okay, okay" Carolyn held up her hands. "I'm giving you

two flakes" – Joan blinked – "the benefit of the doubt. Five minutes to make a halfway sensible case out of all – all this…" She waved her hand at the book. "If your best shot fails to convince, then I'm off. And you, Mr Hotshot Reporter, can either then fulfil your earlier promise for this evening or else find your own way home!"

Jake glanced quickly at Joan, who nodded almost imperceptibly. "Fair enough, Carolyn, start the clock."

"First, why Barguest?"

"Regional identity," the historian intervened, slumping onto her chair. "The word is a corruption of barrow – or gate – ghost. Elsewhere…" She shrugged. "Skriker, Trash, Black Shuck -" She stopped, both eyes opening. "Of course, how stupid of me!"

"What is it, Miss Winspear?"

"Cappel, Jake. In old Westmorland the black dog went by the name of Cappel or Capelthwaite."

"You mean like the priest?" Carolyn appeared rattled for the fist time. Then: "Surely a coincidence…I mean, it's not that rare a surname, is it?"

"No, of course not, young lady, just another link. But at what point do all the links become strong enough to form a chain?"

"Let's return to the facts." Carolyn tapped her slim Cartier. "How come they can appear and then just vanish like that?"

"That's less certain and opens the debate somewhat," the old lady conceded. "Apart from the apparent psychic nature of the beast we're getting into earth energies here."

"Sorry? Earth energies? What?" She looked from one to the other.

"Yes, the natural forces that surround us – magnetism, gamma rays, radiation of sun and stone, also includes lines of energy as yet not fully understood but certainly quantifiable. I can show you some examples…" She made to get up but Carolyn stopped her.

"Okay, we'll pick up on that one later. Go on."

"That the black dogs are ancient guardians left at significant centres of energy. They re-appear for reasons which are still not clear. Some claim they are guarding treasure of a spiritual rather than material nature. You see, Carolyn, energy is force and force is power and power is the most sought-after treasure of all. In days long gone people were closer to nature – they understood it and a few even learned to control it. Most of that ancient wisdom has been submerged beneath layers of so-called civilization but it exists – just as potently as it did then. It's *we* who have lost the sensitivity to perceive it."

"But if we can't even detect its presence then how can it harm us?" protested Carolyn. "Surely its power – accepting for a moment that what you say is true – lies merely in the fear it engenders, undermining our confidence, flawing our judgement. If you refuse to believe then it's – it's like butterflies against your window pane while you sleep."

"Wrong, wrong, wrong!" Joan slammed both hands down on the table. "You can't detect 'flu or cholera till it strikes you down. Only then can you put up a defence against further attacks. We are not talking here about some African tribesman conditioned into a decline by a witch doctor's hex. There are people on this planet, Carolyn, who are truly, truly dangerous, so practised in the black arts that they can call upon forces in such concentration and strength that nothing – nothing! – can withstand them. Hammer Films and Hollywood have a lot to answer for. You must believe me; switching off your TV set does not make them go away. They laugh at crucifixes – spit on them! These people can stockpile demons like governments hoard chemical weapons, and if they decide to unleash them…" She sank back, spent, eyelids drooping as if she were about to nod off.

"Miss Winspear?" Jake said. No reaction. "Miss Winspear!"

The old lady blinked. "Where do the black dogs figure in all this? I mean at the moment? Do my accounts from Alec and Gerry Malone fill in any holes for you?"

"Yes…right. Let's take events in chronological order: at approximately 16.45 hours your surveyor friend swears he and his boss were involved in something frightening and inexplicable. Less than a half a mile away and – as near as we can establish – at exactly the same time Sarah Branthwaite was being terrified almost to death by lightning striking the church roof. Some thirty minutes later Sister Dymphna swerves off a straight road with no other vehicles involved and tragically dies. Then a young girl alleges she was chased by a huge black rottweiler near Sowerby Bridge and last night the Mother Superior of the convent testifies that a giant black dog appeared – and disappeared – within a burglar-proof building. Any disagreement on the sequence?" As both listeners tried to speak Joan raised a hand. "I said the sequence. I am providing a skeleton here, a framework on which to hang more facts and theories. Now…fact: Hobb's Barrow derives from hob – an old name for the devil -"

"So the barrow gets its name from some ancient legend or superstition surrounding it?" Jake interjected.

"Almost certainly. Fact: the church of St Michael's is built on possibly the strongest convergence of ley lines in the area. In fact, it's quite literally constructed around a marker stone placed there thousands of years ago. So…a place of great mystical significance. Fact: the nun died at Hayman's – formerly Hangman's – Cross, another ley line concentration, ditto Sowerby Bridge and Littlebeck Convent."

"Are you seriously suggesting that this – this thing, whatever it is, is appearing at particular points on the landscape?" Carolyn looked from one to the other, raised her hands, palms upwards. "Why?"

"It responded to some call, some trigger against its will. That's why it's hostile and aggressive," Joan grunted.

Carolyn slid a sideways at Jake. "Are we talking parallel universes here?"

"Not exactly parallel," Joan rejoined matter-of-factly. "That would imply they never actually touched. In this case – as in many others – there is abundant evidence that both worlds not only impinge but occasionally overlap."

"Phew! This is too heavy for me, lady."

"Why, Carolyn? Goethe has written a scene in Faust of a black dog with eyes like live coals. Do you deny Goethe? Do you deny the concept of *bete noir*, an individual's personal dread? Why black beast? Do you know there is a village in Devon actually called Black Dog?"

Before Carolyn could form a retort Jake said, "But if what you say is true – and I don't disbelieve it, mind! – then how or why?"

"Well…it seems that the combination of electrical storm" – she stabbed a finger at the open book – "your friend's formation of a pyramidal shape with the measuring instrument's legs as a cap to the barrow – very powerful magic, that. Then the laser's energy directed downwards and whatever was being conjured up in the nearby church, was all enough to break the seal, as it were, on one of those psychic dogs. As to why…" She paused, then: "I went to see Sarah Branthwaite this afternoon. We were at school together for awhile back there in the late forties. I told the nurse I had promised her brother in Scarborough I would look in on her for him. She didn't look too good, very still, eyes closed and somehow shrunken-looking, and connected to all those instruments. I sat there quietly for perhaps twenty minutes, just holding her hand, when Father Cappel entered the room."

Jake was alerted straight away, sensing there was purpose in Joan's measured tones.

"The priest was obviously surprised to see me sitting there. Having seen him I can understand better your views about him... He appears to be under a great deal of strain, far more than is consistent with the fact he is a total stranger in the valley's evacuation. And then his hands...they were those of a gentleman suddenly thrust into manual work – broken nails, scraped knuckles. Anyhow, he regained his composure and said, 'Oh, I beg your pardon, I thought...' and then his eyes went beyond me, to the patient, and at that point all the monitors decided to go berserk."

"What? You mean Sarah's vital signs?"

"Yes, Jake, heart, brain, pulse rate, whatever...all went off the scale and alarms started to go off. Sarah herself became extremely agitated; her hand tightened in mine and her eyelids flickered as though her eyeballs were trying to get out. She made what I can only describe as a kind of whispering sound. I began to speak to her, ask her if she could hear me but just then a bevy of medical staff charged in and we were both ushered unceremoniously out into the corridor. I hung around, really concerned for poor Sarah – for anybody trapped in such a dreadful situation – but the priest..." She paused at the memory, then shook her head and continued. "He acted most strangely for one of his cloth, avoiding my eyes, not speaking, even when I tried to engage him in conversation. He expressed no concern for Sarah's plight, indeed, he muttered something about another appointment and strode out of the building. I waited around until a nurse eventually emerged from Sarah's room to say she had unfortunately not survived this latest seizure, and could I shed any light on her sudden relapse, when all the indications were that she was responding to treatment. I said no but it was almost certainly the sound of Cappel's voice triggered her demise."

Jake got up and paced the cramped kitchen as much as he

103

could, running fingers through his blond curls, tousling them in a way that was seemingly a long-established aid to thought. "Poor Sarah, I'd rather hoped she was going to make it. So…you're saying – if I read you correctly, Miss Winspear – that whatever it was that initially brought about her collapse was more to do with the priest than the lightning?"

"Sarah was always a devoutly Christian person. She had total access to St Michael's. The death of Father Scanlon at this particular time would have been a great source of sorrow to her. Cappel's tenure just prior and after that event may have some significance here -"

"But surely you can't – you're not suggesting…" Jake gazed at both women and then coloured as Carolyn – staring at him in feigned, wide-eyed innocence – silently mouthed the words 'foul play' before arching her eyebrows theatrically. Luckily for them both Joan missed this little by-play as she replied. "I believe, given the facts as we know them, Father Cappel was engaged in some form of unholy ceremony when Sarah intruded. The shock of whatever he was doing, on the very altar steps where Father Scanlon died, was compounded by the appearance of the Barguest which – conjured up either intentionally or accidentally – was enough to tip her over the edge. Her interruption may have caused Cappel to abort the ritual at a critical point and what he got was a conduit to a different part of hell than the one he bargained for. And when I say bargained I mean that literally; he will have made a pact with the devil himself and must pay…one way or the other."

Carolyn's eyes said it: That's it, the old bat's flipped! I'm outta here. Are you in or out, Jakey boy?

The young reporter strove manfully to retain his grip on logic and reason. This was getting too far out for him, and way past any point that old Gus would countenance…even if it were true! And yet…he had witnessed Cappel's bizarre behaviour,

104

exposed those inexplicable deceptions, seen the burn marks on the church door.

"You're saying he was involved in some form of black magic, is that it?" He raised a restraining hand in Carolyn's direction as she made to get up from her chair. "How can you possibly sustain such a hypothesis? I mean, in this day and age -"

"Of a global plague of paedophilia? Of more covens and child abuse across the land than at any other time in history. A satanic ritual is just like any other form of words or actions to achieve an end. If done in the correct and *proven* manner it will work. What's the problem, Jake, can't you handle that concept?" The old lady peered fiercely from her one good eye and tore at another confectionery bar like some latter-day gold prospector with a chaw of baccy.

"Miss Winspear," Carolyn said. "I've sat here, against my better judgement, while you two have batted back and forth a series of hypotheses which – if they were building materials – would make for a very shaky structure. Then having constructed this flimsy edifice, you place a whopping great roof on it that makes the whole thing insupportable. You've destroyed your own credibility by simply going too far. Black magic, satanic rituals…hocus pocus!" She stood up. "Are we going, Jake?"

"Just one thing before you go, young lady." Joan was impassive. "You have a rather fancy machine out there. How many separate parts would you guess it is comprised of…six thousand…seven thousand?"

"What? Why, what has that got to do with anything?" Carolyn stared at Jake in exasperation.

"Its manufacture is a form of ritual, yes? I mean, people wearing their assigned…robes are involved in each stage of its construction – a nut here, a switch there, wiring A to B to C and so forth. Every human operation is proven and formalized to the point of ceremony and all are essential to the final product arriving before the adoring masses in its purpose-built temple – the showroom – as its designer conceived it. But if there is just one error in the sequence…say, a cogwheel inserted the wrong way round or two wires crossed-connected then the eagerly awaited product will not appear as promised. So sorry, there has been a slight delay, sir. Can you wait while we try again? In short, it has fallen short of perfection.

"And you, Jake, have you never watched your mother when you were a small child as she baked a cake? All the ingredients to begin with, set out in their various proportions. And then she mixes them all together…in the right order! Then she places it all in a sort of magic cabinet and sets the time and temperature. If she has done it all in the correct manner, Hey Presto! You have your favourite cherry cake. But if she is distracted by your chatter and forgets to put the eggs in, or the salt instead of the sugar…well, what then? Disaster, fit only for the dustbin." She leaned forward, her hands on the table, staring at them in that lopsided way. "It's ritual, tried and tested, from the taking down of Jericho's walls to the successful launch of another space shuttle to the act of making love. Do it the right way and it works, get it wrong and there's a price to pay – the immutable law. Cappel cocked it up and we have two dead women, numerous terrified people and a hound from hell on the loose. So, go on, walk away, say it doesn't concern you. Go about your gadfly lives whilst one more element of evil stalks the land." She stopped, breathing with difficulty, picked up her brandy glass, then pushed it from her. She looked very tired.

"You really believe all this, Miss Winspear?"

"Young lady, I'm far too long in the tooth to speak of things purely for effect. For all we know the powers of darkness are already aware of our interest in their machinations. If so" – she raised her hands from the table and let them fall back – "then to paraphrase loosely, the game is already afoot. Knowledge conveys not only power but responsibility too." She sighed, and to Jake it was as if all the stuffing had been knocked out of her. "Perhaps you are wise to laugh at my wild imaginings, the young always think they are immortal…long may it remain so."

The almost expressionless interchange between the young couple didn't take long, just enough to commit them to a course of action they both felt instinctively as seminal.

Jake spoke first. "What do *you* think Cappel is after?"

"Difficult – no, impossible to conjecture at this stage. Personal power over someone or some thing. Material wealth or its whereabouts, a vision of the future…perhaps even a solution to a very real problem he has. But I'm convinced in my own mind the Barguest was not part of his plan. The priest's doings may never even impinge on our lives but the dog…" She squinted at them in an almost comical manner, but her voice was deadly serious. "That creature is trouble and will have to be stopped."

"How?"

"There are several alternatives, Carolyn, but they depend on the phantom's purpose and location. Although it assumes solidity I believe it is basically psychic and/or electrical energy. Like all energy build-ups it can be discharged by metal or water, or perhaps some sort of negative polarization…don't ask me what. But that alone wouldn't necessarily ensure its permanent elimination, it would simply neutralize the immediate vicinity."

"Then what about exorcism?" suggested Jake. "I believe I read in the files somewhere that any spirit can be banished for good with the right …"

"Go on, Jake," the old lady prompted, a sparkle returning to her one good eye. "Say it. The right form of words? You don't mean a good old ritualistic spell, do you?" She allowed him to squirm for a few seconds, then relented. "But you're right. The case you're referring to was probably at Kettleness -"

"Yes, that's it!" he exclaimed. "Back in…when was it…the fifties?"

"Yes, one of the country's foremost exorcists, the Reverend Donald Omand, performed a service on the cliffs at Kettleness – not far from here, Carolyn, over near Whitby. There had been sightings of a giant spectral hound there for generations. After the exorcism the reports ceased. Incidentally, Bram Stoker is supposed to have derived his Dracula idea from that particular phantom. If you remember, the vampire comes ashore there in the form of -"

"A huge hound!"

"My God," breathed Carolyn. "Then why not try it on this – this Barguest?"

"Two things, mainly. Making a credible case to the right person. Look at the trouble I've had trying to convince you two! Secondly, we need to be sure we're exorcising at the right place -"

"But the barrow…"

"Was where it emanated from, yes, but where is it at this precise moment, hmm?"

Their crestfallen expressions were a measure of their recently forgotten cynicism and doubts.

"But all is not lost, children, come here." She lumbered to her feet and trudged through to the front room. Jake and Carolyn gazed at the woollen, wrinkled back in surprise before obediently following. The girl's reaction on entering the untidy interior was predictable and made Jake smile, remembering his own introduction to the scattered books and files amid the rickety furniture.

As Joan rummaged in the corner by the bookcase, a column of badly stacked books crashed to the floor, raising a cloud of dust. After much muttering there was a muffled, "Ah!" and she drew forth a rolled-up map. She shuffled back to where they stood next to the old, badly varnished sideboard. Sweeping aside the chrome and oak biscuit barrel, gaudily ornate silver-plated cigarette box and the view of Bridlington harbour bordered with seashells, she spread the map out.

"I believe the creature is confused and angry, hence the attacks. It must instinctively want to return to its resting place. The conflicting abundance of today's energy sources – power lines, aircraft transmissions, cable TV and so on – can't fail but have a disorientating effect on it. But it is following some pattern that I can see. Look!" She stabbed with her stubby forefinger. "This ordnance map shows all the places where Barguest appeared…Hobb's Barrow, St Michael's, Hayman's Cross, Littlebeck Convent and Sowerby Bridge. Now watch!"

Grabbing hold of a cheap moulded plastic tray with 'Souvenir of Scarborough' painted on it, she used one edge as a ruler to draw a line with a stub of pencil across the paper. She stood back a little to allow the other two access. Carolyn and Jake leaned forward, peering at the detailed contours in the low wattage light available.

Then the girl clutched at Jake's sleeve as his sudden intake of breath almost smothered her whispered, "I see it but I don't believe it!"

"Why not, Carolyn? You believe in facts, surely." Joan was obdurate. "You can't have it both ways." She moved forward again, her bulk establishing a kind of bridgehead by the sideboard again. "A dead straight alignment, near as dammit. Remember, the earth's moved a bit over the last few thousand years. All these points lie on a very strong ley line and that means energy, rising and fading over each twenty-four hour period. The creature is sticking to it like a heat-seeking missile because it is its only link with the past. It's trying to get back but it hasn't the directional sense – or paranormal guidance – to go the right way. If it fails to do this it will become omni-directional, perhaps do a kind of psychic sweep to pick up other energy sources, like some random electron whose path could cross and alter a molecular structure, maybe even triggering a similar chain reaction."

"What d'you mean?" asked Jake, trying to absorb what had gone before, in the light of what this remarkable woman was now throwing at them.

"I mean…what if our Barguest lands on a new psychic square, so to speak, activating some other guardian spirit, and they in turn re-activate another…and another?" She allowed the concept to sink in as she almost staggered to the only easy chair and flopped onto its over-stuffed seat. She wiped her face with one hand and wheezed.

"Then what do we do, Miss Winspear?" Jake ventured the question, half-dreading what – if any – answer there might be.

"I have a few ideas. But you'll have to go away while I ponder them. In the meantime, bear in mind the valley gets flooded in a few days. If that happens before we get the genie back in the bottle…" She raised her hands. "It will have no home, wreaking havoc where it will…or until Father Cappel tells it what to do."

14: PARTICIPANCE

Renton Cappel should have felt relieved, freed for awhile from his exhausting, disappointing labours to unearth the Chalice of Akeldama. He was beginning to have frightening doubts about success before the valley became submerged. Worst of all, the fear of what the reporting of such failure could mean for him.

Yet here he was, driving into…what? The devil's domain? His last telephoned instruction had seen him completing the destruction of the remaining ground floor room – the kitchen. He still had the wit to appreciate the irony of this, the kitchen having become a kind of animal's lair, to which he would retreat, lick his wounds and sleep. Blessed sleep; now, alas, as elusive as his goal. This refuge too was now in a ruinous state, only retaining its electricity, plumbing and access. He'd been wearily considering his dwindling options when the nearby phone jangled him off the draining board, spilling his tea and smashing his one remaining mug in the process. He'd hesitated about lifting the receiver, assuming it to be another council official checking through the valley phone list for any stubborn or returned evacuees. But something compelled him.

When he heard the soft, menacing voice he forgot his soaked trouser leg and placed his other hand on the instrument, unconsciously squeezing it as he listened.

The mock-Georgian pile that was Brookefield Hall looked as forbidding as its master. Built to house the Brookes family, who had figured large in the community for several generations, garnering their wealth from the local ironstone deposits. That was old money, gone now, Sir Nicholas being the last of the line, with no issue. By an almost poetic twist of fate the building was

111

returning to the earth that had produced it, one section already subsiding into the old mine workings deep below.

As Cappel negotiated the curving driveway he could see no lights in the big house, intermittently obscured by the row of tall cypress trees flanking him. Another clouded night, with no indications of habitation from the windows across the valley. Only the faint yellow glow of last-minute activity around the completed dam, several miles further down. He fancied he could just glimpse its shallow white curve, smiling enigmatically, it seemed, at his useless efforts.

The old Volvo slid to a crunching halt by the large, stone porch, its arrival triggering the security lighting system as he applied the handbrake. He got out, aware of the slight breeze sighing through the trees. Were they whispering a warning? 'Stay away, stay away'. He straightened his black jacket, wincing at the reminder of split fingernails, and walked to the entrance. The carved wood doors were opened and through the inner hall glass he could detect light at the far end of the passage. He poked at the small white circle in the dark stone and heard its indistinct *br-r-r* somewhere. The dim area of light altered, moved with shadow, and then a bulky shape loomed towards him.

Suddenly the porch light came on, momentarily blinding the priest; he put a hand to his brow to shield the glare and watched Sir Nicholas move towards him in that deceptively fleet manner he'd noticed earlier.

"Renton, my boy! Come in, come in." Brookes held a pale hand out. He was garbed in some flowing black gown that buttoned up to the neck. "Through here." Cappel was ushered into an old-fashioned drawing room – over-stuffed upholstery, wood polish and antimacassars. "Mrs Sykes is away this evening. You have the photos?" He stared pointedly at the large brown envelope in Cappel's left hand.

"What? Oh, yes." As he held the envelope out it was almost snatched from him, Brookes fumbling with the unsealed flap. Several glossy monochrome photographs of various sizes spilled onto the heavy green velvet tablecloth; groups, couples, single figures, standing, seated.

"Ah!" The large man, looking more ecclesiastical than his messenger, selected a full length portrait, gathered up the rest and consigned them to the log fire that blazed in the hearth, increasing the warmth in the already stuffy room. He glanced sharply at Cappel, all the while moving the curling, blackened prints around with the end of a brass poker. "You weren't recognized, were you? I mean, you did conceal your identity, wore civvies and so forth?" Anxiety was plain on the swarthy features, even more satanic in the flickering light. The long black hair merged with his gown, lending the effect of some large nocturnal beast disturbed at its kill.

"Ye-es, naturally. Nobody knows me at the *Clarion* office." Cappel spoke jerkily, aware once more of how vulnerable he was in this man's presence, how intimidated. Whatever life might be allowed him after this mess depended entirely on Sir Nicholas Brookes. He had few illusions about his own lasting usefulness and whilst the salvation of his immortal soul was one thing, his immediate concern was simply living long enough to actually repent. "There's only that cub reporter…Ransome? I told you about him." Brookes nodded. "I kept a lookout, of course, but saw no sign. Photo requests don't entail going through the newsroom -"

"Don't dwell on Ransome." Brookes rammed the poker back in its holder. "I'll be taking care of him first thing tomorrow." He held up the 8"x10" print. "You know why I need this likeness?" Cappel nodded dumbly. "There is definitely someone close who is threatening our enterprise. This Winspear woman was asking searching questions at the hospital after the cleaner died and my subsequent enquiries have linked her to our budding Clark Kent. She is knowledgeable in our ways and determined, with none of the usual family ties we might use as leverage. She must be stopped. A man in my position can – ah, um order various services through third parties but even I cannot risk crossing certain boundaries. For this I require psychic assistance, the perfect crime in law!"

Cappel had a vision of Father Scanlon lying at the foot of the altar, eyes wide open, staring into eternity.

"But now that Sarah is no more…surely nobody can put two and two together in the remaining…" His heart quailed at what he guessed Brookes was about to do.

"We don't just have one loose cannon slewing around the deck, Cappel," Brookes snarled, turning away from the fire, making it flutter and smoke. "We have three!"

"Three?" Cappel repeated weakly.

"Three!" Holding out a spread hand Brookes counted them off on his fingers. "Your bloody dog, this reporter and…her!" He held the photo up. "And you are mistaken when you dismiss the danger because of the time factor. What I have in mind for our chalice will have ramifications for a long time to come and I don't want any unfamiliar ghosts rising up to haunt me. This…this is the one who can thwart our efforts – if not by actual intervention then by later exposure. As to the beast…when we have more time we can perform a ritual to either have it confined, returned to its resting place, or neutralized. The chalice will also assist us greatly in that, as in so many things."

He crossed to where Cappel stood, transfixed by the radiating power of the man, and then he was gripped again, just as before. His arms clamped to his sides, he knew it was useless to resist. "We're almost there, my boy. I too have called up this Asmodeus and it confirms what you say – the chalice is somewhere beneath the building. Everything points to it. You have two more days and if – when – you succeed, believe me, Renton my boy, your career within the church is assured. You want to remain there, fine. You wish for higher office…a place in the Vatican perhaps? You shall have it. I can make it happen!" The darkened pupils and surrounding whites, the gleaming teeth in the swarthy face, all made Cappel imagine for one wild moment that he was caught up in some interpretive scene from Othello.

"I-I'd better be getting back then -"

"No! No, not yet, my boy, not just yet. I need you to assist with this ceremony of exorcism."

"Oh, no, please, Sir Nicholas, let me go -"

"You have showered and fasted, as I instructed?" The hypnotic eyes demanded the correct reply.

"Yes, but…"

"No buts, Renton. We have to stop this woman and two adepts are better than one when it comes to controlling the demons we may have to deal with. You know the responses. Come." He released the terrified priest but only to alter his grip on one arm, steering him out of the room. With Cappel half-walking, half-trotting, the ill-matched pair went out into the passage and then turned left, Sir Nicholas striding along, snapping lights on as he passed, dragging his unwilling accomplice through a series of rooms. They stopped by a dark brown door set in the wall of a bare room. The door frame had two sections of planking nailed across it, criss-cross fashion.

Sir Nicholas stopped for a moment. "You okay?" Not waiting for a reply he went on, "We're in the east wing, and what lies beyond this door is what's called, I suppose, a no-go area. Little do they know!" He chuckled. "The surveyor's report said this end room – formerly the music room in the old days – is no longer fit for normal use because of slippage in the foundations. Well, Renton my boy, I have no desire to upset their notions of

115

normality. Hah!" He laughed outright this time but there was no joy in the sound. "Besides," he grunted, as he eased the boards away from the jambs on either side and stood back to swing them clear of the door, "I quite relish the idea of working on the edge of eternity. Don't you?" Carefully opening the door he stood aside to allow Cappel precedence. When the priest shook his head and backed off Brookes gave that laugh again and slipped through. He switched on the lights; only then did Cappel reluctantly follow.

Brookes had converted this sealed room into his own private chapel. But as an adept of the Seventh Degree its transformation far outshone anything Cappel had ever seen before. Perhaps twenty feet square, with every surface so coloured and designed as to diminish or enhance the spatial effect, depending on which wall you faced. On two opposing walls were painted murals – one of snow-capped mountains, the other a lake and forest scene, all rendered so faithfully as to invite touch and smell. The floor was painted green and the ceiling a sky of deep blue sprinkled with clusters of silver stars.

In the centre of the floor, painted in gold, was a large six-pointed star – sign of a high degree practitioner – enclosed within a silver circle. Standing on this was a wooden altar, composed of two cubes stacked one on top of the other, perhaps four feet high, its sides brightly coloured and, as far as Cappel could make out, sub-divided into squares to accommodate Dr John Dee's Enochian hieroglyphs. On the altar's top a marble slab supported a five-branched candelabrum with red candles.

As Brookes rummaged in a wardrobe behind the door the younger adept had a few moments to dwell upon the other walls. The east wall had another Tree of Life, with a stylised representation of the ten fruits to mirror the ten facets of God. The remaining west wall was the most striking; taken from da Vinci's depiction of Vitruvian Man it was life-size, full frontal, the penis proudly erect. Arms and legs outstretched it fitted neatly inside the silver, five-pointed star whose points touched the edges of a green square. In turn the square's corners reached the vast blue rim that encircled it all from floor to ceiling.

Cappel was familiar with the symbolism; the man-enclosing star signified the five elements of fire, water, water, air and spirit. The green square represented the four corners of the material world and the all-encompassing circle was an emblem of perfection, continuity and God. The male genitals placed exactly at this centre of the universe established the dynamism, sexuality and the generative force in Man and Nature. The well-drawn, muscular figure was an advanced adept's personal statement to the world, the triumphant face boldly staring down was Brookes' own, demonstrating his mastery of the elements and his oneness with the Almighty, Supreme Architect.

"Here!"

Cappel turned back; Brookes swiftly shed his clerical robe and instead donned a rough hessian shift in scarlet, a black cord around his ample middle. He indicated the young priest should do the same.

"You have the Bible?"

Cappel took the much-thumbed book from his jacket pocket and reluctantly handed it over. Brookes strode to the altar as Cappel undressed. The cheap fabric scratched his skin and he knew it would create friction and discomfort once the ceremony began, presumably his master's intention – a mood-set for violence and chaos.

"Hurry, hurry!" Brookes was within the gold star, setting up the small iron pot with charcoal, on which he would crumble a dried mixture of pepper, aloes, benjamin and flowers of sulphur. Possessing no power of itself the compound would merely enhance the atmosphere of fire, blood and conflict with its acrid odour.

Cappel stepped inside the circle, his proximity to Brookes and the already fuming smaller censer a combination he found difficult to endure. But he knew he had no choice, like a rabbit trapped in a car's headlights, there was no alternative but to keep going down the path indicated, until hopefully some means of escape presented itself.

While Cappel reinforced the other's incantations his mentor left the circle to prepare for the demon. Facing north and with red chalk he drew a triangle and inscribed the name ABAD-DON within it. The throat-catching odour of the mixture was permeating the room, so much so that the priest was only hazily aware of the other's ritual progression – from affirming his will-power and control to producing a barrier between the two worlds. The banishing ritual dispensed with, Brookes sum-moned and assured himself of the guardianship of the Lords of the Watchtower against potential elemental forms.

Then, standing before the Tree of Life, Brookes visualized a cloud of light rising before him. He held his arms out towards it and felt his fingertips tingling as the luminescence touched first them and then his brow. Making the Cabalistic cross – navel, right and left nipple – he imagined himself growing, swelling out of the room, out, out above the physical world, repeating the Hebrew words for the kingdom, the power and the glory – *Malkuth…Din…Hod* – until the very earth itself assumed the proportions of a footstool.

Time ceased to be, until, totally enveloped in this inner pow-er, he resumed his normal size, and with the sword removed from within the altar he saluted the Watchers of the Universe to the north, south, east and west. With a reinforced conviction that the force was with him he then took out a crown, a smaller version of the six-pointed star worked in silver. This he carefully pressed onto his head.

He moved to the north of the altar after sprinkling the remainder of the odious compound in the altar censer. The guttering candles and the smoke coiling up from the pot in the triangle combined with the smaller censer to make the room's atmosphere almost offensive, charging the air into seeming layers of oppressive pressure.

He reached inside the altar again and switched on the small CD player. Immediately it was as though the smell had transmuted into sound – a raucous cacophony filled the room, disruptive, discordant, nerve-jangling. Chosen like the abrasive cloth and the nose-wrinkling incense to heighten the mood of dissent for what was to come. No smooth transition into elemental contact, this was an attempt to call up the antithesis of order.

Like a physical blow the jarring sounds assaulted the senses. Cappel felt an inrush of the terror that had gripped him on other occasions when the point of summoning drew near. Even the most able adept could not guarantee the appearance of a spirit form; the energy, the will-power, the time of day or night, date and previous usage – all these had a bearing on the outcome. For a result there would be, failure being just as tangible as success; it would be noted and a reckoning due sometime. As a priest of the Holy Roman Church, schooled to believe and accept a more conventional form of sinful confession and penance, the frightening implications of an occult calling-up was a giant leap into the unknown.

But for Brookes it was akin to greeting a lover. A life-long schemer and seeker after new sensations, his ascendancy through the levels of the New Order had only whetted his appetite. As each new door opened into larger rooms of knowledge his only anxiety had been of mortality prematurely terminating his chance to experience them all…and he was convinced he was nearing the solution to even that final barrier.

So now he willingly absorbed the terrible din, allowing it to do its work, inflaming his already aggressive personality, taking it down inside, until his very tissues responded to its vicious, agitative force. The civilizing shell was stripped away in the raw, primitive rhythm, stirring in him a nameless kind of hatred. Snatching up a thin-bladed dagger he began to slash the air about him as he allowed the atavistic anger to bubble and boil its way out. Oblivious to his acolyte's nervous and evasive tactics, Brookes growled and stamped his feet in a parody of some child's war dance. Apart from any immediate danger Cappel was forcefully reminded of the very real peril beneath their feet. But he knew it would be even more dangerous to try to interfere in his mentor's actions. Brookes' features had darkened, turning purple as the frenzy took hold; he whirled and stamped, slashing and stabbing, eyes bulging and breath coming now in short gasps. But he hadn't lost control completely – daren't – for the most crucial sequence was yet to come. One tiny part of his consciousness hung on as he gave up the rest of his body and mind to the basic urge that now possessed him. He grabbed Cappel's Bible with fingers that were now almost talon-like, scrabbling through the pages to where he'd already marked the passage and – holding it near the candles – began to scream the words.

"And he opened the bottomless pit and there arose a smoke out of it, as the smoke of a great furnace, and the sun and the air were darkened by the smoke of the pit. And there came out of the smoke locusts upon the earth, and unto them was given power, as the scorpions of the earth have power. And it was commanded that they should hurt not the grass of the earth, neither any green thing, neither any tree, but only those men which have not the seal of God on their foreheads."

His breath came in great shudders as he strove to retain some semblance of control. His long hair flailed his face and sweat ran down his cheeks as he plunged and reared, the holy book brandished as though the bloodied head of some enemy slain in battle. Cappel shrank before such a demonic scene but he was constrained by the psychic barrier of the circle. The forces were already gathering, the surrounding air charged in a way that was unmistakable. The incense hung in sickening layers about them, their circle seeming to spiral in to the centre of their own universe. He sank to his knees, holding his face in his hands but afraid to say or do anything that might in some way abort the ceremony. He dare not incur further satanic disfavour; he just wished it to end.

"And then it was given that they should not kill them, but that they should be tormented five months, and their torment as the torment of a scorpion when he striketh a man. And in those days shall men seek death and not find it, and they shall desire to die and death shall flee from them.

And the shape of the locusts was like unto horses prepared unto battle, and on their heads were crowns of gold, and their faces were as the faces of men. And they had hair as the hair of women, and their teeth were as the teeth of lions. And they had breastplates of iron, and the sound of their wings was as the sound of many horses and chariots running to battle. And they had tails like unto scorpions, and there were stings in their tails, and their power was to hurt men five months.

And they had a king over them, which is the angel of the bottomless pit, whose name is…ABADDON."

Cappel clung to the altar as the demented adept jerked and stamped, howled and shrieked the words from the Book of Revelation. Brookes's body shook with successive waves of blind, mindless rage. His face a deep purple, mouth strained further open as he thundered and gulped in air to sustain his exertions. The floor shook, dust mingled with the nauseating smoke of the incense that swirled about the scarlet-robed figure. Somehow the altar crown remained in place as the tousled hair, now slick with sweat, whipped his face.

Then – at the very threshold of seizure and before his last

121

control deserted him – Brookes projected every atom of his conjured-up hatred and fury out of the circle, and directed it towards the triangle. The almost viscous column of smoke rising from the charcoal pot seemed to bend under the force.

"Abaddon, Abaddon, Abaddon!" Brookes screamed. "Abaddon, appear, I command you!"

Before Cappel's fearful eyes the smoke twisted, coiled, and a shape began to form – tall, leathery, enormous bat-like wings enfolding it. A face that was not quite human, framed in seaweed hair, smiled, fang-like, across the abyss that divided them.

Brookes raised his left arm, shaking back the loose sleeve. With the dagger he sliced at the pale skin of his inner forearm once, twice, five times. He held the lacerated flesh over the small censer and as the first drops of blood fell he stared across the intervening space at the spirit form, howling in a peculiar, dog-like way. The thing inside the Triangle of Exorcism twisted in its fury as the evil that was inside Brookes was flung outwards as an almost separate entity. This was the most dangerous time; part of him externalized, with a will of its own. That will was to destroy, and Brookes knew he must not allow it to turn back on himself. It, too, appeared to the terrified Cappel to be materializing outside the circle. Or was it the smoke? He could not be sure as the shadows gyrated in the red-lit gloom.

Brookes turned his attention to the photograph of Joan Winspear. With his bared forearm still dripping above the sizzling censer the stench of burning blood mingled with the reek of the room. In a magisterial tone he thundered at the triangle, "Abaddon, master of the bottomless pit, ruler of all who torment women, hear my will and obey. Give this woman a glimpse of hell before consigning her to her doom. Torture by fire her every part until her strength is burnt away. I give you her head, her eyes, her tongue, her teeth, her mouth…"

As he ran through the litany he skewered her likeness on the tip of his dagger, then offered it to the candle's flame, corner by corner, until the glossy paper caught and began to curl as the flames licked their way through it. Cappel watched, spellbound, as the malevolence in Brookes crackled across the space.

"…so that she may never again speak or make sign I give you her neck, her arms, her upper parts…heart, liver and lungs. Let the fires of damnation consume her woman's parts, her thighs, her legs, her feet…"

The photograph, now almost charred completely, he allowed it to slide off the blade and onto the marble top. When the last of the paper had reddened and died it began to dissolve in the waves of psychic force that whirled across the room.

Brookes looked exhausted, the scarlet robe plastered to his belly and buttocks as he rallied his remaining strength for the dismissal.

"Abaddon, you have heard my will. Do my bidding or I will banish you back to whence you came, there to be chained through all eternity. Now begone!"

The column of incense and it evil messenger wavered, swelled, then disappeared, sucked from the room at its master's command, leaving only the obnoxious smell.

Wearily Brookes took the long sword and began the final ritual – thanking the Watchers for keeping him safe from the random elements that his calling-up would inevitably have mustered. Moving around the circle to the four compass points he made his obeisance, feeling unutterably weary and more drained as the seconds passed. It was always this way but tonight had been especially arduous, even with his unwilling acolyte's help. Thoughts of Cappel made him turn, sensing something wrong. He was alone in the room. Then the sound of a car's engine starting up outside made him nod his head slowly as he resumed his duties.

15: APPEARANCE

"Y'know, this is crazy," she said, shrugging into her Barbour jacket and slamming the car shut. She stamped her feet to get the feel of the green wellies she'd only worn once and then just to please Dolinda Morgenthau, who'd had a fleeting thing about polo after reading Jilly Cooper.

"Our age group are allowed to be crazy." Jake stood by the car and listened to the hot metal's tick fill the surrounding night. He could just make out her head, silhouetted against the background glow of Teesside. "In fact, I suspect it's expected of us." He laughed to cover his nervousness, his back to the waiting Eastby Moor, invisible but palpably there, a thing sensed rather than seen in the almost Stygian gloom. "It's only when you get old that aberrant behaviour is taken seriously…and then usually by the wrong people for all the wrong reasons."

"Perhaps we could discuss this new philosophical side to your character over some Italian rosé and Tagliatelle Carbonara." She tested the high-powered flashlight, inadvertently blinding him.

"Dammit, Carolyn!" He put both hands up instinctively.

"Sorry." She sounded genuinely contrite, extinguishing it.

For several seconds he was totally disorientated, the night's blackness punctured by pinwheeling yellow and red spirals that felt as though etched on his retina. "Dammit!" he repeated, pressing his eyeballs with a forefinger and thumb until the silent fireworks display slowly faded.

"Look, I said I was sorry." She came round to his side, stumbling in the unwieldy boots. One hip struck a door panel with a dull thud. "Shit!"

Jake reached – groped – out as she fell into his arms. They burst out laughing, only to be silenced by a vixen's scream, somewhere off in the darkness. She shivered, remembering why they were there.

"Look…" He ran his hand over her hair, savouring the rare fragrance it gave off. "Maybe this wasn't such a good idea after all, and I did promise you a supper out at a restaurant of your choice. As it happens, there's a highly recommended hostelry, The George, just a couple of miles further on -"

"And have you moan over your apple crumble or whatever about what a great story it *might* have been?" She looked up at him with those enormous eyes that seemed to monopolise what little light there was. He could almost taste her lip gloss. He leaned forward; she drew back, disengaging with practised ease.

"Which way, O master?"

Dammit, she was wrong-footing him again. Each move he made appeared to distance him further from his evening's objective. What the hell *was* he doing on the edge of a bleak, dismal heath anyway, with only probable embarrassment and ruined shoes to show for his bravado? Whose influence was he most under – the old dragon or the young witch? He sighed; he was no good with women. One forceful female at a time was one more than he cared to deal with. But two…two was traumatic. What had made him do it?

He knew *when*, that was easy; driving away from Joan's, car warming up nicely, her profile almost unearthly in the soft glow of the instruments, his only immediate concern had been securing the least uncomfortable position for his long legs. Then she had taken a left instead of a right at the intersection. "Shit!" she'd responded, with no great emphasis when he'd mildly pointed this out.

"No problem," he'd reassured her. "A mile and a bit further on you can double back." Those few minutes had done it –

critical path indeed! To put her more at ease – it was obvious she was not totally in control of the Porsche – he'd half-jokingly broached the subject of their recent visit.

She remained silent as she carefully negotiated another country bend, the powerful headlights picking out the jewelled eyes of some nocturnal creature in the hedgerow as they flashed past. Then: "She almost had me going back there…especially with that darned map." She clicked her tongue at the memory of her cupidity, shaking her head and making the night-black hair swirl. "Spectral dogs…lines of force…natural vortexes…or should that be vortices?" She glanced quickly across at him, wrinkling her snub nose. It was about there he reckoned he'd blown it. That look had said, 'Hey, I'm getting to like you, let's forget that fusty old bat and her loopy ideas. What say we head for the bright lights, maybe add up all the points of mutual interest, see if they make a worthwhile score.' Remember your Desmond Morris, read the body signals. She was reaching out, you cluck, for something attainable, familiar. After an hour of fantasy and fright she wanted reassurance of the real world, with an identifiable role model. Okay, so you're not George Clooney but you're in the frame, she knows nobody else up here. You want a gold embossed invite? So what do you do, eh, what do you do?

"Well, I don't know, Carolyn, Joan Winspear is a much a respected historian around these parts. Eccentric perhaps, strong-willed certainly, but that doesn't place her in the crop circle camp."

"Neither was Sir Arthur Conan Doyle but wasn't he taken in by those two school girls who faked the 'Fairies at the bottom of our garden' photographs?" Her face had tightened, the moment gone. Jake smacked his knee in exasperation at his own ineptitude as she concentrated on her driving once more. Then she went on, "You could make a very large omelette from the egg scraped off the cheeks of those so-called experts who have pronounced on subjects outside their chosen fields."

"But that's just it, Carolyn! Can't you see?" In for a penny, dope. "Joan knows whereof she speaks. This is her bailiwick, she's not just spouting off about UFOs or the Bermuda Triangle but the land she knows and loves. She supported her argument with documentary proof -"

"Evidence," Carolyn cut in, flicking her high beams at an oncoming road hog, waited until the inevitable defiant horn wailed its way past them before continuing, "Documentary evidence is not proof, Jake. It may lend weight but it doesn't tip the balance for me."

"What will?"

"Pardon?" She cast a sidelong glance.

"I said, What will? What will it take to convince you there is some substance to Joan's claims? Seeing the dog for yourself, perhaps? Would that suffice?"

"You mean...?" Her hands jerked, sending the powerful machine slewing across the centre line for a few seconds before she regained control. She rolled another sideways look at him. "You can't possibly mean -"

"The Three Sisters? Why not? It's not far from here. If her theory is right then the dog – or whatever it is – should manifest itself there tonight."

"You're not...you can't be serious!" When she saw that he was she gritted, "Listen chum, I'm returning to London in the morning and I don't intend dicing with death, bleary-eyed on the motorway after a sleepless night spent on the Yorkshire moors. I need my sleep, I told you -"

"But who said all night? Look, Carolyn, we don't know if these – these appearances are transitory or protracted, whether they're time-related or initiated by the energy emitted by humans. It's a bit like the old philosophy chestnut: When a tree falls in the forest and nobody is there to witness it how can we be sure it made a noise hitting the ground?"

"What?" She stared at him for several seconds to gauge his seriousness. "Where did you get that crap?" She shook her head and swore as they squished over a recently deceased hedgehog; leaned forward and slowed as the cruciform outline of a sign post loomed.

"Listen, all the reports have occurred with people and they're all in alignment. Reason and logic -"

"Hah! Spare me those sacrificial pawns."

"Reason and logic says it appears when there is a need for it to do so."

"Or else it's there all the - shit!" She realized the trap she'd set for herself.

"You know Joan can't make it up there herself. Hell, I'm not telepathic but it seemed to me she was asking for help but too proud to voice it -"

"One hour."

"I'm sorry...?"

"I'm giving up one of my last – I hope! – evenings in the neurotic north. After that, Jake Ransome, you'd better come up with some good food and an open fire somewhere cosy or you're gonna be on my Christmas shit list...and that's not a good place to be – Hey! Where did you say that Three Sisters place was?"

"Eastby Moor. Why?"

She braked. The T-junction sign read: *Teesside 5 miles* on one side and *Eastby Moor 2 miles* on the other.

"Say...are you sure I took the wrong turning back there?" Her look was full of accusation. "Why, you sneaky, presumptuous son of a..." With a savage wrench she accelerated into the new route, giving her passenger no time to refute the charge as he'd scrabbled frantically for a handhold.

"Hey, dreamer! You want the burning eyeballs bit again?"

"What?" He realized where he was. "Oh, sorry, this way. It's not far but I'd better have the torch." He took it from her before she could protest and led the way.

"Hey, wait for me, Sir Galahad." She stumbled after him.

As he'd promised it was not far but it was arduous. The boots didn't help. The high-intensity beam revealed a stony cart track angling upwards, not too steeply but enough to demand concentration because of the sharp, jerking surface shadows. After a few paces her independence gave way to common sense; she grabbed a handful of his dark jacket and he – relenting a little from his own frustrated attempts to control her – took her hand in his.

They crossed a stile, relying completely on the hand-held torch now as the jungle of fern and gorse began in earnest on the other side. There was the barely discernible semblance of a narrow track, still rising but veering to the right. Jake breasted the fronds easily but had to protect Carolyn from repeated whip-backs as he guided her through them.

She battled gamely on behind him, without protest, only glancing back once through a break in the foliage. The twinkling lights of the industrial area seemed quite distant now, and infinitely more inviting. Headlights swept past where her car was parked. All comforting signs that familiar scenes were still within reach, should she decide to call it off. Then the strong grip drew her onwards and the option faded. A springy frond swiped her cheek and she involuntarily gasped.

"You okay, Carolyn?" The light's beam turned back for a moment, but directed downwards.

"How much farther?" she puffed. She didn't want to complain but the condition to which she'd referred earlier was real, and she knew from experience how limited her vitality was. If she could just rest for a few moments.

"We're almost through…ah!"

Suddenly they emerged onto open heath, only recognizable as such by the lack of restraining undergrowth. The darkness seemed less than total now, with more space, but there were still no focal points to compare or relate to. Then Jake raised the beam and some detail sprang into sharp relief; a dry-stone wall to their left, broken down in places and running away from them out of sight. Clumps of gorse dotted about ahead and to their right. Broken, dried bracken flat and underfoot everywhere. The cry of some bird broke the stillness, startling her.

"Wh-where's the stones?" she whispered.

"Over there…look!" He raised the torch and the foreground regained some of its colour and substance as the luminescence spread and flattened. The rise ended some hundred metres ahead, and outlined on the near horizon were the Three Sisters, indistinct at the limits of the beam but grey-black and upright, two near and the third obviously some distance back, appearing as only half the height of the others.

"Just one more hurdle," he muttered, starting forward again. Before she could pursue this enigmatic remark its meaning became clear. Half trotting across the dry, crackly scrub in his wake she barely avoided crashing into his outstretched arms as he stopped.

"Yep, it's still there," he said, shining the light on the shallow, three-metres-wide beck that bisected this part of the moor. "You've got the wellies…fancy giving me a lift?" He chuckled at the idea. "There used to be some stepping stones around here some place." The light ranged back and forth. "There they are." He caught her hand again and moved to the right. Some flat grey stones showed above the surface. "You going to try them out, then?" He pointed to her footwear.

"I think it'll be safer than those slippery things," she grunted, tentatively easing into the water as he shone the light. She stumbled, lost her balance and wailed, "J-a-a-ake!" before he reached across from his stone to guide her. The water's chill seemed to seep through the rubber within seconds and she was glad to make the far bank unscathed.

"That's it, well done, city girl." She could see his grin. "Now for the summit."

"What I don't understand is," she grumbled, "if you did plan all this beforehand why couldn't you have included a thermos of coffee and an inflatable cushion." But he was gone, striding ahead. She sighed and squelched after him.

The stones up close were formidable, like giant petrified surfboards, rammed carelessly into the earth and forgotten, and now through time tilted slightly out of true. As the two stood within their confines they loomed around them, at least four metres high, with perhaps the same distance separating each from its sister. Even with his height Jake felt insignificant looking up at them, presumably the objective of their architect. The light revealed the usual graffiti, but some pre-aerosol and more permanent – linking initials and hearts etched in the time-honoured way humans everywhere attempt to enshrine a record of their existence. Evidence of several camp fires, the ubiquitous squashed and empty aluminium cans, two used condoms and a faint smell of urine.

Carolyn wrinkled her nose. "I'm not impressed," she said, plunging her hands deep into her pockets. "What self-respecting spirit would have a one-night stand here? Can we please go now?"

"You did say one hour, Carolyn." Jake was quiet but firm

She groaned. "What can we possibly do for an hour -" She stopped; she was certain she could detect his quizzical expression in the gloom. "I mean, is this it, for the next sixty – hold it…fifty-five minutes?"

"Can't you *feel* anything, Carolyn?" Jake leaned forward, touching her sleeve lightly.

"What? What d'you mean?" She was genuinely puzzled.

"You're resisting," he replied. "Open up your senses, listen to the wind, turn your face to the sky -"

"And inhale nature's perfume," she said sardonically. "I didn't realize ammonia was your particular brand, Jake. That should make my Christmas prezzie list that much easier."

He sighed. "I used to come up here when I was younger…well, young. Before all this…" He waved his hand at the evidence of recent visitors. "Sometimes – even in daylight – it made me feel I was in some special place. When the wind was from the west -" he pointed to one of the slabs – "it's like there was someone or some thing, singing softly far away but somehow also close." He shook his head, looked at her in surprise, then laughed self-consciously. She didn't respond in like manner, sensing his sincerity. But she was also unsure as to what she should say and still appear neutral.

"Of course, I was shorter then…" He smiled. "That makes a difference, I suppose."

"Well, I didn't hear anything except my tummy rumbling and a feeling that these tights definitely do not go with wellies."

"Right, to business then." He brought both palms together lightly. "We don't know what – if anything – to expect, but one thing's certain…if it does happen here I want to be somewhere else! How about you?"

"Affirmative, but where?" She looked around her as the beam ranged through 360 degrees, throwing distorted, elongated shadows across the bracken that was shivering slightly in the chill wind now sweeping across the exposed ground. No singing, not even softly. She was determined to maintain her attitude of uncommitted observer only in the time remaining to her in the company of this likeable but increasingly puzzling young man. It was obvious he fancied her, a sexual chemistry she was all too familiar with wherever she went. She was attractive, even beautiful to some eyes, she knew that and used it to her advantage whenever the occasion warranted. This brief interlude away from her usually hectic lifestyle had been such an occasion. Initially his provincial awkwardness had amused her, and the prospect of a dull, solitary evening in that creepy old mansion, with its locked-up rooms, had made her forgo her usual caution. She knew from experience how it would end and didn't want that. No tacky, unfulfilled relationships, she'd had quite enough of them. But it *should* have been safe – a few hours' diversion in the company of a malleable male before the inevitable lassitude allowed her to exit gracefully.

So what on earth was she doing in this Wuthering Heights scenario, and it way past her bedtime? And Jake, who was certainly a stranger to begin with, becoming more unfathomable with each passing hour. The sexual interest was still there; in his deference to her views; his patience with her often snide remarks and especially the way he gripped her hand. She wondered if the contact affected him as much as it did her. And that was the most mysterious part – the comfort and security his touch brought. Was this the beginning of the Big L word? Is this how it starts? Not the electric thrill as two glances lock across a crowded room, not even the slow build-up of affection over shared interests, but a closeness born of mutual unease…even inner terror.

He was speaking. "…over there seems the perfect spot for a hide." She followed his directed beam. Some fifty metres along the ridge was a break in the section of dry-stone wall.

"We should be safe there," he said cheerfully. She grumped her way along behind him. The freshening breeze was dispelling the cloud cover and with the appearance of stars the visibility also improved. Though they were still too far over the rise to actually glimpse the conurbation, its faint pink glow did fill the northern sky like some *aurora industrialis*. It lent shape if not substance to some of their surroundings. Looking back at the stones she could now get a clearer perspective; all three leaning like weary time sentinels.

"Yes, this should do nicely, Carolyn," he murmured as they reached the wall. The jumble on either side was a partially buried minefield of jagged rocks with bone-snapping potential. He helped her pick her way to the end of the section, then guided her to the far side of the wall. There was a patch of closely cropped grass and a few sheep droppings. He found a clean spot and motioned her to try it.

"You mean sit down…in these designer pants?"

He shrugged. "It will be out of this wind and your jacket should pull down over your, er, more vulnerable parts." He grinned hugely, the first time for hours, it seemed to her. "Look, there's a nice flat stone and I'll pull out some of the wall to give us a viewing port. That way neither of us need get up for a squint." He quickly showed her his intention, easing out several stones until he had an irregular hole some twenty centimetres across to see out.

She peered through; a short distance away the Three Sisters were clearly delineated in the stars' gleam – tall, narrowly elliptical, like gigantic black fingers thrusting up out of the earth, reaching for…what?

"So what's the plan, *mon general*?" she enquired wryly. "For the remaining" – she held the slim watch up to her face – "forty-nine minutes?"

He laughed again, his nervous one. "You're not taking this research in the right scientific spirit, Carolyn."

"Research? Science?" She snorted. "Don't start me on that again, Jake. I keep asking myself why I'm doing this. I can assure you it's way out of character."

He pulled her gently down beside him. She submitted reluctantly. But she did submit, he noted.

"Have you ever thought it might be your true character coming out, freed from any big city artifices?" He looked directly at her.

"Big city artifices," she repeated slowly but with no real malice or scorn. She settled grumpily but submissively on the makeshift seat before meeting his gaze. He was a handsome guy, no argument. Honest blue eyes and that gold wire crinkly hair, full mouth – she liked that in a man – and a slightly crooked nose that indicated at least a passing experience with outdoor activity of some kind. Why wasn't he already involved with some nice, uncomplicated baby-maker around here? He seemed normal – whatever *that* meant these days! Behaved with conventional male insensitivity plus a large dollop of gaucherie. Contrived? Perhaps, but nothing that wasn't irredeemable; plenty of encouraging material to work with. Pity it was doomed from the outset. Is this my subconscious way of putting him out of his misery, stringing out these last hours in a situation of sexual apartheid, instead of a straight put-down?

"There you go, revealing all those hidden depths again." She smiled that smile and his heart lurched, wanting to hold her before she slipped away from him as he knew she must. "You think I should be more mysterious, maybe let you discover them for yourself? That would imply an extension of our relationship beyond tomorrow. Is that negotiable?"

"Jake." She touched his hand lightly. "The only thing I want at this moment is to return to something resembling normality...warmth, comfort, food, drink. You know, what everybody else down there is most probably sampling in varying degrees right now. And in exactly, um, forty-four minutes I intend moving towards that end." She grinned impishly and put her hand in her pocket, drew out the car keys and angled them. "It's up to you, ghost buster."

"Okay, okay" He put up his hands in surrender. "This isn't

exactly my idea of a fun evening either, and I'm beginning to bitterly regret sacrificing a chance to get to know you better. You'll never know how much." He turned away, too embarrassed to meet her gaze, glanced through the makeshift window. "I only wish…"

"What?" She gripped his lapel, jerked it. "Wish what? Finish it, you infuriating -"

"It's there!" he whispered. "Oh, my God. It's out there."

"You lie!" she hissed fiercely. Still gripping his jacket she pulled herself up to the hole, squeezing her face against his to peer out.

"There…look!" His voice was low and urgent. "Can you see something?"

She did see, instantly but indistinctly; something black, blacker than the surrounding night, between two of the tall stones. As she tried to focus better the shape altered, lengthened. It was an animal; she made out a large, dog-like head and a longish tail. It moved, disappearing behind the extreme right-hand Sister. They both exhaled, slumping back against the rough stonework.

"It – it could be just what it looks like," she gulped, not looking at him, still staring fixedly ahead. "Some animal on the loose, after sheep." The voiced thought lent courage and she rallied. "Yes, and then there's those escaped panthers you read about" – they turned slowly, reluctantly, to their peep hole – "roaming at night and terrorizing farms -"

It walked back into view, over to the left-hand stone, seemingly searching. Not a sound, the silence was unnerving. Never a nocturnal rustling or screeching when you needed it, he thought. "If that stone is – what? – four metres, and the creature's head reaches almost halfway up, it means…" he leaned away from her slightly in order to turn his head. "It's taller than you. Even the Baskerville hound would step aside for that baby."

The unease in her eyes mirrored his. "Look!" she hissed in his ear.

The creature turned its massive head in their direction for the first time and Carolyn gave a whimper, seeing two glowing red spots where the eyes should be. Even at this distance they seemed to pulse, flaring and dimming as though responding to some inner turbine.

"What -" His mouth went dry. "What do we do now?" he croaked.

As if in answer the creature went rigid and the two orbs seemed to blaze in intensity.

"Why don't we just duck down here out of sight until it goes back to wherever it came from?" she implored, pulling at his sleeve. "Then we can crawl away and I swear I'll sign any kind of affidavit you care to draw up. Huh?"

"Too late!" He gripped her arm. "I think it's seen us."

It was true, she saw; having apparently pinpointed their presence it was moving in their direction.

"Oh, Mother of God!" she moaned. "What do we do?"

"We run, it's our only chance," he whispered urgently. "Listen…listen!" He shook her out of her fright-freeze. "If we can find another break in the wall we can slip through. There's no other escape route that I know. Okay?"

"But what will it do to us?" She was almost crying.

"Do you want to stay here to find out? Move!" He grabbed her ice-cold hand and jerked her into motion at a half-run, bent double. She stumbled after him, too distraught to protest.

The relatively short distance to the end of the wall's run seemed to take forever, Jake searching desperately for some break in its line. They couldn't stay this side of the wall; it ended at the stream's edge and the far side was thick, virtually impenetrable undergrowth. Their only chance was to find the stepping stones.

"Ah!" About twenty metres short of the wall's end some stones had fallen out, just enough for them to clamber over.

"Over here, Carolyn." He stopped to catch his breath and drew her to him. She was gasping like a landed fish and trembling uncontrollably.

"Quickly, before it comes through the opening. It won't be far to the stepping stones from here."

"Maybe it's gone now." She was like a child needing reassurance that there was nothing in the dark that wasn't there in the light.

He didn't answer; whatever was out there was not benevolent.

He clambered over the loose rocks, dragging her with him. Emerging on the far side he cautiously peered along the wall's length, back to where they had hid. There it was, just approaching their previous position. He held his free hand extended to her, cautioning silence. Carolyn wheezed, one hand pressed to her chest. The creature moved through the opening, disappeared, its long bushy tail flicking out of sight.

"Come," he whispered. The line of stones across the stream was just visible, some fifty metres away and below them. Casting one last glance along the wall to make sure they were still out of sight he began to walk slowly and carefully across the crushed bracken. It crackled and snapped like rifle fire in the still air.

It re-appeared at the opening, eighty metres away. The eyes glowed red and then it shrieked, raising its great head to the sky. The sound froze the blood in Jake's veins and Carolyn screamed, unable any longer to contain her fear. The sounds mingled, clashed, seemed to trigger off reaction in all of them. The creature leapt forward and Jake ran, dragging the sobbing girl in his wake. One glance after the first few strides told him they weren't going to make it; it was gaining on them with frightening speed. The stones seemed no nearer.

He changed direction.

"Where are you going?" she screamed.

"The water…it's our only chance!"

"But – but the stones -"

"No!" he shouted. "The water's the key, Joan said." He panted, looked behind. It was almost upon them, the shaggy, angular head clear now in the gloom. The wide-open jaws and teeth, those horrible red eyes, all the time fixed it seemed, on him.

Staggering a few more paces the beck was suddenly there. Pulling the girl roughly to him he launched her into the black, smelly water. She fell, one hand going out instinctively. Her balance went and she turned over, almost slowly, it seemed to Jake as he turned to face the beast. It sprang, rising up, filling the night like some ragged black cloud as it descended.

He flung the torch as he threw himself backwards into the water and there was an enormous flash and clap like thunder above his head. Then the icy water striking though his clothes, Carolyn's screams and an awful sulphurous smell were the last things registered as his skull struck the rock.

16: VENGEANCE

The sporadic *clack-clack* of the battered Remington vied with the more measured *tick* of the long case clock in the corner, threatening to jerk it from decades of somnolescent stupor. Joan Winspear liked to get her thoughts down on paper as soon as possible, and this evening had seen an unusually high flow of ideas and discussion. The mental stimulus of the young couple. Were they an 'item'? Sexual energy was important in all forms of magic. It all provided much to record and initiate further research. The admitted diabetes was only part of her problem. Her GP was in despair at her lifestyle, particularly since she'd moved her interests from botanical field trips to local history. Given the state of her rapidly-constricting arteries and inexorable rise in blood pressure she knew her old pump might not pass another M.O.T.

But she was not a troubled spirit, having led a full and active life in the fields of her choice. Born plain, rebellious but of independent means and realizing, early on, the invisible bonds of domestic duty, she had accepted her limited options, immersing herself in the mysteries of moorland and mountain. As her contemporaries married, matured and produced more aspirants for the dream of empire she was already carving her own niche. Her discovery of edelweiss so far from its Alpine habitat had been comparable to the thrill of wedded bliss; her first published work on the mosses and lichens of Northern England as painful but satisfying as childbirth itself. Her social life – seldom active – went into terminal decline in her desire to know everything about this wild, unforgiving but beautiful land.

She was old now and past achievements no longer served as a

comfort in her isolation. Her evening class lectures were rendered more through guilt than enthusiasm these days. But here – now! – was something to engage her jaded senses; a very real and present danger she knew few were qualified to recognize, much less equipped to combat. That young reporter, with his brash, tough attitude was really too idealistic for his own good. Now the girl, she seemed to have a bit more steel beneath that impatient and vapid exterior. But her denial of the facts was a weakness others could so easily exploit. The secret lay in determining who one's real enemies were. The whole was a complex web, touch one strand here and it vibrated the fact to… where…who? The girl's name, for instance: Draycott. Something she should remember there, she felt, but that particular part of her, too, was losing out to the onset of age. She would need to rummage through her chaotic 'filing system' later. But first…complete her notes of this evening's debate and some pointers for tomorrow. That meant necessary fieldwork; she wondered if Colonel Granby could still crank up that old Austin Princess of his. She sighed and resumed her tapping, the clattering sound over-loud, echoing off the flagstone flooring.

She became immersed in her work, willing brain and body to comply, although she was extremely tired. The thought of bed grew ever more seductive as the clock gonged its way through midnight. She started, straightened up in the worn, sagging easy chair. She was aware that her posture – seated too low and crouched forward over the ceramic tiled coffee table – was an ergonomic mess. But she had typed her articles, theses and books for so long in this manner it was too late to change now. Besides, there was no one to see or scold her, one of the many advantages of living alone.

Alone. The thought made her look up. For some reason she didn't feel alone. Not all her senses had atrophied and something wasn't quite as it should be. She realized it was way past her bedtime; her glance fell on the clock. Three? Never! Where had the hours gone? She drew the threadbare cardigan closer and returned to work. Probably only the residual ambience of those exuberant spirits. She was unused to such visitations. Now *that* was something she should encourage more often. Youth could be tiring but on the plus side it was impossible to completely ignore their zest and hope. As with all uplifts, however, there was an inevitable downside. Yes, that's it, their presence was fading. She sighed again. Pity, sometimes knowledge of the natural laws can prove counter-productive.

But she found it difficult to get back to her typing, or thinking. Something was getting in the way and the room was becoming decidedly cooler. Oh, my God! Truth struck her like a handful of hail. She pushed against the chair arms, to rise up and reach for the ritualistic banishing artifacts she kept in the sideboard. But before she could act the heavy oak coffee table slammed against her legs below the knees, making her cry out in pain before toppling her back in her seat. Thoroughly scared now she rocked forward, attempting to get off the misshapen cushion that had sunk in the chair frame over the years. But she was effectively trapped by the coffee table, with its even heavier typewriter.

Sobbing while reciting the Lord's Prayer she pushed the machine across the tiled surface until it slid over the edge and crashed to the stone floor. As if in answer the unseen force being applied against her legs increased, crushing both tibias until she screamed in agony. The old chair casters, stuck in the floor cracks, were moved against their normal inertia, trundling the chair and its captive backwards until it fetched up against the wall. Joan screamed again as the shattered bones were ground by the uneven movement.

Through waves of pain she somehow rallied, knowing she must get help before she passed out. She twisted her head, gasping in agony; the front window was just over a metre from her right shoulder. The old man in the adjoining cottage was stone deaf, no help there. But Jack Shepherd – she rubbed at her face and tried to ease her legs back and whimpered with the pain as the pressure increased – it was about time for the retired chemical process worker to exercise his little Scottie along the lane.

"Help! Jack…Jack, are you there? Please help me." She screamed as loudly as she could. "Is anybody out there…? Please…somebody help me…p-please…" She was weeping now, the realization of her plight folding in on her. She was in mortal danger; even the pain rippling through her entire body could not swamp the knowledge of what she could be up against. She screamed once more at the window, pushing ineffectually at what had her pinioned in place. Then she flopped back, her weak heart pounding with the effort.

There was a frightening chuckle inside the room, the first corroborative evidence that it wasn't all some terrible nightmare. The sound was deep, full of arrogance and devoid of pity.

"Please…w-why are you doing this?" she whispered hoarsely. "What is it – oh, God! Three o'clock…the demonic hour…the crucifixion!" Just that chuckle again and the table pressed harder. She screamed as the splintered bones came through the flesh, making her nails dig through the chair's fabric. She cried out once more for succour but there was none. Through the curtain of pain she strove desperately for some means of escape. The fire irons! Fashion a crude cross, call upon the powers of light to hear her plea. But before she could even attempt to lean across the hearth the single light bulb suspended above her began to dim. She stared up in horror as it slowly faded, drawing the room's illumination back into itself.

"No!" She cried out in terror at the power that could so easily demonstrate its superiority over humankind's technology, the filament losing its incandescence, becoming merely a dull red before dying altogether. The only light remaining filtered through the unwashed window panes in the gap left by the curtains, barely enough to identify the room's contents; the sideboard that she'd cleared so recently to illustrate her theories, the book-cluttered table by the far wall, the standard lamp in the corner by the hearth that hadn't worked for such a long time. It was so cold now that the perspiration from her straining efforts and pain cooled almost instantly on her body. She shivered, aware of the very real danger to an old, and infirm body such as hers. It made the mind wander, like that illusion of something in the centre of the floor. What was it…a spider? Spillage? Spillage from what?

Instinctively she tried once more to extricate herself, the bone fragments grating till she almost passed out.

As though hypnotized she was drawn back to the uneven floor. There it was again! She strained her eyes in the near darkness. A shadow was forming in the join between two flagstones. No, it was some kind of a stain, seeping outwards, an ooze bubbling up from somewhere below. Oh, my God, she sobbed, her upper body going stiff with terror. She started screaming again for somebody – anybody – to come to her assistance. But all through the agonized writhing her gaze never left that only other movement in the room. The dark liquid was rising more swiftly now, as though sensing her urgent resistance. Then the smell invaded her nostrils, making her gasp for air. She pushed unavailingly at her imprisonment, fell back in the chair, exhausted, repelled and yet inexorably her eyes turned back to whatever was spreading across the floor.

It was no longer black, now it appeared to be darkish-green, and its wetness lent it a certain sheen. But it also appeared to be thickening, congealing like cooling lava. Now, too, her failing faculties registered the change in temperature. It was growing warm, uncomfortably so. It's coming from that – that evil stuff welling up from below. She moaned, her head turning from side to side in her despair. She watched it creep out in all directions, covering the floor like some revolting carpet, filling every crack and crevice in the floor's surface. She kept crying out every few seconds, but with less and less hope now. A terrible fatalism had taken hold, pinned as she was, like some sacrifice of old, waiting in fear and trembling for…what?

The temperature continued to rise, sulphurous fumes and yellow smoke drifting up from the ooze. Where the floor dipped in one corner the dark green sludge ran more quickly, touching one leg of the sideboard. Immediately the wood began to smoulder, and then with a small crackle burst into flame. Joan whimpered at the sight, knowing now what her fate was to be.

The flames licked up the furniture, gathering energy from the ages-old wood. The varnish bubbled along the drawer front and in a sudden rush flared, revealing the room. It was then that she saw the full horror of whatever it was that was spewing up from below; it seemed to have a life of its own, swelling in places, faint popping noises issuing from it as its surface burst and then subsided. Then the centre of the floor started to rise; an enormous abscess, suppurating and expanding within seconds. A clearly discernible head was forming, topping the obscene excrescence that was now filling the entire room. A mouth hole appeared and more of the filth dribbled out. She screamed and screamed, then began to choke in the poisonous atmosphere. Her hands went to her throat in an effort to ease her breathing.

She gasped out the words of the Lord's Prayer again, looking frantically about for something to make a cross with. She remembered the fire irons by the hearth. If she could just…reach…the poker and tongs.

With a crash the sideboard toppled over as the burnt-through leg collapsed. Doors fell open and the drawers slid onto the gunge that was everywhere round her feet. Scarves, gloves, old letters, books – all provided instant fuel for what awaited them. With a WHOOMPH they ignited, sending bits of burning paper up and outwards like incandescent spores from some new and deadly plant, spreading and infecting everything else in the room. The curtains, the wallpaper, every combustible element now seemed to be aflame. A wall of fire ringed the old lady as she began to die from asphyxiation and heat.

But the flames from hell had not quite finished with her.

As the room turned into a furnace the front window exploded, sending countless glass shards lancing out into the cold night air. Through scorching skin she could faintly hear shouts and bells clanging. Too late, she knew, for that – that evil was still in control. The roaring conflagration turned into mounting laughter as the oozing tentacles touched her feet beneath the coffee table. The leather shoes burst into flames and already blackened extremities began to melt, the skin shrivelling back, the very bones calcinating in the intense heat. Then suddenly small blue flames appeared on her shoulders, like tiny wings. The pain was so penetrating it transcended everything else; she tried to reach this new torment with her hands, to beat them out. But it was no use. More blue flames appeared on her chest, her arms, her thighs, spurting through her clothing, as though an oxy-acetylene torch was being applied. Her body was burning now from within, flowering with brilliant blue lights that were fuelled by her own body fats, eclipsing the roaring inferno that was around her.

As the last oxygen in her lungs was sucked out by the all-encompassing fire she screamed, "God, no-o-o-o!"

17: AVOIDANCE

Jake had difficulty fitting the key in the lock of the ground floor flat. "C'mon," he gritted. "It's just the cold, pull yourself together."

The girl behind him, teeth chattering and almost shoving him up the two steps, didn't help.

"There!" The key slid home and in one motion he twisted and leaned forward, pushing at the heavy wooden door. They almost fell into the short hallway. His hand went automatically to the light switch.

"Don't!" Carolyn whispered. "Not just yet."

He turned, surprised. She put her hand up to her hair in a nervous, embarrassed gesture.

"I must look a mess." Her voice trembled. "Oh, my God, Jake, I'm so frightened." And then she was in his arms, a sensation that almost compensated for the nightmare drive from Eastby Moor. He'd taken the wheel while she had crumpled into the passenger seat, staring straight ahead, not speaking. He had not disturbed her mood, his own thoughts in a turmoil as he wrestled with the unfamiliar steering and power.

She trembled again and he was brought to the present and their sorry state; he was soaked through and she wet from the knees down, where she'd floundered about in her attempts to drag him from the brook. The blow to the head had only temporarily stunned him. Its effect would undoubtedly have been longer but for the almost simultaneous shock of the freezing water.

"Let's get inside, I'm okay now," she murmured.

He led her through into the small living room, flicking on some lights. Quickly kneeling he ignited the coal-effect gas fire, turning the flames to maximum. Vigorously rubbing his hands together he straightened up before turning back to her. The svelte, haughty veneer of a short hour ago was gone, and in its place the haunted, fear-wracked face of a child, with damp, straggly hair stared back. She caught his look and smiled wanly.

"You think I look bad…" She pointed to the mirror above the fireplace. His reflection was dirt-streaked, the normally crisp, curly hair had begun to dry out in the heat of the car – but only in places. Some had sprung back to its former style while the remainder seemed undecided. His jacket – being black – appeared relatively unscathed but felt terrible, heavy and smelling of brackish water.

His eye caught hers in the glass and they both burst out laughing. "We have to do something about ourselves, Jake."

"What? Oh, sure, stupid of me. Come, through here." He took her hand and opened the door to the self-contained toilet and bathroom. "Shower." He pointed. "Bathrobe…towels!"

His relief at the reasonably clean ablutions made him make a mental note to slip Mrs Branson from upstairs and extra four-pack of strong cider tomorrow. It wasn't what her doctor would prescribe but that would just make her appreciate it more.

"But what about you?" she protested. "I'm really only cold and slightly damp. Ten minutes in front of the fire -"

"Rubbish!" He gently pushed her towards the cubicle. "We mustn't ignore the therapeutic effect. Just make it quick." He winked and turned to go, saying over his shoulder, "I'll be taking most of these off and putting on some coffee -" He stopped, realizing how silly that sounded and laughed. "You know what I mean, you have about two minutes."

Stripping off his sodden clothing he dumped it all in the linen basket. Perhaps I should make that two four-packs, he mused, reaching for his old 'reporter's special' trench coat, a relic from his 'Front Page' period. Slipping into it the remedial effect was almost instantaneous, and as he padded about the tiny kitchen his brain began to function at something approaching its usual level. Coming round after the crack to his skull had been as traumatic as his last flash of consciousness before temporary oblivion had blotted out everything else. Carolyn was bending over him, crying and pleading as she strained, hands under his armpits, to drag his dead weight from the water.

He'd thrashed about in panic, arms flailing, trying to recall where he was. He gasped at the cold, only fleetingly aware of Carolyn's almost tearful joy at his recovery. The dog...the dog! He twisted in the water, sliding half-under on a slimy rock, looking everywhere at once.

"It's okay, Jake, it's gone."

"What?" He sat up, leaning back on his arms as she trudged through the knee-deep water to face him. "What happened?"

"I'm not sure." She held a hand out; he grasped it and then she used both hands to help him stand upright. "I was halfway across and looked back to see it launch itself at you..." She shivered. "It was like some black lion, all shaggy, great open jaws and those eyes...oh, my God, those eyes..." She began to sob in delayed reaction.

"Here." He took her by the arm and they stumbled to the bank. "We'll talk later. Let's get back to the car."

The kettle started to pipe and he twitched, pulled the trench coat a bit tighter. Quickly making the coffee he took the mugs into the living room just as she emerged from the bathroom, looking even more gamin in the enormous bathrobe. Her wet hair was tied back with what looked suspiciously like one of his tennis shoe laces, and the rich, dark red of the towelling set off the pale creaminess of her skin.

"I feel tons better. Mmm...hot coffee. You sure know the way to a distressed girl's heart." She avoided his eyes. "Your turn now."

When he rejoined her ten minutes later on the settee, clad in blue jeans and white T-shirt, the coffee was still delicious and warm.

"I've put your duds over the radiator," he said between sips. "You may never regard them as glad rags again but at least they'll keep you decent."

She glanced sideways at him; he smelt clean, soapy. The curly hair was still damp and tousled, the clear skin with a scrubbed look, reminding her of her first boyfriend, Max Cusler, a banker's son from Lucerne. The same blue eyes and fair skin. But there the resemblance ended; her seated companion was no callow youth, despite his boyish looks. In his casual clothes he appeared lean and fit. I suppose he needs to be, she mused, if this was a typical example of his lifestyle.

As though reading her thoughts he said, "You never finished what you were saying back there…about the dog, I mean."

"I–I don't think I want to talk about it, Jake," she faltered, burying her face in the still steaming mug.

"I don't think we have a lot of choice, do we?" he replied quietly. "Whatever it is it exists – on some sort of plane. The last frame in my memory is of some Gothic horror bent on our destruction." He paused to allow her time to come in on this but she remained withdrawn – almost determinedly so, he felt. He reached over and touched her hand. She started, looked down and then up to give that small smile again. "It's okay, Carolyn, we're safe here."

Her expression, while not entirely disbelieving, registered a healthy doubt. But she responded to his gesture and placed her hand over his. She sighed. "I–I looked back… I was halfway across the stream, yes?" He nodded. "You had twisted round to face…it." She gulped, pushed her hair back, then slowly drew the back of one hand across her brow. "From…oh, about twelve feet back it sprang at you. I remember screaming but couldn't hear it somehow. You threw something – I saw your arm swing over… The torch? Yes, the torch. Then you either fell or flung yourself back -"

"Yes, I remember…" he whispered. "The torch seemed to go through it and then there was this brilliant flash and a clap like thunder -"

"Maybe that's why I couldn't hear myself scream." She laughed, gulped again and raised the mug. "The nearest I can describe it is when one of those jets goes through the sound barrier at an air show. A flash, a thunderclap and then… nothing."

"Nothing?" He stared. "Just like that?"

"We-ell, except for the awful smell…a sort of chemically, burning stench."

"Of course, it was something Joan Winspear said." His excitement overcame his nightmarish recollection, "These entities can't abide running water, that's why I told you to change direction. I knew that you at least would reach it first. At that moment it seemed our only chance -" He stopped then, a strange look in his eyes.

"What is it, Jake? For God's sake don't go all enigmatic on me now." She scowled. "I don't think I could stand it."

"I'm sorry, Carolyn." He got up and began to pace the room, running his fingers through his hair, destroying its former order.

"Ja-ake…" she said plaintively.

He stopped, looked down at her. Then, going down on one knee he gripped both her hands in his. The blue eyes seemed to glow. "What if it wasn't the water? Or…not solely the water?"

"What d'you mean? Please, you're hurting me." She eased her hands free.

"Oh, sorry." But he didn't get up. "What if it was the torch – or rather, the energy in the battery cell? That thing must be composed of energy of some description. Isn't that a fundamental law of physics? Maybe my reflex action of hurling it actually short circuited…fused its own energy structure."

"I still don't see -"

"I must speak to Joan!" He straightened up and went out of the room, came back with his cell phone, tapping it and shaking his head. "Knackered! Bog water over technology equals junk. Is yours all right?" She nodded and threw it over to him; he deftly caught it, winked at her as he tapped in the remembered digits and waited. Then his face went blank; he checked the number, shrugged and tried again. After several seconds he slowly flipped it shut and handed it back.

"That's funny."

"What? Dammit, Jake, what's so bloody funny?" Her exasperation got to him.

"The line seems dead, a disconnected tone, the nice lady said the number I want is unavailable. But I know she's not - I spoke to her on that number yesterday."

"Hmph…maybe it's just as well." He looked at her, puzzled. "Have you seen the time? She was tired when we left her. I'm sure she's in bed by now and wouldn't thank you for being dragged out of her sleep to debate which is the best way to disintegrate a ghost - running water or a nine-volt battery! She didn't have a mobile – she's probably just unplugged it, if she's got any sense."

He ruffled his hair ruefully, came over and sat down.

"Yes, I guess you're right. Whatever it is it can wait till tomorrow–" He held his hand up. "Sorry, today. So-o…what do we do now…about our shared experience, I mean?"

"Well, I don't know about you, hotshot, but you can have my share of the experience – gratis and willingly!" She sipped at the last of the coffee, avoiding his surprised expression. "Like I said yesterday, I'm off to London in a few hours."

152

"You're still going, after this?" He was genuinely amazed. "The most exciting -"

"And frightening!" she interjected. "Don't whatever you do forget frightening…or – or maybe even plain scared shitless!" She got up and walked away from him, flinging her arms wide. "Jesus Christ, I don't believe you!" She turned, eyes blazing. "We have just escaped from what will arguably be *the* most scary episode of our lives and all you can think of is its news value, its – its storyline significance." She came towards him and caught his upper arms. Up close he was once again trapped by those luminous great eyes. Two spots of colour on her cheeks accentuated the pallor, as though with some fever. The lips glistened and he was irresistibly drawn to her as before. She pulled away. "Don't start that again, dammit. Were you asleep during the body language lesson?"

"From where I'm standing you're a young woman asking to be held and comforted," he said quietly. "I'm sorry, Carolyn, about misplaced enthusiasm. Perhaps you're right." He made a gesture of helplessness, waving his right hand. "I'm locked into this thing now, for whatever it takes. Apart from it tingling my news nose" – he laughed self-consciously – "there's an old lady out there who believes whatever it is, it's evil. Now, she may be eccentric and old-fashioned, even contemptuous of our generation, but one thing's for sure…she's not stupid. She needs help, Carolyn." His eyes pleaded and she dropped her gaze, knowing she was going to have to disappoint this disturbingly attractive man, maybe even hurt him.

"I'm sorry, Jake, even if I wanted to I can't stay. I have to get to the city. I have a pretty heavy interview for my Registered Representative exams tomorrow…today."

"I'm sorry, what are they?"

"It's a qualification required to operate more fully on the Stock Exchange. I did say I was in media market analysis, remember? Well, my firm, Hesketh and Wise, are pushing me through earlier than the norm and I have to respond to the pressure or drop out." She shrugged. "It's all part of the prevailing philosophy. So you see, even if I wanted to…"

"At least we have tonight." She looked at him, started to shake her head as he took her hand and led her towards the bedroom.

"I don't think that's a very good -"

"Ssh!" He loosened the lace and gently pushed her onto the bed and lay alongside her, pulling her to him. As she protested again he kissed her. Instinctively her left hand crept up behind his head, holding the moment. Then she broke away.

"I–I'm sorry, Jake." She squeezed her eyes tight shut as the familiar images threatened to swamp her psyche. The long-held fear rose up between them. "I'm really attracted to you but I–I can't…"

He leaned back slightly, stopped caressing her left breast, as firm and warm as he'd imagined.

"Do I need to ask the obvious question?" He tried to make light of it.

"It's a matter of timing, really, that's all." She looked directly into his eyes.

"Timing…?" The penny dropped. "Oh, you mean…you've got…"

"Let's just say you've picked a singularly – er, bad period to initiate a sexual relationship," she said wryly.

He slumped back against the headboard, desire and detumescence struggling for supremacy. She noticed the change and tightened her grip.

"All is not lost, hotshot," she whispered. "There's more than one way to a woman's heart. Here, let me show you…"

Her dark hair cascaded as she leaned over him.

18: COUNTERSURVEILLANCE

The dark blue Ford Transit van with tinted rear windows had
been parked halfway down the cul-de-sac for two hours, since
just before midnight. The short street was never busy, even in
daytime. Not merely having one end sealed off, all one side was
a high brick wall, the shell of an old swimming baths, awaiting
redevelopment. Residents normally left their cars, rubbish skips
and wheelie bins along its length. One more anonymous vehicle
raised no eyebrows.

The three men inside – one driver, two technicians – were
becoming restive; having observed their quarry arrive at
Number 26 and monitored their progress from the front of the
flat to the rear, they had switched to the electronic bug fixed to
the window pane of the bedroom.

It was now 01.57.

"Strewf, Mick," Solly the cockney said hoarsely. "She's some
mouf mechanic 'n' no mistake. That lucky barstard must be
dehydrated by now. Wot chance wiv my ol' lady if I play this
tape to 'er, eh?"

"No chance, not when she looks up and sees the same old
five-two skinhead with shit-brown eyes!" The lean, dark one
chuckled and prised the headset from a reluctant Solly and
applied himself to his task. Ex-SAS, he didn't speak much unless
it was to do with his work, and listening to others' couplings had
long since ceased to turn him on. Of late the remotely recorded
grunts and sighs showed signs of having a counter-productive
effect on his own libido, and he had developed a technique of
only picking up on the sounds where they affected his equipment – too loud, too low or unidentifiable. These particular

155

transmissions could have fallen into the latter category but for the exclamations of the happy recipient.

As the decibel rate subsided he turned aside. The driver was West Indian but retaining his pure African blood. The wide-brimmed black hat and matching polo sweater rendered him almost invisible. The ganja joint he sucked on gave the only point of reference in his face.

"Denzil, do you have to smoke that shit in here?"

Gleaming teeth flashed in the gloom. "Man said no booze, nuthin' 'bout in-hay-lay-shun! 'Sides, Ah think Ah'm in lurve. Ah'm jealous 'o that dude in thar. Way she workin' on him gal's good enough t'be brown sugar. One thing fo' sho'…she ain't no vegetarian!" And he burst out laughing.

"Well, she's doing all the work but it's sure taking it out of him," Mick said wryly. "I say we'll be moving in…say, fifteen-twenty minutes. Any takers?"

The other two were silent; nobody was better than Mick when it came to his job. Nineteen minutes later he switched off the recording equipment.

"Show time, Den, let's go." The engine coughed into life and they quietly reversed out of the street, no lights. Turning left and then right into the alley behind the flats Denzil had to resort to sidelights to avoid bins and split plastic bags. Number 26 was in darkness and the two technicians clambered to the rear of the van as it stopped. Solly carefully hefted the gas cylinder down to the waiting Mick. Scanning the alley's length they then pushed open the rotten wooden door set in the backyard wall and slipped through. Having already marked the obstacles – rotating washing line, old bicycle and disused cold frame – they approached the bedroom window. A last check with a stethoscope by Mick before nodding to Solly, who carefully stood the cylinder on its end. The six-millimetre hole they had drilled in the lower window frame showed up clearly against white paintwork. Solly slid the long, steel tube through the hole. When it was fully inserted he pushed the cylinder's flexible hose over its end. Glancing briefly at Mick, who nodded again, he slowly opened the valve, using its knurled knob and peering at the two small gauges. Satisfied that the pressure was dropping he lowered the cylinder to the ground. He went back to the van, returning within seconds with two air breathing sets and small LED lamps with elastic bands.

Mick checked his watch and Solly looked at the gauges again, tapping the left one with his finger. He gave the 'thumbs up' and they both donned the apparatus and head lights. Solly silently turned the key in the oiled back door lock, motioning Mick through first. They both switched on their lamps, heads down, and made their way along the short passage, past the bathroom and into the bedroom. Mick noted the bedroom door hadn't been fully closed, which would have marginally slowed the effect of the halothane. But the anaesthetic was still quietly hissing out of the tube's end a mere metre from the headboard, a fact previously considered in his calculations.

The heavy, stertorous breathing told its story. Mick played the beam briefly over the couple; lover boy was on his right side, inhaling the full force of the gas; the girl lay supine, mouth slightly open and snoring gently. Slowly, carefully, Mick drew back the duvet until she was fully exposed. Even the normally self-controlled technician's breathing rate increased behind the face mask at sight of the flawless form. Her right arm was resting on her lover's left hip, the left arm bent across her lower rib cage, as though consciously cradling the firm breast that showed little sign of the usual flattening in such a position. Her left leg angled outwards and was drawn up, hinting at the mysteries below the small black arrowhead of pubic hair. The slim waist and slightly flaring hips were in perfect proportion to the rest. Aroused and sexually receptive she would be totally irresistible – as the recording testified.

He sensed rather than saw Solly's movement and grabbed him by the arm. He pulled at the rubber sealing his mouth just long enough to whisper, "Not this one, dickhead. Remember her condition – you'll leave traces."

Solly snatched his arm away with an audible snarl. He went searching for her clothes while Mick unfolded the silvered survival sheet. He spread it on the floor by the bed as Solly came out of the bathroom and flung her things into it. Mick motioned to her feet and the other took hold whilst he placed his hands under her armpits and gently eased her to a sitting position. Her head flopped to one side and she groaned, a dribble of saliva trailing across her cheek. They froze for several seconds, Mick remembering the opened door and its diluting effect. Then he nodded and in one carefully practised movement they deposited her on the sheet. Wrapping the sides tightly about her slack body they quickly fastened the wide Velcro straps.

They were about to take her out when Solly waved at Mick and then made a scribbling mime with one hand. Mick hit the side of his head lightly with one palm before straightening up and going across to the dressing table. Taking out a lipstick and using the head torch he quickly scrawled the message.

They carefully carried the drugged girl out to the van, placing her in a space already cleared among the tools and technical equipment that took up most of the interior.

Going back to the flat Mick went inside with his respirator still on whilst Solly turned off the gas and removed the steel tubing. Mick gave the flat a final once-over; he went to the window, flipping the security catch and pushing the frame outwards at the bottom a few inches. Taking a small tube of white all-purpose filler he squeezed some into the drilled hole and smoothed it level with one finger. He did the same on the inside and closed the window. He pushed the bedroom door fully open, doing the same with all the other rooms before finally pulling the back door shut and locking it.

The van moved at a snail's pace until it was out of the alley, following the instructions supplied. Twenty minutes later Denzil slowed as they approached a T-junction.

"Left here, Den," Mick directed.

Parked round the corner of a country road and just inside the gateway of a grass field was a dark green Jaguar. Its rear was to them, boot fully raised and darkened, registration plate completely covered by black sticky tape. As ordered they reversed into the field, lights off, where Mick and Solly got out and quickly transferred the silver bundle.

The Jag's driver side window was down and the aroma of expensive cigar wafted back to them as they carefully lowered the boot lid.

"No problems?" The voice was low and cultured.

"Silk, sir, as promised. Now -"

"Tapes!"

"Oh, yeah, sorry." Mick drew the casette from inside his zip-up and handed it through. Lapses like that could prove detrimental to their continuing reputation.

A large Jiffy bag was thrust at them. The head never turned. "As agreed, gentlemen. Safe journey."

"Yes, sir, thank you." He almost saluted as he backed away.

Before getting back in the van Mick peeled away the white lettering stuck to both panels. As they drove away the tension eased. Denzil slid in a reggae disc whilst Mick tore open the envelope. Switching on the courtesy light he riffled the edges of the used twenties.

"Seems to be all here," he joked. "Thirty grand. See, Solly, you can buy a dozen like her when you get home."

"Not like her, Mick." The cockney shook his head emphatically. "I'll never be able to afford one like her." He slammed the dashboard. "Fuckin' lunar cycles!"

19: DISAPPEARANCE

The insistent warble of the spare phone penetrated Jake's submerged state. As though through layers of silken netting he clawed his way to the surface, fumbled for the instrument and tried to locate his ear beneath the duvet. He fell asleep instantly.

The voice seemed to be inside his head but he knew it couldn't be so. Why would he be calling out his own name? He groped about for the source, eventually touching something that lit up an unearthly blue in the darkness under the cover. He blinked and groaned.

"Jake? Jake, what the fuck's the matter with you? Are you all right?"

"Oooh…! Timesit?" he mumbled, his eyes now open but with nothing to see.

"Time you were getting your arse down here smartish, my lad. Where's your other phone? Who knows, you might even still have a job. Jake? Are you listening to me?"

"Gerry?" He hand-heeled his eyes. "Jesus, where am I?" Realisation hit him as he twisted to look at the other pillow. "Carolyn?"

"Carolyn! Look, tell me about this change in our relationship later…like from your next place of employment." *Click.*

"Gerry? Look, I'm sorry…oh, shit!" He raised his wrist and squinted at the watch face. 11.22 Holy cow! He flung the cover aside and rolled off the bed, stood up and staggered slightly. Jesus, he muttered, that was some night. Talk about sex being a drug. He called her name again but instinctively knew he was alone in the flat. Then he noticed the dressing table mirror and padded across to peer at it. Although the message was writ large he couldn't seem to focus. He concentrated, screwing up his features; the comical reflection mocked him. He didn't feel humorous.

Sorry – have to fly. It was wonderful. Ring you soon.

Love, Caroline.

"Damn!" He tottered towards the bathroom.

The newsroom seemed somehow different as he made his way to his desk, two gulps of coffee and twenty minutes later. His colleagues' derisive greetings were the same for anyone arriving late and obviously hungover. And yet – yet there was something in the air. What was it? One or two stared at him as he passed.

He put it aside, finding it difficult enough to cope with his woolly head. His memory of the night was fine, especially the pre-sleep hour! So vivid and enlightening he didn't think he would ever forget – didn't want to ever forget it! To say that she had amply compensated for her apologetic confession would be an injustice. Replaying the highlights whilst waiting for the lights to move along Southfield Road had brought on an unaccustomed arousal, so much so that he had incurred the wrath of a bread van driver, who had mistaken his disbelieving expression as a criticism of the other's driving. He wasn't sure whether he was in love with her or her amazing expertise – although a little jealous of previous recipients. Did it matter? Besides, if she was like that on reduced power how would she perform on all cylinders? He got hot again just visualizing it.

"Hey, wunderkind, sit down before old Gus finds out you're here."

"What?" Gerry was beckoning frantically from across their desks.

"Get your frigging head -"

"Ransome! My office – now!" The editor's stocky figure disappeared behind the frosted glass and the door slammed. Jake looked helplessly at his friend and drinking partner. "What's going on, Gerry? I've only slept in, for Chrissakes."

161

"I know naw-theeng." Gerry gave his Manuel shrug before reverting. "But it's not simply because you've been stacking the old zeds."

Even more mystified Jake went across and knocked before entering. His boss was sitting reading some proofs – or pretending to; his gaze fixed and the paper held almost rigid, knuckles white. Jake stood there, knowing that a storm was brewing; he'd been through them before. But why this time? So much had happened in the last twenty-four hours but none of it was directly related to his job as yet. He had hoped to broach his theories to Gus later today, after he had tried once more to contact Joan about the events on Eastby Moor. His mind drifted; those glistening lips, that wickedly educated tongue…

"Well, sunshine, you really blew it this time, didn't you?" Gus was glaring up at him, all pretence of normality aside. He made a show of going through the pipe routine but his heart wasn't in it and he flung it on the desk.

"I'm sorry, Gus, I really don't know what you mean. Wasn't my piece about the dog laws not up to scratch -" He stopped, aghast at the unintended pun, but the old news editor didn't notice. That was serious.

"Dog laws my left nut!" Gus yelled and as Jake flinched he glimpsed heads beginning to turn in the outer office.

"If it's about Joan -"

"Joan? Joan? What are you running in your leisure time – an escort agency?" Gus had risen to his inconsiderable height to glare and rant. "I took you here against my better judgement. I've always prided myself on being able to pick a good newspaperman…someone who will be guided, channelled, respond to the blue pencil, cut out adjectives and not use words of more than four syllables in human interest stories. In short," he roared, " SOMEONE WHO WILL FOLLOW ORDERS!"

People were now beginning to stand up for a better look

without actually appearing to do so; leaning over monitors to confer with colleagues or – if their backs were normally towards the editor's office – finding reasons for suddenly requiring something elsewhere.

"But no, out of regard for your mother and our friendship at university" – Jake blinked – "I took you under my wing." The phrase seemed to stick in his throat. "Under my guard, more like…and this is how you repay me." He rubbed his face all over with one hand, noticed for the first time the avid audience outside and turned to let them have some of it as well. "Get back to work, you idle bastards, we have a paper to get out!" He pointed. "You, sit down!"

"I'm sorry, Gus, but apart from the personal embarrassment in front of my colleagues I haven't a clue what the complaint is. If this is some formal disciplinary charge -"

"Son, this is goodbye."

"Goodbye," Jake repeated weakly.

"It's what I mean about compromise, Jake. Nothing's simple any more, if it ever was. I daresay it's always been that way but lately…" He rubbed at his face again. "Bottom line is you're no longer employed by Northern News Group, as of six minutes past six this morning."

"But – but why, for Chrissakes?" Jake felt like he'd been punched in the gut. Too much was happening in his life right now; he was simply unable to absorb what Gus was saying. His hands pawed at the air as a drowning sensation swept over him. "What have I done that's so terrible?"

"Of all the broads in all the gin joints…" The older man looked at him with genuine sadness. "How well do you know your Casablanca?" The lad was still struggling, he could see, so he waved his hand. "Forget it. I never was very good with this end of the job." He sighed, sank back in his chair. "Rule Number One, son: Never fuck around with the boss's daughter."

"I still don't understand, Gus." Jake was pleading now.

"You really mean to say you don't know who Carolyn Draycott is?" Gus demanded. "You really don't know, do you? What's the matter with you kids today – don't you ever come up for air? What about breakfast?" He held a hand up. "Scrub that, don't tell me, I don't want to know."

"That's the point, Gus, she was gone when I woke up. A lot of shit happened last night – no, I don't mean that! What's all the mystery anyway?" He was becoming angry now. "I simply met this girl up on the moors yesterday and asked her out. Big deal. As for her being somebody's daughter… Well, that's where I know you're on the wrong track. Her parents are dead, she was brought up by an uncle – Nicky, she called him…" Something started to surface at the back of his mind.

"Nicky, she called him!" Gus mimicked, exasperation showing again. "I venture to bet nobody else in this big world of business is allowed to call him that. A lot of things, yes, but Nicky… You see what I mean about your lack of 'nose'." He tapped his own broken-veined example. "Who has so recently bought out our beloved newspaper group – that Nicky."

"You – you mean Sir Nicholas Brookes?" Jake felt for a chair, sat down slowly.

"Or as you will no doubt soon be saying, 'Brooksie to his pals'!" Gus returned sourly. "Carolyn Draycott is his only family and – not only that – she apparently suffers from some rare blood disorder. She tends to kick over the traces of her strict medical regimen from time to time, as is only to be expected from a young and beautiful – she is young and beautiful?" – Jake nodded dumbly – "a young and beautiful lady who is the sole…heiress…to…his…entire…fortune." He splayed the fingers of both hands on the desk and stood up before coming round to stare down at Jake. "I'm angry and sad, Jake. Angry because I'm not used to being roused from my slumber at six

164

a.m. by overbearing press barons who control my pension rights and use the threat of forfeiture of said rights to coerce me into acceding to their unreasonable demands. Sad because I'm probably an old man by your standards, who realizes there's more than one way to feel impotent. I can't help you, son, against a billionaire's bully boy tactics, except to say I have extracted one concession – three months' salary in lieu, which should give you some breathing space and get the union off my back. I'll help all I can to get you fixed up elsewhere. Give me a ring in two–three weeks' time. But in the meantime clear your desk in case he decides to drop in and give us the once-over."

"You mean he's in the area?" Jake kicked his brain into gear, bringing Gus's worried features back into focus. "Carolyn said something about him being in Rome."

His ex-boss shrugged. "Well, I'm only guessing but his personal jet was reported at the airport last night."

"But she's already left, some time early this morning. She was gone when I…" He reddened.

Gus patted his arm absentmindedly and turned away. "You're a fine lad, Jake, and a credit to your mother but do seriously consider an alternative career. Science, engineering, something like that, you have the qualifications. Try one of the new Arab firms over on Wilton site. I have friends – hey, Jake!"

But the young man was gone, walking unseeing to his desk, oblivious to the curious stares. Gerry Malone, for all his brash exterior, had the honed perception of a lifetime's skill at reading faces. He allowed Jake to slump in his chair.

"You've been pumped! Why? Expenses, moral turpitude…too tall?" When his friend failed to raise a spark he rasped, "C'mon, kid, you're not the first cub reporter to be fired. Hell, I moved five times in as many years and whilst I wouldn't have believed so at the time it didn't do me any harm."

Jake just stared into space. In exasperation Gerry threw one of his mutilated paper clips at him; it struck its intended target on the chin and Jake started, seeing his colleague as if for the first time. He shook himself and looked around; everyone plunged back into their work.

Gerry stood up. "Let's go, kid, tell papa all about it – away from these inveterate newsy parkers. Bags I the scoop, they can read all about it tomorrow."

"I–I'm sorry, Gerry I've got to clear my desk." Jake's misery almost found a long-dormant heart string in his older companion but it was easily suppressed.

"Balderdash and poppycock. Leave it for now and come back this evening when all this lot have gone home to become ordinary people once more, instead of chroniclers of history in the making. Who knows, you may even have found alternatives by then to jumping in the river or throwing yourself into the printing rollers. Come."

He gripped the unresisting arm and steered the rest of Jake out of the building. Gerry didn't allow him to talk until he had placed a double Jack Daniels and soda in his fist and forced him to drink some. The unaccustomed taste shocked Jake into something resembling life. He shuddered.

Gerry sighed. "That's a terrible waste of a tenner but I'll put it down to experience – yours! Now, what's this all about? If it's crime I naturally get first keyboard rights. Over here, before those bloody suicidal estate agents come whingeing in." He pulled him over to the window seat and, slowly at first but with mounting animation, Jake related the events of the previous evening. Gerry heard him out, only altering his expression at mention of the dog's disappearing act. He sipped his beer, studying the younger man's face. He seemed to have been through a lot, all right, something around the eyes and mouth was different. Not lines, certainly, but an emerging hardness perhaps. Yes, definitely some loss of innocence. And why not?

How often should a young man compress so many disparate experiences into twelve hours? And he knew it wasn't over yet. He sighed again.

"I know why you couldn't contact Joan Winspear last night," he said quietly.

"I'm sorry?" Jake's mind had been elsewhere. Jerry's company and unorthodox but effective therapy were already working.

"She's had an accident, Jake."

"Accident?"

"A house fire. The news came in just before you did this morning. The fire service was called out around midnight."

"How bad is it?" The young ex-reporter didn't really want to hear any more bad news.

"The baddest, I'm afraid. She didn't make it. The old cottage went up like a Roman candle apparently. My contact said he's never seen anything like it in his seventeen years experience. I'm sorry, Jake, I know you had a soft spot for her and you don't need this after... Anyway, all you can say is she was quite old and it was probably quick -"

"No!" The look of horror stopped Gerry more than the denial as Jake swept frantic fingers through his hair. "No," he said again, more quietly. "It was no accident."

"What?" Gerry sat forward, his beer forgotten. "Oh, c'mon, Jake, you've just had too much thrown at you in a few short hours. But get things in perspective, son, house fires among the very young and very old are statistically -" He stopped and grimaced, reached for his beer.

"No, Gerry, she knew she was in danger." He gripped the other's knee in his urgency. "She knew it and she was scared, but she was brave too. We...I–I can't let it lie there, I must do something."

"Do something? What the hell are you talking about?" Gerry's expression said he was losing some of his sympathy as the other's implications ran through his newsy mind. "You're strung-out, not thinking straight. Your desire to express sorrow for a friend is understandable, I would think less of you for being otherwise. But you don't mean that, do you?"

Jake was silent.

"You demand some kind of accounting, make someone pay, is that it?"

"Isn't that usual where there's been a crime?" Jake's face was set in lines Gerry had never seen before.

"But there is no crime!" Gerry exploded. "Or there can't be until Scene of Crime Officer and Forensics have done their thing and that could take days…weeks."

"We don't have days, Gerry," the other replied grimly. "I'm going there now." He stood up; he had a purpose; there was an enemy. He owed someone and he was a free agent of temporarily independent means. He buttoned his jacket and glanced down at his friend. "Are you in?"

"Yeah…in the shit." Gerry sighed, took a last look at his beer. "You can't drive after a double whisky on an empty stomach." He rose and reached for his hat.

20: FRAUDULENCE

Carolyn's reaction on waking was one of panic. She was not back in her small but airy little flat in Hampstead; certainly not looking out onto a dingy backyard in Middlesbrough. Instead there was this high, old-fashioned bedroom with ornate coving and ceiling rose, a tall, heavily curtained window and some Victorian furniture. Jake! Memory cascaded back – she put a hand out as she turned to him but he was no longer there.

Oh God, she groaned, guessing where she was. This had happened before, after a particularly boring but dutiful appearance at one of her uncle's London banquets. Surrounded by the great and the good of society's cross-section, she'd been overcome with fatigue and wine to the point of passing out, eventually coming-to in one of the bedrooms, dreadfully weak and blanked out. That hadn't been too bad – Uncle Nicky saying afterwards how sympathetic the elderly guests had been about her welfare.

But this… How on earth had he found her, for a start? Mrs Sykes, probably. Can't really blame her, I suppose, the old dear has nowhere else to go. She peeked under the sheets. Oops, who put the nightie on? She was still frustratingly modest; her deep-seated reluctance to sleep around was something that had disturbed and indeed frightened her for the last few years. Even with men to whom she had been sexually attracted there had always been some kind of mental barrier preventing her from completing the act. Apart from the confused signals this had led to, the various reactions had shed no light on her dilemma. Having no female family to turn to and never having been one for dormitory confessions she guessed it was somehow linked to her post-pubescent debilitating disorder. She had only resorted to masturbation in times of desperation, her expertise in partner satisfaction acquired only as a means of self-preservation from being branded some kind of sexual freak.

Last night had been different; the bizarre events and irresistible chemistry with Jake had taken her over the edge and into an area where she now knew she could no longer ignore her sexual needs. A solution to her problem would have to be found, the 'perennial period' excuse was wearing thin. She was falling in love and experience told her men like Jake rarely came into her life. But would she have the courage to face Uncle Nicky over this? She looked around for the bell push that was in all the rooms in Brookefield Hall.

Before she could do so the door opened silently and he came in, dressed soberly as always – dark suit, white shirt and dark striped tie. The magnetic eyes and bulky figure transfixed her as usual whenever her vitality was low. It was obvious where his success in the business world came from.

"Ah, Carolyn, how good to see you awake and rested. I was so concerned that you had gone too far this time." The voice, although low and modulated, had an underlying roughness to it she could never quite pinpoint.

"Too far, Uncle Nicky?"

Something in her voice made him falter in his smooth approach to her bedside, but he continued and lowered his bulk onto one corner. The pressure transmitted itself like a shark's detection system in reverse. He was the predatory one; the very stillness of his vast form belied the swiftness with which he could move when necessary. She'd seen film footage of him evading soft fruit missiles during a journalistic dispute; his associates had all been struck between limousine and entrance but his nifty footwork across the pavement had infuriated his assailants as he quickly slipped into the building.

"Yes, my dear." He leaned forward to grip her left ankle

through the bedclothes. "In London your little – ah, flights of fancy were more easily understood. A pressure release that Professor deBono assured me could even be termed therapeutic…just so long as we could reach you in the event of an emergency – such as this."

"But you said my previous blackouts had not been harmful, merely a bodily response to fatigue." She wished she had the nerve to ease her leg from his grasp. He seemed to sense her discomfiture and took his hand away. "What happened last night? How–how did you find me?"

He raised one of his small pale hands and let it fall on the bedspread as if in resignation. "Your new friend – of which more later – became alarmed when he failed to rouse you this morning. In a bit of a panic he phoned a colleague at the *Clarion* office." He laughed deprecatingly. "I dare say at that age a young man's thoughts don't go much beyond getting a girl *into* bed! He had no contingency plan for a medical emergency -"

"Just how bad was I, then?" she demanded, annoyance creeping into her voice. She felt perfectly fine now, a slight 'head' but that could be attributed to one or all of the events associated with last night. More recollections trickled into her clearing brain. That dog! Oh, my God, that dog. She shuddered.

Mistaking her emotion he hurried on: "Nothing organic, the doctor says, just nature doing its work. Your deep sleep state bordered on the somnambulistic apparently, and in this condition you were potentially self-threatening -"

"You mean I might sleepwalk out the window, right?" The bite in her tone made his eyes turn wary. "A bit difficult, don't you think, in a ground floor flat with the window locked?"

He spread his hands. "I was unaware of your precise location, simply glad to find you safe…and sound asleep!" He made light of it. "We can fly back as soon as the doctor says you are fit." He stood up.

171

"But if I'm medically okay," she protested, "I can get up now." She threw the covers aside.

"No!" His cry stopped her. Realising his error he put his hands out, placating. "No, Carolyn, you must rest for a little while. This evening perhaps, hmm?"

She sank back slowly. Something was wrong, she could sense it. It wasn't concern for her welfare either. She'd had to rely on him totally over the years since her parents died; she couldn't deny her debt to him but she could never love him in the way she felt he would want her to.

"Why am I not in my usual room, Uncle?" she asked quietly.

"I – we thought this room more suitable to your current needs." She was about to speak and he hurried on: "We've brought all your things." He waved at the old rosewood wardrobe and dressing table. "And there is an en-suite bathroom." He moved the silk screen aside to reveal a door.

His eyes locked on hers; she knew she was being held against her will. But *why*? It was tantamount to – to kidnapping. Once again he seemed to read her thoughts.

"Perhaps we should get a few things straight, my dear." He said it softly, but the menace, the steel, was unmistakable. "I'm a very busy man. This latest distraction has probably cost me an incalculable amount of money. You know how the stock market works – not only must I not be easily seen to be diverted from my multi-faceted investments, but most importantly must the reason for my absence remain secret. You know I've always striven to direct the beam of public curiosity away from your private life. We agreed upon this together, yes?" She nodded, not speaking. "But the money is incidental, I assure you." He raised a hand. "This is not the time to debate that particular point. I had hoped that your new career in the city would instil a more mature attitude to your responsibilities."

"I'm sorry – what responsibilities, Uncle?"

"Oh, come on, Carolyn," he replied impatiently. "It's not been discussed formally but the Brookes Communications empire rests on my broad but still merely mortal shoulders. I have no male issue but I'm no misogynist…as those other tabloids will testify. It could all ultimately devolve on you…should you be worthy of that honour."

"Don't I get a say in this – this global inheritance, Uncle?" Her anger rose at the arrogance of the man. She was not so foolish as to disregard the advantages of her position and its undeniable influence on the rest of her life. But she was not boardroom material, not at the age of twenty-two anyway. In truth she had no firm idea what she foresaw as her future. Perhaps if she could just throw off whatever it was that was sapping her strength…

He was still talking. "…more circumspect in your choice of bedmate – however transient." She flinched at the implied rebuke. "Your friend Mr Ransome, for instance."

"What's Jake got to do with any of this?" she demanded, something catching in her throat.

"More than you think and hopefully less than he would have liked." Sir Nicholas's face was set and grim, the curiously hooded eyes almost slumberous, but she knew that was a most deceptive sign. The feeling in her throat moved, slid down to more tremulous regions.

"What do you mean?"

"I mean he might have been employed by the *Clarion* but he was actually working for one of our rivals, tasked to dish the dirt on you, just as I am about to finalise a major takeover with the New Millennium Christian publications consortium. I found out just in time. Imagine my horror when I discovered he was last seen with you."

"You're lying!" The cry was from her heart, strident and ragged. "Jake is one of the truest, finest -"

"- actors you'll ever come across," her uncle finished harshly, approaching the bed. She shrank away, her world falling apart, desperately seeking something of last night that could not be misconstrued in the light of day. Surely her lassitude had not allowed her female intuition to falter? He cared, he really cared. Nothing he could say would sway her from that view.

"I'll return later with the file we have on young Jake – which isn't his real name, of course. In the meantime I must know how far you went with him."

"What?" His bluntness almost robbed her of whatever reasoning powers remained. "How dare you -"

"Stop it, Carolyn!" He gripped her upper arms, the look in his eyes blurring the pain. "This is too important for niceties. I have to know the extent of his duplicity, else how can I combat it? Did sexual intercourse take place?"

She turned her head away. "I can't -"

He shook her and her head snapped back, striking the padded headboard with a soft thud.

"Answer me!"

"No! No, godammit! Something stopped me as it…as it always does." She was sobbing uncontrollably now, the dam burst, her emotions streaming out in a liquid mix that cleansed but didn't clear, swamped but failed to hide.

Brookes left her there, quietly closing the door after him.

21: REFULGENCE

They could see the still-smouldering ruin before they got there. Driving up the steep lane revealed the blackened windows, like smudged mascara on a ravaged face. The shiny, bright red fire tender contrasted with the generally dilapidated air of the 19th century row of cottages. Gerry parked the car beyond the lane's opening, up on the grass verge behind a grey BMW and the crime squad's white Peugeot Boxer van. He clipped his Press pass onto his breast pocket, nodded to the young police officer in the Rover as they walked past and up the lane. It was an all-too-familiar scene, even for Jake – the police barrier ribbons, the pitiful remnants of someone's life scorched and strewn across the road for all to see. Except that nobody there was interested in the victim's possessions, reduced as they were to pulp and splinters. Fire fighters were still active, sweating and shouting as they struggled with the heavy hose pipes on the slippery surface.

Two senior officers – one fire, one police – were conferring with a stocky man in grey cords, flat cap and dark green duffel coat. They all wore rubber boots.

Gerry jerked his head at them and spoke out of the corner of his mouth, still walking, "Scene of Crime Officer, Fire Prevention and Forensics. Leave it to me."

The trio turned at their approach, the taller saying something to the others before frowning at Gerry.

"Good morning, Malone. Surprised to see you here. We've already had a visitation from the media. What's the matter – lack of communication?" He flicked a thin smile at his companions to establish acquaintanceship but distance between their respective professions. "Gentlemen, I'm sure you know Gerry

175

Malone, our crime chronicler from the local daily." The others nodded perfunctorily.

Gerry smiled his newsman's smile, accepting the level of the other's commitment, knowing that tomorrow they could well be sharing pints and swapping yarns at some municipal function.

"Morning, George…Martin, Mr Gillespie. You might already know my colleague, Jake Ransome. Yes, I take your point, George, a tragedy, certainly, but little to interest that prurient section of the public known euphemistically as" – he hooked his fingers – "our readership. No, it's just that Jake here was a personal friend of Miss Winspear and was naturally upset to hear of the accident."

"Oh." Chief Inspector George Murcell turned his attention to Jake. "Sorry to hear that, Ransome. Terrible business, whatever the circumstances, and these…"

Gerry's antennae twitched. "Something out of the ordinary, George? I was led to assume -"

"When did you last see Joan Winspear, Jake? There was a fancy red sports car reported here last night. Yours, by any chance?" The SOCO fixed a gimlet stare on the young ex-reporter. His eyes, although still bright, seemed twice as old as the rest of him.

"N-no, sir." Jake, caught in the middle of contemplating the destruction of Joan's house, almost gave himself away. "It certainly wasn't mine." He laughed, he hoped reassuringly. "Still got the same old battered Escort, staggering along from one M.O.T. to the next. Tell me, sir, did she suffer, d'you think, before she – she…"

"Hmm, too soon to tell. The remains were quite badly burnt. She was found still sitting in her armchair. I don't normally make pronouncements on the victim – that's Mr Gillespie's province, any road" – he turned to the civilian deferentially – "but under the circumstances it probably doesn't take a lot of

176

guesses as to cause of death. I believe she had a history of ill-health, hmm?"

Mr Gillespie grunted and turned to go, his professionalism ruffled by this break in protocol. Murcell, realizing his gaffe, followed, only pausing to say, "Usual rules, Gerry, touch nothing and don't hinder the fire crew in their duties."

The duo watched them retreating. Gerry pushed his hat further back on his head and whistled softly. "Something is in the wind and it isn't just ash, ladies. What brings Forensic Science Service all the way out from Wetherby at a cost of around five grand to the county and almost as much per item analysed? I still don't buy all your story but I've seen enough house fires to know there was something in that little exchange that says all is not as it seems."

Jake glanced about him in something close to despair. Joan's cottage appeared to be gutted, so there couldn't be much there that would be of use. The hawthorn and blackberry hedge on the other side of the lane was peppered with bits of a window frame, shattered glass glittering like jewels in the grass at its base. Scraps of paper were impaled like Tibetan prayer messages. What was it the SOCO had said? "…sitting in her armchair…" The only armchair was in the front room, near the window. Wait a minute! There was an old Remington set up on the coffee table in front of it when they had gone through to the kitchen. If she had been sat there typing when…

He shook his head; his whole world seemed to be imploding – Carolyn gone, job gone and now this. Poor Joan, what could have been her last thoughts? Did she have any warning at the end? She must have lit a fire. Then what? But he'd noticed the floor had been rough stone, no rugs or carpets. So how come? If it had happened the other way round she would hardly have flopped into her easy chair and continued typing. No, it must have been the former. So what could she have been typing at the end? Surely something as a consequence of their meeting. One of the tiny pieces of paper detached itself and fluttered towards them, settled at his feet. He looked down; it wasn't charred but jaggedly torn at the edges, with typescript on it.

He breathed deeply. "Nothing's changed, Gerry, except that now it'll be even more difficult." His friend gave him a strange look, sensing there was a change. "I need these scraps of paper." He nodded at the hedge.

"But you know -"

"I know what I said to *you*, Gerry." Jake's stare was direct, even disconcerting, to the older man used to a more pliant junior colleague. "I believe this – this confetti is in effect Joan's last testament, and might have been meant for me." His friend was about to speak again but he gripped his arm so hard that Gerry winced. "Jesus, Gerry, it's all I have left. Don't you see?"

"Okay, Jake, okay," the other said slowly, prising himself free. "Do what you have to do but do it quick. I'll chat up the Bill while you get on with some early blackberrying. But remember, if the firemen cop on, you could still be in deep doo-doo." He walked back along the lane.

Jake bent down and picked up the paper, three incomplete lines of type, a few words on each. None of it made any sense except for the middle line, which read "...the purpose of the Dragon Proj..."

Proj? Project? He shrugged and then began a slow walk in Gerry's footsteps, veering towards the hedge as he did so. Nobody was paying him any attention; three fire fighters were still on the scene, two busy rolling up a flattened hose and the third still directing a stream onto a smoking door frame.

Up close the various bits of paper seemed disappointingly smeared and scorched, and far too deeply embedded in the thorny hedge to be easily freed. Glancing down at the wet grass beneath the hedge he spotted some less damaged scraps, but only a few appeared to be other than blank. He knelt to fiddle with his shoelaces, checked to see if he was being observed before quickly scooping up several with his left hand and stuffing them in his jacket pocket. He looked up; the man with the live hose was giving him sidelong glances as he moved the nozzle back and forth. Jake smiled and straightened up, giving a brief farewell wave as he strode past.

Gerry was leaning into the police car's open window as he turned the corner.

"Ah, there you are. Paid your respects to the old lady, Jake? Just been telling Graham here." He nodded to the PC. "We'll be off then. See you around, Graham, probably at the rugby 'do'. Okay? 'Bye."

They got into Gerry's blue Mondeo and drove off. Jake was trembling slightly, with trepidation or excitement, he knew not which.

"Well?"

Jake repeated the lines on the first piece.

"Dragon Project?" Gerry flicked him a glance. "Does that mean anything to you? Mentioned last night?"

Jake shook his head and then slowly drew out the two crumpled scraps he'd lifted from the hedgerow, smoothing the damp paper carefully. Three short lines on the first one...*Phoebus Car*... Then below that...*right Stones near*...and finally...*due to strange chan*...

He read these out slowly several times before quickly displaying it for Gerry to see. He shrugged and partly lifted his hands off the steering wheel for a moment. The last one was shaped roughly like an inverted miniature Africa. Two lines...*from magic.* Beneath this and to the right what looked like part of a name *Arthur C....*"

"Is that it? Here, let me see." Gerry held his hand out. Scanning them all quickly he handed them back. "Umm...well, that last one's a bit less enigmatic than your Dragon Project. It could be a quotation."

"Quotation? You mean from a book?"

"C'mon, Jake, what did you graduate in? Yes, you know, famous quotations of the twentieth century kind of thing."

"Of course! Arthur C Clarke." He struck the fascia lightly with his fist.

"You got it – Space Odyssey, et cetera. Old Arthur was never one to hide his laser under a bushel basket. Anyway, soon check it out with Google. Unfortunately, it's too late to call Sri Lanka collect, now that he's dead."

They chewed over the other clues for the rest of the journey but came to no conclusions. Gerry dropped him off at the rear of the newspaper building.

His laptop search didn't take long. "Thanks, Gerry, I owe you," he breathed. *Any sufficiently advanced technology is indistinguishable from magic: Arthur C Clarke.* Without pondering its meaning he printed it out. He went into the bedroom and flopped onto the bed, instantly reminded of her fragrance as he disturbed the pillow. He sat up and scrutinized the quotation more closely. Any sufficiently advanced technology is indistinguishable from magic. Hmm, debatable but certainly food for thought. Was it meant for him and if so, why? Perhaps if he had more pieces of the puzzle – or paper.

He spread the few torn sections on the duvet. Dragon Project appeared to be the only solid pointer to something. But what? He sighed, pushed himself back against the headboard. Was just about to Google it when the lipsticked message on the mirror seemed to beckon. He read it again, a frown trying to crease the unlined brow. There was something wrong…what? God, his brain was reeling from so many unanswered questions. Was he imagining this one? He gritted his teeth. C'mon, concentrate, dammit. Then it hit him. Of course! He leant across and grabbed the phone, quickly found the number and dialled it.

"Welcome to Hesketh and Wise, we value your call. If you want Marketing press one, if you want…"

He groaned as the recorded voice droned on and waited for the tape to re-play several times before a real voice – female and cultivated – cut in, as he knew from experience it would. "Yes? Hesketh and Wise. How can I help you?"

"Oh, hello, can I speak with Miss Draycott, please?"

"One moment."

This time a male voice answered. "No, she's not here. Is it personal?"

"Yes, it is, actually. Where is she – at this Representative exam she mentioned for today?"

The voice, now slightly mollified at the other's knowledge and obvious familiarity at some level with Carolyn, grunted, "She should be but she's not – never showed. Mr Malcolm is not best pleased, all things considered. Do you know where she might be?" The voice sharpened at the prospect of a possible shared criticism.

"N-no." Jake's mind was in turmoil. "Look, you're obviously busy, I'll call back later. Oh, before you go – how does she spell her first name?"

"Pardon? Now look -"

"No, please, this is serious. I need to send her an official invite for a company bash we're organising next month. Is it *l-y-n* or *l-i-n-e* at the end?"

"I've only ever seen her spell it *l-y-n*."

"Thank you, thank you very much." He rolled off the bed and went over to the dressing table. *Caroline*. Now why would she have spelt her own name incorrectly? He had only seen it once, hand-painted on the fascia of her Porsche. Why would she do a thing like that: leave without a word, misspell her name and apparently opt out of a very important appointment? A sudden chill swept through him. Unless… Oh no, please, not Carolyn too.

He began to pace the room distractedly, seeking some more clues to her departure. Under and around the bed – nothing. He straightened up, stared out the window and into the backyard, only then feeling the slight draft against his legs. The lower sash raised a few inches. That's funny, he knew it hadn't been him; this wasn't exactly neighbourhood watch territory. Hmm, must have been her needing some air during the night. He bent over to press the frame shut when a lighter spot of white caught his eye. He peered closer. It appeared to be a small circular dent or hole with some kind of filler, smoothed over to blend in with the rest. He touched it and a slight powdery residue ended up on his fingertip. Lips now tight he hurried out to the yard. The hole was clearly visible on the other side of the frame, a few curls of fresh wood caught in a spider's web beneath the sill. He went to the door set in the back wall that led to the alley. It was unbolted and recently oiled…but not by him.

Frantic now he went through the whole flat and finally found a pair of tights that had slipped down between the shower curtain and the bath side. He held them to his face and closed his eyes, endeavouring somehow to conjure Carolyn up before him, or at least receive some sign that what he feared wasn't true. His imagination stopped short of what might have happened, but he was convinced that somehow – while they slept – she had been spirited away. God, why had he thought of 'spirited'? No, whoever had done this was closer to his world. There was too much physical evidence. But this was insane. Here he was debating the pros and cons of whether someone he loved had been taken without his knowledge and against her will.

The cell phone rang, making him jump. He considered ignoring it, loath to open up the prospect of any more bad news, but then picked it up.

"Yes?"

"Jake." Relief washed over him at the sound of Gerry's voice. "Jake?"

"Gerry. Any news?"

"Some. You?"

"You were right about Arthur C Clarke." He repeated the quotation. Gerry was silent for a few seconds. "Mean anything?"

"Not at this stage. You?"

"No, but it might tie in with what I found out about one of your paper puzzles - the bit about stones and Phoebus Car?"

"Yes, yes, go on," Jake urged.

"Well, Gordon Robinson – you know, he of the amateur dramatics aspirations? Writes our scientific snippets…has a -"

"Gerry…"

"Right, I transferred what I remembered onto my terminal, moved them around the screen with my 'paste' option, y'know?"

"Hey, good idea, Gerry, I'm impressed."

"I thought so, I thought so, college kid," the other's wry tones came back. "Anyway, there I was, pasting like billy-o when the bold Gordon stumbles by, groping his way along the desks the way he does, when he spotted what he termed my 'uncharacter- istically adventurous use of a PC'. Cheeky sod! Anyway, cut a longish story he picked up on the Phoebus Car bit."

"And? Yes, go on, dammit!"

"It's actually Phoebus Cart, which still meant nowt to you or me, but Gordon's interests naturally lie in directions other that booze and birds – apart from the aforementioned. Anyway, it's a London-based theatre company -"

"Theatre company?"

"Si, *señor*. A few summers ago they were rehearsing for an open air production of The Tempest, to be played inside an ancient stone circle near Chipping Norton in Oxfordshire called -"

"The Rollright Stones!"

"You've heard of them?"

"Some place, maybe it was the same news story. Sorry, go on."

"Well, it seems some very strange things happened to members of the cast. Production assistant Andrea Duncan was quoted as saying, 'It's weird.' The rehearsals were disrupted for some time when a dancer fainted, several performers had inexplicable memory lapses and – get this – their watches either stopped…or speeded up. It goes on to explain that the Rollright Stones are renowned for being at the centre of controversy, due to their alignment along – and I quote, 'strange channels of energy called leys or ley lines' unquote. So-called experts say the stones give off high levels of natural radiation at various times of the day and night, as well as a powerful form of magnetism."

Jake listened with growing excitement, then: "Right, Gerry, I have to assume that was meant for me. Any other conjecture leaves me nowhere, especially now that Carolyn…"

"Carolyn? What's the matter with her? I thought she was back in London…?"

Haltingly, Jake relayed his fears and told Gerry what he had found in the flat. For once his friend had no banter to relieve the situation, knowing how much Jake cared. Unfortunately he had no real alternatives to offer, either.

Jake repeated the Clarke quotation and was about to break the connection when Gerry suddenly said, "Hell, I almost forgot, with all this going on."

"Gerry, what?"

"Well, it might not mean anything, but that young priest – you know, the one you saw about Sarah Branthwaite's collapse – was apparently in here yesterday."

"What d'you mean, apparently?"

Jake could almost picture him scratching his scalp the way he did. "Jim Cooper was the one who actually saw him – or thinks he did, because he wasn't wearing any clerical garb. Nothing significant there, not these days, I suppose, except he remarked on how dishevelled and furtive he looked."

"The priest? What did he want? Was he looking for me?"

"No, that's the funny part. He was actually after Joan Winspear – or rather, a photograph of her."

"What?"

"Yes, you know the photo service we provide for the public on any photographs we may have used in the paper. Well, he said he needed a likeness of her for an article he would be writing on the history of St Michael's. The thing is, he didn't just buy one, bought a dozen or so snaps of her. Now what on earth would he need all those for?"

Jake sank back on the bed, his mind racing. What did this new development mean? It must have something to do with Joan's death, and certainly confirmed his earlier suspicions of the priest.

"Look, Gerry I've got to go. Ask Gordon if he knows of anyone local who is into ley lines, magnetism, natural radiation, that sort of thing. Ring me soonest."

"Why, what are you going to do?"

"I'm going to see this troublesome priest first," Jake replied grimly. "After that, who knows? Perhaps it's time our local constabulary had their penn'orth. Oh, and find out if Sir Nicholas's jet is still parked on the runway. 'Bye."

22: UNACCEPTANCE

Sir Nicholas Brookes flung the cell phone from him in a fury; it bounced off the top of the leather chesterfield and dropped to the floor. The rage built up inside him the way it always did when thwarted. Usually he could sublimate it into some form of action – such as firing someone or issuing a stream of new directives whose implications around the world he could luxuriate in at leisure. This was different; he was impotent, cut off from the source of the problem.

He got himself under control, consciously slowing his breathing, thinking of success to counteract the more morbid alternative that seemed to hover about his head. He walked across the carpet and carefully bent to retrieve the handset. It was no good, he *had* to consider Cappel's failure to find the chalice. It had been days now, he must get back to London; anyway the valley was due to be flooded tomorrow at noon. The weather forecast predicted heavy rain before dawn, greatly increasing the filling process from the nearby mountains, which traditionally drained swiftly through the valley but would now be contained by a zillion cubic metres of reinforced concrete.

His new-found local rag was making great copy of the event. Exquisite irony, he had to concede, being continually appraised of his impending loss – and all at his expense. Dignitaries and district councillors, police and parishioners, all converging for Man's second favourite attraction - after fire – water.

In truth it wouldn't be much of a spectacle, merely the simple blocking of a smallish river. No doubt some avid student of such things would have already calculated just how long it would be before the rising waters completely submerged the deserted village. Correction: *almost* deserted village. That inept cleric was still futilely digging up floors in the presbytery and declaring in his hysterical voice that the access to the chalice simply wasn't there, at the same time contradicting what seemed to be an unshakable faith in Asmodeus. He swore that the spirit form had no reason to deceive him. Fool! Hell's helpers were unsurpassed in the art of deception. It wouldn't have done to remind Cappel of this fact; slim though it was, the priest was his only chance now, a tenuous link to something that might just be a few measly metres from the wretch's reach. The hours were slipping away fast and he could feel the grip of disaster in a way he had no wish to contemplate. In Rome he had been carried away by his own rhetoric, sweeping Franz along with him on a tide of greed. If he failed now...

He shook himself. He must not give up at this stage, it was not his way. All the clues pointed to the chalice being there. He'd impressed this upon Cappel, took him back through his progress, room by room. How far down had he dug? Had he inadvertently piled rubble on untried flagstones? Where was he now? The front hall? Was there *any* other place – in any of the rooms – untouched?

"N-no," the priest had faltered. "Only...?"

"Only?" Brookes had pounced. "Only what? Speak, man! What have you overlooked?"

"J-just the fireplace in the kitchen, Sir Nicholas. It has this big ancient stove in the chimney recess, but it's so huge, so heavy, I can't -"

"You must!" the satanist raged, squeezing the phone as though it were the other's throat. "That's exactly the sort of escape Julius Marr would have appreciated, a kind of passport through hell. Yes!" The more he thought about it the more he was convinced. "Can't you use a crowbar, rig some kind of hoist?"

"I-I'm sorry, Sir Nicholas," Cappel wailed. "I'm exhausted, I haven't slept for days. Perhaps if you assisted -"

"Don't be a fool! You said yourself the area is all zoned off now." His tormentor's tones were withering. "Hi-Sec security have been through on a final sweep, haven't they, the last few Green protestors rounded up? Only missing you because of the dreadful state of the building. How can I…? Argh, I'll get back to you."

He was about to break off when Cappel almost screamed, "Please! I can't stay here much longer on my own. At least conjure up some help. You are the Master, you are out there and I'm…I'm…" The voice tailed away into sobs and Brookes spent a further two minutes placating him before flicking off the connection.

Hence the rage, the feeling of helplessness. But the more he recycled the dialogue the calmer he became. If the entrance was the fireplace then realistically Cappel couldn't be expected to get at it unaided. If he could somehow manage to infiltrate the area then the actual exploration process shouldn't take long – an hour, two at most. But the risk of detection was great, he was not exactly an inconspicuous figure, even in a crowded city. Here…

He paced the living room of the old hall, the very room in which Cappel had given him the historian's image last night. Hmph, that part had worked, at least, it had been on the local TV this morning. Another tragic geriatric unable to cope with living on her own! What a pity our old science can't somehow incorporate some new science and be able to visually record the results of such conjurations! Something to work on there, nothing is impossible in the 'New Age'.

The realization that he really only had one option made things much easier to consider. He *had* to go to the valley, if only to silence Cappel. The man was now so unreliable that he couldn't allow him to live. The presbytery would become his tomb, his body easily buried under his own rubble. The encroaching waters would seal it. Hah!

Brookes appreciated the irony. But before that he needed to know exactly where the chalice lay. If it was beneath the hearthstone then he required the other's physical assistance and but a little corroboration of that fact beforehand. He sighed and glanced up at the ceiling; his abduction of Carolyn had been motivated partly by the intuitive feeling that he might ultimately have to call upon her services to aid him in his quest for the Judas Cup. The conditions for such an enterprise were less than ideal but the stakes were high enough to risk it. It could mean and end to her usefulness, her place in his future plans.

Perhaps that too was destined; she had proved resistant and difficult to work with. A pity, he mused, on form she was the best he'd ever known. There would be others, of course, that was part of the joy of it all – the not-knowing but at the same time the absolute certainty that some day, somewhere, another sensitive like her was waiting to be awakened.

But first... He reached for the phone; the authorities must be informed of his concern for his ward's safety, in view of her medical history when last seen in the company of a disgruntled – maybe even vengeful – ex-employee.

23: CREDENCE

Jake returned to his research, to try to dig up something – anything – on a Dragon Project, and think things through before deciding how to go about finding Carolyn. He was convinced she was not far away, most likely at Brookefield Hall. Even cats as fat as Sir Nicholas must have limited options when it came to abductions. But he couldn't just go barging in there – at least not in broad daylight. She would be guarded; Uncle Nicky would not be short on that option!

He was getting into something deep, no question. But what? If her uncle was behind it then who would believe it of him? He'd phoned London again but the news was still negative; her office had tried to contact Carolyn at home but her flatmate had not seen her since she'd announced her departure for the north several days ago. Another call to a friend in police traffic at Ladgate Lane headquarters had also drawn a blank. But that only meant no reported incident, of course, a relief certainly, but nothing more.

He sat down on the bed again and tried to put it all together. But rational thought seemed to elude him. He'd touched her mirror message before he'd left, his fingertips smearing the lipstick before bringing it to his lips, remembering last night. It tasted sweet. Had she tasted as sweet when he kissed her? Truth to tell, that experience had agitated so many hormones he couldn't swear to it. He'd not recalled her wearing any make-up after her shower. He thought he would have noticed such a lurid shade, somewhat out of keeping with her style. He punched the bed and stood up, running his fingers through his curls in frustration. It was no good, he was destroying himself here, like a blunted drill bit, grinding away ineffectually at the same spot, producing heat but little else. Whatever he was to do, any chance of success would reduce with each passing hour. If the police wouldn't help then the onset of night would leave him with scant – if any – other options.

He presented himself at the Cleveland Constabulary police station with no little trepidation, unsure now of his reception. No longer the glassed-in cube on Dunning Road, with easy-going George Tancred leaning on the wooden counter ready to listen to any reasonable request for information before giving you the benefit of his thirty years experience. If registering high on his plausibility scale he gave a wink and phoned somebody in the inner sanctum to come out or – rarely but better – gave you the 'thumbs up' and a room number through the back.

Like all good things, it couldn't last. The new building was 'over the border', a cleaned up area once notorious for sin-seeking seafarers, shady ladies and Saturday night punch-ups. The only visible legacy of those nostalgic nights was the Club Bongo, still clinging to a demand for respectability, now that it had the organs of the state close by. The large blue, silver-grey and brick cop shop, with its six towering silver tubes that supported the multi-pointed roof, resembled a new-style football stadium that had run out of money before completion, leaving only the frontage to intimidate all who had even the slightest doubt of their place in society.

And that included him. Jake knew that Gus would not yet have circulated the revoking of his Press credentials but Sir Nicholas obviously wanted him neutralized soonest. That fact alone put his name in the frame as suspect Number One.

The reception lobby was all glass, uncomfortable airport-type seats and quotes and slogans from various sources, all to do with the community and those who served it. It all smelled like a new car. A WPC was ensconced behind glass, with a small

191

hinged hatch at counter height. This was open but her demeanour was not encouraging; it spoke of all human weakness laid
out here, day and night, without cease, and she the main
recipient. But when he spoke she smiled and Jake was heartened. But he guessed this was automatic and would only alter –
if at all – once the nature of his visit was stated.

He tentatively requested a few minutes with Detective Inspector Reid. Although having no Missing Persons Unit as such,
Frank Reid had gained something of a reputation over the years
at locating those in the community who had inexplicably
disappeared, usually females. A reluctant minor celebrity, he'd
nevertheless attained a certain level of expertise in human
behavioural patterns under stress. Jake felt that his natural good
sense and lack of pretentiousness would make him more
approachable in a matter as delicate – and insubstantial – as
this.

The middle-aged woman glanced at him keenly. "Is it something official? Is there something you wish to report – a crime, a
complaint, sir?" Belatedly he fished out his credentials. Her
manner changed instantly. "I'm sorry, Mr…Ransome? You
know the policy." The policy was not to give *anything* to
reporters except through the official police 'spokesperson'.

"No, ma'am, it's something personal." He looked the woman
straight in the eye, amazed at his own audacity. "The DI's views
on it might just prevent me from making a fool of myself."

She relaxed slightly but continued watching him as she
phoned through. Then: "He can spare you a quick five, Mr
Ransome. Don't abuse it, he's up to his ears at the moment.
Through there, on the right"

Jake went down the passage, found the name plate, knocked
on the door and entered. The bent head, with its thin grey hair
brushed right back, didn't lift for a few moments. He initialled
two pages, closed the file and placed it on top of a thicker file to

his right. He straightened up, removed his dark-rimmed spectacles, pinched the bridge of his thin nose and smiled. Pale face, eyes the colour of his hair, deeply etched lines running down to a surprisingly well-sculpted mouth, he gave the impression of having seen it all and yet still believed in his fellow man. His colourless countenance belied a lively mind that of late was increasingly occupied with disappearing people – mainly young and usually located, if not returned.

"Well, young man, what can I do for you?"

Haltingly at first, Jake told the detective of his fears for Carolyn Draycott; how he'd met her and who her uncle was. At mention of Sir Nicholas, Reid's eyes widened.

"You say Sir Nicholas Brookes is up here and his niece should be in London but isn't – or rather, you can't confirm that she is?"

"I'm not sure about Sir Nicholas's current whereabouts but I assumed he was in the area. He's been in touch with the paper this morning -" He realized where he was taking the inspector and changed tack. "But then again…" He quickly ticked off the clues he had discovered in his flat.

Reid had a ready and plausible explanation for the mirror message and tights but at mention of the freshly drilled hole he paused. The young reporter was so intense and genuinely agitated but then, that too was par for the course. Imagination, by definition, tends to dwell on the worst possible construction of events. After a night of heavy sex and perhaps a little pot to heighten orgasmic nirvana he would have been less alert and reluctant to accept her furtive leave-taking. But that hole… His brow cleared.

"A TV aerial cable! The previous occupant had one in that room and you've never noticed it before. Why should you?" He stood up and came round the desk, taller than he at first appeared.

"The hole had just been drilled, sir, the filler not quite set, excess wood still caught in a spider's web." Jake was dogged. He knew it wouldn't be easy. "Besides, I've been there two years now and the previous tenant was an eighty-six year old bachelor, whose only concession to technology had been an electric kettle."

"But are we talking abduction here... conspiracy?" Reid spread his his arms. "Isn't it more likely she simply took off, sought some space, perhaps needing some time to think things through about your relationship? Believe me, son, it happens, only too often. Why don't you -"

"She was with me at Joan Winspear's last night," he blurted out. "I don't believe Joan's death was an accident and Carolyn's disappearance is somehow connected."

This rocked the inspector back a little. "You mean that old lady in the house fire? You were there?"

Jake quickly went through the gist of the evening's visit. Reid went back to his desk, the better to listen and study Jake. As the other's account of why he had been with the historian unfolded he relaxed somewhat but became more perplexed. He wasn't involved professionally in the poor lady's demise but had seen the morning report. Preliminary forensic evidence suggested it wasn't absolutely straightforward; both leg bones had been crushed beyond reasonable explanation and the condition of the burnt material around the body was inconsistent with the state of the corpse itself. He had remarked on the report's error in stating that everything but the hands had been totally consumed, whereas most of the chair she had presumably died on had not shown signs of scorching, much less charring. That was crazy. Now this garbled account of ley lines and mysterious black dogs... Maybe they'd started on the *drugs* before they'd gone visiting!

"Have you told anyone else about this...theory?" Reid asked gently.

"Anyone else...?" Jake stopped in mid-flow. "Well, apart from Carolyn and of course poor Joan, there's…" He was about to say "Gerry" but stopped in time. It was clear that he'd come on too strong with the inspector. He had to admit how ridiculous it could look from a non-participant's standpoint. Gerry wouldn't thank him for calling his sanity into question. It could spell professional suicide for him. "Look, sir, I realize how mad this could sound but believe me there are strange things out there we don't know about – perhaps shouldn't know about." He ran his hands through his curls distractedly and began to walk back and forth. "I just don't know how else I can convey the sense of danger I have over Carolyn Draycott. For a start she's not in the best of health and if they have carried her off -"

"They?" The inspector kept his voice neutral. "You know, young man, this is really the nub of the problem. I can see how concerned you are but have you honestly considered the most likely possibility? That she's had a change of heart – both with this job interview…and you?"

"Me?" Jake ceased his pacing. "Me?"

"If you'd both been on dope or drink then she may have viewed the morning with less joy than the night -"

"No!" He saw the reaction of the policeman and temporized. "No," he repeated more quietly but with great emphasis, even to the extent of leaning across the desk. "Please, Inspector, we hadn't been drinking or sniffing or shooting up. I've never tried the last two and I don't believe Carolyn has either. If anything I was careful to show my best side. I like this girl, like her a lot…perhaps more than I'd care to admit. We were not stoned in any sense of the word. What I said happened, happened. You've got to believe me." He banged the desk top. "Something evil is out there. Take this priest at St Michael's. He arrived and then Father Scanlon dies on the altar steps – listen!" Reid had attempted to interrupt. "Sarah Branthwaite died as a result of something that went on in there in the presence of Cappel. He said it was lightning striking the roof." He paused to get his breath. Then: "Inspector, lightning did not strike that roof, I checked. Furthermore, said priest came to the *Clarion* office in disguise yesterday and bought a dozen different photos of…guess who? Joan Winspear, that's who! Now why would a man of the cloth do that, just a few hours before she died. Another plausible theory, Inspector, hmm?"

Reid had gone red, but whether through anger or embarrassment he would have been hard pushed to say. *Could* something strange be going on? There had been two reports of giant black dog attacks. Received wisdom said released canines of suspect pedigree due to new legislation or, of course, hysteria. He would need to obtain more precise information. In the meantime there was this Jake here and his genuine concern for Brookes's ward. He started to speak but the young man had spotted the large detailed ordnance map on the far wall. He almost ran to it and after searching intently for several seconds turned to Reid.

"Joan accurately pointed out the current path of this dog's appearances, beginning with the church. Carolyn and I proved it last night on Eastby Moor – probably as Joan was dying in that horrible fashion." His eyes were grim. "Please come here, Inspector."

As though hypnotized, Reid did as bidden. "See here." Jake jabbed a finger. "And here – and here! These are all places where the dog has manifested itself and then vanished. If we take the church as the release point…Sarah Branthwaite. Recognise this one? Hayman's – formerly Hangman's – Cross, where the nun died." Reid started. "Anyone reported others…say here…and here? Well," he continued, not waiting for a reply, "I am going to make a prediction, Inspector, purely as an act of faith. Tonight – probably around midnight – the hound from hell will materialize…there!" He placed one finger on the laminated covering. Reid leaned forward, despite himself, drawn by the other's intensity. It didn't register for a moment, then he almost stammered. "But that's…"

"The airport! But what was there before the age of strip concrete? A standing stone in some farmer's field? Whatever, I sincerely hope it's not now the control tower – or worse, a section of runway…with a KLM flight for Alicante about to lift off. No pilot is trained to cope with a giant black dog leaping at him out of the night." Jake paused for breath, seeing the effect his words were having on Reid and went back to the desk; the detective walked to his chair and slowly sank onto it. Jake began to speak but the other put up a hand for silence while he considered.

"If – and I said if – even some of what you say is true then I have to concede an investigation will take time -"

"But that's just it, Inspector, we don't have any time!" Jake felt he was going mad with all this inaction, this battering against an impassive wall of bureaucratic process. "We have to find Carolyn and we have to somehow get that canine genie back in the bottle before the valley is flooded tomorrow."

"Flooded? Tomorrow?" Reid's brow wrinkled. "Why should it depend on the reservoir's inauguration?"

"Its home is in the vicinity of St Michael's. Water repels it. With the church submerged it could roam this whole countryside for ever, looking for its place of rest…and wreaking havoc every step of the way."

The detective shook his head as though to clear it, then said, "And just how do you propose to do that -?" The phone rang. He snatched it up with some relief. Jake turned away in frustration. Damn, damn! He had almost convinced the man, had seen the doubt fading from his eyes. He barely refrained from slamming his fist against the cream-and-silver striped wall. He turned at the familiar name.

"Yes, Sir Nicholas, of course I know who you are." Reid's tone wasn't so much unctuous as careful as he looked at Jake. "Ye-es, you say your ward has vanished…well, abduction is rather a strong charge at this stage – yes, yes, I do understand." Then: "Excuse me one moment, Sir Nicholas." He placed the phone against his chest. "Wait outside a moment, will you, Jake? Don't go away, this won't take long." He remained in that position until Jake slowly backed out of the room. As the door closed the dialogue inside resumed.

Wait outside…don't go away…wait outside…don't go away. The two commands beat at his brain as he stood in the corridor. Wait outside…don't go away. The friendliness had evaporated with the phone call. He'd lost it, goddammit, so close to achieving official acceptance and possible assistance and it had slipped away. No, snatched away by that bastard Brookes. It didn't take a genius to guess what was going on in there. Even a clever person might place a totally different construction on what he had just divulged. And Reid was just such a person, especially after talking to a dominant and persuasive manipulator like the press baron.

He almost ran down the passage, then restrained himself at the corner before turning into the reception suite. The WPC looked up from the little old lady who was protesting that, no, she didn't want counselling, she just wanted her 'bloody window box back'. She nodded at him, then reached for the phone as it rang. Jake saw her expression change as she listened, look startled, then at Jake as the latter broke into a trot.

But Jake was gone, off and running. He nimbly evaded two WPCs as they approached the entrance, smiling to allay their conditioned responses. Then he was across the paving, fiddling with his door and cursing the lack of central locking. Please start first time, he prayed as he made himself turn on the ignition in the usual way. It caught and he rammed it into gear. God, how many people scream away from a police station on two wheels and with the safety belt flapping? He kept glancing in the rear view mirror but his manoeuvres made clarity difficult. Thank heaven for police cutbacks, but that didn't necessarily mean there wasn't a call out for him right now. When Reid found out he'd go ape shit! Credibility zero, evidence ditto, chances of support? Forget it.

Carolyn, he thought. Where are you? Wherever you are I promise I'll find you.

He pressed his foot down as the traffic lights changed.

24: PUISSANCE

Brookes placed the tray gently on the ornamental side table in the corridor. He re-locked the heavy door that separated the upper storey of the condemned east wing from the rest of Brookefield Hall. He knew she would still be secure in her room but he was a meticulous man in some ways, a trait at variance with the more commonly held view that he was only interested in the broader issues and bottom lines.

He carried the tray to her door and carefully unlocked it, trying not to alert her. He could quite easily subdue any escape attempt but the ensuing violence – no matter how trivial or transitory – would spoil the mood he sought. The chloral hydrate in her orange juice would hasten the pre-hypnotic state as it always did. Animosity or aggression would not only prove counter-productive but downright disastrous. It was tonight or nothing – and nothing wasn't an option. He *must* be in London tomorrow; his reliable look-alike – with the camouflage of his usual minders – would not bear close or prolonged scrutiny whilst running interference for the media in the Midlands. But his reappearance had to coincide with the fade-out of his 'clone', and he had committed himself to Sunday, a slow news day. Even the paparazzi needed sleep and sex sometimes.

As he slipped inside he thought for one moment she had somehow managed to get away, then he heard the lavatory flush. He relaxed. Perfect timing, a good omen. "Oh!" She had emerged from behind the screen that hid the bathroom, having changed into some of her other clothes – denim skirt and dark blue sweatshirt, white trainers. "I didn't hear you come in." Her gaze went to the open door. Brookes almost chuckled at the transparency of her intentions.

"Come, Carolyn, you're not a prisoner," he murmured, putting the tray down. "At least not in the sense your overheated imagination might lead you to believe. This is all for your safety, really."

He straightened up as her shoulders went down slightly in submission. Good. She came over to the bedside table and sank onto the bed. She still hadn't recovered from the savagery of his outburst a few hours ago. The intervening period had provided time for her to re-assess her relationship with him. All the little things that over the years had seemed insignificant now took on a whole new meaning. The early years when he'd quite demonstrably loathed her presence – this pigtailed, teeth-braced encumbrance to his burgeoning business career. Sometimes she would visit him at his sumptuous town house in Belgravia, or at his mansion in Melksham, occasionally here. He always had elegant women in tow, most of whom regarded her presence with amused tolerance, some even courageous enough to poke sly fun at this, 'Uncle Nicky's' new and hitherto hidden side. This he usually accepted with ill-grace, grumpily asking if she had no riding lessons to occupy her, or friends to visit. There was always a chauffeur-driven car available.

But then his attitude towards her began to change. She had just returned from Switzerland, sixteen and already showing signs of a dark, intense beauty inherited from her mother. She had been robustly healthy then, into hockey, riding and swimming, had fallen in love once already, hopelessly, and predictably not quite over it when she'd spent the Easter weekend at Melksham. He'd had his latest mistress, one she was to see again and again over the years. Older than his usual stable, strikingly beautiful, with flame-red hair cascading onto bare shoulders; skin like alabaster, slanted green eyes and a

201

figure Carolyn would have died for then. At their first meeting Mrs Fenella Franklyn – or Voluptua as she would henceforth secretly think of her – had not reacted to her arrival in the familiar pattern. On introduction Carolyn felt herself under almost piercing scrutiny, then a series of pointed questions, delivered in a more relaxed manner, about her life to date. She remembered the particular interest in her recent romance, almost to the point of rudeness. Seeing her discomfiture Mrs Franklyn had changed tack to go on to more mundane matters, finally dismissing her as others invariably had done.

But from then on, she recollected, her uncle's manner had altered, a change only noticeable in retrospect. It started with invitations for her to remain in their company at parties past her usual 'banished to bed' hour. After the initial novelty of listening in on what powerful and successful people did at such affairs – shop talk of the stock market or gossip as to which married partner was currently cheating on whom – it all became stultifying to one more used to the outdoor life and the trivia of one in her teens. But then the party games crept in, the search for the most suitable hypnotic subject, all the peals of laughter, the ouija board game, the healing hands tests and demonstrations. She must have, if only gradually, noted the changing composition of her uncle's guest list; not so many old fogeys but a gratifying sprinkling of interesting men – albeit still in their middle years – who didn't totally deter a sexually awakening young miss, all still upwardly mobile in their chosen spheres. And some of their women – hardly ever their wives – were certainly not what she had been educated to believe were ladies in the accepted sense. She was eighteen by then and the strange malaise that was to plague her made its appearance. She would drink too much, fall ill and invariably waken next day dreadfully hung over and listless. Memory lapses were another symptom that worried her. She saw a succession of specialists but to no avail; she was sent to Switzerland again, this time as a convalescent, to a famous clinic where – on a controlled diet, alcoholic abstinence and plenty of rest – she recovered. On her return her uncle arranged for her to work in the City, presumably to learn some tricks of the money market trade. She went to no more parties for a while, she suspected because of a scandal around Melksham involving two local women, divorcees, found dead in a car, clasped in each others' arms. A post mortem revealed they had both died from heart attacks.

But then the parties resumed in Belgravia, much more digni-fied and select. She started being invited again, this time purportedly as an extended element in her marketing know-how. Unfortunately, her medical malaise re-surfaced too, this time without the alcohol. There was nothing organically wrong with her, she was re-assured, that a more leisurely lifestyle wouldn't put right.

It was here that she began to doubt his motives, as he had indicated a more than casual interest in her sex life. She could have answered him shortly that her sexual relationships were actually a mess, but instead told him it was none of his business, to which he responded by backing off hastily, merely muttering something about avuncular concern. Which brought her almost full circle, she reflected morosely.

"It seems you want me…intact in every respect, uncle, doesn't it?" Her chin lifted and she met his gaze, which for once he seemed loath to meet.

He laughed. "Oh, that…sorry, Carolyn. Perhaps I'm getting jealous in my old age. They say there's nothing worse than the company of a once dynamic person in decline. Not that I feel such a description fits me, mind!" He poured out the orange juice, tapped two tablets onto his palm and held them out. His matter-of-fact manner in what was a well-used routine made her automatically accept the medication that always followed one of her lapses. Tossing them back she gulped down the juice, almost gasping at the coldness of it. He grimaced. "Sorry, I know you dislike stuff straight from the fridge but Mrs Sykes has gone to some filling station for some provisions."

"Where's the doctor, then?" she asked dully, viewing the tray's contents. Scrambled eggs, wholemeal toast, bacon, two bananas, coffee.

"Oh, once your medical details were emailed from London he felt satisfied he could do no more than prescribe your usual pills. You will, naturally, be seeing Professor de Bono directly on your return."

"I'm not going anywhere until you explain about Jake." Her obdurate expression brooked no argument and he sighed.

"I had hoped to spare you this, Carolyn. We all make mistakes in our relationships." He laughed ruefully. "I ought to know, it's cost me millions for the lessons! But…" He slid the blue paper folder out from under the tray. She took it with numbed fingers. Inside were three sheets of A4 paper, giving in CV format the details of Jake Ransome's youth and adult life. From Borstal, paternity suit to broker fraud, it was all there. He'd drifted into acting, some provincial repertory and one small part in a TV holiday commercial. Between acting stints he had driven a mini-cab, been a stable hand and a summer guide for the ghost haunts of old London town. It all seemed so – so comprehensive. She leaned back against the padded headboard and felt reality slipping away from her.

Brookes watched her intently. The drug was working, her barriers crumbling. Good. It would not affect her latent powers. Soon he could aid her transition into the required state. He moved closer.

She heard the floorboards creak and opened her eyes; saw the white sheets of paper. Her gaze fell listlessly on the typewritten lines again and then stopped. Stable hand… Stable hand? But…?

"This can't be right!" She levelled the challenge at her uncle. He – caught in mid-stride – was non-plussed for a moment. Then: "What d'you mean, child?"

"This!" She waved the page at him, sitting up. "Jake could never have worked as a stable hand, he was – he is – absolutely terrified of horses."

"How could you poss -"

"This is all lies, isn't it?" She flung the papers from her and sprang from the bed, her eyes flashing angrily. "You've made the whole bloody thing up in order to keep me quiet, forget about him or poison whatever memories I have Well, whatever your game is it won't work." She easily evaded his outstretched grasp and ran to the open door.

Anger bubbled up inside him like bile. Damn, damn! Of all the luck… But he made himself wait patiently, already adapting to this new development. The mood he'd endeavoured to create was now hopelessly compromised. He listened as she rattled the passage door handle, followed by footsteps running past the bedroom door to the sealed-off window at the far end. A few moments of silence, then the sound of fists hammering ineffectually at the thick Perspex sheeting. More silence, then muffled sobs.

He walked slowly out into the passage and she was there, crouched in the corner, grimy and tear-stained. She slowly raised her head. "Why?" she whispered. "Why are you doing this?"

"Come," he said gently. "I wanted to protect you from this until you were more robust – physically as well as mentally. Unfortunately, events have overtaken my plans for you. It's time to grow up, Carolyn."

He led her back to the bedroom, where she allowed herself to be seated on the only straight-backed chair. He went to the old walnut wardrobe and unlocked the door that had defeated her in her preliminary search. Inside, the lower half housed an expensive sound system with shelves for CD, DVD and video storage. The upper section was occupied by a large plasma screen television set and combination recording facility. Her lack-lustre eyes followed his movements without interest. He turned back to her, noting her condition; his lips tightened. This was bad and it could get worse. The drug was reacting with her low physical condition, psychological resistance and hypertension. He would have to give her a booster and risk the circumstances. She took the pills like an automaton, a state she would have to be jerked out of quickly if she was to perform adequately.

"Carolyn...Carolyn!" She twitched. He took her chin in his hand and made her see him. "I have administered a very powerful drug, to which your system is accustomed. Your response will be as it always is – total obedience. But first I am going to show you something which should explain, if not satisfy, your curiosity concerning your mysterious medical condition." He saw a measure of focus creep back into her eyes, her neck muscles losing some of their tension. Slowly he released his hold on her jaw. She rubbed her lips with one hand.

"What – what d'you mean?"

"I mean, Carolyn, there is nothing really wrong with you that a cessation of certain – ah, activities wouldn't rectify."

"Activities? But Professor de Bono -"

"Is a senior adept of the Hermetic Seal of the Golden Dawn, and as such says whatever I tell him to say. Similarly with those other specialists attending you."

"I don't understand any of this, Uncle Nicky. Where is Jake Ransome...Mrs Sykes? Why are you keeping me here against my will?"

"You are here against your will, my child, because you refuse to join us, body and soul, thereby resisting a door I have been trying to hold open for you, a door that leads to unimaginable power and self-gratification. Something – a psychic guardian perhaps – is constantly between you and the acceptance of our terms. Until you do so freely and with conscious desire then your services to us must needs be controlled via your psyche. You have been a source of much pleasure to me and my group these last three years, only marred by your lack of appreciation of our cause." He left her and then walked around the room, collecting his thoughts. His bulk made the floorboards protest as he paced, hands plunged deep into his jacket side pockets.

Carolyn remained seated, compelled by his enigmatic remarks and the realization that there really was nowhere for her to run. She must gain time; Jake was out there somewhere and please God a free agent. If so he would be searching for her. He was no crook; she'd stake her life on it. She gulped – perhaps she was doing just that! Who else would come looking for her? Nicky was powerful; people would accept – if not believe – whatever he told them. She had gone backpacking in Thailand; she was a deck hand on an unstated sailing ship bound for the Caribbean, with appropriate postcards arriving from various ports of call. Or she had entered a Buddhist monastery to sort out her messed-up life How long before someone had the curiosity or courage to question him and backtrack her movements?

"There is nothing organically wrong with you, Carolyn. We are simply using your amazing psychic gifts to a degree very rarely experienced by mortals. In your case it is exacerbated by the aforementioned resistance. But – as the Americans say – you're the only game in town."

"Please, I still don't understand any of this. What d'you mean – psychic gifts?" She wrung her hands and wailed, "I have no knowledge -"

"Hah! Knowledge. There you have it, girl." He turned to her

triumphantly and stopped his pacing. His eyes searched her face for tell-tale signs of rising response to the booster. With Carolyn it was all roulette, part of her mystery. "You remember when you first met Fenella Franklyn?" She nodded dumbly. "It was she – bless her...no, curse her! – who perceived what my continued proximity had missed. She picked up your vibrations immediately. You may recollect that some of her questions on that first meeting were a bit confusing – even silly. Did you dream a lot, did you sometimes feel you knew what another person was thinking or about to say? Your views on death and sex. You were still a virgin and yet your aura was that of some-one a thousand years old! You have in you the reincarnation of at least four famous mystics and practitioners of the Ancient Wisdom. It cannot be pure chance you were chosen and placed in my care. There has to be a reason why our destinies are linked. I should have known, should have spotted it, but I was consumed with other, more material things." He shook his head "Missing you could have led to great punishment for me." He saw she was about to speak and went on: "But fate also inserted a wild card, a joker if you will, in your psyche. We still haven't isolated or even identified the counterbalancing psychic force from another age that has access to your personality. Whatever, I simply do not have the time right now to go down that path. You see, Carolyn, you are the perfect conduit – given the right rituals and preparation you can open the gates to almost every garden of delight in terms of pleasure, profit and procurement."

"You – you mean you have been using me to foretell the future?" She was aghast and yet involuntarily fascinated by the concept. Was he mad or merely fantasizing? He wasn't by nature a humorous man. But then, what did she actually know of his true nature? She only saw him infrequently and then in a public or formal situation. She never joked or drank or cried with him; he was always so remote.

"The popular misconception!" He laughed mirthlessly, as if to endorse her thoughts. "Nobody can really foretell the future, my girl, not on a controlled basis. Oh, yes, there are those who have prophetic dreams or can sometimes plug into a fold or warp in the time continuum and get a glimpse of events not yet within our present vision. But there is no detail, it's all so vague. An air disaster…soon! Some natural catastrophe like an earth-quake or flood, somewhere in the world, the assassination of a public figure – but no distinguishing features to zero in on. Only in retrospect can the medium tie the label to the event. Dreams, fragments, portents – pah!" He snapped his fingers in dismissal. "No, Carolyn, you are the gem who can switch channels into what is happening…now! A much more precise method, and practical. Because it's occurring at that moment, the right receiver can tune in, a fly – no, a camcorder! – on the wall. Can you appreciate the potential of that power in the right hands…in anybody's hands?" He didn't mention the fact that with the Judas Cup in his possession too he could perform his own psychic channel surfing, without anybody's knowledge or worry should something happen to her.

He noted her puzzled frown, came across and knelt down in front of her, hoping for some emergence of the drug's effect. "Look, girl." She tried to back away but the chair constrained her. "Look, in business, to know the opposition's strategies, in romance to point out whose spouse is disenchanted or casting an eye elsewhere. You can blackmail, exploit, manipu-late…there's no end to it!" He stood up.

"And I can do that?" Tears welled up in her eyes at the enormity of what he was saying and her part in it.

"Yes, but against your will, unfortunately, that damned inner defence. You were perfect once we'd overrode that brake to our progress. For that reason we had to have you placed in the proper state of readiness…and also remain a virgin."

"A – a virgin?" The dawning look was not lost on Brookes.

"Well, for one thing the psychic energies were considerably enhanced if you refrained from satisfying your otherwise normal healthy appetites."

"So that's why I can never go all the way," she said, almost to herself. "I couldn't figure it out but I knew it wasn't me. I mean, there were times -"

"I'm sure there were!" he boomed. "There must have been, you're a very beautiful young woman. It's a testament to my hypnotic powers that you resisted so well."

"How do I know any of this is true?" she countered. "I have no recollection of any of what you say. Maybe you're mad or you desire me for yourself. Is that it?"

"Believe me, I desired you a long time ago but as Fenella pointed out, killing the goose that was continually supplying the golden eggs was not only impractical but outside the spirit of the Golden Dawn. I sometimes had the devil – pardon me, Master! – the devil of a job restraining other members from doing likewise."

The lewdness in his tone made her cringe. "Why – why should they desire me because I am just revealing secrets to them? Wasn't I just sitting at a crystal ball or something?"

He laughed that laugh again, but this time it chilled her to the heart. "Like I said earlier, child, it's time you grew up. Perhaps, when you see what you are indeed capable of, your resistance will become compliance, thus making our group the most powerful in the western world. Carolyn Draycott…this is your life!" With a flourish he withdrew his right hand from his pocket and pointed the remote control at the TV set.

The screen flickered, went snowy for a few moments, then coloured into life. Carolyn wasn't sure what to expect and looked up at her uncle. She was beginning to feel unwell but he motioned her towards the TV set.

Reluctantly and with a sense of foreboding she did as bidden. The scene – taken from on high – showed a large room, with what seemed to be a seascape mural filling one far wall; a moonlit, wave-whipped sea that was strangely compelling in its use of greens and blues. The floor was black, uncarpeted, with peculiar geometric designs configured in silver on blue. Some kind of table took up a central position in the room, completely draped in deep red velvet.

The camera began to scan the room and she started; men and women ringed the perimeter, all facing inward and at first anonymous in their sky-blue robes. Then, as their faces came into focus, Carolyn's hand went to her throat. She recognized them as being members at that last party in Belgravia. Two men – if she remembered correctly one a high court judge and the other an Assistant Deputy Commissioner of the Metropolitan Police – stepped forward with a padded board some two metres long by one metre wide, placed it on the table and fixed it securely with some snap fasteners. She could plainly hear them click into position. Then two women – a fast-track barrister and a fashion editor – came into the picture, each carrying two very tall silver candlesticks with lighted candles. These they placed, one at each corner of the table, and then remained standing next to the first couple.

The room's lights began to dim until the only illumination was by the soft glow of the candles. This more natural light seemed to bring out features in the wall paintings she had not noticed before; the waves looked uncannily mobile and the fruits mouthwatering. The circle of people started a low chant whose words were inaudible to her.

"What are they doing, Uncle Nicky?" she whispered, wanting to avert her gaze but somehow unable to do so. She knew now that she was in some way connected with what was going on down there. But to what purpose?

211

"Preparing for the unveiling of the goddess, my child...you!"

"Me? But -"

"Sssh! Look."

A bell rang somewhere and – distorted at first – two figures emerged from below and came into camera range. The Carolyn gasped in recognition; even at that acute angle she saw that one was herself, and her uncle's bulk and shoulder-length hair was unmistakable. They were both robed like the others. Sitting on the chair in front of the TV set she drew her knees up to her chin, reverting to childhood as she did whenever threatened or frightened.

The quartet around the table took up new positions, went into what appeared to be a well-rehearsed routine. While one traced a large circle on the floor with the point of a sword, others did the same with what looked like incense, then sprinkling water.

Her uncle spoke: "The circle has been made secure, the Guardians of the Watchtowers invoked. I am the Lodge Master, you see me now making the Cabalistic Cross" – he was touching his forehead, navel and both nipples before joining his palms in front of his face – "and say, To thee the Kingdom, the Power and the Glory for ever." He turned again and went to the head of the table, between the two women. "Who will offer herself as the path to the gate of vision?"

The other Carolyn – for only as such could she envisage herself – answered in a voice full of vibrancy and confidence, "I will."

"Then be thou our path."

The filmed Sir Nicholas leaned back and pressed something. Instantly music – wild and primitive – filled the room, sending a ripple of anticipation throughout the gathering of robed figures. But it was Carolyn in the centre who responded. With a simple, practised movement she unclipped her robe, allowing it to slip

212

from her shoulders. The watching Carolyn gasped at the picture of herself; completely nude, perfectly still, breasts pointed and proud, trim waist and swelling thighs, her skin glowing in the candles' soft light. She felt strangely voyeuristic, possibly because of the others' reactions to her nudity. Some of the younger ones were clearly affected by the sight, a few swaying forward as though physically drawn to her.

"A woman made for love." It was her uncle, beside her, whispering to himself. It broke the spell; Carolyn tried to get up, intent on switching it off, in mortal fear of what might follow. But he instinctively reacted, clamping one hand on her shoulder.

"No! Stay. You do yourself a disservice by trying to deny your chosen destiny."

"Chosen? By whom? You and your filthy friends! Let me go!" She twisted away from him but he grabbed her head with both hands and forced her to face the revelation that was unfolding.

Her filmed image smiled, took a step forward and commenced to gyrate in time to the now frenzied music, leaping and whirling with an energy she wouldn't have believed herself capable of. Moving clockwise she circled the floor within the wall of watchers. Faster and faster she danced as the drums, cymbals and flutes carried her on, bounding into the air with fierce abandon, her hair flying about her face, her firms breasts bouncing. And as she rose and dipped with the jungle rhythm her passing made the candles flicker and writhe also, so that a veritable troupe of shadows competed with her efforts on all four walls.

But soon the pace began to tell, her tortured rasps of indrawn air rising even above the wild tempo as she passed the camera. The music became wilder still, rising and quickening, the charged atmosphere of the room infecting all, almost tangible to the real Carolyn, compelled to witness it all.

A crescendo was fast approaching and her filmed self, pounding the floor, twirled faster and faster as the drums rattled and the brass section held the notes at an almost unbelievable pitch. Rivulets of sweat poured down her breasts and thighs, her dark hair slicked with it, as she somehow kept up with the music. But the strain was beginning to show; no longer that expression of pure ecstasy that began it. Mouth gaping she now strove desperately to match the tempo, still somehow managing to leap and twist as the music at last reached a fever pitch and then suddenly stopped. The dancer faltered, stumbled and almost fell with the impetus of her stride, but the two men at the table sprang forward and held her at the armpits and waist. She slumped and the attendants had to be assisted by the two women as her weight sagged. Her head flopped to one side and it was only with great difficulty that her limp and sweat-streaked form was laid on the padded board. Her eyes closed, only a slight flicker indicating some inner activity. Her limbs were arranged as she lay on her back; arms by her side, palms upward, the soles of her feet pointed inward, her knees parted to expose her sex to the camera's lens.

The Lodge Master faced the seascape and raising his arms intoned, "Powers of Malkuth, be beneath my left foot and within my right hand. Hod and Netsah touch my shoulders…"

As he droned on her uncle said, "I am invoking the shining powers, Carolyn, from the earth up towards the infinite." He was looking down at her. She had gone pale and yet her cheeks were burning as her gaze was drawn back to the TV screen. Brookes smiled knowingly and placed a gentle hand on her shoulder. This time she didn't flinch.

Her other – filmed – uncle was still intoning. "…blessed Queen of Heaven, whose ebbs and flows control the rhythm of our bodies, whether you are pleased to be known as Ceres, Harvest Mother, or Artemis, the healer or as celestial Venus, who couples the sexes in mutual love." He must have touched a switch by the table, for a pure lilting female voice rose, like a lark on still air, filling the room with an almost fragrant tonal reverence, rising and falling, a hymn to agape love. The women, placed at the unresisting Carolyn's feet, gripped her ankles firmly while the two men further up proceeded to stroke and fondle her shoulders and breasts, deftly smoothing and squeezing, her still-damp skin greatly aiding the process. Brookes moved to her mid-section and ran one pale white hand across her belly, whilst the other one slid down between her thighs.

On some given cue the camera zoomed in and the watching Carolyn gasped at the close-up view of her most private parts. Slowly the slick and clammy appearance of her skin faded, to be replaced by a warm glow as the stimulation reached her inner psyche. A soft flush seeped downward from her cheeks to suffuse neck and breasts, the latter beginning to firm up even more than they already were, as they rose and fell rhythmically, the yielding flesh of her stomach and inner thighs starting to tremble. Her thighs instinctively attempted to spread in order to accommodate Brookes's searching fingers. Watching, Carolyn moaned with the shame of it. Her uncle chided her gently. "You are not sinning, child, merely responding as a young healthy woman should. Believe me, you are not the first but you are the best." He sighed. "A woman made for love. What we are doing is sexually charging you, like a car battery, if you will, your loins storing energy for a specific purpose." He squeezed her shoulder again. "No, not for the sex act. Indeed, the whole ceremony will be counted a failure should you achieve orgasmic release."

The hands about her nipples, thighs and pubis relaxed their ministrations for a few moments, enabling the four to observe their charge's state. Her level of arousal was now obvious to all those grouped about her, her hands fluttering and gripping the red velvet material as they strove to free themselves from her captors' hold.

Her servers recommenced their task, more a duty of love, now evidenced by the renewed massage, purposely designed to maintain but not increase her high peak of stimulation. Her limbs were now shaking so violently as to make their efforts to restrain her nearly impossible; her hands kept trying to reach down to bring about some welcome release. The women were clearly stronger than they looked; whilst thwarting Carolyn's needs they continued gently to fondle and stroke her erogenous zones. Brookes greatly aided this process, his area of responsibility being the most critical. Their prisoner-victim had reached new heights of awareness, her subconscious psyche having to come to terms with the terrible conflict raging inside and outside her body. The earlier small gasps forced from her by the stimulus were now magnified into cries of painful pleasure, palpable pleas to her tormentors, growing stronger as her body squirmed and bucked into long, wave-like convulsions. Cries of sheer ecstasy were wrung from her corded throat.

Sensing the time was right her uncle raised his head and in a deep, resounding voice said, "She shall appear in the sky; she shall be side by side with the gods of the stars; she shall have a place in the boat of the sun…it is so written."

He then began to stroke her again, ever-so gently. Her real-life uncle, watching the video, explained it thus: "There are six important centres of life energy in the human body. We call them lotuses or buds, capable of blossoming into an altered state of consciousness. These flowers of awakening are classified by colour and petal variety, just as with nature itself. My expert stimulus is now channelling this potent sexual energy upwards towards your navel – blue with ten petals – and on to your heart level, where you will now be feeling the lotus blossom inside you with a twelve golden petal radiation."

And indeed she saw that her other body was no longer thrumming as though to some inner instrument; sensation had passed, to be replaced by a perfectly tuned metabolism, with glowing skin and a musculature taut and ready for whatever might be asked of it.

"The energy is now moving to your throat, Carolyn," he said quietly, not wishing to disturb the mood being projected. He glanced down; she was rapt, lost in wonder at the transformation wrought in the body that was hers. She had no memory of the sensations he was describing but then, why should she? If she was on a different plane – and it was obvious that currently this was so – it might just as well be happening to a stranger.

"And this is why I was never allowed to submit to a man in the normal way, when I desperately wanted to sometimes?" She was looking up at him, eyes glistening, imagining all the lost love she might have known in her few brief years of sexual awakening. "What other reasons?"

He looked blank for a moment.

"You said, 'Well, for one thing…' back there."

"Oh…no, child," he said softly, placing a hand on her head like some form of benediction. "It was significant, perhaps, but not the most important. It would have made you more difficult to restrain certainly, your pre-orgasmic spasms more violent, triggered by experiential memory. But no, sadly the reason is more mundane, sordid even…a product of the times we live in. We simply couldn't risk our star sensitive exposing herself to any sexually transmitted disease. Any suspicion of AIDS, even HIV positive, would have been sheer anathema to a group such as ours. Nothing moral, you see, purely a matter of hygiene."

She was about to speak, shocked – even disgusted – by what he said, when he raised his hand. "Look now, the energy is passing up to your throat, where you will be sensing the bud of the purple lotus with the sixteen petals, passing upwards to the final centre, the sixth, between your eyebrows, where you will visualize the opening of a pure white lotus with two petals.

217

Inside, you will be experiencing the sound of gentle gongs, signalling the approach of stillness. You will – as I have instructed – hold that point as it swells to a pearl of thought, like some intangible bubble, growing larger…ever larger."

She watched her televised uncle slowly draw his hands away from her brow and indeed she did appear as one transfigured, an expression of utter peace and tranquillity flooding her beautiful features. Her breathing became deep and regular, a body in repose, no longer racked by sexual storms; having crossed a psychic threshold and entered a world few have ever experienced, much less remembered.

"Many have attempted this ritual, Carolyn, even reaching various levels of success before having to abort. Some – men too – have known ecstasy and the mounting excitement promised by expert stimulation. The adepts who pass through the gate of vision and survive give sterling service to we lesser mortals. You are a vessel of our desires, child, and we cherish you. You see, Carolyn, every last scrap of life energy is needed to open that door, allowing others to pass through. You are the best, the purest. Watch!"

Brookes stepped away from his recumbent ward and the women released their hold on her ankles. Immediately she sat up with all the grace and fluid movements of a ballet dancer – legs crossed in the classic yoga lotus position. Her eyes, bright and clear, stared ahead, the rest of her body in complete repose. Her watching self felt strangely narcissistic, taking in the beauty that was hers. For she was beautiful, breathtakingly so. But it was a beauty owed in no small measure to an almost aura-like glow that emanated from her. She exuded good health. Now she understood why her day-to-day vitality was always below par – it was all being used up in these…these rituals. She had a sudden revulsion then, in this vision of herself, brought from an animalistic, lustful creature, thrusting her open sex at the nearest object for gratification, to this – a serene example of wholesome, compliant womanhood. Who *were* these people, that they could do such things?

One of the men – the Assistant Deputy Commissioner – came forward and stood in front of Carolyn, where she waited calmly to act as a visionary conduit to others' worlds.

"Do you see something, Carolyn?"

"I see what there is," she replied in a loud voice, her large, lustrous eyes seeming to stare right through the man.

"Open the gateway to my world, Carolyn."

The goddess of the lifted veil said nothing for several long moments. My God, thought her watching self, she's – I am! – like some psychic computer, trawling through people's minds, seeking access.

Then: "The face is sly, a friend is too. Someone is seeking to undermine you."

"What?" The grey-haired, military-looking man straightened his back. "Someone close, you say? In the force, you mean…to do with my new appointment?"

"The mountain can bring you terrible woe. To avoid *dis*appointment strike hard the first blow." No flicker of emotion, she spoke like an automaton.

"Mountain?" The man half-turned to the Lodge Master. "Oh…Sir Henry Mountain! Of course, he's supposed to be sponsoring me. You mean…he will renege? Disappointment…yes, I see. How do I counter this threat to my career then?"

"The solution's more data, his old alma mater."

"Alma…? You mean there's something he did whilst at school…?" He glanced again at Brookes and was about to continue but the Lodge Master indicated his time was at an end by motioning him back. The man bowed to Carolyn and retreated into the group.

The old judge was next; he stopped, seemed to sway as her eyes swept through and past him. But then he stiffened at her uncle's audible impatience.

"How-how can you help me, Carolyn?"

"Friends all adore you, children much more. Therein lies the danger, outside your door."

"Children...danger? Why – I..."

"Your sickness is known, exposure draws near. Fate is unbending, choose you not to hear."

The old man trembled, bowed his head, but not in gratitude. Her uncle moved forward and murmured something in his ear; the latter nodded and stumbled away.

Her uncle flicked the remote and the sound faded. He looked down at her. "That should suffice for now, Carolyn, to illustrate your unique qualities, not to mention your stunning physical attributes."

"Have I...have I been with...?" She couldn't bring herself to say it.

"With me? Them?" He glanced down at her again and smiled. But she was not reassured. "You mean did it all end in a bout of orgiastic sex and perversion? Is that what you want to see? Shall I fast-forward -"

"No!" She shrank away. "No."

"Compose yourself, child, did I not say you were a virgin? Here, you are distraught; this has all been a bit too much for you. I misjudged the timing of our...little private screening. I'm sorry, here, have some coffee." He quickly poured it for her and handed the coffee across. She gulped it without thinking and it seemed to do some good. She closed her eyes in an effort to make some of the recent images go away. In so doing she failed to see her uncle's secret smile. She was taking the chloral hydrate in the coffee too. He had never put so much of the hypnotic preparation into her before – the need had never been so great. Heaven – sorry, hell! – knows what she would be good for after he'd wrung her dry but once he'd confirmed the location of the chalice it wouldn't matter all that much. And after all, did he really need her alive – the one remaining member of that family on which his vast financial empire was based?

He leaned over her. "Carolyn," he whispered silkily. "I need your help. After this you really can join your Jake. I promise this sincerely, on your mother's grave. Look at me, Carolyn. I command you, child, just one more time…"

Against her will Carolyn's head came up.

25: NEUROSCIENCE

Jake wasn't sure how long he drove around; up Linthorpe Road, towards Stockton, back through Thornaby. The sky was lowering, heavy and overcast, and it soon began to rain. Traffic and turnings became a blur of lights and street signs wavering through his partially wiped windscreen. Somewhere along Corporation Road he realized he was heading back towards possible recognition and veered off again. He was no good at subterfuge but he knew he would have to develop new skills – and fast. She was out there and in trouble of some kind, he could *feel* it. He pulled into the car park of a pub near Yarm. Surprisingly for a Saturday afternoon there was nobody in the bar. He ordered a half of Everards and asked about a payphone, saying his mobile was off charge. The dour landlord jerked a thumb towards the side entrance passage.

Gerry answered almost instantly, lowering his voice conspiratorially when he recognized the speaker.

"Hey, Jake, where the hell are you?" He quickly corrected himself. "Don't tell me, I don't want to know! I might break under torture; you know how I can't stand pain…or worse – withholding my daily beer intake."

"All right, Gerry." Jake was weary, the tension draining out of him now, with no rear view mirror to stare into, leaving a sense of loss and hopelessness in its wake. He sipped absentmindedly at his beer. Gerry picked up the sound.

"Is thou suppin' ale, lad?" he asked incredulously. "Here's half of Cleveland Constabulary beating the bushes for you, senior officers recalled from sabbaticals in Spain, mistresses left in mid-lie, local footie derby at the mercy of supporters, et cetera, and you're calmly ensconced in some hostelry with a pint -"

"Half."

"Pardon?"

"I said half, Gerry, not a pint."

"Gawd, you must be in trouble, lad, you need counselling. Suppin' halves…or have they already got you and this is part of the torture -"

"Enough! I'm sorry, Gerry, but no jokes, please. All right?"

"Okay, sorry, Jake, sensitivity never was my strong suit. I guess that's why I'm so good at this job - luckily for you."

"What?" Jake perked up. "You mean you've got something for me?"

"Something, kiddo, you decide whether it's good or bad. Firstly, usually reliable sources inform me that you-know-who's personal jet left our friendly local airport this morning. Kemo sabe?"

"Oh shit!" His spirits sank at the implications.

"Still there?"

"Sorry, Gerry, just mulling over the options."

"Not a lot, as our home-grown magician used to say." Jake grunted.. "Cheer up. Source said no female was reported in the departing party, just himself and assorted lowbrows humping luggage. Not conclusive but…"

"Oh, well, that's something; we could still be in the race. I have a plan of sorts but it needs a few holes plugged before it will float. Anything else?"

"Yes, your Dragon Project. It seems it does exist. Our boy Gordon came up with a semi-expert – is that possible? – on the subject, right here in our fair metropolis. Name of…" – there was a rustling of paper – "Professor Leonard Dolgun." He spelt it out. "Lectures in physics at the university here. Gordon knows him through his column, has asked his advice several times. Says

223

he's very approachable, if a little odd about his pet subject, which is sound, apparently."

"Sound?" Jake tried to assimilate this whilst pondering his main concern.

"So he says." Jake could easily visualize his friend giving that familiar dropped-shoulder shrug, a quirk he'd unconsciously picked up from watching too many repeats of Robert Redford in 'Butch Cassidy and the Sundance Kid', just before they'd jumped off the cliff. "He's arranged for you to see him…or at least he did, before the Crimewatch bulletin went out."

"Crimewatch!" Jake was aghast until he realized it was a wind-up. "Bastard! When am I due to see him – and where?" He put some more coins in the phone, his own phone switched off for fear of superior police technology. He shook his head, finished the last of the beer and pushed through to the bar. The big old clock whose face advertised a long-gone farm seed company registered 4.06. He would have time to get something down on paper for Gerry, in case the worst happened. The landlord was eyeing the TV gloomily whilst pretending to polish an empty tankard.

Jake nodded at the beer pump and shoved his glass across the counter. "And do you have a sheet of paper I could use, please? I need to leave a message for someone."

"Aye, lad, one pund twenty-five for ale, ten for paper."

Jake sighed; some things never changed.

The house was imposing, like a former vicarage, with an untended garden, in Cambridge Road. High roofed, narrow windows with stained-glass panels, some of the brickwork facing north beginning to crumble. A porch in similar style but greater need of repair shielded the heavy oak door. As he reached up to use the small gargoyle brass knocker he saw the door was ajar.

He hesitated for a moment before knocking. Immediately a deep voice from somewhere within bade him enter. He did so, pushing the door shut with some difficulty. Inside it was almost dark; relying on the day's fading sunshine through the coloured glass. A long passage, with several closed doors leading off it, except for the one at the far end. A ribbon of light there encouraged him to knock on the door jamb and peer through the opening.

It was a large room. Seated at a cluttered desk was a vigorous-looking middle-aged man. High forehead with grey wings of hair accentuating the prominent cheekbones. He looked up. The rimless glasses didn't quite hide the piercing gaze.

"Yes? Gordon's colleague, is it?"

"That's right. Jake Ransome. We spoke on the phone, Professor Dolgun. I'm sorry for the intrusion -"

"That's perfectly all right. Come on in. Won't keep you long."

Jake smiled tentatively and approached the desk. The room appeared to be a study-cum-laboratory; two walls taken up with work benches and racks of electronic equipment – oscilloscopes, calibration consoles, external power supplies, two laptops. The third wall was an extensive library of books, videos, DVDs and audio tape cassettes, floor to ceiling.

The lecturer was watching him, seeming to read his mind. Jake coloured. "Quite a set up you have here, sir."

"Yes, I am extremely fortunate in being paid handsomely to drone on about something that is now almost a consuming passion."

"What-what is your particular field, Professor?"

"I have been many things - doctor of medicine, psychiatrist, mathematician and biophysicist. But these have now condensed into one absorbing task…well, quest really. Before I die I intend to write the definitive thesis on the nature of sound in Man's existence – from his first awareness of a mother's heart beat in the womb to the handful of soil tossed onto his coffin…and beyond."

"B-beyond?" Jake stared. "I don't understand, sir."

The scientist laughed gently and stood up. He *was* tall, with no hint of a scholarly stoop. The wrists poking out of his checkered shirt cuffs were muscular, the hands large and bony. He reached across the desk and switched on a small recorder.

"Perhaps later. First I think you should tell me what it is you want of me. How can I help? Sit down, please, and speak." He indicated a dilapidated captain's chair and resumed his seat. "Ignore the recorder, it's merely for reference and you can delete or take it away with you later if you wish. Please…sit."

Jake complied slowly, instinctively slipping into the other's calm manner; his personality was one of such command that he felt protected somehow, safe within these walls. "I–I would like you to tell me something about the Dragon Project."

"The Dragon Project? Oh, yes, Gordon mentioned your interest there. Stated simply it's not nearly as mysterious or romantic as its title suggests. A few decades ago a bat expert was returning after a night vigil. Passing a group of megalithic standing stones his portable ultrasonic monitor suddenly began registering a regular pulse. Surprised he swept the area but could find no explanation for it. Then the sun came up and the signal faded, disappearing altogether. Puzzled, he left the scene, unsure if indeed he had witnessed anything.

"A chance meeting with a writer in so-called earth energies made him recall the incident. The writer passed the titbit to a group of other scientists, who were working on the Dragon Project. This group had been actively engaged in trying to determine the full nature of the stone circles, megaliths, dolmens, et cetera, that figured so large in earlier civilizations.

"Encouraged by the bat man's clue, they built a wide-band and extremely sensitive ultrasonic detector. It was field tested for the first time on the Rollright Stones in 1978 -"

He stopped as Jake twitched but continued as the young man waved him on.

"They filtered out local radio, grid power lines, geological fault lines and so forth. Basically, the Rollrights radiated a consistent pulse just before dawn on any given day. This only varied at two specific times, the mornings of the March and September equinoxes, when the signal went into sonic overdrive and lasted for several hours." He paused and reached for a bottle of spring water, poured some, looked at Jake, who shook his head. "There are records of equinoctial rites being held at Rollright even in prehistoric times."

"You mean the two times of the year when day and night are of equal length?" Jake was desperately trying to make some sense of what he was being told.

"Exactly, of considerable importance to the people who lived then and believed in the sun and moon's influence on their lives. You see, Jake, prehistoric communities were not merely pastoral; their feet was of necessity planted firmly on the ground, certainly, but their vision...ah, their thoughts were up there among the stars. They had macro-chip technology. After all, they had the whole universe as a template!

"But at Rollright the Dragon group made a breakthrough. They progressed from ultrasonic to radioactivity; using a Geiger counter they mapped out a pattern of radiation that altered, depending on the time of day or night. They encountered 'cold spots' of unusually low radiation around Kingstone -"

"I'm sorry... Kingstone?"

"An isolated menhir in the group. Then there were hot spots of flaring beta-radiation in certain areas of the stone circle, in some cases so high as to exceed that of a radioactive isotope."

Jake felt he had to intervene. "I'm sorry, Professor Dolgun, I don't wish to appear rude but I feel this is all getting a bit over my head." He laughed nervously. "Science was never my strong point at school, I'm afraid. That's why I'm doing what I'm doing now, I suppose."

The scientist was not upset; he smiled and sipped some more water. "The evidence seemed to suggest that the siting of these stones was neither arbitrary nor haphazard. The natural field of energies that comprises our universe were not only known to ancients but manipulated by them. The arrangement of the stones somehow shields whatever is inside the circles from cosmic radiation bombardment…and whatever else is out there." He pointed a finger. "This shelter extended not only within the physical constraints of the stone barrier but above it. A canopy, invisible but powerful. Our ancestors were no dummies; they somehow conceived, designed and built what were in effect Stone Age Faraday Cages."

"But why, Professor?"

"Ah, the big one!" He stood up and began a slow walk of the room, stopping from time to time to touch a dial or fiddle with a pair of leads. "People have made and lost reputations speculating and writing about that. A form of religion? A space message? Some kind of magic devised by tribal whiz kids to delude and control the natives? All we know for sure is that it all happened three to five millennia ago. They link up with similar sites across Europe and Ireland. But their science is still very much of an enigma to us." He turned to face Jake, almost looming over him, his back to the window in the rapidly fading light. "Is there anything else you want to know, young man?"

"Well, er, yes, if you don't mind, sir." Jake looked up at the not unkind but nevertheless strange face. "I don't see the connection with dragons." He shrugged at his own ignorance.

Dolgun threw back his head and laughed, startling Jake. He went back to his chair and sat down, still chuckling. He leant across and switched on the desk lamp. The effect was somehow cosier, reassuring, revealing more of the scientist's eyes; they were light grey.

"I'm sorry, my boy, I got carried away by my own oratory, an occupational hazard with lecturers, I'm afraid." He leaned back. "Why Dragon Project? Well, it's a term from Chinese geomancy to indicate the active elements that are accepted as being an integral part of their landscape."

"I'm sorry, sir, did you say…geomancy?"

"Yes, a name given to the study of earth energies, leys -"

"Leys! D'you mean ley lines?"

"Yes, why?" Dolgun looked keenly at Jake. "Is that really why you came to see me, Jake?"

"I don't know what you mean -"

"Look, young man, don't treat me like some decrepit old fart who spends his waning years all wrapped up in his own obscure little world." The eyes glinted dangerously behind the glasses. "I know a great deal about your world too. You arranged to come here rather than meet me at my place of work, unusual for a reporter researching an article, don't you think?"

Jake tried to speak but an imperiously raised hand stopped him.

"When you do arrive you are devoid of tape recorder or notebook – indicating negligence, duplicity or great stress. Another hobby is this scanner, permanently tuned to local police frequencies." He paused to let this sink in; Jake's face changed colour. "Would you like to tell me who Carolyn Draycott is?"

Jake sat stunned. His mouth tried to work but nothing came out. "Mr Ransome, if you did have something to do with this young lady's disappearance it could be for a few very obvious reasons, but none of them would bring you here today, would they?" His tone was gently chiding. "Come now, we have most of the evening ahead of us, and believe me, I'm neutral." He sat back, obviously prepared to be patient.

Haltingly at first but with increasing confidence Jake poured out his miserable tale, only holding back the true extent of his

229

feelings for Carolyn. Dolgun was silent throughout the whole twenty minutes, only evincing surprise at mention of the Barguest and Joan's death.

He was so lost in despair at his own failure to influence this growing catalogue of events that it was only Dolgun's reassuring hand on his shoulder that registered the end of his story He looked up, trying to conceal the very real torment he felt.

"Can you help me, Professor, in any way at all? Should I go up to Brookefield Hall, even though he's probably taken her back to London with him? And what of the Barguest? Was Joan right to say its continued freedom was a threat to us all?"

For long seconds Dolgun said nothing, then: "First, let me commend you on your candour, Jake. Your story is a strange one. I have heard stranger but not in this country, and certainly not from one so young. The fact that you also say *who* you are counts in your favour." He paused and smiled gently. "Perhaps the spirit of Joan is looking after you in sending you to me."

Jake stared at him, unable to speak. The calm grey eyes regarded him coolly. Somewhere extremely distant the faint wail of a police siren broke the spell. "Maybe I should leave, sir, and thank you for at least hearing me out. All I ask is that you allow me five minutes start before you inform the police of my visit."

"I don't know if I can help you, young man," he replied quietly. "But my services and experience are at your disposal. I knew Joan Winspear only slightly but I was aware of her historical work and passion for this area. As I see it there are two separate problems. First, there are all those things that seem to flow from the church and its impending submergence. Secondly, the seemingly different situation concerning Miss Draycott. Both elements have a dangerous aspect, one physical and real, the other of a more…umm, esoteric nature. Let's take the second first, if I may. Sir Nicholas Brookes is potentially a very dangerous man. He knows how far to go with his writs, injunctions and so forth, how to destroy at a distance with one phone call or email.

"But the rarefied atmosphere in which he now operates could be his Achille's heel here. If he has had Carolyn abducted then he may feel obliged to come down to ground level, where those with long memories are waiting. This isn't big city life here, he will have to take certain risks, maybe even improvise. That means possible mistakes under pressure. So yes, go to Brookefield Hall. If they are not there he may have left some clues. But if nothing comes of it you must seriously consider resorting to the police for assistance. That has to be Plan A. Right?"

Jake nodded; the professor had already crystallized what he had more or less decided. But it was uplifting to hear it voiced so authoritatively.

"While you are doing that I will apply myself to the other, more elusive, question." He stood up suddenly and went to the bookcase lining the doorway wall. After a few moments' search he selected a magazine from a pile and returned to the desk. He flicked through the pages, found what he wanted and grunted. He removed his glasses and pressed the bridge of his nose for a few seconds.

"Your surveyor friend's experience, the church priest and Joan's theory are all connected, and to my mind valid. Father Cappel's need for several likenesses of Joan just prior to her death suggests to me…" He shook his head. "No, I'm going too fast here. But I do know what she was referring to with the Dragon Project. The term dragon has come down to us by an extremely circuitous route, undergoing many changes in different cultures. It's actually from the Greek for serpent – draconis. A loved and respected creature in pre-history and mythology, only later reviled by religion to eliminate it as a rival to new philosophies."

"You mean the Garden of Eden?"

"Yes. In early cultures the serpent symbolized the flow of energies, the same energies we were discussing just now and what we refer to as ley lines. Early stone carvings depict spirals – the coiled sleeping serpent – and zigzags, or serpent in motion. Through time the serpent became a somewhat different entity, folklore granting it horns, wings, crested, and finally our full-blown flying, fire-breathing target for roaming knights with more than time to kill."

"But why or how did this happen?" Despite himself and the urge to get out and drive to Brookefield Hall he still had some pieces of the other puzzle to fit into place.

Dolgun laughed briefly. "Our old friend Christianity will ultimately be found guilty there. Megalithic man's powers were still very much in evidence two thousand years ago. There were sacred sites, revered and handed down through the generations. Organised religion failed to subvert Man's inherent pagan beliefs. So…if you can't fight 'em, fool 'em. Get the pagans to join the Christians without too much conflict of interest. We all now know that Jesus Christ was was not born on December twenty-fifth. But this particular time fell in with a very significant pagan festival. Earth energy sites were obvious places on which to erect churches, tried and tested as they were by the local -"

"But they can't have built churches on every single place of convergence -" Jake stopped, realizing he was instinctively using one of Joan's phrases.

"Exactly! Those places proscribed as being outside their areas of interest had to be tainted in some way, vilified and condemned as places of the devil. That's why there are so many earthworks and long burial barrows with devil prefixes – Devil's Ditch, Devil's Bed…ditto Basin, Den, Ring, et cetera. The hitherto accepted natural forces quite literally driven underground. But those shrewd ancient psychologists went one step further. Recognising Man's great need for symbolism in a largely illiterate society the early church iconography depicts the slaying of the serpent stroke dragon, i.e., the old practices, by the new conqueror – Holy Church. Saint George is the Christian form neutralizing megalithic man's very real powers."

"But where is all this leading, sir?" protested Jake, the light at the end of the tunnel now assuming the proportions of an oncoming express train.

"Right, to cases! Our body is a microcosm of our planet; just as our human system has an inner protected core and several layers of shielding skin, so too this Earth…even to the pressure vents! And as with the human chakras or acupuncture points, the globe possesses a nodal equivalent, where vortices of multi-dimensional forces exist. These are capable of stimulation by ritualistic techniques, places where the spiritual influences which literally underlie our physical world came into being. Now one of the main properties of certain earth chakras is that they can be activated and channelled by a particular sound frequency. As you are no doubt aware from your own school days, all matter has its own unique resonant frequency, the critical point at which its very molecular formation can be altered."

"You mean like those bridges that we see on television break-ing up from earthquake vibrations?"

"Yes, exactly. Given the right amount of rhythmic oscillation such structures can be made to resonate, sway and eventually pull themselves apart."

"So how does this tie in with earth energies, and more par-ticularly, black dogs?"

"Well, I have my own theories on that, Jake, a bit extreme for some of my colleagues to accept. They have yet to be tested in the field. Perhaps this is as good a time as any to start. I come from Poland, brought up near a place called Grzybnica, among the northern forests. We too have our stone circles and as a child I was personally affected when inside and around them. Perhaps I was over-sensitive, for nobody else in our family could feel the same buzzing as I approached and then this complete absence of any external sound once within their confines. This triggered my initial interest in the subject. Accounts from early western travellers over a hundred years ago in Tibet tell of the combined tonal cadence of monks moving heavy stones. Polynesian fishermen charming schools of dolphins up onto beaches with a certain chant, and so on."

"But -"

"I know, I know." Dolgun put up a hand. "I am digressing although not as much as you may think. I have compiled over the years a library of recordings that is probably unique. Just about every human, animal and plant sound ever emitted is there. Even so-called inanimate objects have their means of registering on the frequency or decibel scale. From shrimps making love to metal under stress, it's all there." He pointed at the crammed shelving. "Vibrations, the Beach Boys struck a responsive chord with that one all right. As you will know, much of the brain's activity is electrical. In fact, a steady pulsing goes on in the old brain box all the time. Each time a person articulates a thought a distinct pattern of brain waves is emitted. Scientists have already located these patterns in the brain.

"Now I have in my possession encephalogram printouts of some of the most famous and notorious personalities of our time. Don't ask me how I obtained these, I couldn't swear my methods fall within strictly legal limits! Suffice to say that my studies and practice have made me something of an adept at reading people's character and possible future behaviour after sticking a few electrodes on their scalp."

"You mean a kind of updating on the Victorian practice of phrenology?"

"Quite a good comparison, Jake. An encephalogram is as unique as an individual's fingerprints and less time-consuming than the eighty-four million-to-one odds with DNA. But in my research with the structure of sound I designed and developed a harmonics frequency analyzer -"

"Whoa!" And again, "Whoa," more slowly. Jake couldn't help it. "I'm sorry, sir, but I'm afraid my scientific studies didn't quite stretch to harmonics."

Dolgun laughed easily, a man happy in the knowledge of his own expertise. "And why should you, Jake? I don't suppose many do. In sound terms a harmonic is a component whose frequency is an integral multiple of the fundamental frequency. Yes? Well, don't worry about it, just have faith for now. It's built, it's there…" He pointed to one of the consoles on the work bench. "But it's still technically in the project development stage as yet."

"What does it do, exactly?"

"Exactly? Well, it sorts out frequencies, their amplitudes – or size – and displays them on-screen, up and down the frequency bands. Or it can be plugged into and EEC machine for brain waves readout. Essentially I suppose you could call it in modern parlance an electronic mind-reader, which can tell you what words or even thoughts are going through your brain at any given moment. I have worked on this quite recently at universities in the States and Japan, who have been working on a programme for long-term patients with degenerative brain diseases. Reading the patient's mind helps relatives communicate when speech and hand signals fail. The machine analyses electrical waves that brains emit when converting ideas into language. Each thought gives rise to a different shape of wave, allowing the trained operator to piece together the ideas in a patient's head. So it's not pseudo-science, I'm not some crackpot with a soldering iron and a pair of jump leads! Come, I'll show you." He stood up and beckoned to the younger man to follow him. Jake, for his part, was less enthusiastic; he glanced at his watch. Dolgun, perceptive as ever, countered: "Believe me, it's very relevant to the help I want to offer you tonight."

"Tonight? But -"

"Don't you know what the date is, Jake?" Dolgun's face darkened at the other's ignorance. "It's September twenty-first, the night of the autumnal equinox, all in balance, stellar alignments…" He sighed. "Look, there will not be a more propitious time to do what we have to. Come." He held a hand out. Jake rose rather reluctantly and went to the work bench, where Dolgun pressed him gently into a hard-backed swivel chair, before going to busy himself around the bank of instruments, switching and tapping to make lights glow and dials come alive, some kicking their pointers like dead frogs' legs galvanically stimulated. From a hook on the shelf above the array Dolgun took down what looked like an Olympics swimming cap, bristling with tiny inverted cones, each one an electrical socket of some kind; it had a chin-strap and Velcro tabs.

Dolgun placed this on Jake's head, pressing it gently but firmly onto his scalp, so that he felt each one of the cold, pointed metal contacts beneath the sockets. The doctor asked Jake to move the cap around until it was comfortable before fastening the chin strap. He didn't pat him on the head like one of those circus helpers before the human cannonball went down the barrel – for which he was profoundly grateful. While Jake did as asked Dolgun was busying himself sorting out the dozens of leads and talking.

"…obviously cannot do an MRI scan or even a PET" – Jake wasn't sure what a PET was – "in these conditions but I had anticipated such a situation. This is an adaptation of a sleep-inducing device to help insomniacs. Professor Giulio Tononi has led the field in this research while I was at University of

Wisconsin-Madison. I hope he doesn't think I am stealing his – ah, thunder! I will not be using all sixty electrodes but will employ a similar electro-encephalograph machine and trans-cranial stimulation to introduce the required frequencies." He looked up and over at Jake, as if suddenly remembering he was there. He stood up and came across to begin connecting the several dozen electrodes. It was only when he reached back across to the bench and connected their circuits to an anony-mous black box that Jake tensed instinctively. It wasn't lost on the Pole.

"Relax, Jake, there are no high voltages involved here. On the contrary, for this demonstration I shall be picking up your brain's electrical impulses and displaying them on this scope. Here, let me adjust this." He gently pulled the cap a little to the left. "You will feel the various pressure points where they make contact -" Jake nodded vigorously. "Okay, not an unpleasant sensation, hmm?" Not waiting for a reply Dolgun switched on the scope to a frequency range. As the console rapidly warmed up several green waveforms appeared and began to flow continuously across the small screen. To the younger man they were almost hypnotic in their snake-like movement. With an adjustment the doctor stabilized the sine waves, so that they stopped moving.

"There, that's better," he breathed, leaning over Jake to do it. "Now, what do we have here? Let's see…" With a ballpoint pen he picked out the fattest curve. "Theta, I think, at about five cycles per second…and this one here at four times that frequen-cy is your Beta signal. This reflects your alertness, if you like, as opposed to being relaxed. You're a bit tense because of your unfamiliar circumstances, so it's rather higher than normal. But it's this one here – Alpha… I need to show you something." He indicated one which registered eight cycles on the scale. "This is somewhat low because of your present stressful state. Now, let me show you something. Here, here, I'll remove these Beta and Theta electrodes…" He unplugged several leads, leaving a single sine wave. "Here we have only Alpha remaining." He straightened up. "I want you to alter your Alpha state, Jake."

Jake almost jerked his head round in surprise. "What d'you mean, sir?"

"By simply relaxing, Jake, that's all." Dolgun smiled down at him. "I'm merely seeking to prove something. Your Alpha indicates your relaxed state, as you can see, eight on the scale. That's rather low, we really want it somewhere around twelve. I've switched to five centimetres per square…see?" He pointed his pen. "Now, close your eyes and really, truly, calm yourself down – think of the happiest occasion from your childhood. Your first real birthday present, perhaps, or the most pleasurable trip to the seaside, or maybe the day when you first realized how much your mother loved you. Anything. Think about it for a few seconds, close your eyes." Dolgun stood back and then went over to another part of the room

Jake gave a kind of mental shrug and decided to humour the man, anything to get out of here and into some positive action, like reconnoitring Brookefield Hall. Some hope, he began to gloom, then realized by the changing sine wave that he actually *was* altering its condition. Sitting up straight lest Dolgun noticed this dereliction he closed his eyes and began consciously to think about some pleasurable happenings from his past. After only a few short seconds he had it. His first – his only – half century at grammar school, when he'd hit that last six of the final over, right into the large sycamore tree to win the inter-house trophy and had been mobbed by pupils and masters alike. But it was afterwards, in the comparative privacy of the locker room, easing his shoes off and sinking back against the cool metal door that the feeling washed over him. Savouring the moment, replaying every movement in slow motion; the *whack* of willow on leather, the dull roar of mounting approbation, as of distant thunder building. A-a-h, God, he reminisced, nothing had ever come close to it, before or since, sex included. Cherished mainly, he knew, because the exact set of circumstances could never again be duplicated. The memory even now brought a warm glow inside his chest -

"Well done!"

He opened his eyes, blinked, immediately aware of the glowing screen in front of him. Dolgun's pen was tracing the changed wave form.

"See here…the frequency has increased in your Alpha to over twelve cycles. Whatever you're thinking it would appear to have been a particularly satisfying moment in your life." The man chuckled. "Don't worry, son, I'm not going to ask you to divulge your innermost secrets. But you do see what I mean?"

Jake nodded; the evidence seemed irrefutable. "But how does it help, Professor?" He tried not to sound churlish.

"Just wanted to show you a little scientific 'magic', my boy" He gave a boyish grin. "Now if I wanted to – and you were so foolish as to allow me – I could have reversed the process by using these other pressure points, injected a different set of frequencies and/or harmonics, thereby triggering off a variety of synaptic impulses within your brain. This would have the effect of making you recall long-forgotten events from your past, bring on feelings of hunger, thirst or even sexual stimulation." He noted Jake's startled expression and gently eased the headset off as a gesture of reassurance. Hanging it up, he continued: "This synaptic stimulation is normally only ever done by accident in the process of brain surgery, but I have practised on myself under controlled conditions and found a certain amount of success with these input frequencies. The important point I wish to make is that I can do all this on a much more powerful scale."

"Why? How would that help me, sir?"

"Come." He walked back to his desk. More rummaging ensued and then he gave that satisfied grunt again, pulled out a rolled map and spread it across the desk's clutter. The effect, on top of the odds and ends, was almost three-dimensional as it rose and dipped. With some surprise Jake saw it was a map of the moors area, similar to Joan's but on a larger scale. Across it Dolgun had superimposed a kind of geodesic matrix, with black dots joined by straight lines. Seeing the other's perplexed look he swept one hand across the paper.

"Joan was not the only one interested in nodal points of energy, Jake, but perhaps for a different reason. Carrying on my thesis on sound I have projected onto this large scale map the convergences and leys." He indicated the places of special note, mentioning names that were now familiar to Jake through Joan's little lecture...when? Only last night? He shook his head and Dolgun gave him a quizzical look before continuing: "You see how close Hobb's Barrow is to St Michael's." He jabbed a finger down. "Well, you may not be aware that the barrow was originally a small island." Jake stared. "That could be of some significance here. The dog may have been a guardian of some Iron or Bronze Age chieftain and it was often the custom to inter leaders under or surrounded by water, for both mystical and practical reasons."

"Oh, how so?"

"Inaccessibility to disruptive elements, basically. The fifth century Visigoth warlord, Alaric, was buried beneath the bed of a temporarily dammed river, to deny desecration from his enemies. Pretty effective, eh? Anyway, it is my belief that this black dog was some guarding entity and our task is to get it back there."

"But if we could return it to its original resting place, then...then..."

"Hobb's Barrow will not be submerged when the reservoir is

fully operational, correct? And that's the problem, Jake, but not an insurmountable one. I go along with Joan's theory of coincidental events that led to its initial escape from whatever time warp or plane of existence it has been part of. But most important is the church's role as a point of convergence."

"You mean because of the menhir set in the church wall?"

"Precisely." Dolgun slapped his hand on the map. "It was obviously established after the burial mound and is of greater power, so the priest's invocation coupled with the stone pulled the entity away from its weakened resting place. The creature only appears to manifest itself during the hours of darkness, which brings a disturbingly evil element into the equation. If we can lure it back into the precincts of the church and somehow bind it to it until the waters cover it all up tomorrow then our task is done." He straightened up.

"But how do you propose to do that, sir?"

"This is where the field testing bit comes in, my boy," the other boomed, with a heartiness Jake felt was a little forced. "It would take too long to explain my theories now; the proper time and place is around midnight in the church." The look on Jake's face made him reach across and pat his arm. "Have no fear, I'm certain we can defeat this thing together, but I must have you in the correct frame of mind. It may need the strength of more than one person to achieve our aims. You must go to Brookefield Hall and satisfy yourself about Carolyn…one way or the other." He held out his hand. "I'll expect you at St Michael's no later than a quarter to midnight. Good luck and God go with you."

26: GRIEVANCE

Mrs Sykes drove around aimlessly, her meanderings unknowingly linked to Jake's, in that their cause was Sir Nicholas Brookes. Her treatment by the media billionaire had left her shocked beyond reason; she'd never seen him quite so angry, and in a long working relationship she drew on considerable experience of his bizarre moods and behaviour. Over sixty years, most of them in the family's service since her husband had died shortly after coming back from Burma in 1945. And now to be virtually kicked out, through no fault of hers, merely because he needed someone weaker to vent his spite on.

The lumpen form, crouched forward in the ancient Morris 1000, gripped the steering wheel so tightly it veered off the country road and across the grass verge, sending several sheep bleating off into the gathering gloom. With a savage oath she wrenched at the wheel, which sent the car lurching back onto the rutted track. It jerked her from her reverie and she braked sharply, her ruined lungs making her wheeze with the effort, the sound almost overriding the rattle from the loose fan belt. She passed a shaky hand across her brow, glanced instinctively over her shoulder to check her luggage. Two battered suitcases; her whole world reduced to this. She began to weep, still bewildered at the traumatic change in her situation. A few short hours ago the custodian of a twenty-four room mansion, virtually her own boss; satellite TV, centrally heated living quarters and access to almost unlimited quantities of gin and sherry. And now this.

She raised her head, realizing she really didn't know where she was. The mist was forming in hollows, the sky obscured by clouds. She had no family, chick nor child; Alfred had been no good that way after the army had returned him to her.

She must find a place to stay for the night, sort things out. She resumed her uncertain way through the encroaching darkness, eventually finding a signpost that told her she was not far from Castleton. A small village clinging to a deep fold in the dales, it would suit her till morning. She parked outside a B&B and lugged her belongings to the front door. Her ring was answered by a small, spry woman in her late seventies, who willingly took her in, the season for ramblers now past its peak. She was sorry, it was too late for a meal, but there was a very nice –

Mrs Sykes shook her head, muttered she wasn't hungry. She heaved one of the cases onto the bed, snapped open the locks and almost reverentially lifted out two bottles of Blue Sapphire gin. Quickly twisting the cap off one she filled the toothbrush tumbler and gulped half the contents straight down, gave a shudder and then carefully placed the glass on the bedside table. She sank onto the bed, her blotchy complexion little enhanced by the tears that now smeared her cheeks.

"What am I going to do?" she whispered into the tumbler before draining it. More was splashed in but left untouched on the table. She stared around the room again, with no greater interest than before. Feelings of panic made her reach for the liquor. She wrapped both hands around the glass and lay back against the worn padded headboard. The noise inside her head began its evening tintinnabulation, the reason for her increasingly slack grip on reality. For five years now the ringing sound that her GP had diagnosed as tinnitus had grown steadily worse, as he had predicted. No cure, her world revolved – sometimes spun – around a daily intake of unpronounceable drugs that helped relieve the symptoms of insomnia, loss of balance and depression. Dr Brewster had reassured her by referring to her secure environment and almost non-existent stress factors on the plus side. What would he say now, she brooded. Homeless, jobless, penniless...future-less. How's that for pressure and stress, Doc?

The thought of having to start all over again at the age of nearly eighty terrified her. What would she do, where would she go? She gulped some more gin, then remembered her medication. Feeling about in her imitation leather handbag she drew forth the two pill bottles and the two capsule blister strips. She sighed, lining them up on the counterpane. It had been such a dreadful day she couldn't recollect if she had in fact taken any yet, much less which ones. She pushed the Loprazolam to one side; that was for sleep, the way she was going she might not actually need them tonight. Now...the long white ones in the foil are Seroxat, for her depression. Huh! She'd better take two of those; popped them in and swallowed some gin. These triangular little jobs...Let's see...mm...En – al – april. Can never remember that one – keep thinking of that Forces singing turn, April Lane! Anyway, they're for the blood pressure. One down – hah! She wiped her mouth. And the Serck are my anti-fall over pills. For all the good they do I might as well stick one in each ear! But she threw one down along with the others, ignoring for the fourth time the warning not to take alcohol or drive or operate machinery, etc.

That done she began seriously to take stock of her options. That bastard, that obscene imposter of a once-proud name, with his filthy goings-on and small white hands like nimble slugs. Who did he think he was, dismissing her with an hour's notice and a measly three months salary in lieu? When she had recovered enough to rally and demand redundancy at least, he'd merely laughed that cruel laugh of his.

"Redundancy? I'm dismissing you for disloyalty and incompetence, Mrs Sykes. Disloyalty for not immediately informing me on her arrival, incompetence for allowing her to go out on

244

her own, knowing her condition." He held a hand up at her expected reply. "You knew my orders and you chose to ignore them. Redundancy compensation, hah! The job isn't disappearing, Mrs Sykes - you are! I'll get someone else. The sooner the better. Look on the bright side; I'm your benefactor, really, saving you from an early alcoholic grave. Where else will you obtain a position that will put so much temptation in your way? Now go!"

Perhaps Carolyn could get me reinstated, she mused, twisting the cap off the second bottle, almost instantly forgetting her own rejection of all things Brookefield. What else could I have done? She was always like the grand-daughter I never had. I knew she wanted to get away from that fat slob. "Som'ing wrong there," she mumbled, "som'ing wrong. Girl wasn't well an' he…he had som'ing t'do wi-ith it. Som'ing t'do wi' east wing, a'ways locked up. But" – she cackled – "I listened when he'd been doin' wha'ever he'd been up to in there. Strange noises, funny chantin', music like I've never heard before. And those smells… Oh, yes, I could tell a tale or two. Who to?" She blinked blearily, trying to focus on the mildewed framed hunting scene. "Newspapers! That's it, show him up for what he is. Oops!" She giggled at the thought, spilling some gin down her navy blue cardigan. "Better make sure first it isn't one o' his!"

She chuckled and drifted off into an alcoholic stupor, misremembering her childhood, her parents, lost loves and opportunities. Eventually her hazy recollections turned full circle and she was back in the cheerless room, surrounded by her few bits and pieces, and a future filled with desolation and despair. She sat up, easing her aching back and triggering off a fresh carillon inside her head. She spotted the pills and haphazardly swallowed some more.

What if something *has* happened to Carolyn? Poor child, a bit like me, with no real family left in the world. At least she can't claim blood ties with that pervert. Oh, yes, she knew his real origins, had done her own little bit of poking around in his absence. Foreigners had foreign ways, not like us. Disgusting. Want wiping out…what we fought the war for. What would Alfred have done? "The Japs, the Germans, Doris," he used to wheeze, "an' all those others who make our world a place of death and corruption. Give 'em a taste o' their own medicine, is wot I say, like they done to those poor Jews an' gypsies. Put *them* in a oven, Doris, that's wot I would do." Then he would fall back, dissolving into those terrible coughs that always broke her heart.

She sat upright, knuckling her eyes, her breath catching in her throat. Good old Alfred. If I'm quick enough he won't have informed head office of my dismissal yet, too busy looking for Carolyn.

She pushed herself off the bed, fumbling with her coat. Swaying slightly she checked her car keys were in her bag, took one last swig from the bottle and made for the door.

27: RECONNAISSANCE

Jake parked the car carefully among the trees halfway up the driveway to Brookefield Hall. He got out and stood quietly for several seconds, listening, still pondering the unexpected bonus of the wrought-iron security gates wide open. Was it a trap? If so, who for? He wasn't quite sure what he was expecting; this – like so much of what had happened to him recently – was so alien to his world that if an owl had hooted he would probably have wet himself. Likewise if a steam engine had suddenly thundered past he might well have merely noted its size, sound and smell. Gordon would probably sniff and murmur something like, "Experiential, old chap, lock yourself into it and remember – nothing is ever wasted."

Somewhere off to the right an animal squealed in terminal fright and he jumped. So much for experiential, he thought, moving forward. There was little light, the moon hidden behind a few scudding clouds. He was familiar with the house in daylight, it was a landmark from most directions. He skirted the driveway, keeping to the grass and angling towards the building. He stopped by a stone statue of some scantily-clad nymph and scanned the house. No car out front, at any rate, but some light over there on the far side, upstairs. Was there a housekeeper? Sure to be but where at this moment? C'mon, Jake, what you gonna do – throw gravel at the windows and hope Carolyn will pop her head out? If she is in there she won't be roaming freely around, will she?

You're wasting time! Taking a deep breath he stepped out of the shadows and headed for the front porch. Instantly the whole front area of the grounds was bathed in glaring white light as the security sensors activated, like some enormous, interminable flash photograph.

He flinched, his hand going instinctively to cover his eyes. "Shit!" He hesitated but only for a second, before running forward to the illusory shelter of the porch. What would he say, how would he explain his standing here, arriving apparently on foot at ten o'clock in the evening at the door of one of the wealthiest, most private men in the country? He groaned, trapped in partial shadow. As he frantically ran through a series of sketchy scenarios in his head the tungsten filaments cut out with a loud ping, plunging the area into even greater darkness.

And still nobody came to investigate, no dogs snarling and slavering, accelerating across the gravel before their final lunge at him in this confined, killing space.

Heartened by this first lucky break of the day he pushed at the heavy front door. It creaked open; no lights on. Poised for flight at every step he slowly moved into the house, stopping every few paces to cock his head and listen for the slightest sound. Nothing. He turned right at the hall's end, towards what he fancied was the lighted area above the stairs. His hand slid along the banister rail until he reached the first floor. A very dim glow somewhere ahead. Even more slowly now, for the floorboards complained each step of the way and he winced along with them. But the house seemed empty, with the possible exception of that room at the end of the passage. Would that be the housekeeper? Somehow the idea of a housekeeper occupying an entire upper storey didn't quite gel with him. But then, nobody else stayed here apart from Sir Nicholas, and then only rarely.

If it was the housekeeper he reckoned he could manage to talk his way round why he was there – provided he didn't give her a heart attack first! There was a large ornate door barring the passage and tried the handle carefully. It turned but wouldn't open. Locked, dammit! Then his fingers touched the key sticking out beneath it.

Hardly daring to breathe he turned it slowly. Opening the door he suddenly realized the implications of what he had just done; it meant there was certainly no housekeeper living behind a locked door. You only lock doors to keep people out…or in! The faint light was seeping from under a door to his right.

He fumbled around the walls on either side until his fingers made contact with a light switch and eased it down slowly, in the fervent hope that any resulting light would be equally tardy in appearing. It wasn't and he blinked for a second; the high old-fashioned chandelier illuminated the rest of the passage, showing a door each side and two side tables. The door on the right was his objective and he approached it now with a thumping heart and trembling hands. It, too, was locked from the outside.

He very carefully turned the key and gripped the brass knob. It was the correct room, lights on…and Carolyn lying across a large bed in the far corner. She was sobbing quietly.

"Carolyn?" he said softly. She went rigid for a moment and then twisted round on the bed to stare at him. Her beautiful face was streaked with tears and blotchy.

"Jake? Jake, is it…it can't be you!" She half-rolled off the bed and slid to the floor, unable to believe her eyes.

He ran to her as she stood up unsteadily, the desperate look in her eyes cutting into his heart.

"It's me, Carolyn, what have they done to you?" he whispered as he took her in his arms. Her whole body shook and heaved against his as the dam burst and she collapsed in tears. He kissed her face, her neck and her ears until her sobbing faltered, stopped, and she began to laugh, despite herself. She hugged him more tightly for a second and then drew back, those gorgeous eyes still wet and brim-full.

"Has he…has he gone…really gone?" She looked over his shoulder fearfully, her hands clutching at his upper arms and plucking at his sleeves, somehow daring him to deny it.

"Yes, Carolyn, I think he's gone, back to London. We're alone in the house. Would you like to sit down and tell me what all this is about?"

"I–I don't know whether you'd want to know it, Jake," she whispered. "I wish I didn't know." She looked up at him as he pressed her gently back onto the bed. "It's all in that cupboard over there."

28: DURANCE

The Morris 1000 turned through the open gateway into Brookefield Hall and made its way unsteadily up the long driveway, stopping at the front porch in the glare of the security lights as they blazed on at her approach.

She did feel a momentary panic, returning to what had been her home for many years, now under such altered circumstances. She wavered, the engine ticking over asthmatically. Then she remembered Alfred's words and her wobbly chins tightened in firm resolve. She switched off the ignition and heaved herself out onto the gravel, grunting and wheezing.

The place seemed empty but it was difficult to be sure with all that bloody glare blinding her. She put up a hand as her balance problem began to affect her in the intense, unnatural light. He'd had all the east wing windows made shutter-tight, so if he was in there he would not be alerted by the lights. It also meant he could still be in there; that was her hope. She had heard him on the phone earlier, telling someone he would be staying up here tonight, before leaving for London in the morning. Whether that was because of Carolyn's 'escape' she wasn't certain. She suspected he wasn't all that concerned about her whereabouts, knowing she would return as she usually did. Better if she stayed away for good, the old housekeeper sniffed, opening the car's boot. The red plastic fuel container was full.

She staggered with the awkward weight to the porch just in time to trigger the lights again as she fumbled with her keys before noticing the large front door was ajar. She rubbed her face, realizing she had been a bit silly with the pills and gin. Then she giggled; she had a plan and shrugged off the mystery of the open door and instead slipped inside, gratefully placing the petrol down for a few seconds in the hallway. Was that a light up there? It was only discernible because the security lights had gone out. She squinted up the stairs but her focus was gone and she waved it away with a flapping hand which upset her balance again, making her totter into the wall. She leaned there for a few seconds, breathing deeply and trying to compose herself. She belched, rubbed at her shoulder and gathered her thoughts. Oh, yes…the plan. Reaching up to the painting of sheep by Farquharson she pulled the edge of the frame towards her. The hinged picture revealed the electronic control panel that monitored the heat and smoke sensors. She keyed them all out and then flicked the hallway lights on.

"That's better," she muttered, bending down to lift the container once more. Wonder why they called them jerrycans? Alfred would have known, but they're plastic now like everything else, so what's it matter, huh? She stumbled round the corner of the hallway, with the intention of going straight along to Sir Nicholas's 'secret room'. But noises from upstairs stopped her. Very carefully lowering the container she looked up the stairs, cocking her head. But the sounds were too indistinct, music perhaps, certainly not voices. To ignore the implications could possibly thwart her plan; even her gin-soaked brain could see that. The air burbling in her lungs, she cast about for inspiration, sinking down on the stairs' lowest step. She didn't feel well but she couldn't go back, not now, after screwing up the courage to come this far, amazing herself at her initiative and determination. What would Alfred have done? She took a deep breath and stood up, began hauling herself up the wide staircase.

The chandelier was lit, but as the connecting passage door was only half open its illumination was restricted. Even stranger…that door was always locked and the key kept by him; a safeguard, he maintained, against anyone being endangered by inadvertently entering an area officially designated as being structurally unsafe. Did this mean he was up there? Please God, let it be so!

The sounds were clearer now, and with a shock she identified them; that same wild pagan music she'd heard before, when he was having one of his secret room sessions. The first door beyond the connecting on the right appeared to be slightly open. So, the bastard was in there doing it now!

She stopped, the excitement and the danger robbing her of breath. She daren't get too close; he seemed to have supernormal senses, even read her mind sometimes. Her first instinct was to turn round and go back to the lodging house, accept her fate and throw herself on the mercy of the welfare system. But no, bugger it, Alfred wouldn't have given in that easily; he was up there somewhere, watching. She wouldn't fail him, and besides, her plan really depended upon him being there tonight. Once back in London his sacking of her would become a matter of record. She was quite certain in her own mind that with his present problems the details of her dismissal would not still be uppermost in his mind. With him gone she would still qualify for a pension as an employee. I must do it!

She approached the open door, could hear a voice now – his! That voice ringing out above the satanic bells and rattles. It gave physical impetus and at the same time made her falter emotionally. If she should fail… Alfred's voice seemed to whisper in her ear, "Go on, girl, one more last effort. You know God's on our side."

She could see the key in the lock. Holding her breath she reached across the open space between her and the brass knob, hooking her fingers over the smooth surface and pulling it quickly towards her till it slammed shut. There was a shout from within, the music was cut off abruptly and she heard footsteps pounding across the room towards her. Frantically she twisted the key in the lock just as he reached the far side and rattled the door knob.

"Open up! Who is this? Let us out right now, d'you hear?"

But she was already lumbering away, her high-pitched cackle drowning out his cries. Quickly she did the same with the connecting door, shooting the bolt for good measure.

"That'll slow you up, you bastard. You're big but you're not fit. A few minutes, that's all I need. C'mon, Sykes," she growled. The hammering on the door and the shouting was still plainly audible but indistinct through the old thick wood.

After pulling herself down the stairs by the handrail she paused at the bottom to catch her breath, but the sound of his battering fists and voice urged her on. Leaning heavily to one side she half-dragged the sloshing burden along the passageway until she came to the nailed-off doorway. She knew what was in there, oh yes, she was nobody's fool, certainly not the mental defective *he* took her for!

It was no good, she had to take a break, no matter what, if only to ease her aching back muscles. But she was almost directly beneath the upper room now and movements could be faintly heard. She swore at him under her breath out of habit and then, unscrewing the cap, began to tip the fuel out, starting with the door and surrounding frame. Immediately the bare room was filled with the pungent odour, the fumes making her eyes sting and triggering off a coughing bout.

"It's not as easy as – as in the fillums," she gasped, as it gurgled and splashed out, landing just about everywhere but where she intended. But the ungainly weight *was* lessening, and she found it easier as she retreated out of the room, dousing the bare wooden floorboards and then the hall carpet.

Almost done, she thought, tipping the last of it out as she reached the front door. Stepping outside she leaned against the porch and gulped in great lungfuls of pine-scented night air, the contrast making her feel quite heady and realize just how saturated the interior was with the flammable vapour. She could hear no sounds from upstairs now.

Flinging the empty container in the car's boot and slamming the lid she fumbled for the cheap cigarette lighter she always kept in her handbag.

"Okay, you bastard," she growled, crunching across the gravel to the open entrance. "You like to play the devil…then go to hell!" Flicking the lighter on and turning the flame to maximum she hurled it into the hallway.

For one brief moment she feared it wasn't going to work, then the woollen carpet suddenly blossomed, rippling into yellow life, a flame running at first towards her, so that she reared back in terror. Then – as though responding to a greater need – it raced away from her, down the hall, throwing the pictures and ornaments into sharp relief. Round the corner the flames leapt and before she could clap her hands in child-like glee there was a resounding *whoomph* and a blast of hot air came rushing back at her.

She turned and ran to the car in panic, alarmed now at the enormity of her actions, to crouch at the far side as the roaring and crackling began, and the whole interior of the centuries-old pile gave out a flickering glow. Glass started to shatter somewhere and she ventured to lean out and stare expectantly up at the first floor, where her captor would no doubt be getting the message, as the noise and heat and smoke rose from beneath his feet.

"Now, you evil bastard," she whispered, her eyes reflecting the flames now licking out through some of the ground floor windows. "Now…let's see you deal with a situation not of your making for once – and no fucking minions to piss on the fire for you. C'mon, big boy," she shrieked, moving out from the car in her excitement and towards the target of her vituperation.

"Where's those godless helpers of yours now, eh? Are you choking yet, Sir Nicholas?" She spat, bending down and scraping up a handful of gravel before hurling it at the upper windows. One pane cracked but that was all. "Whatsamatter, isn't your spell book fireproof, then?" She cackled at her own wit, then felt a sudden vice-like pain that made her clutch at her chest, slowly slumping forward onto her knees, toppling to one side, her head striking the gravel. Saliva trickled from one corner of her mouth and her eyes gazed unseeing at the tongues of flames now spurting outwards from the upper windows.

"I'll…see…you…in…hell…you…bast…"

29: THERMOLUMINESCENCE

"It must be Sir Nicholas! Who else would want us both held prisoner?" Jake was equal parts anger, puzzlement and fright. He couldn't admit to the latter but there was something wrong about all this. It didn't seem to fit the media magnate's style, what little he knew of him. Sure, he was easily quite capable of it, but then to go away, not to gloat over their predicament – but then who the hell else? He furiously rattled the door knob again and shouted at the thick door, pounding the carved wood until his hand hurt.

Truth to tell he was afraid to turn round and confront her. Watching the clip had made him want to weep for her anguish, yet admire her courage as she forced herself to sit through the whole degrading spectacle. But at least it was all that much clearer now, and thus curable – or at the very least treatable. He had just been impressing this fact upon her when the bloody door had slammed shut. He'd caught a glimpse of the sleeve in his peripheral vision across the flickering TV-lit room.

He turned; the look of utter rejection and surrender on her pale face entered his heart like a lance. He didn't need to be a mind reader; why hadn't he taken her away as soon as he'd found her? The recordings could have been taken along with them – anything, just to get away from this awful place.

"What are we going to do, Jake?"

He looked at the high windows but before he could even think or form a question she told him about the thick Perspex panels. A quick check confirmed this and he felt the first twinge of despair. What was it all about, really? The man was a lot of things, but surely not reckless enough to risk all by this dabbling in the occult. How could such a hard-headed businessman be drawn into such claptrap? Did he even believe it? Carolyn certainly did – for the moment anyway.

He must raise her spirits, priority one. The face that seemed to plead for reassurance was still the beautiful one that had first captivated him, gazing down imperiously from that enormous hunter. But something had gone, perhaps forever, and in its place an awareness of the world that nobody – least of all a young and carefree girl – should be exposed to. The knowledge of what she had been a party to, over and over again, would haunt her dreams for a long time to come, perhaps forever. She would need a lot of help and, above all, understanding. He just hoped he was up to the job.

He went across to the tear-stained face and kneeling down he gently wiped her cheeks, kissing her tenderly and murmuring love words, words he'd never used before last night.

"C'mon, love, we'll beat this together. You've survived things that most others have never even heard of, much less…" He gulped. "I mean -"

"It's all right, Jake." She squeezed his hands, smiling bravely. "I'm just feeling a bit sorry for myself, I suppose."

"Good girl. Besides, I have to be somewhere in" – he glanced at his watch – "less than an hour."

"What do you mean?"

He quickly told her about Dolgun, but before she could begin asking any further questions he stood up and sniffed the air. "Can you smell smoke?" He sniffed again, went quickly to the door, placing his right ear against the carved surface. She was beside him, all thoughts of self-pity lost in this new and fundamental fear.

"Oh, my God, Jake," she whispered, clutching at his arm, her big eyes seeming to draw him in. "Something's burning!"

"I can hear it…something crackling," he replied grimly. "The insane bastard has torched the place." He faced her, staring beyond, eyes ranging the room once more, but this time with an urgency that had risen by several notches. The whole building would go up like a lumber yard – old furniture, floorboards, threadbare curtains.

"The smoke detectors?" She gazed up expectantly at the sensor in the ceiling. "This place has one of the best fire and security systems available. It should kick in…"

"Then why haven't -" He regretted his words as soon as they came out. Her face crumpled and she pressed the knuckles of one hand into her mouth, backing away from him, her head shaking from side to side.

"He wouldn't do this, not even Uncle Nicky," she stammered. "I'm all he's got…"

"Maybe, Carolyn, but I think he wants more than that. A matter of priorities perhaps. Maybe it's somebody else – is there anyone other than him in the house? That housekeeper…?"

"Mrs Sykes. She was here when I arrived but I haven't seen her since last night. He probably sent her away for a few days until…until…" He took her hand and squeezed it gently.

But his despair grew as he inspected the electronics cupboard, the walls and finally the bathroom and toilet. It was unfortunate that all the furniture and fittings were from the pre-flat pack era. At any other time he might just have appreciated the robust manufacture of the heavy oak bed with matching chair and table. Likewise the bathroom hand basin and bath in ceramic and brass, the ornate shower unit, looking like some version of a Victorian telephone, hand-held spray resting on its cradle. But right now he would merely hurt an already bruised hand by slapping them in his frustration.

She squeezed his arm. He turned, willing something encouraging to enter his head. Her over-bright smile made any attempt at such tenuous thoughts impossible.

"Perhaps some kind of alarm did get through to the fire brigade," she ventured. "You know…a sort of fail-safe device." Her palpable need for reassurance spurred him as never before; he steered her out of the small bathroom, pointing to the high, protected windows.

"Yes, you're right! We have to work on two fronts, me to check out these windows more thoroughly and you…" With an animal-like ferocity he went to the bed and flung the bed clothes off it and in her direction. "You soak these. Fill the bath up. When they're saturated we'll spread them across the floor." Her frightened expression lent him even greater urgency. "We have to damp down the effects of the heat and smoke until help arrives – and it will, I promise you, Carolyn. At worst it will be ten minutes before we're spotted by someone across the valley -"

"But there's nobody there any more, Jake," she wailed, pulling at her face again. He went round the bed to her and gripped her hands, kissing them and then her face with a tenderness that wasn't feigned. She clung to him, returning the touch of his lips hungrily, her fingers clawing at the back of his head, in his hair, the better to cleave to him. He wrenched his head back and her eyes snapped open in shock, unfocussed, unseeing, for a brief moment. He shook her gently.

"Carolyn, Carolyn, don't lose it now, we're going to make it, believe me. Somebody will ring in the alarm. Remember there is a security presence in the village." He glanced down; smoke was snaking up between the cracks in the floorboards. "But we do have to shorten the odds a little." He pushed her away slowly. Then: "Move!"

He left her there and went to the bed, dragged the mattress onto the floor. "We'll try to get this wet too." He had to raise his voice above the ominous crackling that didn't appear to be so much under them as all around them. Please God make it an acoustic anomaly, he prayed, as he grunted and heaved the cumbersome oaken bed frame over on its side, straightening up to grab it as it overbalanced. Gripping the upended frame with both hands he proceeded to push and pull it across the room, towards the nearest of the two windows. He judged the distance and then toppled it – end-on – so that one corner crashed against the protective Perspex. It shivered but showed no sign of weakening.

Gritting his teeth and dashing the sweat from his dripping brow he backed off and tried again. Once more the transparent panel bulged under the onslaught but held firm. He saw at once that the trouble was; only hitting it at the lower section, where it was firmly fixed on three sides, thus giving it greater strength at the edges. That and the fact that he couldn't really get enough impetus into the frame.

Groaning with despair and frustration he shuffled the frame around and leaned it against the window. As a crude ladder it served him better and he climbed up it until he could stand on its upper side, teetering, face pressed to the warm surface. His finger sought one edge, feeling for a possible loose point in its installation. But the wide-headed bolts were screwed tight. He gave up after several fruitless minutes.

He lost his balance and fell backwards, twisting awkwardly in his instinctive attempt to avoid landing at an angle. Carolyn heard the crash and emerged from the bathroom.

"Are you okay, Jake?"

"Yes, dammit," he groaned, clambering to his feet. "And so is that bloody Perspex! How are we doing with those bed clothes?"

Before she could answer the lights went out, plunging the room into a darkness that was eerily split from below by the flames' light where the floorboards' cracks were. In the brief instant before Carolyn screamed the air extractor cut out.

"Don't panic, Carolyn," he shouted, moving quickly, cutting across the light beams spearing upwards as he did so. There was no bed in the way but he forgot about the mattress. "Damn!" He stumbled before reaching her outstretched arms, pulling her to him. She buried her head in his chest, her muffled sobs vibrating through his clothing and ribcage as he stroked her hair.

"It was to be expected, love," he soothed her. "I should have warned you. Some of the wiring had to go first but other circuits may still be live." This did not placate her entirely but her sobs did subside into a more acceptable snuffling. Their eyes were becoming accustomed to the strange conditions; the growing rumble and flickering streaks of orange and yellow from beneath their feet.

"Look!" She drew back a little; the floorboards were distorting in the heat, a broad ray of light and heat bursting through, a pillar that separated them by its suddenness until Jake stepped over it to hold her again. "It's – it's like hell is opening up for me!" she whispered. "A punishment for all the terrible things I've done." As though in answer there was a series of popping noises from below, followed by a crash. They both jumped.

"Stop it, Carolyn!" He shook her roughly; he mustn't lose her now. "I've told you…it wasn't your fault. We'll beat this together…together! D'you hear me?"

Her thick dark hair flopped about her and then she steadied.

"C'mon, kid, we don't have a lot of time. Get those sheets while I fetch the curtains." He tore down the velour fabric drapes from one window and dragged them into the bathroom. Carolyn was struggling, barely able to shift the sodden sheets. Stooping over her he quickly hauled them from the filled tub and into the bedroom, where he proceeded to spread them across the floor, the dripping water hissing and bubbling from the cracks in the floor. Starting with the gap under the door he worked towards the centre of the room. They immediately started to steam, confirming the reality, the probable futility, of what he was attempting to do. The stifling heat and dull roar all around told him the flames were in full control now. But he knew he had to do something, if only for her sanity's sake. Only outside assistance could really affect their hopeless situation, and pretty damn soon at that.

He raced back to the bathroom to do the same with the curtains. This time it was more difficult, the heavy material soaking up an amazing amount of water.

"You'll have to give me a hand with these," he gasped. "Leave the water running, we'll need all we can get to damp down the floor. Just pray the plumbing is of the same quality as those bloody window frames! We're due for some luck, eh?" He kissed her cheek and then took one end of a curtain. It didn't take them long to stretch all four sections across the remaining floor space. If nothing else the overall effect should – however minimally – reduce the rising temperature and deaden that hideous crackling and popping from beneath their feet.

Back in the bathroom he grabbed the ornate shower spray and proceeded to smash its sprinkler rose on the edge of the bath. A few good whacks did the trick.

"What are you doing, Jake?" She was standing in the doorway, her eyes two orbs in the uncertain gloom.

"That wet curtain effect won't last long, love," he panted, ramming the changeover valve across. With a soft *thunk* the flexible hose quivered, stiffened in his hand before the water gushed out in a semi-solid, spurting stream. Dragging the hose as far as possible towards the doorway he directed the water jet into the room. It hit the nearest part of the floor, where it steamed for a moment before the sheet became saturated once more. As slowly as he dared he moved the stream back and forth, then raising the trajectory to obtain a farther reach. Hissing and steaming the room resembled for a short few seconds a sauna, almost drowning the sound of the greedy flames below them. Carolyn crouched against the bathroom door jamb, her hands to her ears, no longer able to cope with this new horror as it hissed upwards in writhing coils of vapour.

Jake realized his dampening-down efforts were only partially effective; something like half the floor was not being touched by the water – even at its steepest angle and height. Unless he could get it to the corners the flames would eat through at some point and quite likely bring the whole floor down, the very thing he was trying to prevent. When help arrived it would have to be via the windows. A fire crew would be able to pierce that bloody Perspex, but would they think it worthwhile, uncertain perhaps that anyone could survive in the inferno? That was his big concern, that nobody would even *try* to get at them. Either he or Carolyn must somehow be there at the windows to let them know they were alive.

First things first though; the nozzle size had to be reduced in order to increase the water pressure. Grabbing the wooden bath stool he proceeded to batter the brass spiral tube's end. The effect was immediate; a thin, more forceful jet emerging. He daren't constrict the flow too much for fear it split along its side.

This time the jet hit most parts of the floor. Although diminished in volume it was getting there. He shouted encouragement to Carolyn, whose expression he couldn't quite read but whose posture indicated dejection and defeat. To jerk her out of it he ordered her to clamber up the bed frame and keep a lookout for the first sign of the fire tender. Reluctantly she left his presence and squelched over to the windows. Jake brought the jet back to the foreground again, trying to be methodical and forget what lay below. He had no doubt they were on a hiding to nothing. The volume of water was pathetic in relation to what was needed to quench the heated hunger greedily seeking new fuel. The irony was not lost on him that in deciding to remain in the bathroom and control the flow he could be cutting himself off from his only escape route should the floor collapse.

Carolyn suddenly screamed and pointed to the door. He directed the stream there automatically as it began to crackle and bulge. The water cooled it instantly but the damage was done – flames were already licking around its edges where it had found a gap. He wiped the sweat away and shouted, "Carolyn, is there no sign of anything out there?"

"I'm sorry, Jake, but I can't quite see beyond the window-sill…it–it's just that bit too high for me…" She began to cry.

"It's okay, love, not your fault." He groaned. *C'mon, damn you, I've paid my community tax. Where are you when I need you?*

The water gave a sort of strangled noise, spluttered and stopped.

"Oh, God, no!" He shook the flexible tube but it was no good. Carolyn, in the ruddy gloom and the steam and noise was unaware of this new – most serious – threat. He cast about for some straw to clutch, a diminution of the fire's ferocity, a distant siren…anything. Scooping up the nearest sheets he flung them back in the tub, which still had some water in it. Soaking up the last of the water he carried them across to the window. Carolyn's stricken face was clearly visible by the moon-lit panel.

"No water?" she whispered.

"Had to go sometime, pet." As he tried to smile reassuringly the door exploded into the room and she screamed again, this time long and high, the sound pure terror as the monster revealed itself. Jake ducked instinctively, expecting shrapnel, or at least debris, to shower them. But it was just a blast of lung-sucking heat that seemed to bounce off the walls before wrapping them in its stifling cloak. He peered back fearfully; orange and red flames were pushing in like unruly lager louts seeking victims. Jake turned her head away and stretched up to stare out through the deeply recessed window. It was difficult, with the reflection of the flames behind them dancing in expectant glee.

Which made the sudden apparition at the window all the

more welcome. Carolyn screamed again at the yellow helmet and face mask and Jake grabbed her as she lost her balance on the shaky frame.

The man waved them back, brandishing a large shiny axe. Jake shook his head vigorously and slapped his hands on the Perspex to indicate the double-skinned window. The fire fighter's puzzled look behind the visor cleared and he nodded; with one gauntleted hand he struck the glass, quickly demolishing the remaining shards around the frame.

They both heard the glass, even above the inferno around them. It was already scorching their backs, Jake shielding the girl's body with his own. Breathing was almost impossible. The bed sheet they held above them was purely cosmetic now.

The spike's point came through the Perspex about a half metre above their heads and they ducked, crouching as low as they dared whilst still retaining their balance in their precarious position. Carolyn's soot-stained face stared into Jake's bravely, trying to ignore the flames leaping up at them like so many ravening dogs. He smiled, realized he must look as bad, and kissed her slowly, endeavouring to instil a calmness he certainly did not feel.

The spike came through again, this time jerking from side to side to widen the hole. The rending screech as the material split and slivers fell around them was the sweetest music to their ears. One edge near him lifted, strained, and then the whole section came away, snapping halfway up with a splintering crack. Jake grabbed it and heaved it over their heads. The noise from outside invaded the room, making a welcome overlay to the roaring flames behind them. He looked up; the man on the ladder waved them to one side and brought his hose nozzle to bear. With a *whoosh* the pressurized stream took on the might of the creeping conflagration. The fireman, who had removed his BA set, shouted, "When I raise the hose get through here sharp as you can. Okay?"

They both nodded.

"Anyone else in there?"

"No!" Jake had to shout as the opposing elements of fire and water fought it out behind them. The nozzle waved right and left to achieve maximum traverse in the restricted opening.

"Right…move!"

As they scrambled through strong hands eased them over the blanket-draped sill and into a world neither had expected to ever see again. Two large fire tenders, an assortment of cars and vans, blue and yellow flashing lights, voices crackling out of radios, floodlights…people. They stumbled down the ladder steps and into the care of two paramedics.

Carolyn was beginning to react to the full horror of their shared experience. She shook uncontrollably in the cool night air as she looked back at the raging inferno that had for a time been her childhood home. Flames were avidly seeking more fuel, licking up through the gutted lower windows, searing the ancient ivy she used to climb. Several hoses were directed into the rooms downstairs but it was clear that all that side of the house was doomed, the stream of water simply being used as a holding operation. She shivered again but not with cold.

The Senior Fire Officer came across, wiping his sweaty face, wanting to know how they had survived so long in such an inferno. Jake told him about his idea for soaking the floor.

The SPO turned to Carolyn. "Young lady, if you're ever caught up in a life-threatening situation again try to make sure this chap is around. Such initiative is rare in one so -"

"Bloody hell, not you again!"

Jake turned to see Chief Inspector Murcell, the SOCO from Joan's investigation site, crunching towards them. The young ex-reporter tried to raise a grin. "You know me, sir, always first with the worst."

"Hmph," the officer grunted, jerking a thumb at the lurid

flames devouring the last of the ivy. "They don't come much worse than that. It begs the obvious question: What's an employee – sorry, ex-employee of the *Clarion* doing *inside* Sir Nicholas Brooke's family home as it burns to the ground? A less charitable person might allow his imagination to dwell on words like hostility, resentment…revenge -" He winced as the roof fell into the body of the fire in a huge welter of sparks and splintering timbers. "Although there are limits, even to my impartial, clinically trained mind."

"Hey!" Jake held his hands out, palms forward. "We're the victims here. This is Sir Nicholas's ward, Carolyn Draycott. When she tells you her story you may wish to re-direct your enquiries." He completed the introductions and squeezed her arm to encourage her. She was recovering fast, youth on her side, and after a false start launched into a full account of what had happened to her since being abducted from Jake's flat. Within seconds of her speaking the officer took them both out of hearing of the ambulance men. Continuing in the police car she wisely omitted her other secret, and the evidence left in the bedroom, now almost certainly destroyed. She made much of her illness and Sir Nicholas's overly-attentive ministrations.

Murcell heard her through, only snorting incredulously at the drugging part and then waving her on until she finally faltered to a halt, gulping in great mouthfuls of air, as though she had just completed a marathon. Jake chipped in here with his version of why he had concluded she could only have been here or else back in London.

"So are you seriously suggesting that one of this country's wealthiest and most influential men locked you both in a room and then set fire to the place, his only family…and his own ancestral home?"

"Well, he's not a blood relative and it isn't his ancestral home, strictly speaking, it's Carolyn's, sir." Murcell blinked but before he could respond Jake went on, "But obviously someone did -"

"Hmph!" That snort again. "Obviously, and she's lying over there." He pointed back towards the front of the house. "We found an elderly lady, dead of a heart attack seemingly, and reeking of petrol. It was only that fact that brought me on the scene…in view of that poor historian's strange circumstances. Housekeeper apparently "

"Mrs Sykes! Oh!…." Carolyn started to cry again. "You mean…you mean she – she..?"

"Looks every bit that way. 'Course we can't tell for sure till Forensics do their thing. There are some elements to this whole affair – and your part in it, Ransome – that leave me greatly puzzled. Your – er, uncle, will have to be informed – wherever *he* is." He looked speculatively at the house, then up at the sky, back to the young couple. "I shall require you both at the station as soon as the medics are finished with you, to make formal statements. Where will you be staying, Miss Draycott? At Ransome's address?" She nodded dumbly. "Right, out you get. Oh, by the way, Ransome, one of my men said to ask you about a large black dog that appeared out of nowhere on the runway at the airport, just as the Alicante flight was taking off… Why would that concern you, hmm? No matter, I don't believe any of us can handle any more enigmas right now. We'll sort that one out later too."

They climbed out of the car and rejoined the paramedics, still standing patiently by their vehicle.

Murcell: "Are these two injured in any way?"

"No, sir, not really. Shock, dehydration, but nothing that a hot bath and a good night's sleep won't cure. We'll take them both in for observation overnight, of course, but tomorrow they're all yours."

Jake didn't like the sound of that; he had less than twenty minutes to rendezvous with Dolgun. Murcell had already turned away, called to inspect something in the wreckage.

Jake turned to the driver. "Look," he said, "I have my car over there -" he pointed vaguely towards the darkened trees – "and I don't really want to leave it here." Seeing the resistance building up in the other's eyes he piled it on. "It's a classic – Ford Escort RS 2000, know what I mean? How about if you take Miss Draycott with you?"

"No!" Carolyn's interjection stopped Jake cold. Surprised, he started to make a case for her but she cut him off with a chopping motion of her hand. "I'm staying with you, Jake, no arguments - wherever you go, I go. Okay?" Their eyes locked and he saw something there he'd not noticed before. One more facet? He didn't have time to argue, he turned to the driver, now joined by his companion, who shrugged at his colleague's quandary.

"We-ell, I dunno." The man rubbed his chin. "It's against procedure, mind. But I guess we can't actually force you if you really object…human rights an' all that. Seein' as 'ow you're neither of you actually injured – hey!"

"Thanks!" Jake was already gone, the girl beside him. The car was still where he'd parked it. "Are you really sure you want to come along, Carolyn? I have to warn you -"

"Warn nothing!" she snapped, hopping in and slamming the door. "Even if that bastard hasn't tried to kill me he's sure as hell got some explaining to do. From what you said earlier he's somehow behind Joan Winspear's death. Even billionaires can't get away with murder, kidnapping, drugging, sexual and physical abuse and – and whatever other filthy perversion he's guilty of." The blaze in her eyes was no residual glow from the flames in the background. "After you've finished with this jiggery-pokery in the church perhaps you'll demonstrate some more of that new-found initiative on my behalf. After what I've been through in the last twenty-four hours I think you owe me that, Jake." Then: "Does this thing still go?"

30: CONCURRENCE

Renton Cappel jerked out of his fear-wracked slumber. Over the last few days the nightmare that his life had become had meant some of his faculties heightened, whilst others had atrophied. He discovered that he could do without food to a large extent; as long as the water remained on tap he could go on. He realized that such situation could not prevail; his wrists were painfully thin and his heart threatened to burst out of his chest whenever he had to heave the heavy floor slabs about, indicating that the demands upon his diminishing reserves were leaving him dangerously weak. But this was still within the limits he had set himself, given the short-term programme for his future. One way or another, by tomorrow his search would be ended, courtesy of the local authority. The patrolling security guards no longer even bothered to look into the ravaged presbytery. He had taken to hiding beneath a jumble of torn-down cupboards and doors until their regular but cursory poking-about took them through the house, stepping over upturned flagstones and commenting on the peculiarly energetic form of vandalism the local yokels were prone to – chucking such huge flags around. But even that, nothing for the last sixteen hours.

But his hearing was now more finely attuned, however, as he waited for Sir Nicholas to arrive. Every tiny external sound, no matter how distant or familiar, had him up and twitching. Their last telephone conversation had left him in no doubt as to his options; the entrance to some chamber or crypt simply had to be through the hearthstone. Apart from the virtual elimination of any other possibility inside the building he had confirmed his belief since putting down the receiver, uncovering the cup-shaped recess with its bar handle, set in the front of the stone where it protruded beneath the heavy cast-iron grate-cum-cooker. It had been filled in and smoothed over with mortar a long time past, being quite crumbly and a different colour from the rest of the floor around it. Digging the material out with a steak knife had taken but a minute. He had trembled all over, glancing up in sudden realization at the blackened pulley wheel set in the roof of the original fireplace. He could find no rope or chain to test his supposition and in any event he would require physical assistance to remove the grate first. He had tried to call Sir Nicholas back on the phone to give him an update but got no reply.

What was that? A new noise outside, heavy and scuffing across the rough stone garden path. He silently skirted the ruins of the kitchen fittings, his sense of direction now almost perfect. The dancing light beam scared him for a moment, but then realized that only someone with a supreme arrogance would be so blatant in such a situation.

The bulky figure, swathed in his usual dark suit beneath a sweeping black topcoat filled the doorway.

"Cappel." The voice was still silky-smooth. Cappel had to admire such presence and command despite his repugnance of the man.

"Sir Nicholas…yes, over here…watch your step." The priest held out a helping hand but it was waved away, Brookes stepping across in his light-footed way over the wreckage the other had wrought. He stood, picking out the fireplace in the beam of his torch. Excitedly Cappel showed him his new find. "Yes, of course," Brookes murmured. He could visualize it clearly, secretly annoyed at not reaching such a conclusion himself earlier. But he had been under a degree of pressure; that damned young reporter, Carolyn's disappearance and then the urgency and stress of reclaiming her. Firing that blasted housekeeper and then having to reveal all to Carolyn, with the possibility that he had closed down that particular rich conduit of knowledge forever. Ah, well, perhaps not, they were still within the deadline and very close; he could feel it. When this night was over then maybe they could all get on with their Brookes-ordained lives!

But there were problems still, he thought, calculating. He was not a physical person, more used to three-hour lunches and limousines.

"Couldn't you have shifted this" – he kicked at the black-leaded grate – "before I got here? A rope, a lever of some kind… How on earth did Julius Marr manage when he did a runner, eh?"

"N-no, Sir Nicholas, this range came with the rebuilt house. The earlier version would have been more basic, some grate bars, a spit, something like that. And remember" – Cappel gulped as he realized he was lecturing this fearsome man who controlled destinies, lives even. "I mean, this was almost certainly only used as a last resort or bolt hole, perhaps joined directly to the church. Such tunnels were common."

"Yes, yes, but how did he – how do we get it out of the blasted way to even test such a theory. I may be big but I am no body builder"

"Look here!" Cappel showed him the pulley. Brookes flashed his torch where indicated and immediately saw the possibilities. "If you have a rope or chain in your car…" Cappel held his breath; the next few seconds were crucial, there would be no time to go seeking lifting gear – even if they could be sure of moving undetected. "We could move the grate first by raising the front end there and – and then placing the chimney tubing underneath to act as a kind of fulcrum. By attaching the tow rope to the rear end to complete the movement I'm certain we could fairly easily take it clear of the flagstone…sir." Silence. Desperately the dishevelled Cappel burst out, "The principle is sound, Sir Nicholas, I can assure you -"

"Yes, I believe there is a heavy tow rope in the car boot. Saw it when I lift – er, it should be okay Here!" Cappel just managed to catch the car keys. "Go now and fetch it." He quickly told the quivering cleric where he had hidden the Jaguar and pushed him out of the kitchen.

Cappel, too cowed to resist, suddenly found himself outside, the cool night air on his face, like a man released after a long solitary confinement. His first impulse was to make a run for it, escape from the fear, the filth he had lived in these past few days. Just go somewhere civilized and normal, a place that knew nothing of the occult, murder and everlasting damnation. Walk in sunlight instead of someone else's shadow. Good God, how had he come to this? He looked back; saw the flickering beam playing on the kitchen ceiling and it all came crushing in on him like a black avalanche. There was no succour, nowhere to run to that would be safe from his master's reach. Like some robot programmed to respond only to its controller there were simply no choices he could make except self-destruction…and that would be a horror lasting through eternity.

He stumbled away into the darkness.

31: ASSEMBLANCE

Getting back to St Michael's was surprisingly easy. Jake parked the car in a copse behind and above the village. He should have ventured closer because of the time factor but instinctively baulked at the idea of leaving the car somewhere below the level of what would soon be deep, dark water. He got out of the car, taking Carolyn's arm in the faint moonlight and feeling Dolgun would most probably laugh gently at his imagination while at the same time understanding perfectly.

There was a well-worn path through the trees. The darkened streets and houses at least aided their uncertainty by not dazzling them in their descent. A soft wind rustled the remaining leaves in the nearby birches. Carolyn shivered and hooked her arm through his, trying to match his long strides in an instinctive effort to reduce unnecessary noise.

"What is it, exactly, that this Professor Dolgun is going to do in St Michael's, Jake?"

He laughed self-consciously. "Truth to tell I'm not too sure. He has this theory…as yet unproven, mind you. Something to do with tapping into the energy lines radiating from the church's standing stone and tracking along them to find our spectral dog."

"Ugh!" She shuddered at the memory. "Not so spectral. And then…?"

The ancient church lay just before them now and Jake sensed something wrong in the silhouette beyond the stone wall. She felt him stiffen and looked up anxiously.

"What is it, Jake?" she whispered. "Tell me!"

"What? Oh, I don't know…something…" He tried not to be

275

alarmed. Then he saw it. "Shit!" He quickened his stride. "It's okay, Carolyn. Just me. In here." He opened one of the double wrought iron gates that led to the rear of the church and when she had slipped through he carefully closed them again.

"Look!" He pointed. The shape that had unsettled him was a battered and dark-coloured van, parked close against the north wall of the building.

"I guess the good professor is here…thank God," he breathed. The rear doors of the van were open and there were several cables snaking out and across to the church side door, which was ajar. Jake led the way and tentatively peered inside; there was just enough night light to see the grey hair and glinting glasses bending over some electronic equipment.

"Professor? Professor Dolgun?"

The tall figure straightened up and turned. He was dressed in a black track suit and trainers. "Come in, come in and close the door as much as possible. Watch your step over those power lines"

Carolyn peeked around Jake's shoulder and Dolgun grunted something inaudible before striding forward, hand outstretched.

"You must be Carolyn. I'm very happy to see you. It means everything is working along the right lines."

"I'm not too sure about that, Professor," Jake replied. His tone made Dolgun whirl, the spectacles flashing in the moon's pale light falling through the old stained-glass window. "Tell me but make it quick, we don't have a lot of time. I've managed to divert security to the far end of the valley by cutting into their frequency but I can't guarantee a time limit. Over here." He indicated some more equipment, not yet connected. Carolyn sat on one of them and glanced fearfully about her. And well she might, thought Jake, following her gaze.

The interior had been stripped of furnishings and fittings, a strange sight, rather like some Gothic barn, with its sweeping arches and columns that seemed somehow more majestic than he remembered from his former visit. Bare flagstones and walls; he turned, a little confused and then realized – even the communion rail had been removed. What for – auction perhaps? Storage, refurbishment…ecclesiastical boot sale? Only the stained-glass windows remained to remind him of its religious origins. What a bizarre goldfish bowl that'll make for the new inhabitants! He started, for the first time registering the significance of the image depicted in the main window behind the altar – St George slaying the dragon. What was it again…the new religion driving the old beliefs and energies underground?

"Jake? Jake!"

"Yes, sir, sorry." Dolgun was back at his oscilloscopes but staring up at him impatiently. He quickly told the older man what had transpired over the last few hours. At first Dolgun had merely continued with his work, connecting and setting up, calibrating, nodding, a terminal screwdriver gripped between his teeth. But as the story revealed the full extent of Brookes's duplicity and the fire he turned to Carolyn, only really noticing their dishevelled state for perhaps the first time. Then he became quite solicitous, quickly checking her pulse and then her pupils with a pencil torch.

"I'm sorry, my dear, I was so wrapped up in this…" He patted her hand. "You seem fundamentally sound; youth is a wonderful thing, the only real answer to shocks of that nature." He turned to Jake. "So now we know, hmm? No matter how much they have it's never enough. Right!" He slapped his side. "If what they say is true he should be here…or near."

"You mean because of the natural energy convergence?"

"No," the professor replied grimly. "Because there are really only two places the chalice *can* be." He swept one hand about him. "As you can see, nothing has been disturbed here -"He caught Jake's surprised, disbelieving expression, even through

277

the gloom. "Oh, yes, the poor place has been somewhat denuded; that was to be expected in a situation like this. But it hasn't been ripped apart in any search, has it? Given the account of Julius Marr's disappearance and apparent demise to be accurate then the chalice would have to be hidden here -"

"The presbytery!" Jake whirled on Carolyn, who was sitting quite still but taking it all in. "Of course, it has to be wherever Marr's body is." He smacked his brow in annoyance. "That has to be where Cappel is skulking – and Brookes is probably there at this very minute." His jaw tightened. "I think I can kill two bastards with one stone…If I'm not back in ten minutes, Prof, start without me."

"Jake! Jake…" Both Dolgun and Carolyn shouted in unison, the latter in sheer terror at this further strain on her already over-stretched nerves. She went to run after him but Dolgun grabbed her. She twisted and screamed, "No! Jake! Jake, please don't leave me…please…" Her voice broke in a sob and she turned, white-faced, to the older man. "What's he doing? It's insane. Please stop him…please… I couldn't bear to lose him now, not after…" She collapsed in his arms, her body racked with grief.

Dolgun's face filled with compassion and he gently drew her tensed arms down, pulling her to him as he did so.

"There comes a time in a man's life, Carolyn – hopefully just once – when he feels he has to prove himself…to himself. When that time comes there's very little anyone can do to stop it…except perhaps pray that he comes through unscathed."

32: IMMINENCE

It took Brookes and his unwilling helper the best part of an hour to crack the seal on the tunnel's entrance. Cappel's plan had proved workable if unwieldy. With the cleric's surprising strength and the other's useful bulk they manhandled the Victorian grate out of position. The heavy cast iron sections separated once upended, and Cappel almost shoved Brookes aside in his urgent need to achieve their objective. The media magnate let him get on with it, standing to one side as Cappel flung the sections out of the recess and onto the tumble of debris that had been the kitchen's interior. Neither of them considered the possibility of exposure, so intent in their focused endeavours.

They worked mainly by the moon's fitful light, having drawn the curtains to allow what little there was to aid their task. The car's torch was only used when absolutely necessary. They hardly spoke, each knowing the other's primary reason for being there and only wanting it to be over.

Finally there was nothing left in the fireplace except a few bits projecting from the blackened brickwork. Cappel, filthy as the chimney sweep he'd almost become, got down on his knees, running his fingertips along the crack that was the main hearth stone.

"Here!" Brookes held out the reinforced tow rope from the car. It had a snap ring at one end, which Cappel engaged in the lifting handle across the cup-shaped depression.

Cappel quickly dragged the pine table across the ruined floor until it was close enough to stand on and lean out towards the blackened pulley. Wordlessly Brookes handed him the rope. The priest's face was gaunt and streaked with sweat, his breath seeming to scrape through his lungs in great gasping gulps. Brookes regarded him with extreme distaste, seeing in him a burnt-out case. The man was clearly reaching the end of his usefulness and couldn't be relied upon to sustain the secrecy required after all this was resolved. The devil only knew what form his fevered dreams had taken, stuck in this virtual prison over the previous few days. Give him his due the man probably couldn't have done much better. But dammit, he had his own troubles to contend with –

"Catch…sir!" Cappel gasped as it looped over and down, where the other deftly caught the rope's end. Cappel jumped down and immediately took up the slack. The bright orange line bisected the gloom in an inverted V. Brookes reluctantly moved closer to the sweating priest and took hold of a section of rope. With a muttered prayer that almost made Brookes recoil in shock Cappel appeared to uncoil like a spring and – grabbing the rope above Brookes's grip – heaved downwards with all his might.

Nothing happened, apart from a thrumming sound from the rope and their rapidly emptying lungs.

"Again…" Cappel whispered, and Brookes leaned back as hard as he could, feeling unaccustomed perspiration bead on his pale brow. Still no movement. Both of them sagged, Cappel's breath coming in wheezing sounds.

"Have you gone round the edge with a knife or something?" Brookes thought it was time he regained control here.

"Y-yes, sir." The other's sunken, haunted eyes met his for a moment before brightening. "But perhaps not enough. Stupid of me." He went to the draining board and rummaged about until he found the steak knife. With both hands he proceeded to score with the pointed blade all along the four sides of the 3'x2' stone. Jabbing and hooking along the crack he grunted, "That's it…I'm…getting…somewhere." Down on his knees now he became engrossed, creeping around the flagstone's edge, ramming the steel tip more deeply as he loosened the ages-old dirt. Brookes stepped back as some of it struck his clothes. The man's like some terrier at a burrow, he thought, gazing through the semi-darkness at the crouched figure. How quickly we slide down from our high station when priorities alter. He tried to make out the time by his watch but the dark dial defeated him. He smiled thinly; there were some disadvantages in the lack of light, he conceded.

"There! That should do it." Cappel straightened up for a moment, easing his back, before going to the rope again. Brookes took up his position beside him and when the other gave an enquiring look he nodded. Taking deep breaths, together they took the strain. For a long, dreadful second nothing and then with a slight but definite jerk something gave. For a moment Brookes feared the pulley was coming out, but then Cappel shouted, "Yes! It's coming… Heave!"

Gritting his teeth Brookes bore down with an effort he'd not have believed possible of himself. He felt a sharp pain in the muscles of his right upper arm. Then – with an almost human groan – the lip of the stone trapdoor lifted above the floor level. An inch…two…and suddenly a tiny gap appeared. They both saw what was required almost instantaneously; Cappel – being closest – kicked a broken chair-back towards the opening, grunting and whispering to himself as he strove to manoeuvre it with his right foot.

"Got it!" With a small whinny of triumph he rammed one side of the broken chair under the raised stone's edge, checked that both ends protruded at either side before twisting round to say hoarsely, "It's all right, Sir Nicholas, you can relax now."

With a barely suppressed groan Brookes slumped backwards, almost slipping on the uneven floor. Ruefully he rubbed his palms together before cautiously easing his shoulder with a circular motion of his right arm.

"I hope that was the hard part!"

"Yes, yes, look." Bending forward the grime-covered cleric gripped the edge and – with both hands – proceeded to lift it further, all the while easing the makeshift wedge along with his foot to hold the increasing angle. When the gap was approximately six inches he stopped and fumbled the torch out of his trousers pocket. He had to slap it against his thigh once before it flickered into life. He knelt forward and shone it into the narrow opening.

Brookes – unable to maintain his aloof stance as the excitement gripped him too – stumbled to Cappel's side and peered down.

"Steps!" he breathed, clapping his companion on the shoulder.

"Yes…and the air seems relatively clean." The other's glittering, feverish eyes shone out of the blackened face. His breath was foetid, reminding Brookes of the solitary nature of the man's search. The poor sod must have gone through… He stopped himself, knowing what lay ahead for both of them. Best allow the man his moment, his enjoyment would be brief; it would also serve to allay any emerging fears or suspicions.

"I think the honour should be yours, Cappel. " He stood up, assisting the other to his feet. Cappel stared at him wildly, a series of emotions registering as they chased each other across his lean, sweat-streaked features.

"I–I...Sir Nicholas…" he stammered.

"C'mon, my boy, our quest is almost at an end." He pointed to one corner of the flagstone and, gripping the other one with both hands, took up a firm stance. Like some schoolboy eager to please his favourite form master, Cappel scrambled as bidden to the other side. At a nod from Brookes they slowly hauled the protesting slab to the vertical position, and then carefully leaned it against the back of the fireplace. Even in the gloom the stone steps were visible.

Standing across from the entrance to all his dreams Brookes nevertheless controlled his breathing enough to say, "After you, Renton." He held out one still-pale hand as encouragement and chuckled. "Any demons down there will be user friendly, I can assure you." As the other still hesitated, unsure how to take this new Sir Nicholas, the magnate's voice took on an edge. "Of course, we can both stand here and just wait for the next security patrol to topple down there first. Come!"

33: CONFINANCE

Jake ran down the gravelled path that led to the presbytery. Oblivious to any potential injury in the darkness he made it to the gloomy-looking building in a matter of seconds, only pausing at the front door, gulping not so much from lack of air as indecision. Now that he'd reached a palpable point of committal the rage had transformed itself into a cooler appraisal of what he must do.

Wiping a hand across his mouth, he licked dry lips and pushed at the heavy glass door. Not only unlocked, it was partially open. Cautiously he pushed the handle; it seemed to be jammed at the bottom. Grasping the door's edge with both hands he slowly but firmly pushed and felt the door give, albeit with noisy reluctance as it rode over the obstruction. Squeezing through the few inches of clearance he blinked, muttering an involuntary "Jesus!" at the scene of devastation.

Gingerly stepping over the wreckage he checked out every room along the hallway, ignoring the stairs for later, should his search indicate that as a possibility. But he thought not; the chalice had to be at or below ground level, and each room he peered into tended to confirm that view. The floor damage was similar in every case. Cappel obviously hadn't found what he was looking for here, he decided, trying not to stumble and clatter against something. He had no illusions about the seriousness of what Brookes and Cappel were embarked upon, having learnt so much these past few days, not least the true nature of evil. How many other lives had the man tampered with, even destroyed? He had few doubts now about Father Scanlon's demise. But the risk! For a man such as he, to gamble all on one missing artifact. Surely it couldn't be *that* powerful. He was reminded of Joan's words. "Most things work if you believe in them enough." Okay, then, Joan, he muttered, I truly believe these two men have forfeited God's gift of life. Give me the strength to do whatever is necessary.

He groped his way to the rear of the big house, feeling his way by touch and what little natural light there was. Each room was like some crazy trail for him to follow – he only prayed he was going in the right direction. This must have been the kitchen; wall cupboards and a draining board by the sink, stuff hanging from the ceiling, a firepl – He stopped, his heart missing a beat. Was that a faint light, over there by the floor in the fireplace recess?

He sank to the floor, his hand carefully feeling about in the rubble for something to use as a weapon. He silently discarded what was obviously a saucepan and then a scrubbing brush. His fingers curled around a very substantial chair leg. Hefting it he crept forward, placing each foot extremely carefully, for he could see almost clearly now in the pale moonlight that one of the flagstones was raised and its underside was reflecting…something.

He reached the steps and slowly straightened, his mind and pulse racing. It looked as though the pair had found what they were seeking – or at least a way towards the source. They must have a light, Brookes was not one to arrive unprepared. He could see no light now though, nor any sound. Obviously moving away, along a passage. It suddenly struck him and he turned, orientating himself.

Of course! If this passage continues in a line from the steps bottom it heads right for the church. That was Marr's escape route. But did he elude his tormentors on that terrible night 150 years ago? Had he had enough time to get down there, pull the stone shut over him, tear along the tunnel and come up somewhere in St Michael's, precious cup clutched to his chest and a contemptuous curse on his lips? If so, then Brookes and Cappel were going to be sorely mortified. They would then – presumably – come boiling back up here before the next patrol came by, or discover Marr's exit and pop up to confront an unsuspecting Carolyn like some vision from hell! Oh, my God, she couldn't handle that; I have to get back.

But what if they *did* find the cup? What if it does have the ultimate power in such a man's hands? He had no alternative, he saw that now. One way or the other they had to be stopped – and he couldn't be in two places at once, could he?

"Sorry Uncle Nicky," he intoned softly. "Let's just say this is going to be the first real test of your belief in the Judas Cup." Grunting with effort he lowered the stone back in position. It dropped into place with a soft thud. Casting about Jake quickly located the nearest uprooted flagstones and 'walked' one of them, corner-to-corner, until he could lower it over the hinged hearthstone. Three more followed, to form an untidy pile. Stepping back he dusted his hands off and surveyed his handiwork before turning to go.

"I sure hope you two get along together."

34: EXULTANCE

"What was that?" Cappel turned to peer back towards the tunnel entrance, now out of sight around a slight bend. "Did you hear it?" he stared fearfully at his companion, who merely gestured impatiently to keep moving.

"Whatever it is we can't really go back to look, can we? Probably just some security stumbling about or looking for a place to pee. He's not going to notice one more upturned flagstone, is he? Or just rats. Let's get on."

"We should have lowered it after us, Sir Nicholas." Cappel's voice was tremulous, and not only because of his diffidence in the company of this man, so dangerous and unpredictable, but in the surroundings, which seemed not to affect his companion one whit. The young priest would have dearly wished for a fraction of his *sang froid*. He had somehow expected – once having seen the steps – that whatever was down there would be equally of a man-made nature. But once below ground it was obvious that was where the craftsmanship ended; the passage was rough-hewn, mainly following a natural fault through the rock but in parts the subsoil. It was here that he felt the peril of their position, for such stretches – although extending no more than a few yards apart at most – were shored up with pit props from the long obsolete ironstone workings. Some of these had collapsed, although little actual soil slippage was evident.

The tunnel was obviously constructed as an emergency escape route, designed to come out somewhere under St Michael's, making Cappel wonder if their search would be in vain. Julius Marr would hardly allow himself to be trapped in such a place.

Brookes pushed him and he stumbled forward, the hand torch throwing the cobwebbed walls into sharp relief. The roof was no higher than his head when standing upright and considerably less in some places, no more than a yard wide anywhere. But the air was clean, probably drawn and warmed by the fire in the kitchen that must have burned almost continuously in the old days.

"It can't be far now, Renton, by my calculations." Brookes's voice echoed strangely from over his shoulder. The larger man was finding it arduous, thought Cappel, and all this unaccustomed exertion was taking its toll. Plus the stress of anticipation and undoubted thoughts of possible failure in the next few minutes. For his own part these recent days had left precious few moments for rational thought. He'd only left the presbytery once, to get the details on Joan Winspear – *Oh, my God, I wonder what has happened to her and that niece or ward of his? When all this is finished…* But that brought him back to his resolution. In his rare moments of lucidity – between the nightmares, frantic digging and dodging army patrols – he'd finally made his peace with God. The last three years had been a kind of purgatory, an interim punishment for whatever was to come. He'd been a fool but that was no sin; what had transgressed God's laws had been his capitulation in the face of a manipulative evil that he had been trained to guard against. It had been *that* woman, Franklyn, she who had reminded him so much of his one and only true love. Teen age he may have been, but when had love been more intense than in those formative years? His naiveté had at first intrigued, then excited, Rosemary Hall. But up close the ineptitude of his initial sexual fumblings had made her impatient, then angry, and finally derisive. Her knowing laughter still rang in his ears, down all the years, had driven him straight into the arms of those who placed no burden of feminine knowledge on his narrow shoulders. Too late had he realized the true meaning of vocation and just how little of it he possessed. However, with a vista of uncertainty before him and his mother with her very definite views on everything urging him on he knew he really had no choice.

And then Fenella had triggered off his dormant sex drive again. The same flaming red hair and bold green eyes. He'd never revealed his attraction but she had tuned in almost instantly, he knew that later, and she had exploited his weakness for all it was worth - which had turned out to be plenty for the west Somerset Lodge of the Golden Dawn.

But no more, he knew now where his salvation lay. And if it meant the ultimate sacrifice then so be it, he was ready to meet his Maker.

The tunnel floor dipped, continuing the fault, before opening out into an artificially-made chamber some three metres square, and there, in the pale yellow torchlight, lay the mortal remains of Julius Marr.

"Holy Mary, Mother of God!" Cappel made the sign of the cross instinctively in the presence of death.

Brookes brushed past him, snatching the light from his slack grip. The partially clothed skeleton grinned up at them in a grotesque parody of greeting, the uncovered teeth catching the light, eye sockets staring into eternity in an expression of perpetual wonder. A black, broad-brimmed felt hat, tilted back on the hairless skull like some halo from hell. It all lay at the foot of more steps, leading up to another flagstone set in the roof. Nearby lay an open bible, most of the pages shredded by rodents. A few paper scraps were scattered about, rejected no doubt after a diet sated on human flesh. Cappel shuddered, wishing himself anywhere but here. His companion was not so squeamish, muttering an oath as he roughly went through Marr's coat pockets, tearing the rotten material in his haste.

"It must be here somewhere – ah!" His treatment of the body

dislodged the skull; it toppled to one side, making Cappel scream involuntarily as it rolled with a terrible clicking sound to end up at his feet. He jumped back in horror, trying to gurgle something. Brookes ignored him, reaching for the polished mahogany box on which the head had rested. With an uncharacteristic reverence he held it in both hands before raising it above his head in tribute.

"Behold, the Judas Cup!"

35: BIOSCIENCE

Dolgun glanced up from his work as Jake came through the darkened doorway. Carolyn gave a small cry and ran to him; he held her close for a moment before leading her back to where the scientist was finishing off his setting-up. She kept touching Jake's arm as though still not believing his safe return.

"Tell me, Jake," Carolyn pleaded. "Did you find Uncle Nicky over there?"

"Never saw hide or hair of him…or that devil's disciple, Cappel." Her look made him hold his hand up like someone in the dock. "Swear to God." He crossed his heart for good measure, avoiding Dolgun's piercing gaze, relatively easy in the gloom. "How we doing, Prof?" He kept his voice deliberately light for Carolyn's sake, who was still regarding him uncertainly.

"We're just about there, Jake." Dolgun stood up slowly and stretched himself, running fingers through his hair. "All we need now is a short period of undisturbed concentration and…a responsive subject. If our friends aren't in the presbytery then that takes care of one big worry for the moment. Strange though…"

"Perhaps they have already found what they were after -" Carolyn stopped, realizing what that could mean for her. Jake squeezed her arm reassuringly, saying, "I'm sure they're far away from here by now, in which case we can deal with them later." He turned to Dolgun. "Let's get a move on, sir, I'm still not fully convinced those construction people know the difference between twelve noon and midnight!"

Dolgun chuckled, despite himself. "If they don't then there will be an awful lot of local dignitaries' wives with new hats and nowhere to go tomorrow. No, that's not a problem. The real concern for us is where the dog is, at this precise moment."

"Well," grumbled the young journalist, "we know where it was about forty minutes ago."

"Yes, well, that's a clue, Jake, I'll admit, and one that I've entered into my calculations. See here…" He unrolled an A3-sized sheet of white paper. It showed up clearly in the limited light. Defined in black marker pen it resembled a ragged spider's web, with some of the intersecting lines highlighted, others named. A north-pointing arrow was in the top right-hand corner.

"See here." Dolgun spread his hand across the paper. "Working on Joan's very apt analogy I have marked where the creature has been reported or suspected as having been seen. The airport runway is of course the latest update – here!" He stabbed the paper with a forefinger. "And this is the centre of the network, our church…or more precisely that standing stone over there." He pointed to the east wall. "But this whole altar area is close enough for our purpose."

"But isn't its focal point the tumulus?" Jake cut in.

"Yes, well done, young man." The scientist patted him on the shoulder. "But the fact that it appeared here I think indicates two things. One, its centre of energy has shifted over the centuries. As I mentioned, the tumulus used to be surrounded by water…right? Two, that stone is here and the dog manifested itself here, so it is reasonable to assume it will recognize the church as its new resting place."

"And all this…?" Jake swept a hand around him. Ranged on either side were two rows of electronic equipment; signal generators, oscilloscopes, power supplies, most of them winking small coloured lights in a beguilingly friendly fashion. The laptop with its cool blue screen dominated. They were all connected to a portable generator housed in the van outside, from which a low throbbing hum now emanated.

292

"Hopefully this is the magnet that will attract our canine customer -"

"And then?" Carolyn couldn't help it, her nerves beginning to unravel in the creepy surroundings. "I mean, this is the original hound from hell. We've seen it…and what's worse, it's seen us. It has some unfinished business with Jake and me. By all accounts this–this paranormal pooch takes on nuns, rottweilers…737s! What are we supposed to do when it appears, say three Hail Marys and hope it will be sucked back down the time tunnel to wherever it came from?"

She began to sob into her hands and Jake was there in an instant, shielding her with his arms and glancing beseechingly at their mentor. Dolgun came across and gently prised them apart. Carolyn didn't want to be separated from Jake but the scientist was too strong and eventually she looked up, sniffed and wiped her nose with a tissue she managed to find in Jake's outstretched hand.

"Look, young lady, I do appreciate what you are going through. Nobody should have to cope with all that you have endured these last few days…and it's not yet over by any means, is it?" She shook her head. "Whatever the outcome here you will still have to address the rest of your life against that fiendish uncle of yours. But Jake and I will be there to help you sort that out, so that has to be a plus, hmm?" She reluctantly nodded, in thrall to the power in this man. If only someone like him had brought her up, she mused, how different would my life be today? The idea caught her imagination and she chuckled, despite herself. Probably somewhere like this!

"That's better." Dolgun patted her arm, releasing her. "Now, as to your somewhat fraught but valid question on how we deal with whatever transpires from all this" – he waved one hand – "you will have to trust that I know what I am doing. If this creature is confused, disorientated, then that gives us an edge straight away." He held up one finger as she was about to speak again. "One of the main factors in power and control is confidence in one's knowledge…and how best to use it. We have that. Okay?"

She nodded dumbly.

"Making it appear against its will automatically gives us an advantage. It will be up to us to seize the moment and use it to best effect. Basically, if I have the technology to pull it back here then I also can *drive* it somewhere else."

"You mean –?"

"Enough, Jake! We are losing valuable time. You remember what is special about tonight, we must move on."

Jake tried to ignore Carolyn's puzzled look and sat where directed as Dolgun produced what he thought of now as the Squid helmet. Quickly explaining its function to her he connected up the various electrodes and put them through the digital converter linked to the computer.

"You see, contemporary physics is forcing us to accept that there are alternative realities to the physical. It envisages 'virtual particles' which can appear for small periods of time before disappearing once more into a non-material or etheric state."

"You mean – you mean from one plane to another?" Jake was incredulous, although why he should feel so with this man who had the seemingly continuous power to amaze, defeated him.

"Yes, in essence, that's why it's referred to as the Salmon Leap. And this particular spirit form we are trying to contact is apparently moving back and forth along this energy line matrix, seeking the correct path back here."

"You mean… Sorry for interrupting…"

"That's perfectly all right, Jake, I'll allow you one more question. Fire away."

"If I read you correctly then I have to somehow 'tune in' to its frequency via this – this Squid thing." He still didn't look entirely convinced. Carolyn shrugged herself out of the debate and sat on one of the warm electronic cabinets.

"Not quite, Jake, and it wasn't a question. It is a pretty basic rule of particle physics we're dealing with here. You have seen the creature, can imagine it. It therefore exists…somewhere, either physically or inside your head." He held up a hand as Jake made to protest. "That standing stone there is continually exerting ultra-sound. It is also pretty unique in that it is what I like to call a high-band markstone. This means it emits energy on several different bands up its length and these can be 'tapped' as it were, to release its energy."

"What d'you mean tapped?" asked Carolyn, interested despite her decision to remain outside whatever was going on here.

"Well, they – the energy bands – move up and down the stone throughout the lunar cycle. Each band has a specific property. The uppermost or seventh band is perhaps the strongest and will deliver a mild electric shock if touched when primed. Such energy can be stored – ideally at sunrise and full moon – and released suddenly. These pulses are called overgrounds and usually transmit in dead straight lines -"

"So if we can use them we can possibly reach our dog, jerk his psychic chain, so to speak," broke in Jake, turning to Carolyn in amazement.

Dolgun chuckled. "Well, I wouldn't have put it quite like that but yes – establish a conduit for it to lock on to and hopefully travel back along it to confront whatever it is that is duplicating its brain waves…namely, you! Belt and braces, as you British so aptly put it."

"And these…?" Jake had just noticed the four loudspeakers placed around the altar space, each one fixed high up on a pillar.

"Ah, that's for the second phase. No more questions! Shall we begin?"

36: DISCORDANCE

Cappel gazed up in horror; Brookes holding aloft the symbol of evil in an obscene parody of the transubstantiation of Christ, the ceremony he had lovingly performed so many times, before falling into the trap of easy virtue and its inevitable price. The chanting. The swinging of the thurible and the incense wafting from it, the Tridentine Mass and the Latin. He could still recite the words, although it was many years now. "…*pro innumerabilibus paccatis, et offensionibus, et negligentiis meis, et pro omnibus circumstantibus*…" He shuddered, a reaction so violent it broke the spell for Brookes, who lowered his arms, drawing the object of so much desire and urgency to his chest before turning and stepping carefully back down to where Cappel stood.

"Here it is, Renton…at last!" he breathed, looking into the other's eyes but not relaxing his grip on the small chalice. "Almost two thousand years of history. What scenes it has witnessed – caused – since Judas held this silver in his hands." He looked up. "Betrayal, murder, revolution, a weapon. Another time a royal seal to overthrow a kingdom? Fascinating, considering its size."

Cappel felt his gorge rise once more, seeing only the reason for his beloved Saviour's agony and betrayal, a trigger for all that had followed, beginning with the death of its first recipient, then Jesus Himself and only God knew how many more since that fateful Sabbath eve. But it was indeed small, no more than ten centimetres high, half of that stem and base. And blackened with age, not glittering as he imagined it would be. The rim was less than five centimetres across and the whole of the outer surface was intricately chased with what at first he took to be Arabic or perhaps Aramaic lettering. But as he raised the torch and rubbed at the rim with his jacket sleeve to see it better he recoiled; the 'lettering' was a continuous series of copulating figures – men with women, men with men, animals... He turned away as Brookes, seeing his revulsion, laughed harshly and thrust it at him.

"What's the matter...priest? Lost the urge? Or perhaps you are really only interested in redheads...or in one in particular, hmm?" And he threw back his head and laughed again, the long black hair swirling about the fleshy face like a dark curtain. The man radiated so much power that Cappel felt like some trapped animal in the confined space. But he must do what he had vowed, feeling for the steak knife in his pocket.

Brookes, misreading the other's mood, became serious. "Right, we have what we came for but before we leave this place forever" – he bent down to return the chalice to its box, a move whose swiftness caught Cappel unawares – "let's establish just why old Julius here didn't make it to freedom." Holding the box tightly he climbed the ten steps until his head was touching the flagstone's underside. "C'mon, quickly, man, you know I can't do it alone." Cappel hurried to obey. Once again he was hampered in his resolve by having to use both hands as they tried vainly to raise the trapdoor. After several attempts they gave up and retreated, back down, Cappel leading.

"Not surprising, really." Brookes was panting. "After all this...time... But there must be a reason why, then. Heart attack?" He rubbed his chin, gazing down dispassionately at the leering skull. "C'mon, Julius, what's the story, hmm? Pegged out at the last fence...? No, I can't buy that...the Master wouldn't countenance such an – an inconsequential finale for one who had served him well and was obviously intending carrying on his work with the Judas Cup." He raised the hinged lid on the polished box and gazed inside for a moment, as though seeking inspiration. He seemed oblivious to Cappel's presence, didn't see or feel the other's hate-filled eyes upon him as he fondled the chalice in an almost sensual manner. He had no doubt that Cappel would have been astounded at where his thoughts really lay at that moment. No parochial performances for this little treasure, destined as it was for the very heart of the Vatican, returned to its place deep in the vaults. With the alarming rise in religious artifacts thefts worldwide the return of this particular one would almost certainly tip the balance for little Franzl, as someone determined to redress the church's increasing deficiencies in the twenty-first century.

"Perhaps this can explain the mystery, Sir Nicholas." The priest knew he had to lure the heavier man down to his level before attempting anything physical. He tried to keep his voice and expression neutral as he proffered the torn bible.

"What...? What d'you mean, man?" Brookes snapped the box shut. "What have you got there? Let me..." He came down the few steps rapidly, reaching for the torch.

"I–I can't quite make it out, sir, but he appears to have left a message, scrawled on the inside cover. It looks like..." He looked up as the thought struck him. "How could he have found ink? It must be blood...he's left a note in his own blood. My God!" He crossed himself again, his lean features registering the repugnance he felt.

"Here, give me!" Brookes snatched the black cover and its few remaining pages from the other's nerveless fingers. "What's a little blood to a man who is about to meet his Master and wants to hand on his most precious possession?" He peered at the faded script, shook the torch and then his head. "It's no use, we need more light..." He cast about, his eyes alighting on the crumpled remains of Julius Marr. With a triumphant grunt he pulled at the legless trousers and the fabric parted easily at the

298

seams. As Cappel cried out over this further desecration Brookes shook the bones from each trouser leg, femurs, tibias, kneecaps and an assortment of smaller bones rattling around their feet. The priest shrank away in horror, his plans driven from his tortured mind as the media magnate bent down and, carelessly grabbing one femur, roughly wrapped a strip of one trouser leg around its end. He took out a lighter, flicked it and the effect was dramatic as the ancient material flared into life. The rough-hewn chamber walls seemed to recede, thrown into sharp relief, the sputtering flame making the shadows leap and dance about them. The skull's teeth gleamed in mute mockery.

"Here, let's see what we've got." Brookes started to read the script, stopped, puzzled, before anger reddened the normally pale cheeks. "It's – it's in fucking Latin!" He glared accusingly at Cappel, including him in this further conspiracy to thwart him. "Come here! Quickly, unless you want me to make a bigger torch!" Reluctantly Cappel moved closer and reached for the bible. Haltingly and then with more confidence he began to translate: 'How humorous life is. The fools above in their ignorance have trapped me. In their search for the chalice they have somehow moved the altar base thus sealing me in this uncomfortable tomb. I am sorely wounded and now must accept my fate. I will greet my Master in the manner expected of a dutiful servant. He will ensure the cup's next owner is worthy of its power. Should he choose to misuse it then he must accept the price, as we all do – if not in this life then assuredly in the next.' Cappel lowered the book.

"That's it?" Brookes growled, receiving only a fearful nod. "Hmph, at least now we know. Fickle fate – Damn!" He dropped the torch as the flames reached his fingers. It smouldered to a dull red glow on the stone floor as Brookes sucked his thumb, brooding. "Still…" He turned to Cappel, the light returning to his eyes. "His loss is my gain, eh?"

299

"What *do* you intend doing with the cup, sir?" Cappel asked quietly, his mind racing as he sought some means to divert this dangerous accomplice to evil. "You never really said."

"Do with it?" Brookes laughed that cruel laugh. "Well, not what you think, Renton, old boy," He saw the other's surprise, savouring the moment. "You naturally thought it was to be used in further acts of satanic devilry perhaps, hmm? I agree that would be a logical extension of its destiny but there are other priorities which militate against the obvious here -"

"Priorities?" Cappel was intrigued, despite himself. Brookes went on to explain his plans for the Judas Cup, gazing at the box with an almost affectionate expression. At first Cappel was amazed, taken once more with the vision and ruthlessness of the man. Then the realization hit him. He took a step back. "But – but you heard Julius Marr's words…you are virtually ensuring the cup's neutralisation by consigning it to the Vatican vaults." Cappel whipped round as though struck, terror ripping through him at the prospect of being placed between the ultimate evil and this man who was about to openly defy it. But there was nobody – no *thing* – there, and he shook himself for being a fool. Brookes's laugh brought him back to the reality of his predicament.

"I think the Master will prove understanding, once I have made my long term plans clear, Renton." The mocking expression he had come to loathe was back. He was being toyed with again. Would the torment never end? "With the new age of media government that Italy has inflicted on Europe I'm certain my not inconsiderable resources plus Vatican Radio's clout can successfully broker a merger with the Italian prime minister's television and communications empire. With such a marriage – if not quite made in heaven! – there really isn't much that any country this side of the Urals can withstand."

Then Cappel saw it all, those millions out there, relatively unsophisticated in the ways of the hard and soft sell, pumped out over the ether every minute of every day. Sex, sadism, false standards, the ultimate pollution, when people no longer cared about virtue, morality and the code of law – because they would never be exposed to it. Satan would bestride a major portion of the globe, poised for total domination. The prophesies from the Book of Revelation would all come true…

"No! No, no, no, never!" Cappel screamed. Drawing the hidden weapon he lunged at his tormentor.

"What? No, Renton, don't…" Brookes recoiled, eyes widening as the knife's blade glinted in the dull torchlight. He threw up his right arm, still instinctively shielding the boxed chalice with his left. He had no time to retreat up the stone steps and for a brief instant he saw all his ambitions dissolve as his attacker's face became a screaming black hole that threatened to engulf him. Then it all changed; tilted, slid sideways as Cappel's final step came down on Julius Marr's skull. The shiny cranium skidded out from under the priest's full weight, skittering to smash itself against the nearest rock face. However, not before the shift imparted to Cappel's impetus had propelled him off balance, his look of incomprehension changing to one of surprise as his head struck the steps by Brookes's left hand. The force accompanying the sharp crack as this second skull shattered was enough to end the life force in the hapless cleric, without the instrument of his attack being twisted up under him as he slid past Brookes's long black coat to the floor. The blade entered his own chest just beneath the sternum, ripping at his heart as his weight drove its path upward. He flopped against the bottom step, his mouth gasping something the other couldn't comprehend before the eyes rolled up, the head jerked back and he died, the rictus smile a reminder of the one whose destiny had drawn them down here.

37: PRECIPITANCE

"It's no use!"

The atmosphere inside the abandoned church was no longer cold and dank. The operating equipment had removed the chill, but there was something else. The radiated energy of three people had added a tension that was possibly measurable on one of Dolgun's meters. The scientist's gaze, however, was now fixed on his young charge, as though willing him to try harder. But this too was without apparent success. Jake was seated, his hands fiddling with the helmet, a look of abject misery on his face. "You know I've never done anything like this before, apart from a few minutes in your lab. I–I'm really sorry, sir."

A great silence descended on the little group as they huddled inside their electronic laager; the ultra-modern technology surrounded by ages-old stonework that seemed now a mocking testament to their puny efforts. Then an eerie sigh broke the spell as a rising wind found a break in one of the stained-glass windows.

Carolyn saw – felt – the anguish in her loved one's eyes and took a deep breath, again for one brief moment seeming to stand outside her seated body as she heard herself saying, "Let me try."

"No!" Jake wrenched at the helmet, flinging it aside as he crossed the intervening space. Grabbing both her hands in his he knelt before her, his face white, so close she could just see the tiny flecks marring the deep blue of his eyes in the near-darkness. "No, Carolyn, we agreed no more dabbling in the abnormal…the unnatural forces out there. Please!"

"But it's all right for you to dabble, Jake, hmm?" She purposely kept her expression and tone tight, believing she already knew enough about this loveable guy to work it to her advantage. She didn't want to, seeing how clearly it hurt him, but they had come too far now to simply give up. Before beginning what should be a bright new phase in their lives she had to cut adrift all that other disgusting baggage. "Look...look!" She squeezed his hands. "I have the gift – God help me – of being able to tune in to etheric forces. Okay, so up till now it's only been used for negative purposes. Let me at least try this once to redress the balance. You must admit there will never be a greater need for us. Don't you see, darling, we've got to finish this here...now! One thing Uncle Nicky was right about, when he said you should never try to run from trouble, invariably its causes are within us – the things we do, say or respond to. We merely delude ourselves by giving them fancy names or push the blame onto others. Eventually you have to turn and face whatever's there. Only then can you walk away without flinching."

"Professor, you talk to her." Jake stood and ran his fingers through his hair. "Make her see the danger. She's physically and mentally strung out, being jerked around by that bastard. If she goes through with this and makes contact can you guarantee her safety?"

"There are no guarantees in this life, son, what can I say about the next one?" Dolgun was calm, but the look that passed between him and the girl made Jake throw up his hands in despair. Carolyn went to him and touched his arm. "Don't, Jake, it will be all right. Nobody appreciates what is at stake more than me." She reached up and kissed him lightly; before he could react she turned to Dolgun. "Okay, Professor, let's get this show on the road. I have other plans for what's left of this moonlight."

He sat her where Jake had been and fitted the helmet – taking a little longer because of her abundant hair – working

303

quickly and explaining its functions as he did so. She nodded several times, only shaking her head emphatically when he asked her if she wished to be deep-tranced.

"No thanks, not this time. If I have the power then just this once I want to fly on manual. You understand?"

"Yes, yes I do, young lady, and I commend your courage. Jake is in for some wonderful surprises with you by his side. I wish I could be there to witness them."

She smiled brilliantly but her eyes were over-bright as she took a deep breath. "Who knows, you may be…for some at least! Okay, I'm ready."

Dolgun patted her arm, fixed the black velvet blindfold on her and then crossed over to the consoles, quickly making several adjustments. He then went through the same process as with Jake earlier; getting her to visualize some episodes from her life he then recorded and punched in the various pick-up points and frequencies from her electrodes. He re-positioned two of the electrodes, checked his findings, ran them through the laptop before nodding in her direction.

"Okay, then, Carolyn, take it gently and concentrate deeply on your image of the beast as you perceived it. Consider its menace and evil intent but also try to input a certain sympathy for its plight, in that you wish to assist its return to its resting place…its guardianship role, whatever it may be." He laughed quietly at his own words. "I must sound a bit like Ken Russell on a film set, eh? But we're not painting in light brush strokes here – we're dealing in pretty basic emotions – life, injury, sheer terror…death. Remember above all this is no game, nor an exercise. The stakes are high and we'll only get one shot at it -"

"For God's sake!" Jake's anguished cry stopped the older man; he raised one hand in mute acknowledgement and turned back to his instruments.

For Carolyn the world quickly became a very small place as

her consciousness slipped into a conditioned reflexive mode. She ignored Jake's helpless expression and the tensed back of Dolgun as he played the electronic equipment like some skilled pianist. At first the oscilloscope sine waves darted about, Disney-like, a sinuous snake, collapsing, reforming, squeezing up and then levelling out as Dolgun strove to accommodate Carolyn's thought patterns as she sought a deep, fixed image of what the black dog meant to her, should it defeat or escape them this night. What if her uncle somehow brought it under his control? Where the hell was he anyway? She sensed Dolgun's agitation as her concentration slipped, held a hand up in acceptance of her drift and plunged inward more deeply still, calling upon her previous experience. Although always otherwise deep-tranced the indoctrinated technique took over immediately, something she had banked on when deciding to volunteer. This was no work for amateurs, and if there was one thing she was good at it was calling upon all her inner resources.

She heard Dolgun's soft "Yes!" beside her and, encouraged, she visualized still further, knowing he was converting and transmitting on full power.

She became aware of the ancient church's altering ambience – the molecular make-up thickening, like soup when more ingredients are added. Her highly developed senses picked it up before the others and she slowly raised both arms, eyes still closed, to draw their attention.

Jake responded first, initially uncomprehending as he instinctively moved in her direction, fearing she was in some kind of danger already. He was mindful of Dolgun's warning not to speak unless it was absolutely necessary. She then – just as slowly – spread her arms, splaying her fingers. Jake's brow wrinkled; she seemed to be including their surroundings. Then he heard – or rather felt – it. The small hairs on the nape of his neck prickled, just as they had on the moor.

Dolgun stiffened, looked up from his manipulation. Seeing Carolyn's signal he twisted round on his seat to confront Jake, who was standing half-crouched in a defensive posture, his eyes darting nervously. The older man quickly pressed a few more keys before leaving his position and going to Jake's side.

"What is it, Jake?" he whispered.

"Can't you feel it, Prof? Something in the air…all around us. Listen!" He gripped Dolgun's forearm

The vaulted, gloomy space above them was coming alive with imagined movement; indistinct sounds but there, sometimes clarified to one word, like "You!..." or "Here…" or a sniggering chuckle as though at some secret joke. The whispering increased in volume but also in multiplicity. It was like being a peripheral part of an enormous dinner reception, with the intimation of some less lucky guests who were somehow partitioned off, to dull the aural perception.

"Jesus, Prof, what the f – ? What's going on here?" His eyes were on Carolyn but still gripping the other's arm.

"Relax, Jake." Dolgun prised his sleeve free. "I'm moving up through the frequencies, using various carrier waves and beating selected frequencies together to achieve a superheterodyne effect." He ignored the other's baffled look. "In the process we are unavoidably alerting discarnate spirits on the lower planes of the astral world. It's called EVP – electronic voice phenomenon. A bit like a deep sea diver passing various creatures on his way to the ocean floor – only in reverse. Don't worry, I've set the gear to 'ramp on' through it as we search. Listen, it's working."

The chattering and chuckling was indeed lessening, and with it the feeling of oppression. Jake began to breathe more easily again, as though a great weight had been lifted from his chest. Carolyn was the least affected, her concentration now so total as to render her oblivious to the surroundings. As Dolgun went back to his seat Jake felt his sense of inadequacy returning. From being the main player – albeit reluctantly – he was now effectively sidelined. Not camera either; she would simply not believe without proof just how bizarre she looked, with her funny plastic bobble hat, perched on a wooden box inside a denuded church – at midnight!

This time there was no warning; the darkness above them began to sparkle. Before he had time to whisper hoarsely, "Look...look!" myriad tiny flashes of light blinked in the gloom about them. Dolgun's composure was beginning to falter, his reassuring grin at his young companion's new panic failing to impress.

The lights' activity increased, soon resembling a night sky in the southern hemisphere. There was no accompanying sound with the display, making it even more eerie. Then the twinkling stars began to join up in groups; strings of glittering pearls held the two men spellbound as the incredible scene began to move in seemingly random patterns. At first gently slipping from side to side as though jockeying for position in the diminishing available space and then – as with a single mind – they all moved.

"The frequencies...they've altered!" Dolgun whispered, casting a quick look in Carolyn's direction. But she – the catalyst around which all this now neurologically revolved – was no longer part of their group, so thoroughly mind-focused as to be heedless to the wonders above her head. Her tightly closed eyes barred her from the spectacle revealed to Dolgun and Jake as the dazzling display unfolded around them.

The patterns had now formed into elongated strips of varying amounts, amalgamating into alliances of even greater intensity, in some cases blazing so brightly that it hurt the eyes. But as Jake held up one hand to shield himself he felt strangely unafraid by this new turn of events. The feeling radiating down to them was non-threatening, even benign.

"What the hell is this, Professor?"

The glittering lights – some now two or three metres long – started to circle each other, as though preparing for some elegant gavotte. At first lazily, but then moving faster and faster. Whilst thus engaged each length formed itself into a loop which started to rotate as it circled. Some captive loops would suddenly burst through their encircling neighbours to assume the role of captor. This manoeuvring accelerated to a bewildering speed of multi-coloured trails, filling the cavernous space above the trio with their movement but strangely not emitting any radiated light, so that the backdrop was still in darkness. Then this too altered, until all the lights coalesced into six whirling cones of merged colours, giving the effect of giant whirlpools as seen from below. Spinning ever-faster they became vortices of brilliance, teetering slightly on their points but maintaining a general equilibrium with each other.

"It's pure energy!" Dolgun breathed. "The ultimate aim of all human thought."

"You mean - you mean…as in…heaven?" Jake gulped at his own audacity.

Dolgun laughed, a little shakily, his gaze never for an instant leaving the glittering performance enacted three metres above their heads. "Not as we know it, Jake. No, more your nirvana, *the* final frontier. Where all human intelligence achieves a state of pure energy, interactive and mutually supportive. Timeless and ever-expanding, like our universe." His rapt attention was beginning to worry Jake, standing there like a supplicant in a temple. Which is what he is, I suppose, conceded the younger man, held almost awestruck by the magical spectacle of countless life forms reduced to incandescent pearls.

"But what about the black dog, Prof, and more importantly, Carolyn over there? Shouldn't she at least have the same chance to glimpse nirvana…or will it still be here when we have become exhausted by the – well, the sheer exhilaration of it all?"

Dolgun's head turned with great reluctance, seeing his companion's anxious expression. He sighed. "You're right, Jake, we've gone too far…in more senses than one. We've somehow found the key to a world that I – for one – am not quite ready for. It's a bit like the fabled Lost Chord. Momentarily we have hit the exact note which allows us to peel back one corner of a different dimensional curtain, where we are privy to what one can aspire to on other planes of existence. But our conversions and transmitted frequencies are ramping on automatically and I fear we may never again be able to replicate those conditions precisely -"

"But surely if it's all electronic…"

"Ah, but it's not, is it?" He pointed to Carolyn. "Whatever her exact thoughts were three – four minutes ago is now gone. In all those billions of neurons where do we find the same synaptic junction? No, you're right, this is not the time or place for such a momentous quest. Who knows, perhaps later… Anyway, we've obviously travelled in frequency terms far beyond the level where we would expect to find our dark friend. I don't think we can ask this poor girl to go through all this again." He moved towards her, and as though to underline their fading hopes the thousands of tiny pulses began to split apart, moving away from each other, growing dimmer in the process, until in a matter of seconds they had all vanished. Dolgun reached up involuntarily with one hand and then let it fall to his side. He placed his hands on Carolyn's and said quietly, "Carolyn…Carolyn? Turn your thoughts to where we are – here in the church of St Michael's just after midnight. You are not in a trance, merely a form of meditation…" He stopped and whirled as a strange sound echoed through the unfurnished building.

Jake heard it too. "What was that?" His voice was shaky.

"A sort of muffled cry." Dolgun was more definite. "It didn't come from above…the opposite if anything."

"What's the matter?" Carolyn was blinking and rubbing her temples. "It didn't work." Her blank stare provoked a reply from Dolgun. "In one sense too well perhaps. Not your fault, my girl, you gave us some wonderful chances, we'll tell you about them later. But the one we wanted just wouldn't come through." He proceeded to remove the Squid. She glanced at Jake enquiringly; he shrugged and then shook his head. She stood up, easing some back muscles with her hands. Her normally pale face was now chalk-like in the dim moonlight. "Mind you, the seating arrangement tends to divert one's area of focus, Professor."

"Yes, I'm sorry." He placed the helmet on top of the transmitter. "It was all rather hastily contrived, but worth a try, I still believe that."

"Do you want me to -"

"No, no, my dear, you've done more than your share. We simply require more rehearsal, more...time." He tried to keep the disappointment from his voice as he busied himself with some controls.

"And that's a luxury we just don't have, eh, Prof?"

"Afraid so, Jake, every passing minute reduces the potential power now."

Jake held out his hand and she came to him. He gently kissed her brow. It was dry and cool. "Here, you're cold." He placed one arm around her and she sighed. He wasn't sure if it was with contentment or regret, there was so much to know about this enigmatic woman. They moved away from Dolgun, young lovers instinctively distancing themselves from the rest of the world.

"So what now, darling?" she asked quietly as they stopped in the shadow of the east wall.

"Oh, I don't know, love, have it out with your uncle -" He stopped, struck by how unlikely that would now be. Then: "You do want us to continue... I mean, are we -?"

"An item, as they say in the gossip columns?" She gave that impish grin and pushed him. "Yes, I guess so, although you may want to reconsider journalism as a permanent career – especially after him…wherever he may be. It's strange he wasn't in the presbytery. What's the matter, have I said something?"

"N-no, I was just looking at this menhir, set in the wall." He pointed to the ancient markstone. "Funny to think that this monolith is the possible start of it all." Anxious to divert her thoughts he went closer, drawing her with him. "Hey, Prof, what was it you said about this being some kind of capacitor?" He reached out to slap it playfully with his left hand.

"No, Jake! Don't -"

The shock was stunning, lifting him off the ground. He was in the air just long enough to be aware of the fact before crashing onto his back – alongside Carolyn. Her agonized scream helped clear his still-racked nervous system. For a further moment he simply lay there twitching, his left hand and forearm still throbbing from the pain, now mercifully gone. His head rang. He shook it, a mistake.

Dolgun came racing across. "Are you all right? Here, let me." He helped the girl to her feet, then Jake, who shook him off angrily.

"Jesus, man, you said tap the energy. That was more like your actual zap." He rubbed the back of his head ruefully. "You okay, Carolyn?"

"Is it always going to be like this around you, Jake?" She dusted herself down wearily. She'd had enough, all she wanted now was a hot bath, followed by a large and comfortable bed and dreamless sleep. She feared the latter might prove elusive. As she looked up she groaned; Dolgun was standing, ignoring them both, his head cocked in the manner of a hunter sensing prey nearby.

"Ssh! Please!" His hand waved at the stone. "It must have

311

become charged up to an incredible degree. You're both lucky to be alive. Listen! Can you hear it?"

The young couple glowered at each other, almost telepathically ready to resist any further involvement. Then Carolyn's face changed, became alert, then wary.

"It's vibrating…a sort of hum."

"And it's getting louder." Dolgun's excitement was contagious. "You've set up some kind of oscillation, maybe even self-generation. It's transmitting…something. If only…"

"If only we could transpose an image of the black dog onto it." Carolyn ran back to get the helmet, Dolgun two paces behind her, immediately flicking on switches and resetting dials. Jake stood where he was for a few moments until the humming stone jerked him from his torpor. He quickly placed several paces between him and it before walking more slowly back to the equipment.

She was already deep in thought, sitting on the box. He sat next to her, careful lest he distracted her attention. Dolgun was talking, more to himself than them. "Of course, you fool! It was there all the time, just waiting for the ancient wisdom to re-activate it. Well, Mr Stone" – he laughed – "you'll just have to settle for some new technology…and a large slice of luck. Please God, take care of the luck…" He continued in this vein as Jake tried to make sense of it all, glancing from one to the other.

But something was wrong, it still didn't appear to be succeeding the way they expected; their strained faces told its own story as the seconds ticked away and Dolgun's skin developed a film of perspiration.

"What is it, Doc?"

"I-I'm not sure, but it appears we're swamped by the magnitude of the signal coming from the stone. Carolyn's thought patterns are not clear enough." He tried frantically to lock onto something recognizable, shaking his head all the while.

Carolyn spoke. "How far will these leads stretch, Prof?"

"What?" He whirled from what he was doing, perplexed by the question.

"The stone and I are fighting each other, aren't we? I mean, in terms of airwaves or whatever." Her beautiful features were serious but amazingly untroubled by the implications of her statement. The stone's hum had settled to a gentle but unvarying note, no longer insistent or threatening. "If we bond -"

"Oh, sweet Jesus!" Jake jumped up in his agitation. "You two are something else. Am I the only one with an iota of sense left around here? We've both just defied the law of gravity and risked injury, thanks to that – that thing there and now here you are considering…" He couldn't complete the sentence, tailing off to a stammer. What he saw in Dolgun's face gave him no cause for comfort and he groaned.

"The stone's initial energy pulse has obviously flattened out but it is radiating something at a constant level -"

"The leads?" She stood up, ignoring Jake's anguished expression, and trailed the Squid's contacts behind her as she crossed the short space to the church wall. She looked back briefly at Dolgun, whose nod was just as short, before slowly placing the palms of both against the set-in stone. There was no repeat of their earlier experience, and after a few seconds she said quietly, "Let's go, Professor."

"Can you feel anything?" It was Dolgun, excited but not absolutely certain of the theory or principle. She nodded and lowered her helmeted head between her shoulders.

At first nothing except Jake's laboured breathing, and then the older man's soft, "Yes!" He made a few more adjustments, pressed a button and straightened up before turning round to them. "We're locked onto something… I don't know what," he said quietly. "It won't ramp through the frequencies, so my part is over, whether I like it or not. It's up to her now."

"But what if something *does* happen…? What if she begins to receive instead of transmit, eh?"

Dolgun didn't respond, his gaze fixed some several metres and to one side of Jake's left shoulder, near the altar base. Jake turned, not really wanting to but afraid of the alternative. At first he saw nothing, was about to chide his companion for being a silly old – There! In the near-darkness that was the bulk of the altar something – what? – moved. No, not some thing, nothing solid but the outline of the altar itself was moving, or more accurately, seeming to go out of focus. He knew this to be untrue, had to be, but…what?

"Oh, my God!" It was Dolgun, behind him.

A shape was materializing before them, like some conjurer's illusion. Jake realized then what it was. He should have been aware instantly, given that it was the object of the whole exercise. But – but it was huge, much larger than the beast that had chased them across Eastby Moor. The head was as large and as high as that of a horse, the flanks leaner but in proportion, the long tail swishing in anger. Then the eyes, seemingly out of nowhere, tiny orbs in the sockets, spinning and growing ever-larger until they threatened to encompass everything in the angular head, glowing and pulsing in that way he remembered with revulsion. And yet it still wasn't solid, the whole shape undulating like some film screen rippling in a draught.

"Move!"

"What…?" He twisted to face Dolgun; the Professor had grabbed Carolyn, the shock on her face was as of somebody being torn from a deep sleep as she staggered back.

"I said move, dammit! I need to alter directional power!" He ignored the look on Jake's face, pulling at the girl until she complied. Dolgun killed the Squid's power and flicked the switches to the signal generator, at the same time bringing in the circuits to the four large speakers mounted high on the pillars around the altar.

Jake saw then what the other meant and dived out of the immediate area, a move more activated by his fear of the rapidly solidifying form behind as any suddenly acquired wisdom. He shoulder-rolled himself upright and went to Carolyn, brushing himself down. They held each other for mutual comfort as the older man took over, adjusting and twiddling frantically.

"Here! Put these on – now!" He threw the ear guards at them, slipped a set over his own head. The noise began very quickly but the creature was forming substantially faster; it looked almost complete, a terrifying vision from a nightmare world that they were all a reluctant part of now. Jake realized the reason for Dolgun's urgency; a race between his skill and the creature's final formation – itself a supreme irony, given that they had in effect commanded it to appear.

The sound and decibel rate from the frequencies that Dolgun was producing still managed to penetrate the foam padding, Carolyn gripping Jake's arm so hard it almost distracted him from the noise being generated.

Suddenly it was quiet, Dolgun taking off the ear protectors gratefully and indicating they do the same. He turned to face the fearful apparition that now stood on all fours in the altar space. It was as high as Jake's shoulder, tail lashing, the red orbs of its eyes trying to draw him into their spinning depths. It trembled like some fractious foal, the angular head with its lantern jaw opening wide to reveal its teeth for the first time. Long, uneven and yellow they seemed capable of crunching through stone.

"Jesus, Prof, let's get out of here!" Jake said hoarsely, his eyes never leaving the beast's features. "Are we still on power? I can't hear anything."

"Oh, yes, I am bombarding it with what I hope will be the resonant frequency of soft animal tissue." Dolgun walked towards the creature warily. "It's molecular structure should start feeling the effects soon."

"But-but can it harm us…I mean if it comes at one of us?" Jake instinctively eased Carolyn to his rear with one hand as he spoke. "What if your plan doesn't work? I really don't think we can beat it to the door – we've already seen its turn of speed once, y'know."

"No, Jake, as long as the sig-jenny operates we should hold it. The directional speakers are effectively locking it there from equidistant points. I don't believe it has enough intelligence to guess there may be areas into which it might escape." He was still behaving like the showman in 'King Kong', pacing around the perimeter of confinement, back-tracking, half-crouching to get a better look. "Amazing. We're making history here, d'you both realize that? We've managed to materialize a spectral entity from another plane of existence and now virtually control it -"

"Virtually?" Jake jumped. "Virtually… Doesn't that mean… not quite?"

"Slip of the tongue, young man. I don't really think -"

The dog howled, a blood-chilling sound that made them all shrink back. The great head lifted, stretching the neck tendons as it again released the fearful cry, and then commenced writhing, the teeth snapping and biting at the air.

"It's started! It knows something is attacking it - look!" Dolgun pointed, without it being necessary. The others were just as stunned by the gigantic dog's behaviour. As though in some terrible convulsion it snarled and bit at itself, plainly confused and frightened. Foam flew from its mouth, it continued to howl and tried to turn or move backwards, but was held by the invisible, sonic bonds. There was nothing spectral about its occupation of the restricted space and Carolyn prayed the Professor was correct in his theory, for it was now undoubtedly attempting to get at them as its focus of torment. The heavy jaws snapped in their direction, the drool splattering onto the stone floor, so much that Dolgun was worried enough to race back to his equipment

"Must get a little more power," he muttered, loud enough for them to hear. He connected up some more leads and shut down unnecessary instruments as he flicked another switch on. Almost instantly the animal howled again and reared up, pawing the air. Then – as though accepting its domination by a superior force – it fell back.

"It's happening...look!"

The twisting shape trapped in its cage of sound was altering again. At first the other two could see nothing different, it still seemed huge and threatening. Then: "It's shrinking!"

"No, Jake, it's sinking." Dolgun's voice was calm again. "There are more planes than we know. It is attempting to escape this physical plane by altering its exact position in space and time. According to my research there is a sealed crypt below the church proper. It will seek some sanctuary there -"

"Oh, Christ!"

"What's the matter, Jake?" Carolyn grabbed his sleeve. "Isn't this what you want?" When he didn't reply she turned to Dolgun. "Isn't it, Professor?"

"Yes, yes, of course, Carolyn. If we can somehow batten it down there until the valley floods in a few hours it will be effectively imprisoned for all time."

The beast now appeared to be on its belly, fast disappearing into the stone as though through quicksand. Its head was moving from side to side, the terrible eyes that were still glowing fiery red watching them with a hatred they could feel. Soon only the head, lower and lower, until the wet snout alone was visible. Then it was gone.

"Jesus!"

"Thank God, I can't believe -"

A frightful scream issued from beneath their feet, making all three recoil in horror, fear and confusion on the girl's and Dolgun's features. Jake's registered a kind of sombre satisfaction that neither of the other two noticed.

"That-that sounded almost human," Carolyn gasped. "In fact, if I didn't know better…" She shook her head, waved the thought away. Then her head came up slowly and she stared for a long moment at Jake. He met her gaze frankly before turning to the Professor.

"What now, Doc? I mean, is that it?"

Dolgun was about to reply when the power failed, robbing the church of what little light there was, but more importantly, shutting down their control over the dog. The professor swore for the first time, running to the half-open door and out to his van. For a second the silence was eerie, the chug-chug of the power generator having been an accepted background noise to whatever had been going on inside the abandoned church.

Then Carolyn whispered, "Jake, the stone! It's humming again – only different somehow."

Clearly now they could the feel the emanations from the menhir in the east wall. It grew within seconds, the humming now accompanied by an uneven vibration. Dolgun rushed back in, about to speak when he immediately detected the changed ambience.

"My God, we've somehow hit the stone's resonant frequency! It will destroy itself. Get out of here – quickly now!" He gestured frantically, made a move to the wired-up equipment, representing thousands of pounds, and then gave up on it. As the young pair turned for the door the stone split asunder with a fearsome crack, taking a large section of the east wall with it, great blocks of stone tumbling inwards and crashing onto the floor. Carolyn cried out as the flagstones beneath gave way under the impact. She started to fall backwards, screaming at the realization of where she could end up. Jake grabbed one arm, tugging desperately to drag her across to where he crouched. The high vaulted ceiling groaned ominously as some of the supporting pillars began to twist away from each other.

"Prof!" Jake's cry stopped Dolgun, who was almost at the door. He turned, hesitated, then ran back, dodging a falling lump of masonry. The girl's terrified face looked up at them both as she slid feet first into the hole that had been the sealed crypt. Spurred by her terror they managed to haul her out and ran with her towards safety. A stained-glass window imploded under pressure and they were showered with coloured shards.

The door was jammed in its half-open position, not enough for more than one person to squeeze through. Jake shoved Carolyn unceremoniously ahead of them, glancing back, not knowing whether to expect a natural or supernatural danger behind them. But his sight of anything disappeared beneath a cloud of debris as the roof collapsed with a terrifying roar, blocks of stone bouncing towards them like styrofoam cubes. Then he was through, the dull boom suddenly deadened by the one remaining wall between them and disaster.

The others were already in the van, Dolgun revving and engaging gears in horrendous fashion as Jake threw himself at the open door. Carolyn grabbed his jacket and the van screeched out of the graveyard, bumping over fallen gravestones and out through the gateway.

"The lights...switch the bloody lights on!"

A blaze of light as the twin beams cut through the haze of night and showed them the deserted village street. Jake twisted round to peer back; they were trailing snakes of several cables that whipped in their wake. Dolgun eased off the accelerator and slowly braked.

"What...what are you doing, Professor?" shouted Carolyn, still back there on the edge of eternity. She shuddered at the memory, plucking at his sleeve like a child. "Let's get out of here...please."

"One way or another, it's over, Carolyn," Dolgun replied, applying the handbrake. "I simply want to write *Finis* to the story. Look!" He alighted and pointed back to the churchyard. She followed reluctantly, after seeing Jake get out on the far side.

The church of St Michael's was rapidly ceasing to exist, the final piece of roof folding in almost gently on the rest with a clearly audible thunder. Dust was rising into the cold night sky as a few granite blocks slid down the pile of rubble and then it all became still.

Jake broke the silence, trying to make light of it. "As they say around here, 'That were bloody close'."

"But is it over? I mean, weren't we supposed to keep the dog trapped down there until – until…?"

"In a crazy sort of way I think the destruction of the church helped us, Carolyn. The dog – in whatever form it now assumes – will have certainly become disorientated by so much released energy when the building disintegrated. The menhir – focal point of the leys – is no more, the very energy grids themselves dispersed, perhaps for all time. Basically it currently has no-where to go and as it has no concept of time it will not be aware of a deadline -"

"You mean the valley flooding?"

"Exactly, and that should place an effective headstone over its demise. As to its possible resurrection should the reservoir ever be emptied…well, that's too far in the future for the likes of me to worry about. I gratefully hand that task on to resourceful young people like yourselves. Shall we leave this area before Hi-Sec wakes up? I still have to get back to the university lab and report a rather unusual break-in. Carolyn, you said something about the remaining moonlight…?" He held the cab door open

"Ye-es, all right, Professor." She got in, then looked across at Jake. "I still think *you* have some explaining to do regarding the whereabouts of Uncle Nicky, hmm?"

"Right." Jake jumped aboard and placed his arm around her shoulders. "Now promise you won't cry when I tell you this…"

38: ACCEPTANCE

The cardinal read the article again and sighed, before going to the high windows and stared through the billowing curtains at the courtyard below. It was a beautiful morning, the sort that made even old men feel good to be alive. He wondered how the very frail Pontiff in the papal chambers was greeting the new day, almost certainly his last, if the country's finest physicians were to be believed. But more importantly and immediate was the disappearance of his secret brother. Sir Nicholas Brookes's body had still not been found, probably never would now. Divers had discovered his Jaguar car in the presbytery garage in that flooded valley somewhere in Yorkshire. The submerged church mysteriously pulled down…thrown down? Who knows what his last thoughts and images were. He had elected to go up against a terrible adversary, he wouldn't be the last to pay the price for failure. As for himself… He turned, picked up the newspaper and threw it in the waste basket. One thing their father had always dinned into them: Never rely on just one route to achieve your ambitions.

There was more than one path to papal power.

39: PERPETUANCE

The boy would never get the hang of it, impaling worms on bent wire – ugh! Then dangling it all in the water until something happened – which so far it hadn't. His dad was further along the reservoir bank, cheerfully waving to him every five minutes as he endeavoured to instil the same enthusiasm that had sustained him all his life.

He could still hear his words to his mom: "The boy is too wrapped up in that damned computer and PlayStation crap. He needs some healthy outlets…like fishing! D'you know what I caught him delving into last night on the internet? The occult! Oh, he snapped it off sharpish when I came in but not fast enough. He tried to tell me he'd stumbled across it by accident. Hmph! I almost wish it had been honest-to-God porn. But that black magic shit… Well, he's going to start coming out with me more often, I can tell you. Now that we've stocked the reservoir and we don't use barbed hooks any more even you can't really complain. It'll be good for him, me too… I don't seem to know that kid these days."

Plop! The boy glanced up, thinking he'd caught something at last. Nope, nothing. Then he saw the ripples and the small dark box bobbing a few metres out. Gee, maybe from the drowned village! They say a man's body is still down there. Maybe it's some sort of treasure. He waded out as far as he could when his dad's back was turned to him and used the tip of his rod to nudge it towards him. He scurried back to the bank and then hauled it the rest of the way with the rod, until it bumped against the shingle. He picked it up. Some dark wood, with a clasp thing in the middle and tried to prise it open. It was too tight, or maybe rusted solid, he wasn't sure. But it would just squeeze into his flap pocket. He could have a proper go at it when he got back to his room. Besides, he thought, there's always someone I can Google if I have a problem.

"Damien! Have you got a bite there?"

"No, dad, just snagged the line."

"Careful now, son we don't know what's down there really. What say we call it a day, okay? Can't expect to be lucky first time out. C'mon, we'll grab a burger and coke. I guess you've also earned some screen time."

About the Author

Author Shaun Ivory has been many things over the years – telegram messenger boy, barman, airman, oilman, literacy aid teacher, instrument technician, instructor, planner, radio troubleshooter, GEC, AEI, ICI, MFI…well, maybe not the last! His writing career was kicked off by a one guinea postal order fee from Al Read, the Manchester radio and TV comedian. Moderate success followed with short stories, articles, speeches, gags, odes, poems, and in 1976 he collaborated on a TV episode of The Sweeney (sadly never filmed). In the 1980s he wrote his first novel Chainshot, a techno-thriller which featured a Soviet nuclear submarine commander who had chosen to defect and bring his prototype vessel with him. At last, it seemed Shaun was on the cusp of blockbuster stardom… until his career was torpedoed by a certain Tom Clancy and The Hunt for Red October.

Shaun lives near the North York Moors and was a founder member of the local writing group. He currently contributes to Ireland's largest circulation weekly magazine. The Judas Cup is the outcome of a year-long novel-writing course at Leeds University. Shaun has just completed a third novel set in Ireland in 1943 and is currently working on a film script about the first black American fighter pilot, who flew for France in the Great War.

Printed in Great Britain
by Amazon